SUSANNA KEARSLEY was a museum curator before she took the plunge and became a full-time author. The past and its bearing on the present is a familiar theme in her books. She won the prestigious Catherine Cookson Fiction Prize for her novel *Mariana*, and has been shortlisted for the Romantic Novel of the Year Award for both *Sophia's Secret* and *The Rose Garden*. *Every Secret Thing* was originally published under Susanna Kearsley's pseudonym Emma Cole.

www.susannakearsley.com

By Susanna Kearsley

Mariana

The Splendour Falls

The Shadowy Horses

Named of the Dragon

Season of Storms

Every Secret Thing
(previously published under the name Emma Cole)

Sophia's Secret
(also published as The Winter Sea)

The Rose Garden

The Firebird

EVERY SECRET THING

SUSANNA KEARSLEY

Allison & Busby Limited
12 Fitzroy Mews
London W1T 6DW
www.allisonandbusby.com

First published in Great Britain by Allison & Busby in 2006,
under the name Emma Cole.
This paperback edition published by Allison & Busby in 2012.

A CIP catalogue record for this book is available from
the British Library.

10 9 8 7 6 5 4

ISBN 978-0-7490-0901-4

Typeset in 11.5/16pt Adobe Garamond Pro
by Allison & Busby Ltd.

The paper used for this Allison & Busby publication
has been produced from trees that have been legally sourced
from well-managed and credibly certified forests.

Printed and bound by
CPI Group (UK) Ltd, Croydon, CR0 4YY

*This book is for Euan, who wouldn't
give up, and my grandparents,
Mary and Harry and Edith and Ab,
who were young, and are never forgotten.*

Speech after long silence; it is right,
...Unfriendly lamplight hid under its shade,
The curtains drawn upon unfriendly night,

W. B. YEATS, 'AFTER LONG SILENCE'

Beforehand

I've been told, by people more experienced at writing, that the hardest part of telling any story is the search for its beginning, and its end. I might add that it's harder still when telling a true story, because truth does not allow for tidy endings.

The beginning was a problem in itself, in that this story started long before my birth. In many ways, it isn't even properly my story; yet I chose, at last, to start where I came into it, and let the tales of those who came before me weave their way into the narrative.

Not everyone who spoke to me survived. And there were stories I learnt later, that were placed throughout the book as random flashbacks, for the sake of keeping everything in order. But for the most part, what I wrote was nothing more than a chronology of strange, confusing days, and what I saw, and what I lived, and what was told to me.

The ending didn't come till I was nearly done revising my first draft.

It came, not in the form of inspiration, but by messenger, with flowers, for my birthday.

The dog heard the knock at the door before I did – he usually does – and I opened the door with a hand on his collar. Without the dog there at my side, I would never have opened my door to a stranger. Not even a smiling young man holding flowers.

But the flowers were roses. Tea roses. And when I saw them I knew straight away who'd sent them. It was, after all, my birthday, and although he was out of the country I knew that he wouldn't have let the day pass without some sign to show he'd remembered.

With the roses came a box – not large, just the size of a bottle of wine, and about the same weight. It was wrapped twice: the first time in tidy brown paper, and under that, prettier tissue, with ribbons.

I sat down to open it, carefully working the knots. The box itself was very plain, and lined with wads of newspaper – Italian, from the look of it. I thought, at first, he'd sent a statuette, some kind of sculpture. It felt heavy in my hand. But then I turned it, and the paper fell away, and I could see exactly what it was.

Time stopped. At least, it seemed to stop. And then, in that peculiar way it sometimes has, it shifted, and it took me with it, back to that first morning on the grey steps of St Paul's, in London.

But that won't mean anything to you, yet – you won't understand, unless I make a better start, and tell the story through from the beginning.

I first met Andrew Deacon on the morning of the day he died.

It bothered me, afterwards, how little I remembered him.

Someone who changes your life the way Deacon changed mine should, by rights, be remembered, imprinted indelibly onto your brain, and I found it disturbing that though I had talked to him, shaken his hand, I could not with closed eyes shape his image; that through everything that followed he remained as insubstantial as a shadow at my shoulder, the impression of a man and nothing more.

How much of that was my fault and how much could be put down to Deacon himself I never would know. His life had depended for so long on his being average, on not being seen, that even if I'd studied him properly, really looked hard at him, it might not have made any difference. I wish I had tried. But that morning in September I saw only one more grey old man in overcoat and hat, and I was busy.

CHAPTER ONE

England

I saw the world and yet I was not seen;
My thread is cut and yet it is not spun,
And now I live, and now my life is done.

CHIDIOCK TICHBORNE, 'ELEGY'

Wednesday, September 13

'Do you have the time?' the voice asked, at my shoulder.

I hadn't been aware of the older man sitting beside me, but when I glanced up he was there. Mentally I registered the overcoat and hat; assessed the voice, an English voice, politely middle class. I glanced at the time display ticking at the bottom of my laptop's screen.

'It's ten to ten.'

'Thank you.' He didn't comment on my accent. Some people did when they were making conversation, but this man said nothing. He had taken a seat a respectable two feet away, leaning forward with elbows on knees, gazing down at the taxis and cars passing by. 'Here for the trial, are you?' he asked.

How he'd managed to deduce that I didn't know – I wouldn't have thought that my occupation was that obvious, but then maybe he'd simply been reading over my shoulder. I gave a vague dismissive nod, not wanting to encourage him. The fact that I'd resumed my typing didn't put him off.

'A most interesting case, don't you think? He doesn't

look the type, but then they don't, always.'

Oh, please, I thought, *not now*, but it was too late – I could sense him settling in and getting comfortable, preparing for a chat.

At any other time that wouldn't have annoyed me. I found the trial interesting myself, and didn't mind discussing it. After all, it wasn't very often we Canadians had something so sensational to follow involving one of our own – in this case a Winnipeg dentist who was, the Crown argued, a serial murderer, having spent fifteen years here in England methodically killing off strangers and assuming their identities, like a hermit crab fitting itself into one abandoned shell after another, discarding them once they'd outlived their usefulness. The case was a hard one to prove, and we journalists were often found debating in the pub around the corner at the end of each day's testimony.

But this morning I didn't have time to debate. This morning the jury, having been out two full days, was widely expected to come back with its verdict, and I, like my colleagues, was sticking as close as I could to the Old Bailey, waiting for word.

It was a good morning for waiting outdoors. Late September in London had always been one of my favourite times of the year, when the sun that so often stayed hidden in summer could suddenly break through for days at a stretch, bringing just enough warmth to soften the edge of the chill morning air.

I liked London. Liked working in London. My very first foreign assignment, in fact, had been here, and I'd fallen in love with the city – the tangible history, the bustle, the pulse

16

of the river, the endless arterial flow of its traffic through streets that smelt sharply of diesel exhaust. I hadn't been here in eight months, and I'd missed it. This current assignment, on that count, had come as a welcome surprise.

Ordinarily I wasn't sent to cover trials – I was only a business reporter – but I'd been covering the latest Bombardier deal in Paris, conveniently close, from my editor's viewpoint. She'd known that I wouldn't say no, even though it would mean another week living out of my suitcase. And I hadn't said no. I knew full well whatever success I enjoyed at my newspaper came from not letting my editor down.

Which was why I was sitting here now, on the broad steps of St Paul's Cathedral, my third morning coffee grown cold on the hard stone beside me, bent over my laptop at work on two alternate articles, one for each verdict the jury might reach, so that when they did finally return I could fire the appropriate article off without delay. I was nearly finished now. A few more lines to go; a few more phrases to be tightened…

The old man beside me went on in his mild voice, 'I should imagine it's a fascinating job you have, observing other people's lives. Telling their stories.' He paused, but I didn't get the sense that he was waiting for me to contribute anything. He was still looking out at the street, not at me. 'I have a story I could tell you, if you're interested. Not anything like this' – he nodded at my laptop, in a reference to the trial – 'but there's a murder in it, just the same.'

'Oh, yes?' I said vaguely, my mind working to come up with a more common word for 'hubris'.

'An old murder, but one still deserving of justice.'

I didn't say anything that time, just made a faint sound.

'But you're busy,' he told me, and started to stand in that cautiously creaking way old men do. 'I'm staying in town the night – ring my hotel if you like, we'll have dinner. My card,' he said, handing it down. His hand stayed outstretched, so I shook it politely, dismissively. Two steps below me he stopped and turned. 'Oh, and do say hello to your grandmother for me. I hope that she's well?'

I looked up at that. Frowning faintly I said, in a slow voice, 'She's very well, thank you.'

'I thought that she might be.' He smiled. Turned away. Then he paused for an instant and briefly turned back. 'You have her eyes, you know.' He'd very clearly meant that as a compliment, but even as that registered he'd started moving off again.

Bewildered, I lowered my gaze to the card he had given me. *Andrew Deacon*, it read, and below that an address in Hampshire that he'd neatly crossed out with a stroke of his pen to write, in its place, *The Fielding Hotel, Covent Garden*, with a phone number. Now how on earth, I wondered, did this man know my grandmother? More to the point, how had he known who I was?

I looked up and called: 'Mr Deacon!'

In spite of his slowness to stand he had moved with surprising speed for someone his age, and had already reached the street, too far away to hear me. He was looking down... he didn't see the car.

It all happened so very quickly. For all the times I would replay that scene in the strange days that came afterwards, the details would never grow clearer or easier to distinguish. There was the car, of course, but I only saw that for an instant

– it came on fast and by the time I'd fully realised what had happened it had gone again, without so much as slowing down, just blending with the normal rush of traffic.

Nobody else seemed to take any notice.

The old man might have been a ghost, I thought, invisible to everyone but me…and I was frozen to my step in shock, unable to be any help. The clock kept ticking on across my laptop's screen but time seemed not to move at all, until at last the first car stopped, and then another, and the kerb and sidewalk swelled with people, bending, peering, murmuring.

I saw a woman kneel to check the old man's pulse. I held my breath.

And then she slowly stood, and faced the others, and I saw her shake her head.

'Look, Kate, I know you've been upset by this, but keep it in perspective. After all,' said Margot, setting a glass of white wine on the table in front of me before sliding into the booth with her own drink in hand, 'it's not as if you knew the man.'

She spoke in a tone I'd become very used to in the three years we'd known each other. Margot liked nothing better than giving advice. It was usually good advice – Margot had been in the business much longer than me. She was tougher, more worldly and, although at forty-four she was nearly twenty years my senior, she remained much more likely to grab male attention whenever we went out together. She was doing it now, on a Wednesday, in mid-afternoon, in this pub where we'd taken to meeting for drinks and a post-trial talk.

She wasn't working this trial. Margot worked for her newspaper's foreign desk, and a London trial wasn't foreign news to her. But she was idling here right now between assignments, and she liked to act, with me, as something of a mentor.

She was watching me.

I moved my glass in aimless little squares across the tabletop. 'But he knew me. He knew exactly who I was. He even knew my grandmother.'

'Did he?' This altered things. Her eyes grew faintly interested. 'How curious. What else, exactly, did he say to you, this...?'

'Deacon. Andrew Deacon.' It seemed suddenly important to remember that, the dead man's name. I'd remembered little else. I'd been trying all day to recall what he'd looked like, without success. I had his voice – some version of it – in my memory, but I couldn't form the face. Each time I thought I caught a glimmer of a feature it would melt like sand beneath a running wave. I frowned, and turned my mind back. 'Well, he said he had a story he could tell me...'

'Oh, yes?' Margot's tone had dried. She, too, like me, had run the gauntlet of those people who, on learning we wrote for a living, backed us into a corner at parties and held us there, trapped, while they went on about their great 'scoop', their great story – 'I'll tell you, you write it, and we'll split the profits...'

I shook my head. 'It wasn't like that, really. He was very sweet.'

'And what was his story?'

'Something about a murder.' How had he phrased it? I tried to remember. '"An old murder, but one still deserving of justice."'

'And where did your grandmother come in?'

'As he was leaving. He asked how she was doing.'

'Ah. He called her by name, did he?'

'No…' He hadn't, had he? 'No, but then I only have the one,' I said. 'There's only Grandma Murray. And besides, he told me that I had her eyes. I do.'

'So one assumes he knew her fairly well?'

I couldn't give an answer then…not then…just as I couldn't tell her how the man had come to know who I was; how he'd known where he could find me.

'Maybe,' Margot theorised, 'if this chap and your grandmother were friends, she might have told him you were here.'

'My Grandma Murray? Not a chance. She doesn't give out information like that, not to anyone. The Spanish Inquisition would have trouble finding out where I was staying.'

Margot smiled. She'd never actually met my grandmother, but she'd heard all my stories. 'Still, I rather think that once you've had a chance to speak with her, you'll find that's what she's done. It's the only logical explanation.' She took a drink. 'How is she doing now, your grandmother? How's she adjusting to having you home again?'

'Fine, I guess. I thought she might have second thoughts, but actually we're getting on OK. And it was crazy paying all that rent for that great big apartment when I wasn't ever there.'

I knew that Margot thought that it was crazier to give up my own place, to live with family. It was something she'd have never done. But then, in her case, I could understand. I'd met *her* family. They were nuts.

She said, 'So, you're heading back when? At the weekend?'

I shook my head. 'Not until Tuesday. My editor wants me to do a few follow-up interviews. Talk to the victims' families, the lawyers, you know. And anyway, I'm booked for Friday night. I'm going down to Kent.'

'And what's in Kent?'

'Patrick's parents are throwing a party.'

The sisterly advising look was back. 'Now, Kate, I thought that wasn't serious. I've told you my opinion of your Mr Damien-Pryce.'

'It isn't and you have,' I said. 'Repeatedly.'

'Then why...?'

'The party,' I informed her, 'is for Patrick's Aunt Venetia.'

'Ah.' She nodded understanding then, and even smiled approval. 'Sorry. My misunderstanding. I thought you'd gone off the rails, for a moment. But I'll permit you to see Patrick if you're using him to meet Venetia Radburn.'

That had, actually, been my main objective since I'd first run into Patrick Damien-Pryce last week at the Old Bailey, or, more properly, since he'd run into *me*, so deliberately by chance that I'd suspected from the outset chance had not had much to do with it.

To be honest, I'd grown weary of his obvious pursuit. Some women would have found it flattering, I knew. The man was gorgeous. And intelligent. And witty. And urbane, in a way that few men were these days – at least, men under fifty. His clothes always fit to perfection; he knew the right places to go, and the people who worked there knew *him*, and I was beginning to think he could walk through a windstorm without it disturbing his hair.

'Rising young star in the criminal courts,' was how Margot had summarised him, when I'd asked. 'Took silk at an early age; has the right pedigree. Very ambitious. His being a lawyer is only a prelude to politics, I should think.'

Politics would suit him. He was slick – that was the only word that fit him – and I'd never trusted men like that.

I would have tried much harder to discourage him, if Margot hadn't also said that Patrick was related to Venetia Radburn, grand old dame of British politics, who even in retirement was regularly entertained by heads of state when travelling.

I'd have given a lot to be introduced to the woman, so the prospect of spending the whole of Friday evening eating dinner with her in return for letting myself be chased round the table a few times by her good-looking great-nephew seemed – to me, at least – to be a bargain.

'Just mind you keep your wits about you,' Margot told me now, her voice not managing to hide her amusement. 'People like the Damien-Pryces are bound to have a pile in the country' – which was British-speak, I knew, for 'giant house' – 'and I've seen first-hand how property affects you. You go all wobbly,' she accused me, 'in great houses.'

'I do not.'

'You do. I was with you at Blenheim, remember? Last year.'

'That's different. Blenheim is a palace.'

'I'm only saying. Certain settings,' she informed me, 'seem to make you lose your proper sense of judgement.'

A male voice above my shoulder asked, 'Which settings would those be, then?' and Patrick himself, pint in hand, slid confidently into the booth beside me, his long body as always looking too cramped in the small space.

'Sorry, that's classified,' I said, immune to the strength of his smile.

Margot, less welcoming, told him he looked out of sorts.

'Yes, well, I was late to court this morning. The police had traffic stopped in Cannon Street, for some inestimable reason…'

I said, 'There was an accident. A hit-and-run. A man was killed.'

'Kate was there,' Margot said; then, dryly, 'She's been traumatised. That's why I've got her drinking.'

'Ah.' He glanced at my wineglass. It wasn't like me to drink wine at this time of the day, but I didn't imagine that Patrick had noticed. Men like Patrick didn't notice things like that unless they somehow stood to benefit. 'So you were an actual witness?'

'Some witness.' I sobered. 'I wasn't any help to the police. I couldn't really tell them anything. Couldn't even give them a description of the car. It didn't stop,' I said again, as I'd said earlier to Margot.

And again she told me, 'Kate, it was an accident. There wasn't anything you could have done.' Above her drink, she said to Patrick, 'You might tell her she needn't take it all so much to heart. I mean, he might have known her grandmother, but still, that doesn't mean—'

'He knew your grandmother?' asked Patrick.

'Look,' I told them both, 'I'd really rather not discuss it. Can we change the subject, please?'

There was a pause, and then, 'So,' Margot said to Patrick,

'Kate tells me you're taking her down into Kent at the weekend.'

'I am.'

'Your Aunt Venetia's birthday, is it? How old would she be, now?'

'No one knows,' he said. 'I should think she'd be close to the Colonel's age, maybe mid-eighties, but you'll never make her admit to that.'

The Colonel, I knew, was his father. Why Patrick called him the Colonel and not Father was a thing I wasn't sure of. It might have been a nickname of affection, or a sign of emotional distance between the two men – I hadn't been able to figure out which from the few times that Patrick had mentioned his family. I had, though, been able to glean that his father was considerably older than his mother, and that somewhere – on his mother's side, I thought – there was a fair amount of money.

He turned to me. 'You've got the map I gave you, right? You won't get lost?'

'I won't get lost.'

'Because if you're worried at all about finding your way you could drive down with me. Take the train back.'

He just never gave up, I thought. Ten to one I'd get down there and find there *were* no trains back up to London. Amused, I told him, 'That's all right. I'd rather have the car. What time is dinner?'

'Eight. But you should aim to get there earlier, to spend a bit of time. I ought to be there myself around six, give or take. We could go for a walk round the gardens…you know, feed the ducks, that sort of thing.'

'They have ducks?' Margot asked.

'And a handful of swans.'

'It sounds lovely,' she said. Then, in casual tones, 'Big place, is it?'

'Big enough. It used to be a priory, in Tudor times, and everybody after that saw fit to add a piece. My mother complains there are too many bedrooms and not enough baths.'

Margot sent me a knowing look, meant to remind me of my alleged weakness for opulent houses. I chose to ignore her, and Patrick, being self-absorbed, missed the exchange altogether.

'I can't stop,' he said, draining his pint. His breath smelt of ale as he leant in to kiss my cheek. 'Want to do dinner tonight?'

'Can't.'

'Tomorrow?'

'I'm busy all day.'

'Right, we'll leave it till Friday, then.'

Watching him stand, I asked, 'What should I wear?'

'Wear whatever you like,' he said. And then, halfway to the door, he turned back to call over his shoulder, 'Oh, and don't forget something to sleep in. I'm partial to black negligées,' in carrying tones that turned heads in the pub, bringing all-knowing smirks to the eyes of the journalists sitting around us.

'You want to watch out,' Margot told me. 'You'll end up a headline yourself.'

She was teasing, of course. She couldn't possibly have known just how prophetic those few words would end up being, in a very few days' time.

I walked through Covent Garden on the way to my hotel. I did it every evening; but tonight, instead of turning at the market,

I went straight on past the Opera House and crossed the narrow street to enter Broad Court, a brick-paved pedestrian passageway running from Bow Street to Drury Lane.

The Fielding Hotel was a small, charismatic place, halfway along the short stretch of Broad Court. An old building, with vines on the front and a dimly cramped entry that gave, on the right, to a cosy front bar, and on the left, to a hole-in-the-wall type reception desk. Everything smelt vaguely dusty, and charming. An African grey parrot, caged near the door of the bar, eyed me warily as I stepped in to the entryway.

The desk clerk, a well-dressed young woman, became wary, too, when I said that I worked for a newspaper. It was always a gamble, I knew, introducing myself as a journalist – some people talked, others didn't. This woman seemed far more concerned with protecting a hotel guest's privacy. Admirable, really, if not very helpful to me.

'Mr Deacon,' she said, 'was a regular guest, yes. We'll miss him.'

'Did he stay here often?'

'Whenever he was in London.'

A diplomat's answer, I thought. I pressed forward. 'Was he here alone?'

'Yes.' A little indignant.

'I just meant…I wondered if there was a friend, or maybe someone from his family, staying with him.'

'No.'

'Did he have a family?'

'I don't know.' She didn't know much, as it happened, or else she simply didn't want to say. Even when I showed her the card Andrew Deacon had given me, she wouldn't confirm or deny the home address by checking the register. 'Sorry,' she said, 'but guest records are private.'

Aware that I'd run up against a wall, I gave up trying. Thanked her. Turned. Then, struck by one last thought, turned back.

'What sort of man was he?'

'Sorry?' she asked.

'I mean, did you like him?'

That question she answered. 'We all did. He was sweet. He always stopped to say good morning; always saved a bit of breakfast toast with jam for Smokey,' she said, pointing to the parrot. 'We all liked him very much.'

I said, 'I see.' And then, although there seemed no point in it, I handed her *my* card. 'In case you think of something else…'

She read my name. 'You're Katherine Murray?'

There was something in her tone that gave me hope. 'Yes. Why?'

'You're staying at the Cheshire Arms?'

'Yes.'

'I've been ringing you all afternoon,' she said, relaxing. 'I *am* sorry. If I'd known that you were you…' Her eyes met mine, companionable. 'We found a note,' she told me, 'in his room, when we were cleaning it. Your name; the name of your hotel. He had today's date written underneath. We thought perhaps he had made plans to meet with you today…that you might not have heard…that you might want to know.'

It surprised me that he'd known the name of my hotel, but I tried not to show it. 'Thank you. That was very thoughtful.'

'But you knew.'

'I did, yes. I was...I was with him, when it happened.'

'Oh, I see.' The desk clerk eyed me a long moment, and then asked a question in her turn: 'He didn't suffer, did he?'

Her face remained impassively professional, but her eyes told me my answer was important.

'No, it was very quick. I'm sure he didn't suffer.'

'Good.' And bending to her work, she said again, as though it were his epitaph, 'We all liked Mr Deacon.'

There was an old man eating on his own, two tables over in the dining room of my hotel. I found that my attention, all through supper, travelled back to him, because of that – because he was an old man, quiet, someone I might easily have overlooked. And because it had occurred to me that Andrew Deacon could have sat there last night, or the night before, and I might not have noticed him, either.

I could, for all I knew, have met him, spoken to him somewhere...at a dinner function – I had been to two since I'd arrived here – or a party, or the library. Perhaps our paths had crossed, and I had simply not remembered.

I was good with names and faces, when it suited me. I noticed people like Venetia Radburn, people who were newsworthy – but with ordinary people of a certain age, my vision seemed to narrow.

That bothered me more than it should have, perhaps. No one likes facing up to their shortcomings, me least of all, and I didn't like admitting I was something of an ageist.

Old people were invisible to me, I thought, unless they were of use to me.

The waiter broke my train of thought by reaching past my

shoulder to retrieve my empty plate, and looking up to thank him I observed with vague surprise that I was now the only person in this section of the dining room. The old man who'd been sitting at the second table over had now gone, his place already cleared and set for the next person, as though no one had been there.

I'd told the truth to Margot when I'd said my Grandma Murray didn't part with information. It was something of a joke among my co-workers, who knew by now it was a waste of time to ask her anything. 'She always comes back with this "need to know" argument,' one of my friends had once told me. 'It's like phoning the Pentagon.'

Grandma's defence was that if I had wanted somebody to know something – how old I was, or what flight I was on – I'd have told them. She kept her own life just as private.

So I couldn't believe she'd have told anybody the name of my hotel in London. Not even an old friend…assuming, of course, Andrew Deacon had been an old friend.

There was only one way that I knew to find out.

It was nearly eleven o'clock when I settled myself on the bed in my room. In Toronto right now it would only be suppertime. Grandma would be in the kitchen, I thought, only steps from the phone. I was right. She picked up on the second ring, her voice as sure as ever. 'Hello?'

That voice turned me into a child, as it always did; took me straight back to the clean-smelling rooms of the old brick house on Barton Ave., to the little back room with its rose-patterned wallpaper where I had slept as a child, and where I would sleep when I went home next Tuesday.

I'd never known my other grandmother – she'd died young,

as my own mother had – and although both my grandfathers had lived to see my birth, the only one that I had any memory of was Grandpa Murray, who, together with my grandmother, had raised me while my father had gone off to do his corporate work in India, the Middle East, South Africa, wherever he was sent.

Grandpa Murray I remembered as a gentle man, a tall man with a presence that was comforting. He smoked a pipe, and often took me walking in the neighbourhood. He knew the ways to whistle like a bird and even once, to my amazement, coaxed a squirrel from its tree to take a walnut from his hand. But these were childhood memories only. He had died when I was ten. And five years after that, my father, in Bahrain, had had his third and final heart attack. Since then, the only family that I'd had was, 'Grandma,' I said. 'Hi. How are you?'

'Katie! Nice to hear your voice. They were just talking about your trial, on the evening news. You're finished, then, are you?'

'Nearly. I have a few follow-up interviews, still, with the families…'

'I'm sure the guilty verdict will have come as a relief to them. They've had to wait so long,' she said, 'for justice.'

'Yes.' I hesitated. 'Grandma…'

'It's a shame that no one stopped him sooner. I'd imagine the police would have made more of an effort to catch him if he had been killing young women instead of old men.'

She was probably right, I thought. 'Grandma…'

'Yes, Katie?'

'I was wondering,' I started off, then stopped and simply said, straight out, 'I met someone today who said he knew you.'

'Really? There in London? Who was that?'

'A man named Andrew Deacon.'

She was silent for so long that for a minute I thought our connection might have been broken...until I heard the quiet creaking of the chair springs as she sat. Her voice was different. 'Deacon?'

'Yes. He said to say hello to you. He asked me how you were.' Feeling as though I had stepped onto less than firm footing, I edged my way forward with caution. 'I kind of wondered, Grandma...that is, he just seemed to know so much about me – who I was, and what I did – I wondered if you'd maybe been talking to him recently, and had mentioned that I was in London, because—'

'No,' her voice drifted in, not as strong as before, as though part of her had moved a long way off. 'I haven't talked to Deacon now for many years,' she said. 'Not since...' The words trailed off. Another pause. And then, 'How is he?'

'Actually, Grandma,' I said, as I worked one finger through the coiled ringlet of the telephone cord, wishing that I could delay the inevitable, 'actually, he...that is, there was an accident this morning, just after he and I spoke, and I'm afraid...' I stopped, and tried again. 'It was a hit-and-run, you see. A car came out of nowhere, and it hit him, and he's...well, he's dead.'

She took a moment to absorb this. 'Dead?'

'I'm sorry. Yes.'

The silence stretched so long this time I had to finally speak to reassure myself I hadn't killed her, too, from shock. 'Grandma?'

She took a breath that shook a bit. And then she did a thing she'd never done. She said, 'Forgive me, Katie,' very softly, and she set down the receiver.

THURSDAY, SEPTEMBER 14

'Were they lovers, do you think?'

'Oh, Margot, please. My Grandma Murray?'

We were having what would likely be our final meal together for this time of mine in London. I'd come out by train to Margot's flat, in Shepherd's Bush, for supper. You had to be a very good friend of Margot's to get an invitation to her flat. Like my grandmother, she had a thing for privacy.

Her flat was in the lower level of a house, its narrow rooms as cosy as a hug, the walls and bookcases and tables overflowing with the evidence of years of travel – wooden carvings from all over, from the Orient, and Africa; clay figurines from Mexico, a painted mask from Hong Kong, and a weaving from Afghanistan.

Her cooking, too, was wonderfully eclectic. I never knew what recipes, collected in the course of her assignments, she was going to try out on me, and every time I sat here, at her tiny kitchen table, with the butcher block beside me on the counter, heaped with peelings, I could not suppress a feeling of adventure.

She reminded me, 'Well, you did say your grandmother's reaction was completely out of character, her ringing off like that. The thing is,' she went on, grating raw ginger into a pot of mystery vegetables, 'you never know what old people got up to, in their youth. Take my father, for instance. When he was my age he was quite the adventurer. He climbed mountains, raced cars, has the pictures to prove it. But look at him now and you'd think he'd done nothing but sit and play bridge all his life. Maybe your grandma's like that – a dark horse.'

'My grandmother,' I said, distinctly, 'did *not* have affairs. She was madly in love with my grandfather.' And justly so, I thought. From the portrait that still hung in Grandma's bedroom, of my grandpa in his Royal Air Force uniform, it was clear that in his youth he'd had the dark-eyed, dark-haired good looks of a young Gregory Peck. Small wonder she'd been so in love with him. 'They made their own little world, those two.'

'So maybe she knew this Deacon character before she met your grandfather.'

'I doubt it. She and Grandpa were high-school sweethearts.'

'So what do *you* think Andrew Deacon was to her, then?'

'I don't know. A friend of Grandpa's, maybe.'

'Ah,' she said, in tones that weren't entirely convinced. Turning on her gas stove with its usual alarming puff of flame, she set the pot to boil and nodded sideways at the little stack of newspapers I'd spread across the table. 'Any joy?'

'Not much.' None of the papers had bothered with more than a few lines of print on the accident. 'Pensioner Killed – Driver Sought' was the dominant theme, in small type tucked away behind flashier news. Because I still had

Andrew Deacon's card, with his address in Hampshire, I'd gone so far as to buy a local Hampshire paper, but even the death notice I managed to find there offered little in the way of information about the man, except for the fact that he'd been predeceased by a sister some years ago. 'Sadly missed by his nephew, James Cavender,' finished the personal details.

I read down the funeral particulars: 'At St Stephen's Church, Elderwel, two o'clock Saturday.'

Margot said, 'You weren't honestly thinking of going, were you?'

'Well…'

'It's a hell of a long way to go, you know, Hampshire.'

'It wouldn't be that bad. A two-hour drive, maybe…'

Margot smiled, reminding me how amusing she found my North American habit of measuring distances in time, not miles – a two-hour drive, a forty-minute walk…'Why do you do that?' she'd once asked me, and I'd had to admit I didn't know, unless it was because we North Americans, in dealing with the vastness of our continent, found time the only measurement to which we could relate. She said now, 'Yes, well, that might not seem much to you, but no self-respecting Englishwoman would drive that far to go to someone's funeral unless she were in the damned will.'

Patiently, I explained that I'd only been thinking of going in the first place because of my grandmother. 'I'm sure she'd go herself, if she were here.'

'Yes, well, I'd have thought you'd be busy enough, without that. You're off to Kent tomorrow evening, aren't you?'

'Yes, but…'

'So a dinner like that might go on till midnight. Then you'll have to drive back here…'

'It's not long, on the motorway.'

'And after that, you're planning to go roaring down to Hampshire for the afternoon? You're mad,' she said, but seeing that my mind was set she let the matter drop and backed the conversation up a step. 'Are you all ready for tomorrow night, then?'

'I can't wait.'

'I'm envious, you know. Venetia Radburn…I once met a former aide of hers, at a party, did I tell you? But that's as close as I got to the woman herself. It ought to be amazing, having dinner with her.'

I didn't need to be told. Apart from my personal awe of the woman and all she'd accomplished in politics, meeting her might open all sorts of doors and connections for someone like me, in my business.

'Hell,' Margot said, with a smile, 'I'd consider sleeping with Patrick myself, if it meant meeting up with his Great-Aunt Venetia.'

I gave her a look. 'I am not,' I said, 'sleeping with Patrick.'

'I hope not,' she said, with her tongue planted firmly in cheek. 'I've got twenty quid riding on your standing firm and not being seduced.'

'There's a pool on me?' I tried, without success, to take offence. 'Who else is in on it?'

'Darling, you know that I never name names.'

My turn to smile. 'Well, never mind. Your twenty pounds are safe.'

'I'll take your word. You're leaving when?'

'On Tuesday.'

'I have a friend,' she said, 'who's flying to Toronto Tuesday morning. Might be on your plane, in fact. He does corporate security…surveillance systems, that sort of thing, very technical. Apparently there's some big conference next week in Toronto, police from all over the world, and my friend was invited to speak. I'll tell him to look out for you on the airplane.' She took a fork and poked the vegetables to see if they were done. 'I'm flying out myself, tomorrow.'

'Oh, yes? Where to this time?'

'Buenos Aires.'

'Very nice.'

'You think so? I'll switch places with you, then. You spend the month in Argentina, and I'll stay and go to dinner with Venetia Radburn. Deal?'

I shook my head. 'No chance.'

'I didn't think so. Oh, all right, then, go enjoy yourself,' she told me, with a teasing wink. 'Just see that I don't lose my bet.'

I sighed. 'You won't…'

'Remember Blenheim.'

'Blenheim was a *palace*, not a house.'

She switched the stove off with authority. 'I'm only saying. Incidentally, you are aware, aren't you, that Venetia Radburn's famously allergic to journalists? Has Patrick told her that he's bringing you?'

'I don't know.'

'Because,' said Margot, 'if he hasn't, you might find the evening proves more interesting than even you expect.'

Friday, September 15

The great house rose out of the landscape to greet me as though it had stood there for ever, a sprawling thing, solid, of weathered red brick that seemed one with the hedges and trees that surrounded it. The approach from the gate, up a long gravelled drive with a pond to one side, gave a leisurely view of the magnificent façade – the gabled wings, the angled chimneys, and the rows of stone-silled windows with their glinting small glass panes.

I turned my small rental car onto the broad gravel curve to the east of the main door, and crunched to a stop.

There were two other cars here, but neither was Patrick's. I looked at my watch. Six o'clock, he'd said, give or take, and I'd deliberately timed my own arrival for nearer six-thirty, to be certain he'd be here before me. Not that there was anything to do but ring the doorbell – I couldn't very well sit in my car in the driveway all evening, waiting for Patrick.

With a house of this size I'd expected a butler to answer the door, but the woman who came to welcome me was clearly not the hired help. She was, for one thing, too well dressed, in a sort of traditional twinset and pearls way. Besides which, she had the same brilliant blue eyes as her son.

'You must be Kate,' she said. 'I'm Anthea. We're so pleased you were able to come.' Patrick's mother held wide the front door, stepping back to let me enter. Her smile was quick and genuine, lending her small face a beauty that transcended age. She'd have been in her fifties, I guessed, though she had kept her figure well and if you'd seen her from a distance you would probably have put her some years younger. She gave the impression of someone who wasn't too eager to age – there was no trace of grey in her soft upswept hairstyle, and her make-up, while not overdone, was nonetheless the kind that took some time to put on properly.

She looked, to me, as carefully preserved and polished as some of the decorative objects that lined the front entrance hall – the scrolled wooden mirror with its hooks for hanging coats on, and the marble-topped table beneath it, and the large Japanese-looking blue and white porcelain floor vase filled with canes and umbrellas.

Beyond the entry I could see a higher-ceilinged, brighter hall, with doors that opened onto rooms as elegant as those I'd seen in British *House & Garden* magazines.

Patrick or no Patrick, I thought, I was going to enjoy having dinner here.

'My son's not with you, then, I take it? No?' She smiled. 'Well, that's a man for you. I don't imagine he'll be long. Please, do come through. My husband's been longing to meet you. He does so enjoy having pretty young girls come to visit.' She said that with fondness, but the statement itself tended to reinforce my earlier suspicion that I was one in a long line of women Patrick had brought down here for a weekend.

Still, the Colonel, to his credit, tried to make me feel I was the first and only one.

He was old, and in a wheelchair, but those details ceased to register the minute he came forward from the windows in the library to take my hand in both of his. 'My dear girl,' he said warmly, 'you are much too beautiful for Patrick. He doesn't deserve you.'

He was decidedly Patrick's father. In his youth he would have been a very handsome man, a womaniser probably. His smile was very like his son's, and so I didn't fall for it. I did, though, from politeness, let him play the part of charming host, and show me round.

We didn't see the whole house – just a few rooms on the main floor, but the brief tour was enough to let me know that Patrick's family was as wealthy as he'd hinted. The giant portraits hanging on the panelled walls weren't copies, and the rooms were thickly furnished with high-quality antiques, with rich veneers and chintz and mirrors and the sort of Persian carpets that you almost hated stepping on. My favourite room of all was the Colonel's study, lined with books on shelves with doors of leaded glass, and quiet light and well-worn armchairs and a writing desk, behind which heavy draperies framed a pair of tall french windows slanting sunlight on the floor.

More wonderful than that, the windows opened onto a broad terrace looking over clipped green lawns and gardens to the tennis courts.

The Colonel, having got me on the terrace, seemed content to keep me there awhile, inviting me to have a seat on one curved stone bench while he wheeled his chair round till he faced me. 'A marvellous view,' he remarked, gazing over it with clear appreciation. 'I always enjoy coming out here, it gives me great pleasure. Especially when I have someone as lovely as yourself to keep me company.'

I smiled, as I was meant to, and wondered whether men like him ever fully realised they were old; that they had aged beyond the point where their good looks and words of charm would bring the women running. It was rather sad, I thought, and for a moment I felt sympathy for Patrick, who would come to this as well, in time, and like his father, probably not know it.

'So tell me, my dear,' said the Colonel, 'is this your first visit to London?'

'Oh, no, I've been here quite a few times.'

'Then how is it my son failed to notice you before this? I should think a face as beautiful as yours would stand out in any courtroom.'

I thanked him for the compliment, and said that my path simply hadn't crossed Patrick's till now. 'I don't usually cover trials.'

'Well, you got rather an interesting one this time,' was his comment. 'Did you think the chap was guilty?'

'The jury thought he was.'

'A diplomatic answer.' It apparently amused him, and he gave me an appreciative once-over before going on, 'I read that he'd had twenty-two identities…is that a fact?'

I nodded. 'That they know of.'

'Twenty-two.' He shook her head. 'Imagine. Keeping all the details straight…'

'He didn't keep the details of the last one straight. That's how they caught him.'

'Ah, quite right. It's all the little things that trip a person up. I remember my elder son, John, when he first got his licence, he took Patrick out for a drive round the lanes. They were going too fast, you know – reckless, the pair of them.

One of our local policemen, a new lad, he pulled the boys over, and Patrick, he thought he'd be clever, and he said his first name was Tom, and the officer asked how he spelt that and Patrick said, "P-A-T-R-I-C-K".'

My smile at *that* was genuine.

The Colonel said, 'Never the sharpest pencil in the box, our Patrick, though he tried. John did so love reminding him of that day, when the young policeman pulled them over.'

I didn't catch his use of the past tense, and so I asked him, 'What does John do?'

'John?' He looked across at me. 'We lost him, I'm afraid. A plane crash. Liked to fly his own planes, John did. Reckless, as I said.'

'I'm sorry.'

'Oh, well, it was years ago. Time heals, they say. I'm not sure that they're altogether right in that, but it at least forgives, does time.' He looked across the wide lawns and the tennis courts with eyes that seemed to see a great deal further. Conversational, he said, 'I think Venetia took it hardest. She was always sure that John would make prime minister.' And then he stopped, and brought his gaze back guardedly, as though he'd strayed too far into things personal. The practised smile returned. 'I do apologise, my dear. I didn't mean—'

'I might have known,' said Patrick, coming through the tall French doors behind us, 'that you'd try to steal my date.'

His father took the reprimand in stride. 'My boy, you ought to be more of a gentleman and not leave such a lovely lady unattended. I was merely seeing she was entertained.'

'I'll bet you were. You know,' he said, to me, 'he's not as harmless as he looks, despite the wheelchair.' It was faintly unsettling having both those faces, Patrick's and the Colonel's, turned upon me with the same slick smile.

Patrick's kiss, I thought, was for our audience as much as me. He said, 'Sorry I'm late.'

'Not to worry,' I told him. 'I've been well looked after.'

'So I see.' He put a half-proprietary arm around my shoulders, so that I felt like property reclaimed. 'Mother sent me out to look for you two, actually. The other guests are mostly here; I gather we're to come inside for drinks.'

'And Venetia?' asked the Colonel, as he turned his wheelchair with an effort, 'is she here as well?'

'Her car was coming up the drive as I came in.'

Which was, despite the view, enough incentive to propel me from the terrace.

Venetia Radburn in person looked smaller than she did on television. Not smaller in the sense of less significant, but physically smaller, more delicate, more feminine, and yet when I was introduced I felt intimidated. During her time in the Commons she'd gained a reputation for not losing her debates, and having met her now in person, I knew why. Like a medieval queen, she moved with a natural aura of power, and gave you the sense she could have you beheaded at will.

'You're a redhead,' she told me approvingly. 'So was I, once.'

There was still a faint tint of it left in her whitened hair, though whether it was natural or not I couldn't tell. She'd aged well – she was striking, and her strong face showed few wrinkles save the crow's feet round her eyes, those eyes that now were trained on mine with such unwavering intensity.

She said, 'You're a reporter.'

'Yes, I am.'

'You know I don't give interviews.'

'I've heard that, yes.'

'You'd like to change that, I suppose.'

Patrick interrupted with, 'Aunt V, be fair. Kate's only here because I asked her. She hasn't got any hidden agenda.'

'Of course she hasn't,' said Venetia Radburn, though I can't imagine she believed it. Still, she didn't seem to mind. She even insisted I sit at her end of the table at dinner.

It was an incredibly wonderful dinner, with all the right wines served in all the right glasses, and candlelight catching the gleaming gold rims of the bone-china dishes that came and went with every course. The dining room was wonderful as well. It smelt of panelling and polish and the dust that settles into velvet curtains, and above our heads a chandelier of perfect crystal teardrops trapped the light and spun it out again against the golden walls in little rainbow arcs that wavered with the slightest breath of movement.

The guests glittered, too…some literally, with jewels, as well as figuratively. There was the dashing white-haired actor whom I recognised from British television; the young woman in the diamonds who had come with the tall bearded man from the House of Lords; and the high-flying stockbroker wearing a suit that I guessed was Armani. I sat across from a very smart middle-aged woman whose plain name – Anne Wood – masked a not-so-plain intellect. She was a lawyer, as well, though her scope was a little bit broader than Patrick's. Next month, I was told, she'd be busy defending an African general on trial for war crimes at the International Court in the Hague.

'It's a difficult thing, war,' Venetia agreed, in a guarded

defence of the African general. 'Most people these days haven't lived through one, they wouldn't know. The things one does in wartime…it's like living in a different world.' Her eyes grew reminiscent. 'I got bombed out twice during the Blitz. Twice,' she emphasised. 'Quite an experience. We had Morrison shelters, great steel things on four legs, with mesh round the sides. You put your bed on top, or used them in your dining room to eat on, and when the raids came you crawled under. Remember?' she asked the Colonel, down the length of the table.

He smiled. 'I did my service overseas. We didn't have Morrison shelters.'

'Well, my point is,' she said, 'that the rules of society change in a war. Look how all of us women were called up to work in the factories and whatnot, in place of the men who had gone off to fight. We had freedoms we'd never enjoyed up to then. The rules of behaviour by which we'd been raised disappeared for those few years.'

Patrick, according to the British rule of seating couples separately at dinner, was a few chairs further down the table, next to the wife of the stockbroker. Looking at his great-aunt with a grin, he asked, 'Did *you* work in a factory?'

'I did many things,' she told him. 'One went where one was told to go, with war work. For a time I even drove an ambulance – I adored that. And then, of course, the war ended and the boys came back, and we women had to give up our jobs, and that was terrible. For me, at least. I'd had a taste, you see, of what life could be like, of independence. Couldn't fit myself into the mould again, not after that. I suppose that's what propelled me into politics.' She looked my way and smiled. 'So there you are, then. The beginnings of my biography.'

45

Anne Wood glanced up, intrigued. 'Are you a writer, Kate?'

Venetia answered for me. 'She's a journalist.'

I saw the heads turn all down the length of the table and remembered what Margot had said about Venetia being 'famously allergic' to journalists. Evidently Venetia's friends were wondering how someone like me had sneaked onto the guest list.

The Colonel – very gallantly, I thought – explained to everyone I'd been in London for the trial. 'She was unfortunate enough to fall in league,' he said, 'with Patrick.'

Patrick's mother, midway down the table, smiled, and then said, 'Patrick mentioned you'd had quite a nasty shock the other day…I do hope you've recovered?'

Not quite sure, I looked to Patrick, who explained, 'She means that accident, the hit-and-run. I did get it right, didn't I…it *was* a family friend of yours that died?'

Anne Wood said, 'You don't mean that poor man who was struck and killed on Wednesday morning, at St Paul's? I saw the aftermath…the ambulance. You knew him?'

'Well…'

'I read about that in the paper,' someone else put in. 'They haven't found the car yet, have they?'

Patrick said, 'I shouldn't think they ever will, unless the driver develops a conscience.'

I was keen to change the subject, and it must have altered something in my face because Venetia seemed to think I needed bolstering. She took the nearest bottle and began to fill my wineglass.

'Oh, no,' I said, 'I really can't. I have to drive.'

She held the bottle poised, surprised. 'You're not thinking of driving all that way back up to London tonight, are you? Not at this hour, on your own?'

The Colonel wouldn't hear of it. 'No, no, we have plenty of rooms, my dear girl. Take your pick.'

'I really couldn't...'

'Nonsense,' said the Colonel. 'Have some wine, enjoy yourself. We don't let our guests get away so easily.'

To be honest, I wasn't really struggling to get away. And while I hadn't followed Patrick's earlier instructions to bring along my negligée, I did, from habit, have a toothbrush with me, and it wouldn't be the first time that I'd worn the same clothes two days running.

'Of course she's staying,' said Venetia Radburn. So it was decided.

The room they showed me to was lovely, very spacious and high-ceilinged, with large windows that at daybreak, I'd been promised, gave a view across the garden to the walnut grove.

I had expected Patrick, being Patrick, might at least attempt to make a pass, but to my great relief he didn't. He didn't even follow me upstairs. Long after the other guests had gone, and I had changed into my borrowed nightgown, having carefully smoothed out my simple black dress at the foot of the bed so that it would be wearable in the morning, I still could hear the timbre of his voice in conversation with his family in the drawing room below. I couldn't make out what anyone was saying, only that it sounded like a very keen discussion or debate that would be going on awhile.

But then again, you couldn't be too sure, I thought, with Patrick. And, remembering my grandmother's advice that you could never trust a lawyer, I made sure to lock my door.

SATURDAY, SEPTEMBER 16

The Colonel saw me out next morning, to my car. It can't have been an easy thing to do, to wheel his chair across that gravel, but he managed it, a holdout from the days when men's behaviour had been bound by rules of chivalry. His parting smile convinced me once again that in his youth he would have been at least as handsome as his son. He said, 'You're sure that you won't change your mind, and stay to lunch?'

'I'm sorry, but I can't. I have to be somewhere this afternoon.'

'Ah, well, I had to ask. I do hate losing all my company at once.'

Patrick had left half an hour ago, and Venetia had gone, too, though not before I'd had the chance to spend some time in conversation with her, just us two. I'd risen early; so had she. Her allergy to journalists apparently did not apply at breakfast. For a long time we had been the only people round the table, and our talk had been wide-ranging, from our favourite Paris restaurants to the state of the economy. She had such a quick intelligence, and such a way with language, that I could have stayed the whole day in that room with her, just talking. But the highlight of it all, for me, had been when she had asked me for my card. 'You never know,' she'd said. 'Perhaps one day I *will* write my biography.'

I hadn't really thought that she'd been serious, but I would have been an idiot to let the pitch go by, and so I'd given her my business card. 'My number's on the back, and Patrick has my address in Toronto, at my grandmother's.'

'Of course.' And then, the icing on the cake, 'Perhaps, if you come back to London sometime in the spring, when I'm not travelling so much, you could have Patrick bring you by my flat for tea.'

And so it seemed I'd scored a minor coup, achieving everything I could have hoped from coming here to dinner. I was smiling now, because of that, and the Colonel, not knowing the source of my happiness, appeared to put it down to his own charms.

He smiled. 'A shame that Patrick couldn't stay to see you off.'

'Oh, well. He works a lot.'

With steady eyes, the old man shook my hand. 'My son's a fool. And you're a lovely girl,' he said. 'Drive carefully.'

He waved me off, a lonely figure growing ever smaller in the rear view as I rumbled down the drive.

It was easily the warmest day we'd had yet in September, and I drove with the car windows open, purposely leaving the motorway early and taking the scenic route down into Hampshire. Tall trees arched up over me, making a tunnel of green that cast cool dappled shadows across my car's windshield, with here and there flickers of sunlight that caught on the late-blooming wildflowers lining the verge. The day and the drive lulled me into a pleasantly semi-hypnotic state, so that I nearly missed seeing the signpost for Elderwel pointing away to the right.

I turned the car sharply, just missing the hedge at the side of the road.

Seen from the crest of a low hill as I approached, Elderwel looked like a tiny toy village of little square houses and small tidy gardens that ran in a line down each side of the narrow main street, with a church in the middle. Drawing closer, I could see more detail – clustered shops, and a one-storey school, and a half-timbered pub, and beside the pub, something that caught my attention: an old greystone house with a neat painted sign at the gate that read simply, 'The Laurels'.

I pulled up across from it, looking more closely. This had been the house where Andrew Deacon lived. In a street of unremarkable houses, it was the most unremarkable. With its quietly ordinary walls and the windows with blinds behind, looking like half-asleep eyes, it stood rather deliberately back from the road, not expecting or wanting attention. No one would give it a second glance, I thought. Just like its owner.

Taking a last look I slipped the car back into gear and moved on up the long street towards the grey church of St Stephen's.

'To every thing there is a season, and a time to every purpose under the heaven.' The vicar, a young man, mid-thirties or so, with laugh-lines deeply carved around his eyes, was reading from Ecclesiastes in a pleasant voice that sounded not the slightest bit funereal. *'A time to be born, and a time to die...'*

In the yew tree at the vicar's back a wren had taken shelter and was watching me with disconcerting steadiness, as though it knew I didn't quite belong. I'd been afraid there wouldn't be many at the funeral, and that I as a stranger would stand out like the proverbial sore thumb, but this corner of the churchyard was thick with people. Keeping discreetly to the edge of the crowd, I manoeuvred myself into a spot from where I had a clear view of the coffin and those closest to it.

'A time to kill, and a time to heal...'

I let my gaze wander the men standing nearest the grave, a monochromatic assembly of dark suits, virtually indistinguishable from each other. Trying to pick out which was Andrew Deacon's nephew, I studied the faces.

'A time to keep silence, and a time to speak...'

The wren in the yew tree tipped its head as though studying *me*, its bead-like eyes betraying nothing of its thoughts. Ignoring it, I narrowed my focus to the three men standing to the right side of the vicar, all of whom looked to be something like sixty or seventy, just the right age.

'A time of war, and a time of peace...'

Watching the three men, it struck me that they were among the oldest people here. I only saw two women and one man who would have been near Andrew Deacon's age. Not many old friends come to see him off. Perhaps, I thought, when you got to be Andrew Deacon's age there weren't too many old friends left.

I couldn't help but feel I'd done the right thing, coming here in Grandma's place, to say goodbye. Though I had to admit it appeared Andrew Deacon had not been too lonely –

there were some thirty people gathered round his plain wood coffin, and it didn't take a journalist to see this was a man who had been well liked and respected, and was missed.

It shamed me to remember just how blithely I had brushed him off; considered him a nuisance...

'For God shall bring every work into judgement,' the vicar was saying, *'and every secret thing, whether it be good, or whether it be evil.'*

A sharp wind stirred the scattering of flowers on the coffin, and the wren shot from the yew tree like a bullet, madly twittering. One of the three men that I had been watching reached forward to straighten a small wreath of rosebuds, then stood back and lowered his gaze to his black-gloved clasped hands.

The nephew, I decided, and felt even more sure of it at the ceremony's end, when the vicar shook his hand first and some others from the crowd stepped up to offer words of comfort. I didn't attempt to speak to him then, not just yet. Instead I followed along to the reception, mingling with genuine mourners amid the plates of sandwiches and polished urns of coffee.

I knew I wasn't one of them – I hadn't known the man as they had; I could claim no real acquaintance that would justify my being here, in what had until recently been Andrew Deacon's home. But I was, as Andrew Deacon himself had pointed out, an observer of other people's lives. It was a trait that I'd been born with and I earned my living from it and I couldn't ever switch it off completely. I was curious to see inside the house where he had lived, to study his possessions and the people who had known him and to judge from them what sort of man he'd been.

I had learnt much in the ten minutes that I'd been inside The Laurels. I'd learnt, for example, that its owner had been a great gardener. In contrast to the bland, colourless face that the house showed the street, the high-walled back garden was filled with a startling and lovingly tended assortment of flowers and shrubberies, artistically arranged in beds that curved around the property in such a way they left only enough room for one trimmed green circle of lawn at the centre, with space for a bench and a birdbath.

I stood at the dining room window and looked at that garden, and tried to imagine the work that had gone into making it – the never-ending daily round of weeding, trimming, watering…of tying off the branches of the vines so that they grew just so against the sun-warmed wall…of digging up perennials, dividing up the roots, and then replanting them…a task for every season. And I tried to picture Andrew Deacon sitting on his bench beside the birdbath, lost in thought, as old men sometimes are, and looking at his flowers, at the beds of tea roses that grew close against the lawn.

He had liked to look at things of beauty. That I knew, from standing in this long room that had served as both a living room and dining room, its walls a pale golden peach colour that warmed in the light and set off the mahogany dining room suite to advantage. He'd hung paintings – not prints, but real paintings – wherever he could. Mostly landscapes, and street scenes, and one I particularly liked, of a little round windmill with wood-and-cloth sails. It didn't look Dutch, I thought. Greek, maybe. Mediterranean.

Andrew Deacon had been to Greece, I knew, because above one low cabinet he'd hung a collection of photographs, all of them black and white, all of them good, all displaying the same eye – his own, I guessed – for light and composition. At least one was from Greece, looking down on the ruined remains of the open-air theatre at Delphi. I'd stood in almost the same spot myself, on my only trip to Greece, and it was strange to see the view again through someone else's eyes; to know that Andrew Deacon had once stood there, too, and seen what I had seen.

The other photographs showed places that I didn't know. Like the paintings, they were mostly landscapes: an avenue of plane trees, deep in shadow, that looked French; a sweep of barren desert underneath a cloudless sky; a curve of coastline backed by jagged mountains wreathed in mist, that felt distinctly Oriental. And there, unexpected, the little squat windmill again, with its round stone walls, backed by the sun with a man's silhouette standing just to one side.

I was leaning in for a better look when a pleasant male voice said behind me, 'They're lovely, those photographs, aren't they? He had a great talent.'

Turning, I found myself facing the vicar. He looked even younger close up – early thirties, perhaps, with dark hair and dark eyes and a warm, relaxed smile. He offered me his hand. 'Hello. I'm sorry, I don't know all Andrew's friends.'

'Kate Murray,' I introduced myself above the handshake, and his eyebrows lifted.

'You're American.'

I didn't correct him. My grandmother always said that there were certain categories of people who shouldn't be corrected, for the sake of politeness, and I was fairly certain men of God fell into one such category. 'I've been working in

London,' was all that I said, and then into the short pause that followed I added, 'That's where I met Mr Deacon.'

'Ah.' He didn't ask for details, but then why would he? I thought. I was the only one who felt a need to justify my presence.

I shifted the talk from myself. 'That was a lovely service, Reverend…'

'Beckett. Tom Beckett.'

I nearly made some remark about his name being well suited to his profession, but I stopped myself, figuring that he probably got it all the time, so I said nothing, and the Reverend Thomas Beckett grinned.

'It's quite all right,' he told me. 'My mother's way of making sure I chose the right sort of career, I think. And I'm glad you liked the service.' With his hands in his pockets, he studied the frames on the wall. 'I always think they're rather sad things, photographs, when someone dies. One is left with the pictures, but none of the stories.'

I hadn't really thought of that before, but he was right. I looked at the pictures with new eyes, wondering when he'd taken them, and why. They were a record of a man who'd travelled widely in his life. I looked for pictures of a wife, a family, but found only one small portrait, framed and sitting on a table, of a young man robed for graduation. Intrigued, I took a step to study it more closely. 'Is that Mr Deacon?'

'No, that's his nephew, James,' the vicar told me, with a reminiscent smile. 'Andrew loathed having his picture taken. Went to great lengths to avoid it, if possible.'

I took stock of the room again – a quiet room, a man's room, with its trappings of a solitary life. 'He was a bachelor?'

'A widower. His wife died long ago, I understand. They had no children.'

'Oh.'

'Here's James.' The vicar stopped a man who would have passed us by, and, putting a hand on my shoulder, brought me forward. 'James, I'd like to introduce Kate Murray, one of Andrew's friends from London. James Cavender,' he told me, and smiled an apology at both of us. 'You'll have to excuse me, I'm meant to be helping my wife with the coffee.'

It *was* the man I'd noticed at the funeral. He'd be somewhere in his seventies, I judged, with a determined mouth, a longish nose, and pale blue eyes. Kind eyes.

James Cavender had kept hold of my hand from the handshake, and gave it back now as he looked once again at me, the kind eyes making a visible effort. 'You're from London?'

'I've been working there, yes. I wanted to tell you how sorry I am—'

'You're Canadian.'

That stopped me, in spite of myself. James Cavender, I thought, had a good ear for accents. 'I am, yes. But how…?'

'You're the journalist.'

I paused at that, frowning myself as I wondered just how…

'I'm afraid I can't help you, Miss Murray.' James Cavender's long face had hardened. 'My uncle gave you everything; I've nothing else to add. And now, if you'll excuse me,' he said, in a flat voice, and pointedly turning his back he walked off.

SUNDAY, SEPTEMBER 17

It was just how he'd said it, I thought. 'You're *the* journalist'. Definite article. Clearly, his uncle had told him about me. But as to the 'everything' he thought his uncle had given me, I had no clue. Very likely I never would know. I had left the reception right after James Cavender's snub, and I didn't expect I would ever be back to The Laurels, or Elderwel.

I hadn't gone there, after all, to cause a scene, or be embarrassed. I had better things to do. And so I'd pushed the matter from my mind, and got on with my work.

I'd spent today in Essex, out near Colchester, interviewing the family of one of the victims of my now-convicted murderer. They'd had a lot to say, and it was going on for seven when I finally made it back to my hotel.

The desk clerk was ready with my room key. 'There's a gentleman to see you.'

'Oh?'

'He's been here since four-thirty. I did ask him if he'd like to leave a message, but he said that he'd prefer to wait. He's in the Bugle Lounge,' he said, and checked his notes. 'A Mr Cavender.'

I crossed the lobby slowly, apprehensively.

The Bugle Lounge had lots of ferns and hunting prints and deep red fabric walls – a warmly masculine environment that made it a relaxing place to sit and have a quiet drink, or read the evening paper. James Cavender was doing both. He was sitting at a corner table, on his own, his chair drawn round to face the open doorway and the bar, so he'd be visible to anyone who entered.

Not that I saw him right away. He was one of a half-dozen men of a similar age, sitting round in a similar style, but when I saw him I remembered him – the long face, the pale eyes.

In spite of his earlier snub, he had old-fashioned manners. He stood as I came across to meet him.

'Mr Cavender.'

He shook my hand. 'Miss Murray. I do apologise for coming up like this, without an appointment. I did try telephoning first – my uncle left your name and number on his desk – but you were out. I haven't caught you at an inconvenient time?'

I told him that he hadn't, though my voice stayed fairly cool. A fleeting smile transformed his features as he motioned me to sit. We sat. Folding his newspaper neatly, he set it aside and studied it a moment, as though he wasn't sure how to proceed. He glanced up. 'May I buy you a drink?'

'You don't have to do that.'

'Nonsense. What will you have?'

'Dry white wine, please.'

He didn't summon the waiter, but rose and fetched the

drinks himself from the bar, a pause that was deliberately designed, I thought, to give him time to organise his mind. When he returned, his face had cleared; his eyes held purpose.

He began to talk before he'd finished sitting. 'I was rude to you yesterday, Miss Murray. I apologise. I'd like you to know that I am not ordinarily rude.'

'That's all right.'

'No, it isn't. It isn't.' He swirled the contents of his glass and took a drink. 'The thing is, Uncle Andrew was the only family I had left. I liked him. We got on together, he and I. We always did.' He said it simply, quietly, the way I'd noticed most men spoke of things that they felt deeply. 'I didn't see the need for him to come up here, to London. It's quite taxing at his age, you know…the trains, the tube. It's tiring. And unnecessary, really, when he could have simply called you on the telephone. I told him that, but he insisted. Wouldn't listen. Stubborn man, my uncle. If he'd taken my advice, and stayed at home…' He left the thought unfinished, but I sensed the conflict in him – his frustration with his uncle, and the guilt he felt for fixing any blame upon the dead. 'When I heard what had happened,' he said, 'I was angry. I still am. And rather inexcusably, I took that anger out on you. At any rate, I didn't sleep too well last night, thinking of how I'd spoken to you. You were only carrying out Uncle Andrew's last wishes, so to speak, and I ought to have helped. So,' he sat back and steepled his fingers. 'I'm not sure what you need, in terms of access to his files. He did keep photographs. Not many, mind you, and I wouldn't know what you'd be looking for, but if you'd like to borrow them, you're welcome.'

I shook my head. 'I'm sorry, but I don't—'

'He would have wanted you to see them, and the papers. I expect that's why you made the trip down yesterday.'

'Mr Cavender...'

'Is it to be a book, or just an article? Early days yet, I know, but—'

'Mr Cavender.' This time my tone of voice registered. Waiting, he looked at me. How did I say this, I wondered?

I came at it sideways. 'Your uncle and I didn't really have much time to talk. We only exchanged a few words. I was busy, you see, with the trial and everything, so he told me I could call him, that we'd maybe go for dinner, but we never got that far because the accident—'

'But that means...' He was frowning as he tried to take it in, what I had told him. 'But that means you don't know...'

I shook my head. 'I don't know anything.'

Andrew James Deacon, his nephew informed me, came into the world on November 11th, in 1918, on the day that the First World War ended. Andrew's mother took that to be a particular omen, and often in later years liked to remark on how peaceful her son's face had been at his birth, as if he'd somehow in his nascent wisdom heard the guns fall silent all along the Western Front. At any rate, he grew to be an easygoing child who never quarrelled, never picked a fight, not even with his older sister, Lucy.

He loved languages, and painting, but being the son of a headmaster meant that there were certain academic expectations, and young Andrew had obligingly fulfilled them, going up to Oxford on a scholarship and coming down with firsts. His father offered him a teaching post, but Andrew, independent, turned it down, and went instead to work in South America. There his passion for paintings allowed him to build quite a reputable name as an art dealer, but after two years in Brazil a nearly fatal bout of dengue fever drove him north, to New York City, where he fell in love and married.

That had been, James Cavender confessed, a shock to all the family. 'I was only a boy at the time, but I remember the talk. My mother had never recovered completely, you must understand, from the King's abdication a few years before, and now here her own brother was marrying some strange American... No one approved.' No one went to the wedding, either, but then of course there was a war on and it wasn't such a simple thing to cross the Atlantic.

But later that year Andrew Deacon had crossed it, to take a position in Lisbon. His newlywed wife, for her safety, had stayed in New York, while her husband, alone, went to work with the famed Ivan Reynolds.

'I didn't know who Ivan Reynolds was, of course, when I was younger,' said James Cavender. 'My mother always spoke of him the way she spoke of royalty. In some ways, I expect, he was America's equivalent. Like JP Morgan, or the Rockefellers.'

Which was, I thought, a good way of describing Ivan Reynolds. His was one of the twentieth century's fairy-tale lives – the American son of a dispossessed White Russian mother and Scottish-born father, he'd made his first fortune in oil and his second in shipping, and had donated most of it back to the public by building fantastic museums to house his own privately gathered collections of art.

I would not for a moment have guessed that the quiet and modestly dressed old man sitting beside me that day on the steps of St Paul's would ever have moved in the same sphere as Reynolds.

'In the end, my uncle didn't work for Ivan Reynolds very long. He went to Lisbon sometime late in 1943, I think, and Reynolds passed away the following spring, of cancer. My uncle came home after that.'

'And his wife? Did she come over from New York, to join him?'

'No, she died that spring, as well. I don't know all the details. My uncle never spoke of it.' He thought about this for a moment, then he said, as though it were important I should understand, 'My uncle was a very private man. A quiet man. He didn't talk much – never said two words when one would do.'

I took my wineglass from the table with a frown. 'And yet he travelled all this way to talk to me, a stranger. Why?'

'I don't think he considered you a stranger. When he mentioned you, he spoke as if he knew you.'

'No, we'd never met,' I said. 'He knew my grandmother.'

'Ah, there you are, then. I felt sure there was a personal connection, from the way he spoke.' The faint edge of a smile. 'He'd had a call from Whitehall, I believe it was from Whitehall, and it left him rather...well, angry might not be the right word...more disgusted, I guess. He said little enough about it, only that things never changed and he shouldn't have wasted his time; should have gone to the press to begin with. That's where you came in,' he said. 'He didn't mention you by name, of course. He wouldn't have. But he did say he knew a

62

journalist in London, a young woman, a Canadian, who was someone he could trust. He said you'd do a better job of it than anyone.'

'A better job of what?'

'Getting it out in the open, I assume.'

'But you don't know what "it" was?'

'No, I don't. I'm sorry.'

We were on our second round of drinks. The Bugle Lounge was filling, but oddly enough the increasing activity around us and the densely layered rise and fall of voices only seemed to make our corner more secluded, more untouched, as though we'd somehow found the calm eye of a storm and were secure in it.

James Cavender's voice didn't try to compete with the noise from the bar, but I heard him distinctly. 'I *do* know it began last May,' he said, and settled back. 'The Chelsea Flower Show. It was my uncle's passion, you know, gardening. His garden. He came up to London every year like clockwork for the show, he never missed it. Only this time, he came back all out of sorts. I noticed it straight off when I met his train, and he didn't say anything all the way home. Not that he was a talkative man, as I've said, but it wasn't the silence, so much as the *way* he kept silent.' He paused, seeking a way to explain. 'I saw a man once, on the news, whose house had crumbled in an earthquake. He'd lost everything, his home, his family, absolutely everything, and all he did was sit there, staring. Didn't say a word. My Uncle Andrew looked like that,' he said, and glanced at me to see that I was following. I nodded, once, to show I understood, and he continued, 'I was worried, so I dropped round after dinner to look in on him. I found him drinking whiskey. Uncle Andrew rarely drank – he only kept a bottle in the house for company. And there he was, with half the bottle gone, and past the point of making sense. He simply sat there, staring at the wall, at all the photographs he'd taken in his travels…and the only thing he said was, "He's not dead. He should be dead."' He took a drink himself, and shrugged. 'Anyway, that was the beginning of it. The next day he got down his boxes of papers and started to write that report.'

I shook my head vaguely. 'Report?'

'Forgive me. I do keep forgetting. I was so sure, you see, that he had given you a copy. It was a fairly thick report, all typed, with referenced letters, documents. He spent a lot of time on it. He didn't do much else all summer, only that and his garden. He sent the reports off the end of July. There were two, that I know of. One went to Whitehall, to someone named Petty. The other went airmail to Lisbon. I posted them both for him.'

'And do you know what was in the report?'

He shook his head. 'No, I'm afraid not. He didn't discuss it, you see, and I didn't intrude. I never did learn who it was who was meant to be dead. But…' His pause had significance.

'Yes?'

'Well, it may have been nothing, but…that night, that first night he came back from London and I caught him drinking, just after the Flower Show, it seemed to me that he was staring at one photograph specifically. And when my uncle told me, "He's not dead", I rather fancied he was speaking of the man who's in that photograph. I had a closer look myself, a little later on, but it was nobody I recognised.' He stopped, then, as though something had occurred to him. 'Unless...' he said, 'unless, of course...I'd quite forgotten *that*.' His eyes began to lose their focus slightly as the memory rose. 'One does forget...'

He raised his glass, but absently, and from his face I knew he was no longer in the present, but had slipped into another time completely, and his next words took me with him.

It had been this time of year, he said, the middle of September, when the mornings started cool and crisp and warmed to nearly sweltering by afternoon, as though the summer was not ready to give in, just yet, to autumn.

It was 1944, and he was twelve. He should have been at school that day, but his mother had taken him out on account of the trip to Southampton. The war years had made her protective, and paranoid. Even when they were at home in the village she kept a close watch from the sitting-room window for fear a bomb, unheralded, would strike the school. It wasn't the idea of the bomb itself that worried her, so much as the idea that they might not die together, that they'd be in different places when it came. She'd been a worrier like that since James's father had been listed with the missing in the fall of Hong Kong to the Japanese. At times she'd come quite close, James thought, to going mad, but then her brother, Andrew, had returned from several years abroad, and life had levelled out somewhat.

James hadn't really wanted, or expected, to like his Uncle Andrew. James's father had never got on with his brother-in-law, and the tensions had grown with the outbreak of war. James could often remember his father remarking that men who stayed safe in New York when their country had need of them weren't men at all, they were cowards, and ought to be damned well ashamed of themselves. And now that James's father had gone missing out in Hong Kong, James himself had grown disdainful, in his father's place, of those men who had never donned a uniform.

He'd met his uncle coldly, accepting him into the house with no thought of making friends, but it was easier to dislike the imagined Uncle Andrew than the real one, than this quiet man who never had an unkind word for anyone; who only had to put his hands upon the earth, it seemed, to make the garden bloom with flowers where before there had been weeds. And though he felt a traitor to his father, James had found that, as the weeks and months had passed, he'd formed a bond with Uncle Andrew that was based, as much as anything, on their shared sense of loneliness.

Where James had been missing his father – and to some extent his mother, since she hadn't for some time now been the mother he had known before the war – Andrew Deacon had been missing someone, too. His wife's death was a wound so raw he rarely even mentioned it, and if somebody else did he would bring the conversation to an end.

'He must have loved her very much,' James Cavender confided. 'He was quite a young man, then, but that was it for him. There were no other women. And he wore his wedding ring until he died. I had him buried with it.'

Anyhow, he carried on, he'd come to feel a kinship with his Uncle Andrew, so he hadn't minded being taken out of school that day to go down to Southampton. There had only been himself, his mother, and his uncle, and the driver of the van they'd hired to bring his uncle's few household effects home to Elderwel.

Andrew Deacon had flown back to England from Lisbon by plane, in the spring, but his paintings and belongings had been left to follow on by ship. They'd twice been delayed, but considering there was a war on, the fact that they'd made it to England at all was a miracle.

James, looking back, had a very clear memory of that afternoon – the busy docks, the ships, the shouting, and the blue September sky...and his Uncle Andrew, talking to a nervous-looking member of the crew. 'What sort of damage?' his uncle was asking...and then they were turning around again, back to the ship.

There were two crates, not large. Sitting there on the quay they looked normal enough from a distance, but close up James saw they were dripping with water. The man in ship's uniform, leading them, made his apologies, made his excuses – a hatch had been left open; no one knew how...

Andrew Deacon took this news the way that he took everything: calmly, no change of expression. He moved to examine the crates, walking round them, and James saw him lean in to sniff at a waterlogged section of wood.

While the adults were talking, James made a careful imitation of his uncle's actions, walking slowly round each crate in turn, hands clasped behind his back. He even sniffed the slats as well, and smelt...well, nothing. He'd expected the seaweedy smell of salt water, but the wet boards only smelt like wood.

Stepping back, he bumped against a man...not Uncle Andrew.

All he would remember in his later years was that the man had been tall, with a moustache and walking stick. The walking stick stayed in his memory because it was carved with a dragon's head handle, an ivory white dragon's head handle with glaring red eyes. This was what registered with the boy James as he stood looking up at the stranger.

The man spoke. A posh voice. 'Hullo, my boy. You're giving them a good once-over, are you? Are they yours?'

James had been spared the need of answering by his uncle's reappearance.

The adult James Cavender paused in his narrative. The lights in the Bugle Lounge seemed to have dimmed. Someone laughed in the shadowy corner behind me; I don't think he heard it. He lifted his head. 'I'd never seen my Uncle Andrew angry. I suppose that's why it stuck with me, that one day at the docks, why I remembered it so vividly – because I'd never seen him look like that.'

James, at twelve, had not known what to do. Andrew Deacon's eyes ignored the boy, and fastened on the stranger, who had, smiling, lit a pipe and raised his walking stick to indicate the damaged crates. 'Some trouble with your shipment, was there? Ah, well,' he said, 'accidents will happen.'

Andrew Deacon, very calmly, had said, 'James, go to your mother, would you? There's a good lad. I won't be a moment.'

But he'd been a long time talking to the man. And then the man had gone, as inexplicably, it seemed, as he'd arrived.

'I never knew his name,' James Cavender said now, to me. 'We never saw him, after that. But it might have been him in the photograph, there by the windmill. A tall man with a walking stick – the outline of the figure's fairly clear. One can't make out the face, but then I don't remember faces from my childhood. Do you?'

I hadn't thought about it really.

'Anyway, I don't suppose that's much help to you. Maybe these,' he told me, 'will be more.' And from the seat beside him, underneath his folded coat, he drew a large manila envelope and handed it across to me.

'What's this?'

'They're the letters that my uncle wrote to Mother, in the war.'

'Oh, no,' I said, and pushed the envelope away. 'I couldn't...'

'Nonsense. He wouldn't have minded.'

I wasn't so sure anybody would want a reporter to read his old letters, but James Cavender insisted I had no cause for concern.

'My mother's dead. Been dead for twenty years,' he said. 'She might have lived much longer, but my father wore her down. He came back to us, after the war,' he explained, 'but he wasn't the same man. He'd been in a Japanese prison camp, all those years, and...well, it would have changed any man, what he went through. He was...difficult.' He left the rest unsaid, and shifted topics to, 'My Uncle Andrew wasn't with us anymore, by that point. He went back to doing business as an art dealer. He travelled. It was only after Father died that he came back to Elderwel to settle.'

'With his garden.'

'With his garden, yes.'

I looked down, at the envelope of letters.

James Cavender followed my gaze. 'They're from Portugal. I thought you might need to know details of what he was doing in Lisbon.'

'I'm sorry? Why…?'

'Well, it must have something to do with Lisbon, mustn't it, this story he wanted to tell you? He sent a report there.'

I nodded, accepting the logic. And then I said slowly, 'He talked about justice, the day that I met him. He mentioned a murder.'

'I wouldn't know anything about that, I'm afraid.'

'He never spoke of any deaths in Lisbon?'

'He never spoke of Lisbon. There was Ivan Reynolds, naturally – he died, but that was cancer. And my uncle's wife, but she was in New York.' He tipped his head as he considered. 'I should imagine there were any number of murders in Lisbon, in the war years. It was rather like Casablanca, wasn't it? A neutral place with people from both sides milling about, plotting things in back alleys…a magnet for spies and skullduggery.'

'And there's nothing in the letters to your mother?'

'About murder? Not that I recall. But you might find a reference that I've missed, when you read them.' He thought of something, brightening. 'He does mention several acquaintances, people he worked with. Perhaps they might be of some help, if they're still living. That can be something of a problem, when you get to Uncle Andrew's age,' he told me. 'Finding people still alive. It's like that poem by Kingsley, do you know the one I mean? "Young and Old", I think it's called. "When all the world is young,

70

lad", that's how it begins, and how one ought to travel, have adventures, fall in love, and then it finishes quite touchingly:

'When all the world is old, lad,
And all the trees are brown;
And all the sport is stale, lad,
And all the wheels run down,

Creep home and take your place there,
The spent and maimed among:
God grant you find one face there
You loved when all was young.'

He pondered this a moment, while he finished off his drink. 'I suppose that's why my uncle came to live in Elderwel again, when he was done with dealing art and all his travelling. My mother was there, and myself. Although,' he said, with faint regret, 'the face he'd loved the most when he was young, I should imagine, would have been his wife's. He wrote a fair bit about *her* in his letters to Mother.'

I looked at the envelope of letters again, and he said, 'Those were the ones that I could find straight off; there may be more that I can let you have.'

I realised he assumed that I was taking on the story, and before I could think of a nice way to let him down gently, he said: 'I'll be going through my uncle's things this next while, clearing out the house before it's sold. If I do come across a copy of his report, shall I send it to you here, or shall I wait till you come down?'

I didn't need more work, I thought. I had more than enough

on my plate as it was, without chasing cold leads on an uncertain story that might, in the end, not be worth half the effort. But I looked at his face, at the pale blue eyes that yesterday had been so cold, and now were so expectant. And I couldn't tell him no. It wouldn't cost me anything to let him send the damned report, I told myself. I didn't have to read it. 'I'm only here till Tuesday morning,' I relented. 'So I likely won't have time to make another trip to Elderwel. But if you do find something, you can always send it on to me in Canada. I'll give you my address.' Tearing a sheet from my notebook I wrote the address of my grandmother's house in Toronto.

He took it, and thanked me. We stood.

We said our goodbyes in the lobby. I could have gone up to my room straight away but I stayed there to watch him walk out through the great glass revolving doors. Not that I really expected that lightning would strike twice, but after all, this was the second time a member of his family had journeyed up to London just to talk to me, and I wanted to be absolutely certain this one got away all right.

He did. There were cabs in a queue at the front of the hotel, and he got into one. I wondered if he'd taken a hotel room for himself somewhere, or if he would be going back tonight, by train. It must have been a nuisance for him, coming all this way and waiting round so long to see me. I decided that he must have loved his uncle very much, to make the effort.

I was thinking this, and walking slowly back towards the elevator, when someone who'd been sitting on a lobby sofa rose to block my way. A small man, slightly built, with a receding hairline over sharp dark eyes.

'Miss Murray? I was wondering if I might have a word.'

MONDAY, SEPTEMBER 18

My temper had calmed by the following morning, but the whole thing still seemed so unlikely, to me, so surreal – this stranger drawing me aside to have a seat with him among the hotel lobby's potted palms, his patronising voice pitched low enough so people wouldn't overhear.

He'd shown me his credentials: Sergeant Robert Metcalf, Scotland Yard. He had been very to the point. 'I believe you are acquainted with a Mr Andrew Deacon,' he had told me, 'and that Mr Deacon may have passed you certain information that he wanted you to publish.'

I had stared at him a moment...then, deciding that what Mr Deacon had or had not given me was none of this man's business, I'd said only an enquiring, 'Yes?'

'The thing is, Miss Murray, that a good deal of what Mr Deacon told you is protected by the Official Secrets Act, and I'm afraid that any attempt to make those details public would be very inadvisable. At best, any such publication would be suppressed. At worst, there might be charges brought.'

'Charges against whom?'

He'd smiled, a condescending smile, instead of answering, but the implication had been clear to me then, as had the threat. It had the opposite effect, with me, from what he had intended. Always had. Just like Pandora's Box – when someone told me that I couldn't look inside, it only made the contents fascinate me more.

I'd placed my own notebook more firmly on top of the manila envelope James Cavender had brought for me, the one that held his uncle's wartime letters home from Lisbon, and feeling indignation flare inside me I had turned to Sergeant Robert Metcalf. Anyone who fired a warning shot across my bow, I'd thought, deserved a full-scale onslaught in return.

I couldn't quite remember what I'd said, what words I'd used…only that I'd been a little fierce, and very probably insulting, in my staunch defence of the freedom of the press. And then, not giving him a chance to speak again, I'd made a perfect exit, putting the whole incident behind me as I'd gone up to my room.

But now, this morning, sitting on my bed in my pyjamas with my breakfast tray in front of me, I wished I hadn't been so hasty; that I'd stayed around a little longer, asked more questions, made an effort to be civil. If I'd kept my wits about me, and kept the man talking, I might have learnt just what Scotland Yard *thought* I'd been told by Andrew Deacon… might have learnt, in fact, just how they'd known I'd ever met the man.

Maybe it wasn't too late. With my toast still in one hand, I reached for the phone and the London directory.

Sergeant Metcalf wasn't at his desk. He wasn't even, the receptionist informed me, in the country. I'd just missed him.

He had flown out this morning, and wouldn't be back until Friday. But if I cared to leave a message on his voicemail…

So I left a message, brief and to the point: I regretted the way I'd behaved when we met; could he please call me when he got back, at my home in Toronto, so we could discuss this?

I left him the number and hung up, faintly frustrated, honestly curious now as to what had been in Andrew Deacon's report. He'd sent two copies off, so his nephew had said – one to Lisbon, the other to Whitehall, to someone named…

'Petty.' I said it out loud, so it lodged in my memory and, taking a moment to wash down my toast with a swallow of coffee, I once again reached for the phone.

This was trickier, and more involved, than calling Scotland Yard. Whitehall wasn't one specific building, it was more of a district – a street, and a place, and a court, lined with government offices, stretching roughly from Trafalgar Square down to the Houses of Parliament. When someone spoke of 'Whitehall' they were speaking of the British Civil Service, but which branch…?

A half-hour of phoning around turned up only one Petty: a Stephen in the Foreign Office.

Stephen Petty's secretary had a friendly voice. I almost hated lying to her, but I was fairly certain people in the Foreign Office weren't inclined to volunteer much information to a total stranger calling, or to journalists.

'Hello,' I said. 'I wonder if I could just check the status of some correspondence that my father sent to Mr Petty, this past summer.'

'Yes, of course. Your father's name was…?'

'Andrew Deacon.'

'Deacon…Deacon…Yes, of course, I do seem to remember that. I'm sure I passed that on to Mr Petty. If you'll bear with me a moment, I'll go ask him.'

I was put on hold, and stayed there long enough to drink a second cup of coffee. I was pondering the wisdom of a third one, when the woman's voice returned, apologetic.

'I'm so sorry. It appears I was mistaken.'

'Oh?'

'There's no report from anyone named Deacon in our files.'

I felt a twang of disappointment. Then, 'I didn't say "report",' I pointed out. 'I just said "correspondence". How did you—'

'The thing is,' she cut in, 'we don't have anything at all from Mr Deacon.'

'Ah.'

'So there you are. I'm sorry that we couldn't help.' And I was hurried off the telephone as though I were a salesperson.

I hung the phone up slowly, while the journalistic sixth sense I depended on began to tingle deep within my mind. Well, well, I thought. There might, in fact, be something more to this affair than I had first believed. I might just, after all, have to begin to dig around a bit, and see what I could learn.

Pushing my breakfast tray down to the end of the bed, I leant over to pick up the big envelope James Cavender had given me, the letters that his uncle had been writing home from Lisbon, in the war. What was it he'd told me? 'I thought you might need to know details of what he was doing in Lisbon.'

I was starting to think that he might have been right.

CHAPTER TWO

Toronto

Come back with me to the first of all...
Let us now forget, and now recall...

ROBERT BROWNING, 'BY THE FIRESIDE'

TUESDAY, SEPTEMBER 19

Grandma's house, like Grandma, never changed. The same scents of paste wax and furniture polish still met me like a wall at the front door, and as always my steps shook the floor just enough to make the chimes ring very faintly in the big old mahogany-cased grandfather clock that stood angled in a corner of the entry hall. Ahead of me, the stairs ran steeply upwards to the bedrooms on the upper floors, while on this level I had a view right straight through to the kitchen.

Pocketing my key, I swung the front door closed behind me, making sure to turn the deadbolt. Grandma wasn't always good with locks – not because she was forgetful, but because her mind was frequently preoccupied with other things. She was a busy woman with an intellect that, I suspected, could run rings around my own. I slipped my shoes off, calling out to let her know that I'd arrived.

She didn't answer.

Normally, that wouldn't have alarmed me. Grandma often did her reading in the afternoon, and nothing short of an earthquake, or the ringing of the telephone, would draw her out of a good book. I wasn't even sure about the earthquake.

But today, for some reason, I felt a little bit uneasy at the silence. I called louder. 'Grandma?'

She wouldn't have been out, I thought. She'd known that I was coming, and besides, if she'd gone out she would have left a note for me on the hall table, the way that she always did. Worried, I set down my luggage and started to search.

She wasn't upstairs, in her bedroom. Or down in the basement doing laundry. She wasn't anywhere, as far as I could see. I was standing in the kitchen, trying to decide what to do next, when a flash of movement past the window caught my eye.

I hadn't thought to check the yard. Grandma wasn't really the outdoor type, and her yard wasn't much of a yard to begin with. When my grandfather had died she'd had it paved with brick, because she hated cutting grass. She'd spared the maple tree, which stood now as an island of natural growth in the narrow space, hemmed in by tall wooden privacy fences that, seen from the windows upstairs, made the back yards of Grandma and all of her neighbours look like rows of those claustrophobic narrow high-walled starting gates they jammed racehorses into. This wasn't living space, by Grandma Murray's definition – just the place she kept the garbage cans and, sometimes, hung her laundry out to dry.

So it was something of a shock for me to see her out there now, and on her knees at that, trowelling topsoil into a raised wooden planter – a new feature – set in the very back corner. I'd never seen her gardening. She looked quite different, doing it.

She didn't look herself. I couldn't put my finger on it,

really, but the difference was enough to keep me there, beside the kitchen window. I sat at the table with its tablecloth of yellow gingham checks with little apples spaced between the squares, and resting my chin on the heel of my hand I watched my grandmother the way I might have watched TV.

She spent a fair amount of time preparing the newly built planter. Her neighbour, I guessed, must have made it for her – he was handy in his workshop, and was always quick to lend a hand to Grandma when she wanted something. Besides, the wood he'd used to make it matched the fence he'd built between their properties. He'd likely had some bits of boards left over, all these years, waiting for just such a project.

Grandma seemed pleased enough with it. I watched her dig holes and take twiggy somethings out of pots, carefully patting the clumpy roots into the soil. Then she soaked the whole bed with a watering can and stood, dusting her knees with gloved hands, looking satisfied. She still had that look when she came through the kitchen door.

'Katie! Sweetheart, when did you get back? I didn't hear the taxi.' Her hug was freshly cold with outside air, and smelt of garden soil and autumn leaves. And it was firm. At eighty-three, my Grandma Murray stood as arrow-straight as always, with her white hair – which had once been red as mine – cut short and styled for convenience. I had hopes that I would age like her, although I knew I'd never match her energy. She asked, 'How was your flight?'

'Fine, thanks. One of Margot's friends was on the plane as well. We managed to get seats together, so at least I had someone to talk to.' As Margot had promised, she'd told her friend, Nick, to keep an eye open for me at the airport, and he, being a security and surveillance expert, had taken her at her word, hunting me down in the check-in line. 'He was nice. He's in town for the international Chiefs of Police convention, and…'

'Oh, that reminds me.' Turning, she apologised, 'Sorry to interrupt, honey, but you had a call today from a policeman. Metcalf was his name. He called at two o'clock, or thereabouts. Now, you know I don't like giving anyone your schedule, but he did say you'd called him first, and that it was important, so I told him you'd be home tonight. I hope that was all right.'

'Of course it was.' I hadn't actually expected that he'd be in touch so soon. Whatever the Sergeant's failings, I conceded, he at least checked his voicemail and answered his messages promptly.

'Something to do with the trial, is it?'

'Sort of.'

'I thought it might be. He had an English accent.' She had her coat off now, and her gardening gloves, and was casting a glance at the clock. 'We have a bit of time before I have to get supper on the go. How be I make us a couple of Caesars?'

I didn't say no. My grandma's Bloody Caesars were her speciality; my weakness. Since I'd moved back to live with her, it had become a ritual between us, having drinks to celebrate my coming home after assignments.

I watched her while she moved to wash her hands and get the vodka from the cupboard, trying to think of a way to approach her about Andrew Deacon. She was not a chatty woman, and if she didn't want to talk about a subject, trying to engage her in discussion could be every bit as challenging as using your bare hands to try to open a determined clam. In the end, I tried to edge in sideways. Looking out the window, I remarked, 'I see you've got yourself a little garden out there.'

'Oh, hardly a garden. It's just the one planter. I thought it might be nice to have some roses.'

Roses…That was better than I'd hoped, really, because it seemed quite natural, then, to reach into my jacket, slung over the chair at my back, and take out the thick paperback mystery I'd carried to read on the plane. 'I brought you something back,' I said, 'from England.'

She glanced round from the chopping board, where she was wedging a lemon. 'Oh, Katie, you shouldn't be wasting your money on gifts, not for me.'

'It didn't cost anything.' I drew a breath. 'I went to Andrew Deacon's funeral, Grandma, and I thought that since…well, since you couldn't be there, you might like to have a little something, sort of a memento, from the grave. So here you are.' I took a small pressed rosebud from the pages of the book, and held it out toward her on my upturned palm.

She didn't take it right away. She set down her knife, and stood a moment looking at the flower lying on my outstretched hand. And then she reached to pick the rosebud up, with something close to reverence.

'Thank you, Katie,' she said quietly. 'That was thoughtful of you, very thoughtful. I…' She stopped, and set the fragile flower gently on the window ledge before turning to busy herself with the lemon again, her hands making rapid and decisive movements. Head down, she asked, 'What was the funeral like?'

I was back on uncertain ground again, feeling my way, but I took my cue from the deliberately conversational tone of her voice. 'Nice, I thought. It was in Hampshire, at a little village church, and the vicar gave a beautiful service.'

'Were there many people there?'

'Quite a few. I met his nephew.'

'Little Jamie, yes. His sister's boy. I had forgotten…'

Which must have meant she'd been a young woman when she'd met Andrew Deacon, if his nephew, at the time, had been a child. I tipped my head, taking a chance with a straightforward question. 'When were you friends with him, Grandma?'

'Oh, years ago, Katie. I told you. We lost touch.' Taking a half-empty jug of clam-and-tomato cocktail from the fridge she filled our two glasses and stirred in the vodka. Usually she rimmed the glasses, too, with salt and pepper, but this time she had either forgotten or simply not bothered. 'Did he have any family of his own, there? Any children?'

'No. He lost his wife during the war, I was told, and he never remarried. As far as I know, he was all on his own.'

She didn't turn; she kept her back to me, but I could sense the change. Her movements stilled. Head bent, she asked, 'How did she die, his wife?'

I'd hit a nerve, I knew, but since I wasn't sure how I had done it I carried on, cautiously, 'The nephew didn't say. He told me no one really talked about her much. She was American, apparently. They married in New York, and she stayed there while Mr Deacon went to Portugal, to work. I think she died while he was there.'

A long moment passed, and her silence was so like the silence I'd heard on the phone when I'd called her last Wednesday from London, that I couldn't help but be curious. 'Grandma?' I said. 'Did you know her?'

A pause. And then she turned her head, and once again I had that feeling that I'd had when I had seen her planting flowers in the yard – the feeling I was seeing someone I had never truly seen.

Her eyes, especially, were almost unfamiliar. They were smiling, but I thought the smile seemed sad. 'Oh, yes,' she said, 'I knew her very well.'

It wasn't the first time we'd sat face to face at the old kitchen table with its cheery yellow gingham cloth, the afternoon sun slanting through the back window. But this time was different.

Maybe, I allowed, the change was not in my grandmother, but in myself. My vision had matured, perhaps. Certainly I seemed to be seeing my grandmother through altered eyes, today – seeing her more fully, without prejudice.

In all the years I'd known her she had always seemed the same, the constant point around which my own world, chaotic as it was, revolved. And with the selfish eyes of youth I'd only viewed her from the angle that applied to me – she was *my* grandmother, not Georgie Murray, woman in her own right. I supposed that she hadn't been really allowed to be plain Georgie Murray for years, not since she'd been twenty-five, when she had married Grandpa. After that she'd always been somebody's wife, somebody's mother, someone's grandmother. In fact, she'd always filled that role so perfectly I'd never stopped to wonder what she might have been before all that…when she was my own age.

I had a feeling I was going to find out now, to get a glimpse at least, because she started out with, 'I suppose you never knew I spent a year in New York City, working, when I was a girl.'

'I didn't, no.' So that, I thought, must have been how she'd come to meet Andrew Deacon, and his wife. I leant my elbows on the table, took a sip of my own drink and waited, knowing that with Grandma you could never rush the process.

She was quiet for a moment, as though trying to decide where she should start the tale. I had no idea, not then, what was coming. Had I had any inkling, I would have stopped her, gone out to the hall, and fetched my tape recorder so I didn't lose a word. In fact, I never quite forgave myself for *not* recording what she told me, afterwards.

But then, I didn't know.

It started simply.

'I went down,' she told me, 'with three other girls, in '43. I knew them from here, in Toronto. We all worked together at a war plant, called John Inglis – they made refrigerators after the war, but during the war they made Bren guns, and we worked upstairs, in the payroll department. Well, one of the girls read an ad in the newspaper, and she asked me, how would I like to go work in New York? It didn't say in the newspaper what the job was, it just said working for the British government, in New York City.'

That, I thought later, was the point at which I should have started taping.

She went on, 'So, we wrote to them. It took a while, but finally we heard back, and they asked us to come for a typing test, to one of the downtown hotels. I remember I was nervous, but I only typed one line, and then they said fine, thank you, and that was that. I had the job. I had to have a medical, of course, and a note from my dentist, and the Mounted Police checked me out.' She smiled. 'My mother found out about that when a friend of hers wrote to ask what I'd been up to, because the RCMP had been round to our old neighbourhood, asking questions. Mother wasn't a stupid woman – I'm sure she figured two and two was four, but she never said anything if she did. But my dad…when I told him I'd been hired for this job in New York City, he said no. No way. In those days you would never go against your parents' wishes, and I thought the world of Dad.

'Usually, he backed me to the hilt when I had set my mind to something, but this time… I think maybe it was because my brothers, both of them, were fighting overseas, and he just didn't want me leaving home as well. I know that when my younger brother, Ronnie – you've heard me mention Ronnie, he's the one who played the violin I keep up in my closet—'

I'd heard his name a few times through the years, and I had seen the violin, but I felt suddenly ashamed that I remembered little else. To be honest, I had always thought he'd been her only brother, and although I knew he'd died before I'd come along, I didn't know much more than that.

'When Ronnie left,' said Grandma, 'Dad had a hard time of it. He kept saying how he couldn't get used to the house being so quiet, with the boys gone; and of course he'd listen to the radio and go to watch the newsreels, and he'd worry. He'd been in the First War, the Great War. He knew what war was. And he knew what my brothers were up against, what it was like for them, how slim the odds were they'd both come home safe. So I suppose when I said that I wanted to go to New

York, to him it just meant he'd be losing his last child, and that must have seemed like the last straw, to him.

'Anyway, he said no the first time. And then, of course, I had to talk him round, because I really wanted to go. If I'd been a man, I'd have done what my brothers did; I'd have gone over to fight, but I couldn't. I had to sit at home and watch all of them, all the young men of my neighbourhood, all the boys I'd played with, gone to school with, watch them all sign up and go off, and I felt like I'd go crazy if I didn't *do* something, if I didn't find a way to help the war effort. That's why I took the job at John Inglis, to begin with, because they made the Bren guns and I thought maybe one of those guns might end up helping one of my brothers, you know? Or your grandfather. Not that he was fighting on the ground like they were – he'd gone over earlier, right at the start of the war, to join the RAF. I'll never forget when he sent me that photograph of him in his uniform, he looked so handsome...'

'Is that the picture in your room?'

'That's right. Oh, my friends were jealous when they saw that. He looked just like a movie star. And of course, we weren't officially engaged then, but there was an understanding, and he'd write me all the time; I'd get a letter nearly every day. He told me what was happening in England...all the bombings, and the deprivations, and I wanted so desperately to do something that would help.

'This was what I tried to tell my dad, to make him understand, and in the end he said all right, that it was useless arguing with a redhead anyway, and that I might as well go if I'd made up my mind to. So then I told the other three girls, and a few days later the four of us left together and we went on the train to New York.

'That was my first time away from home – people didn't travel then, the way that they do now – and I cried all the way down on the train. I guess I looked funny to other people, but Dad had taken me to the station, and when I turned back he was tipping his hat to me, saying goodbye, and that got me going. I cried all the way to New York.' She still looked half embarrassed to admit it. 'I tell you, Katie, I was so homesick the first three weeks I thought I'd die. It's a terrible thing, homesickness.'

I'd never really felt it much, myself. Maybe if I'd had the sort of home she'd had – a father, mother, brothers – then the pull to home, for me, would have been stronger.

Behind us, in the living room, unseen, the mantel clock chimed off the half-hour with a melody so delicate it sounded like a music box.

She said, 'They put us in the Beekman Tower Hotel, on First Avenue. We were allowed to stay there for a month, I think, and then we were supposed to go out and find apartments for ourselves. Well, I'd never been away from home, like I said. I didn't have the first idea how to go about finding an apartment. But one of the girls I'd gone down with was older, quite sophisticated, and she found us a place. We lived in a brownstone, on East 54th. It was just what you see on TV – you could hear the garbage cans rattling and all, and there was a nightclub on the corner, it was really something else. But it was exciting, the time of my life.'

I couldn't help but call her on the contradiction. 'I thought you just said you were homesick.'

'Oh, only for three weeks. And then I fell in love with the city. There's no other city in the world like it. I'll never forget the first day we were there. It was spring, just a beautiful day, and the four of us thought we'd walk down for a first look at where we'd be working, and on the way down there we went past a bar. I can't remember who suggested it, but somehow we got the idea to go in and each have a drink, to celebrate our arrival in New York. I didn't know what to order – I'd never had alcohol – but they had a drink called a Manhattan. Well,' she said, 'I thought I'd die, it was so awful.' Grandma had the greatest laugh; I'd always loved her laugh. 'That was my first drink and I've never forgotten it.' As if to erase the memory, she took another long sip of her Bloody Caesar. 'Anyway, after that we walked on to Fifth Avenue, 50th and Fifth, to the International Building at Rockefeller Center. It had only just been finished a few years before, you know, and it was stunning, with that big statue of Prometheus outside. So we stopped, and we had a good look at the building, to see where we'd be going, and then the next day we started work.

'We worked for BSC – British Security Coordination. They had part of the mezzanine floor. There were offices upstairs, as well, but the mezzanine floor was where they had the passport office, and that was the cover. Anyone coming in would have just seen the passport office; they'd never have known what was really going on, behind the scenes. Most of the real work went on in a huge room we called the TK room, a big open room filled with teletype machines, and blacked-out windows so no one could see that we worked round the clock.

'You had to be a British subject to work there – that's why they recruited so many Canadians, you know, because we all had British passports in those days. There was no such thing, then, as a Canadian passport. Most people working at BSC were Canadian – some Aussies, some English; the executive level were nearly all Brits. Aristocratic Brits...*very* aristocratic.

'We reported to a British Major who had us sign the Official Secrets Act. I don't know that it hit any of the other girls the way it hit me, but this Major said, "I don't care if it's twenty years down the road, and you're working in an office, and someone asks you, 'Who was the person at the next desk to you, when you were with BSC?' – you know, casual – *Don't tell them!*" He had me afraid to go out on the street.'

'So it was pretty secret stuff, what you were doing?'

'Well, we were working for Sir William Stephenson.'

She floored me with that single, simple statement. Sir William Stephenson – the Canadian millionaire hand-picked by Churchill himself to control British secret intelligence out of New York in the Second World War, and whom Churchill had code-named 'Intrepid'. The Man Called Intrepid. There'd been a bestselling biography written of Stephenson, under that title, some years ago, and a television miniseries too. I'd read the book, and seen the movie – real exciting cloak-and-dagger stuff, as I recalled, if not always entirely accurate. His business had been training spies and saboteurs, and intercepting enemy messages and breaking codes. My grandmother, on her teletype machine, might have been passing on the secret location of a German submarine to the navy so the sub could be destroyed, or she might have been relaying the instructions being given to a Japanese commander.

It made me view her wartime job in quite a different light.

I think she understood. She said, 'We didn't know, you realise that, what we were going down to. We had no idea we were going to work for such a wonderful man, for Sir William. He was like nobody I've ever known. Not then. Not since.' The living-room mantel clock chimed its light melody into the pause as my grandmother searched for the proper description. 'He was a small man, physically small. You could pass him in the street, you wouldn't know him. He had a way of making himself almost invisible, really. A curious thing. He would stand very still, and he wouldn't make eye contact, and honestly, you wouldn't see him; wouldn't know that he was there. I know – I shared an elevator with him, once, and I nearly jumped out of my skin when he spoke. I'd thought I was alone, you see.

'I only met him – face to face, I mean – one other time, and that was when I went to a cocktail party at his penthouse. I was working on the thirty-sixth floor, then, the floor that Sir William was on, and he gave this party and I went to it, but other than that our paths didn't really cross. He was really on another level, someone to admire. Nobody up on the thirty-sixth floor ever used his name, that I recall. He was always called DSC – Director of Security Coordination. It was a mark of respect, really – we all respected him. At times he seemed almost superhuman. I don't know how many times he crossed the Atlantic, during the war, but I read somewhere, I think, that he made more than forty crossings, and he was always back and forth to Washington. And the things that he did...

'I didn't know everything at the time, mind you, but I knew more than most of the girls. They were downstairs, most of them, in the TK room, with the teletype machines, and everything down there was in code. No one knew what messages were coming in, what details they were passing on, but up on the thirty-sixth floor it was different. All the things I saw upstairs were in English. So I knew, then. I knew what we were doing.

'It's a powerful thing, to know that you're helping save lives. I really felt, at last, that I was helping to fight the war. Not in the same way my brothers were, of course, but in a way that was important.'

More important than most people knew, I thought. I wondered how many women like my grandmother there were across the country, still – living anonymous, ordinary lives; rubbing shoulders with people who had no idea of what they had done in the war.

'It was interesting work, on the thirty-sixth floor,' she went on. 'I was the assistant to the secretary for one of Sir William's top men. But my friends were all down in the TK room, and it was hard to get together, so I asked for a transfer and I went down there. In some ways, it would have been absolutely fantastic to have stayed upstairs, but they were mostly private-school girls, upstairs; they didn't laugh as much as we did. And, actually, the way things turned out, we couldn't have had more fun.'

She smiled again, recalling, 'We worked shifts. There were three shifts a day, and our group stayed together, we rotated round all together, fifteen girls to a shift. We used to go out at four o'clock in the morning, over to Hamburger Heaven – they served cakes like you wouldn't believe. Oh, the butterscotch! You would have died, Katie. It was the best. And we'd go to the movies... I remember after one midnight-to-eight a.m. shift, a few of us went to the Paramount. I don't remember all of what we watched – there was one movie with Robert Cummings in, I *do* recall that. That was sad. But anyway, we got there at eight o'clock in the morning, and we left at eleven-thirty at night and went back to work – we'd spent nearly sixteen hours at the Paramount! And in the summer, we used to go right from our eight o'clock shift to Jones Beach. It got so hot in the city, in the summertime, really hot, so we'd go to the beach, and one time I went I got sunburnt, I'll never forget...I fell asleep, I guess. That night I stayed off work because I was so badly burnt, and a nurse came to the apartment. I thought I'd get all kinds of sympathy, but no, I got reprimanded, for not taking care, because there was no one else to relieve us. So I didn't do that again. But oh, how I did love to go to the beach. I remember I had a two-piece bathing suit...'

'In 1943? I don't believe it.'

'I'll prove it.' She rose and went into the hall, and I could hear her digging in the cupboard by the stairs. I thought I'd seen all of her photograph albums, but the one she returned with was new to me – one of the old kind, with red leather covers and black paper pages, and little square photographs held in by gummed paper corners.

'There,' she told me, opening the book between us; pointing to a picture. 'That's when I was twenty-one, instead of eighty-three.'

I'd known that she'd been pretty, in her youth. I'd seen a photograph of her at twenty-five – her wedding picture, taken with my grandfather beside her – but by then she had matured. She'd looked respectable. At twenty-one, standing by the doors of Union Station with a suitcase, she'd still had a girlish look about her, young and fresh and innocent. She was wearing a dark-coloured suit, with a blouse and a skirt, and her hair was swept up at the sides and piled high on her head, with the back left to fall in loose waves to her shoulders.

'I love your hair,' I said.

'Oh, that's a pompadour. Everyone did it like that, it was easy.' She turned a page. 'Here you go. This is in front of the office, and there we all are, one shift. That's Molly, there, and Joan…you'll know the two of them, at least. We get together every now and then, for lunch.'

The two young women in the photograph did bear a strong resemblance to my grandmother's best friends. I'd never questioned how they'd met, or how long they'd known Grandma. I had always just accepted that they turned up every month or so; they went on trips together. If asked, I would have guessed they'd met at church, not doing secret wartime work in New York City, sixty years ago. I looked at them with new eyes, as I searched the fifteen faces for my grandmother's familiar one. I found her. Raised my eyebrows.

'You smoked?'

'Oh, sure. Most of us smoked. When I went down, I was the youngest of my group, and I was always teased about being the baby, and so I started smoking. Cigarettes were rationed, then. So many things were rationed. We bought stockings on the corner, and cigarettes, too – we lined up for them. But then, we were used to lining up for things in New York. We lined up to see Frank Sinatra – a block long, to see him, and New York policemen on horseback patrolling the crowd. It was something.

'Now, this is the beach,' she said, pointing, 'Jones Beach, and I'm in a two-piece red and white bathing suit.'

She was, too. I couldn't tell the colour from the photograph, of course, but it was definitely in two pieces. I would never have imagined that I'd see my grandmother, at any age, in a bathing suit like that, any more than I would have imagined us ever having this kind of conversation. It was faintly surreal still – not only that she was talking about things so openly, but that she was talking about them to *me*. It was almost as if Andrew Deacon's death had flipped some hidden switch inside her; as if, like him, she'd suddenly decided that the time to keep silent had come to an end. It was now time to speak.

'And this is a nightclub,' she said, moving on. 'I don't know the name of it. And I don't know who these men are, either. I think they came from Belgium, because they couldn't speak English, and they came off a ship and I think somebody arranged for us to go out with them.' She looked closer. 'This was taken not long after I went down, because I'm wearing my Toronto suit, my dark brown suit with the pinstripe, and the short skirt and the collar out. And here again, that's me, in a gold suit. I remember the colours,' she said, with a smile, and a nod to the black-and-white pictures. 'Clothes were a very big part of our lives, in New York. We all became very fashion-conscious there. We all had cocktail dresses, and we all had lounging pyjamas, which we had never had before. We had great clothes, and they were a lot cheaper – you could get some good deals in New York, then. We used to go to Klines, down near Grammercy Park, in the Village – that was a wonderful place. And I bought a hat at Saks once. I had a love affair with hats, then, and besides, all of us, on our first visit back to Toronto, we simply *had* to have a hat box with us, just to be impressive. We were being paid well in New York, more than what we were used to – BSC gave us thirty-five dollars a week – but we spent every nickel.'

'You said, "first visit back to Toronto",' I said. 'Did you get home a lot?'

'I only went home the once. But my mother came down. All our mothers came down to see how we were doing, and we had a lot of visitors. We took them to every part of New York we could think of, and got to know New York very well, better than even Toronto. It was such an exciting city. There was the Empire State Building, the Rockettes, Radio City Music Hall, and the jazz places, down in the Village – I absolutely fell in love with jazz, that year. And the Latin Quarter…that was a real nightclub. It was owned by Barbara Walters's father, and we'd take people there, for the floor show, and dancing. And then of course New York had all the operas, and the plays – I remember I saw *Lady in the Dark*, a play that starred Tallulah Bankhead, and there was this hilarious fellow with a small part, no one knew him but he stole the show. In later years, I found out that was Danny Kaye.

'We saw a few celebrities like that, in the embryonic stages of their careers. Sinatra, like I said…and on 52nd Street there was a restaurant, the Toots Shor restaurant, where we used to go, and at the end of the first showing of a play, the actors and actresses would come in and sit there in fear, waiting for the first edition to tell them whether they were in, or whether they were out. We saw some faces there that you'd recognise.

'And Walter Winchell…you know who *he* was? A few of

us were in the drugstore – and drugstores in those days had bars where you sat to have soft drinks, and milkshakes – and Walter Winchell was sitting beside us. He had such a loud voice, really piercing, and he said, "You girls are from Canada, because of the way you say your 'oots', and 'aboots'", and then he said, right out loud, "I know where you're working." Well, there was dead silence, and then we just kept on talking, and he didn't go any further, but it was a close call. Because you had to be very careful…there were places you didn't go, things you didn't do. They were very strict at BSC. They kept tabs on us, even when we moved into our separate apartments. We were checked all the time, we were followed. We weren't aware of it, but we realised it did happen, because if you did the wrong thing – talked to the wrong sort of people, or went to the wrong sort of place – they knew about it. Once our whole shift, the gang of us, went out for dinner, for somebody's birthday, and we sat at one long table and just laughed and laughed and had a really good time, and the next day we were called on the carpet and told in no uncertain terms to never do a thing like that again, to never make ourselves conspicuous. And a few girls – not anyone from my shift, but a few girls were even sent home. They just went overnight, and we never knew why.

'So we tried to be careful. We never told anyone what we were doing at work; we never discussed it, not even amongst ourselves. I didn't know what the other girls I roomed with did, and they didn't know what I did.'

'How did you manage that, living so closely?'

'I don't really know, we just did it. It's hard to explain, to someone young like you, who's never been through a war, but we just did it, we kept quiet. There were posters around in those days that said, "Loose Lips Sink Ships", and for me, I was always aware that my brothers, the two of them, might be on one of those ships. So I watched what I said.' She shrugged. 'When people asked what I did, I always said, "Oh, I work with passports." I never saw a passport. But people don't really want to know what you do.'

She paused a moment, thinking; then, 'It wasn't until years later, when the books about Sir William started to be published – *The Quiet Canadian* was the first, I guess, by Montgomery Hyde, and then the Intrepid one – and then I felt that I could talk about what was mentioned in the books. Not what I did specifically, but what was in the books. And even then…my parents died, and never knew. They never knew exactly what I did.'

I sensed a bit of sadness there, as though she would have liked them to have known, to have been able to take pride in what she'd done to help the war effort, the way they had, no doubt, been proud of both their sons in uniform.

'What about your brothers?' I asked. 'Did you tell them?'

'I didn't have the chance. My elder brother, Mike, was killed in Sicily the summer I was in New York, in 1943. And Ronnie died at Juno Beach, on D-Day. I went home after Ronnie was killed. It was hard on my parents, especially Mother. She needed me home.' She paused, and then, as though the talk had veered too far in a direction where she didn't want to go, she deliberately lightened the mood as she turned a fresh page in the photograph album. 'Oh, here, I was meaning to show you this one,' she said. 'This is my glamour shot. It was taken by a photographer on Madison Avenue.'

This picture was larger than the others, professionally posed, like all those old studio shots of the Hollywood starlets. Her hair was still swept up into the pompadour, her make-up picture-perfect, and her dress cut low, its sweetheart neckline squared with metal clips.

'My black dress,' she said. 'Black was very popular in those days. On the shoulders – you can't really see very clearly – but it was jet beads, all jet beads, made into an epaulette, like on a soldier's uniform, and the beads all hung down in a fringe.' She traced them with a finger and a reminiscent smile. 'I loved that dress.'

She tipped the page to look at it more closely and two papers slid out from between the album's pages, slipped across the table, and would probably have landed on the floor if I hadn't reached out to collect them. The top one, the smallest one, turned out to be a hotel menu.

Grandma glanced up. 'I'd forgotten I had that. Just look at those prices,' she told me. 'Full-course dinners, thirty-five cents! At a buck and a half, you were really living it up.'

'And what's this?' I asked, flipping the other sheet of paper over. It was larger. Official. Some kind of a letter.

'Oh, that's just a certificate, acknowledging my service in New York. That's signed by Sir William himself,' she said, as I began to read it. 'He was a very gracious man. They held a reunion, you know, at the Military Institute in Toronto, back in 1984, for all of us who worked for BSC. Of course Sir William, by that time, wasn't well. He couldn't come, but he sent a video tape, and they showed it on a big screen, and he welcomed us.'

I frowned, not really listening, as I read the certificate.

She went on, 'That was one of the nicest things we could have gone to, at the Military Institute. There were a hundred and one in attendance, including Sir William's secretary, who came from England, and his grandson, who came from Bermuda, and all of us women – we came from all over. They can't have had an easy time finding us, because there were no real records kept, you understand. Everything had been so secret. And then a lot of the girls who were single back then, well, they'd married, and had different names, so it must have been difficult, tracking us down. They did it all by word of mouth, really, and letters. They got a long list together... everybody passed names, of the women they knew of—'

'Grandma,' I cut her off, 'speaking of names...'

But she'd already started her next thought. 'And it was the funniest thing – this was the fortieth anniversary, you know, and there's a sort of a nucleus of at least six of us who've kept in contact over the years, and when you're with people all the time, they don't change. It's like watching your own children grow up, you don't notice the change day to day. So the night of the dinner, the six of us got all dressed up, and went down, and walked into the room and thought, "My gosh, they all look old!" Grey hair, as far as you could see!'

She was chuckling about this when I finally got her attention.

'The name on this certificate...' I said.

'Yes?'

'Well, it says "Amelia Clarke".'

'Yes, well, that was my maiden name, Clarke. You knew that.'

'But your first name is Georgie.'

She shook her head. 'That's just a nickname. My big brother, Mike, was so keen to have another boy in the family he simply refused to believe that I wasn't one. He wouldn't call me by my name – instead he called me George, and that just stuck. Even your grandfather…well, he was good friends with Mike, so he knew me as Georgie, from when we were kids. I was never Amelia, to him.'

All these years I'd assumed that her first name was short for Georgina, or maybe Georgette. My frown deepened as I tried to understand fully. 'Your name is Amelia?'

Something in my tone must have struck her, then, because she looked over. Met my eyes, levelly. 'Yes.'

But I still had to say it, out loud. 'I've read all the letters, the ones Andrew Deacon wrote home to his sister in England, while he was in Lisbon. He mentions his wife all the time, every letter. And *her* name,' I said, 'was Amelia.'

Lots of people, I knew, could have had the same name. Certainly, in a city the size of New York, there would have been any number of Amelias back in 1943. But my journalist's radar was active enough to have picked up on something…

A hunch, nothing more; but I'd built my career on such hunches.

She didn't say anything, not right away.

She looked out the window, to where she had planted the rosebushes, against the back fence, and her eyes began losing their sharpness of focus, the way that James Cavender's had when he'd talked of his childhood. Watching her, I wasn't altogether sure that she still saw the window, or the yard. I wasn't sure that she still knew that I was in the room.

Until she spoke.

'You have to understand,' she said, 'that it was wartime. I was working for the government. I went where I was told to go, and did what I was told to do. And Deacon…' For the first time since she'd started talking, I could see that she was having difficulty. She paused, and her breath came out soft, on a long, weary sigh. 'It's been sixty-two years, Katie. And you want to know what happened, and I'm not sure how well I can tell the story.' Still looking out the window at the rosebushes, she confessed, 'I think sometimes, we had it so ingrained in us, to never talk to anyone, that now it can be so hard to remember…'

She did remember, though, how it began.

It was the first day of November, 1943. Her alarm clock broke that morning, and that set the tone for everything that happened after that.

By the time she got to work, she'd lost a button from her coat and banged her knee and scraped her ankle on the kerb, which tore her stocking. And to make things worse, her supervisor met her at the door to the TK room, with a letter in his hand.

'They need this upstairs, on the thirty-sixth floor,' he said. 'Run it up, would you? You know where things are, up there.'

She knew enough to know that her appearance, harried and dishevelled, would be bound to raise some eyebrows on the upper floor, among the British secretaries. But her supervisor was a man; he didn't think of things like that.

Resigned, she took the letter from his outstretched hand and turned away again.

There were two other women on the elevator with her, but they both got off together at the fourth floor. After that, she had the whole car to herself...or so she thought. Relaxing a little, she took out her lipstick and tried to at least make sure *that* looked all right. Even with the mirror of her compact angled back and past her shoulder she had no clue there was anyone behind her till the man's voice said, 'Good morning, Miss Clarke.'

She wheeled, surprised.

She'd only met the chief of BSC one time. She wouldn't have been sure, this time, that it *was* William Stephenson, except she'd been impressed at that first meeting by his eyes. They were distinctive – long and grey and heavy-lidded, filled with a dispassionate intelligence. The kind of eyes that saw more than they ever gave away.

She wondered what they were seeing now, looking at her.

She wasn't at her best this morning – not the way she would have liked to look, to meet her boss. But when she'd managed to recover from the unexpected jolt, she was able to greet him, in her turn, with a reasonable degree of composure.

He nodded at the envelope she held. 'Is that for me?'

It wasn't, but she let him have it all the same. He read the name, and gave it back. The fact that he'd known *her* name wasn't really a surprise. He had a reputation for knowing everything there was to know about the people he employed. It wasn't for nothing that some of the women had taken to calling him 'God'.

He asked her, 'So, how are you liking it, working downstairs?'

She wasn't sure how she should answer. After all, she didn't want to imply that she hadn't enjoyed working up on *his* floor, but…she opted for honesty. 'I like it very much, thank you.'

'Good.' He watched her quietly, then said, 'Your young man's in the RAF.'

'Yes, sir, he is.'

He nodded. 'I was in the RFC, last war. The Royal Flying Corps.'

Georgie had the impression that wasn't the end of his statement. She waited. She still felt amazed he'd said anything to her beyond that 'Good morning'. He *didn't* have a reputation for conducting small talk.

They had fifteen floors left to go up. He stayed silent for five of them. Then he said, 'I was shot down, over France, and captured. Put into a prison camp. I managed to escape, though, in the end. It all came out all right.'

The grey eyes held hers, levelly, a moment. Then they slid away, the contact finished.

Georgie turned away more slowly, not quite certain what the purpose of his speech had been. She might have asked him, but his silence was the private kind, not welcoming intrusions. And besides, they'd reached their floor.

She had expected he'd step off with her, but when she turned, the elevator door had closed, and he had gone. She couldn't see him anywhere.

The afternoon was fading, and the sunlight slanting through my Grandma's kitchen window held a tinge of red. Her glass was empty now. She laced her fingers round it, very carefully, and studied them.

'The telegram,' she said, 'came two days after that, to tell me your grandfather's plane had gone missing, shot down over France.' The pain she'd felt that day must have been easy to revive because I felt her sadness touch me in the pause that followed. She looked up. 'He knew, you see. Sir William knew. I don't know how...but I know he was trying, then, to give me comfort, give me hope. I never did forget that. Never will.'

A week after the telegram, her supervisor sent her upstairs again. No letter this time; just herself, with orders to report to one of the secretaries.

Georgie couldn't think why anybody was wanting to see her. She hadn't done anything wrong, that she knew of. She'd been like a robot the past several days, but it hadn't affected her work. If anything, bad news increased her level of efficiency, because her mind sought solace in routine, and found distraction in the constant rhythmic clatter of the teletype machines. That had been how she had coped, last summer, with the news her brother Mike had died while storming the Sicilian beachfront, and it was how she was coping now. Not that the two situations were really identical – with Mike they had known from the start he was dead, but this time, with her Kenneth, the message had said he was missing, which meant there was still that uncertainty, still room for hope. How much of that she owed to those few minutes with William Stephenson, when he'd planted in her mind the notion someone *could* survive the crash, the capture, and could make it out alive, she didn't know. She only knew that this time, she felt different; not as shattered as she'd felt when Mike was killed.

She wasn't perfect, though. The tears still swelled behind

her eyes and clogged her throat a little when the secretary upstairs said she'd heard about Ken's plane, and she was sorry. With a sympathetic smile the secretary led Georgie into a small, empty office, and left her to wait.

When the door opened ten minutes later, the man who came through was the same British Major who had given Georgie the Official Secrets Act to sign, on her first day at work, and who had frightened her to death with all his warnings about secrecy.

'Miss Clarke.' He nodded shortly, looking at the file he was holding. There was no preamble. Straight away, he said to her, 'We're sending you to Canada…'

Her heart sank. She didn't want to leave; to be sent home in disgrace. Determinedly, she blinked back any trace of tears and told him, 'But I'm fine. I'm really fine.'

His upward glance was brief, one eyebrow raised. 'We know that. We wouldn't be sending you otherwise.' Lowering his gaze, he carried on, 'You'll leave by train, tonight.'

And then came the instructions.

She was to go immediately back to her apartment, and pack a single suitcase. To her room-mates, she should say that she was going home for several days, to be with family. Nobody would question that, considering the circumstances. At ten o'clock, a taxi would be sent to pick her up. The taxi driver would pass over certain papers; she would put those papers in her suitcase, and she'd keep that suitcase with her on the train, at all times…

She actually became a little paranoid about that suitcase. Even though they'd given her a private berth on the overnight train to Toronto – high luxury, compared to the way that she'd travelled the first time she'd gone home to visit, renting a pillow to sleep sitting up in a regular seat – still, she couldn't stop worrying someone would come try to steal what it was she was carrying. She would never have made a good spy, Georgie thought. She was nervous enough as a courier. God only knew why they'd picked her to do the job.

Despite the comfortable berth, she got almost no sleep, and was glad when the morning came.

She had to change trains at Toronto, and carry on east a short distance, to Oshawa. There, she'd been told, she'd be met at the station.

The platform was nearly deserted at midday, and cold from the damp wintry wind blowing in off the wide, white-capped shore of the lake – Lake Ontario – just out of sight to the south. Georgie wanted nothing more than to set down her suitcase. Her arm ached. But caution and a crushing sense of responsibility for whatever it was she was carrying kept her standing there, the suitcase held in front of her with both hands, while she waited. As the train pulled out behind her she heard footsteps, and a woman – young, like her, but wearing military uniform – approached with cheerful confidence.

'Miss Clarke? I thought so. If you'd like to come with me, I have a car around the front.'

An army station wagon, big and draughty. As she settled herself in the front passenger seat, Georgie wedged her suitcase in the space between the dashboard and her knees, glad that she soon would be rid of its worrisome contents. This was, she knew, the last leg of her journey. According to the briefing in New York, the woman corporal at the wheel would now drive Georgie to her final destination.

She was curious to know where it might be, but she knew better than to ask. Instead, she watched the scenery pass: a country road, with blowing grass that scurried south to meet a line of trees that parted, now and then, to show the choppy frigid blue of Lake Ontario.

At length, the car itself turned south, and took a road that ran towards the lake.

The woman corporal said, by way of an apology, 'I'm sure you'd like to go to your hotel and freshen up, but the Major wanted to see you first.'

Georgie's heart sank a little at the thought of *another* major. Maybe this one, she thought, would be a little less intimidating than his New York counterpart. At any rate, all she had to do was give the man the papers that she'd brought, and let him give her, in return, whatever it was she'd be carrying back to New York.

It must be important, for them to have sent her here in person to collect it. And 'here' (although she wasn't really certain where she was) seemed like a place that might house things of great importance. She'd spotted the huge transmitter tower first, far off. And then the sign that warned the area they'd entered was 'Prohibited'. The station wagon turned again, along a narrow road that on the surface looked quite innocent – a farm road, with an orchard full of twisting, bare-branched trees on the left – but through the window now she saw a scattering of huts and buildings sprouting from the landscape, unexpected in this rolling lakeshore setting.

'Here we are,' the woman corporal said as they drew level with the guardhouse. 'Welcome to The Farm.'

* * *

'The proper name,' my Grandma Murray said, 'was STS 103 – STS for "Special Training School". But people called it other names. The Farm—'

'Camp X?' I cut her off, incredulous. 'You're talking about Camp X?'

Like many people in this part of the country, I knew the famous spy school had existed, though I'd never been to see the site. There had been books written about it, and television documentaries, detailing how the camp – the first spy-training camp in North America – had been set up by the British to train agents in the arts of sabotage and secret war. It had been built before Pearl Harbor, before the States officially came into the war, and I knew that the maverick head of the American OSS, 'Wild Bill' Donovan, had made use of it to train his own clandestine corps of agents, who'd evolved into the modern CIA. Ian Fleming, the naval intelligence officer and writer, creator of none other than James Bond, had reportedly been to the camp, and countless secret and dangerous missions in occupied Europe had been planned and orchestrated from that one small bit of farmland near Toronto.

My grandmother, having already amazed me by the things she'd told me of her time in New York City, now amazed me further by the matter-of-fact way she spoke about the spy school.

'Camp X, that's right. Sir William was in charge of that, as well. I didn't work there, but I worked *through* there, you understand – the radio transmissions, all our messages, were sent through there. So afterwards, I took a special interest in the articles that people wrote...the books. I still save everything. It's so much more exciting than the work *we* did.

The men who went there,' Grandma said, 'were taught to kill. Kill or be killed. Of course, some of them, like the Yugoslavs, had lost their families, so they wanted to get back, but oh, dear, the things that they went through to learn. They were very brave men.'

The musical chimes of the clock in the next room broke into the silence, the only reminder of time passing on in the present.

My grandmother said, 'It's a shame, in some ways, that the buildings weren't saved. We don't value our history enough, I don't think. In England, you can go to see the war rooms… you know, Churchill's war rooms, underground. They've kept them as they were. But here…' She shrugged. 'I know some of the small things are in a museum, and they did build a monument, down where the camp used to be, by the lake. I remember we were all invited to the dedication of that, all of us who worked for BSC, but I didn't go. Some of the others did, but I've never been back. Never even had a look at it. It wouldn't be the same,' she said.

Georgie felt, that day, that she had entered a forbidden place, as when, in childhood, she had strayed beyond the boundaries of her own safe neighbourhood. But here, instead of barking dogs and unfamiliar faces, there were guards with loaded guns held at the ready.

It was clear she'd been expected. The station wagon she was in was waved through without ceremony, and a few moments later, before she'd had much chance to take a good look at the buildings around her, she found herself – and her suitcase – being politely but insistently ushered into the presence of the camp's commandant.

His office wasn't large – a desk and a couple of chairs, and a filing cabinet, but the rigidity of military protocol still made the space seem formal. The only contact Georgie had ever had with soldiers (apart from her two brothers, before they'd been shipped overseas, and they hardly counted) had been with the young men that one sometimes met in New York, in their uniforms. But she'd met them in civilian settings. This was her first time on the other side of the fence, within the structured world that was the army.

The importance of rank became immediately obvious – regular soldiers were not on the same plane as officers. The woman army corporal who had brought her from the station became very deferential and received only a brief acknowledgement before she was dismissed.

Georgie, having no rank at all, wasn't sure how to behave, but the Major soon let it be known that he was not expecting her to keep to protocol.

'Have a seat,' he said. 'Make yourself comfortable.'

There was only one chair in the room besides his. Georgie took it, and waited.

He came round and held out his hand for her suitcase. 'You have something for me, I think.'

When she gave him the papers, he walked back to his desk and, without looking at them, shut them in a drawer. Resuming his seat, he leant back and began, in a friendly way, asking her questions. How had her trip up been? Had there been anyone interesting for her to talk to, to help the time pass? 'Deadly things, trains,' he said, with a smile. 'So boring. I much prefer flying, myself.' His tone and easy manner were inviting her to chat, but her BSC training would not be so easily overcome. She found herself responding as she would have if she'd met him on the street – revealing nothing, in politely brief replies. It didn't seem to put him off. Instead, he talked about New York.

He'd been down to the office before, evidently. He asked after one of the women who worked on her shift, someone Georgie knew well, but she didn't admit to it. Remembering what she'd been told when she'd signed the Official Secrets Act, about not discussing her co-workers, she told the Major simply that she didn't know a lot of other people where she worked.

'Ah, well, maybe she's in a different department. Big place, is it?'

'Well…'

'I'm told you get some quite important visitors,' he said. 'Someone said Noel Coward comes to see your chief, from time to time. And Lord Mountbatten.'

Georgie had heard about Noel Coward, and had actually been fortunate enough to see Lord Mountbatten pass through the offices. Like everyone else, she had thought him quite dashing and handsome, though nobody, really, compared with her Kenneth.

Still, she didn't think that discussing the comings and goings of people of influence was such a wise thing to do during wartime. Excusing her ignorance with a smile and a shrug, she said, 'I wouldn't know. I only work with passports'.

Then the Major smiled, too, and stopped his questioning to measure her approvingly with one long glance. 'You'll do,' he said. 'I thought you might, when I heard you'd been selected by Bill Stephenson himself, but even so, I like to be sure. Now,' – he glanced at his watch – 'I expect you're tired. I'll have somebody run you up to your hotel. You'll get a bit of rest, at least. The train to New York won't be leaving till later tonight.'

He was standing, dismissing her. Georgie frowned. 'But...'

'Yes?'

She nodded at her suitcase. 'I thought...that is, I was told you had something that I was supposed to bring back.'

He looked at her in vague surprise. 'That's all they told you?'

'Yes.'

He sat again, reaching for his phone while, in his turn, he gave a nod toward her suitcase. 'Well, it won't fit in that, my dear.' Into the phone, he instructed, 'That package we're sending to New York, could you locate it for me? That's right. In my office, please.'

They didn't have to wait more than ten minutes, but to Georgie's confusion the man who stepped into the office came in empty-handed. He was older than she was, but not by too much – not yet thirty, she guessed – neatly dressed in civilian clothes: white shirt, grey suit. His hair was neither blond nor brown, but something in between, just as the man himself was neither tall nor short, but simply medium in height and build; nice-looking in a quiet way, with nothing unremarkable about him.

Unless, she thought, one made allowance for his eyes. He had blue eyes, intense and intelligent. They looked at her, then travelled to the Major, with a question.

But the Major spoke to Georgie, first. 'Miss Clarke, meet

Andrew Deacon. Andrew, this is Miss Amelia Clarke. She'll be escorting you down to New York.'

Through the polite exchange of nods, Georgie tried to adjust to the notion that the 'package' she'd be taking back was human, while the Major continued, offhand, 'We might be wise to keep you here another day, and send you back tomorrow. Give Miss Clarke a little time. She didn't come prepared.'

She turned her head, and asked, 'Prepared for what?'

The Major smiled. 'For being Andrew's wife.'

They didn't actually have time alone together until they had boarded the train on the following evening. And it wasn't until they were seated in the dining car for dinner that they had their first real conversation.

The dining car was very nearly empty. There were only three couples, including themselves, and the others were seated at tables some distance away. They could speak in lowered voices without being overheard.

'This has all been a bit of a shock for you, I expect,' Deacon said.

She had taken to calling him Deacon because it made everything seem much more businesslike, much less uncomfortable. Not that he'd been anything except a perfect gentleman, but still, the fact remained that she was travelling in intimate close quarters with a stranger.

'It's been a shock for me, as well,' he said, in his evenly pitched British voice, with a faint smile that told her that he, too, felt awkward. 'I didn't plan on marrying this year.'

The marriage wasn't real, of course. Somewhere, she

knew, there would be papers stating otherwise, to bolster the charade. And there would also be the photographs the two of them had posed for in the camp commandant's office earlier today, Deacon in his grey suit and she in a dress borrowed for the occasion from a local shop.

She could have tried refusing, she supposed. She could have told them that, although there was a chance, a good chance, that her boyfriend might be dead, this whole scenario felt wrong, to her. Disloyal.

Or she could have tried to argue that she didn't have the skills for this. She wasn't trained to masquerade as someone else; she wouldn't be convincing. *Why me?* she'd wondered once again, and as before, had found no one to give her any answer. She only knew that this was *not* what she'd signed on for, when she'd gone to work for BSC.

Nonetheless, she'd gone along with it. Hers not to reason why, she reminded herself. Besides, she didn't know what mission they were sending Deacon on – she'd been told simply that he was going overseas – but it was possible that what this man was being sent to do would be important to the war, and that her role, however small, might make a difference.

She found it difficult, looking at him across the white-clothed table in the dining car, to judge what kind of job he might be going to. He was not the sort of man who made a definite impression on her at first meeting, but rather he revealed his personality in stages, like an image that was blurry to begin with but came into focus more and more the longer that one looked at it.

He was, she thought, a quiet man; a little shy with people, but not lacking in self-confidence. His smiles were swift but genuine – they always touched his eyes. And she thought that she'd detected, underneath the calm reserve, a rather wicked sense of humour that would make him fun to be around.

He noticed people; watched them, not suspiciously, but – so it seemed to her, at least – because he found them interesting. And it said a lot about him that he'd spoken to the waiter in the same way that he spoke to everybody else, with natural politeness and respect. He might be English, with an educated accent, but he wasn't, to her great relief, a snob.

She hadn't been told much about him. He lived in New York, she knew that. He had friends there, whom she would be meeting. He was an art dealer. That seemed as good a place to start as any, Georgie thought, and so she asked what sort of art he bought and sold.

His upward glance was friendly. 'Paintings, mostly. Some sculpture. I have a particular interest in Spanish art.'

While they ate, between the comings and the goings of the waiter, Deacon talked about the shop he'd had in Rio de Janeiro, describing some of his more colourful customers in such detail she felt she would know them on sight if they ever passed by her. He didn't say much about the dengue fever that had driven him out of Brazil, but she had the impression he must have been very ill indeed to have left a place he obviously loved so much. His second shop, in New York City, didn't seem to hold the same appeal. 'It's still my business, but I hired a chap to manage it last spring,' he said, 'when I went up to Canada, and he's done such a brilliant job that I intend to let him go on doing it.'

So he had been up at the Training Camp for several months, she thought. She didn't ask him what he had been doing there, because she knew he couldn't tell her *that*. She did know, though, from her time on the thirty-sixth floor, that South America was of special interest to BSC, so she reasoned his stay at The Farm might have somehow been linked to his time in Brazil.

The waiter came past and a family of four took the table beside them. They didn't discuss much of anything after that; only concentrated on the meal, which was excellent.

It was snowing when they left the dining car. The heavy flakes turned instantly to water on the windows of the lurching narrow corridors as Deacon, with a hand at Georgie's elbow, led the way towards the first-class sleeping coach. Georgie hadn't given much thought to the implications of their having a private compartment before, but it occurred to her that, while they'd been at dinner, the compartment would have been made up for night-time, and the berths pulled down to sleep on, and the thought of that arrangement made her even more uncomfortable than she had been before.

There was no real alternative, she knew. Her job was to convince others that she was Deacon's wife, and she'd never do that if she went to pieces every time they had to share a room.

Another couple pressed past in the corridor as Deacon stopped outside the door of their compartment. Stepping close to shield her, he reached down to put the key into her hand, and in a voice that wanted to be overheard, he said, 'I'm not quite ready to turn in yet, darling. Think I'll go and have a brandy. Do you mind?'

She said she didn't, and the other couple passed by, out of hearing.

'Right, then,' Deacon said, and smiled. 'Goodnight, Amelia.'

Her real name, unfamiliar, sounded pleasant in his accent. It was, after all, the name by which she had been introduced to him, but Georgie had a feeling that he wouldn't use her nickname even if she tried correcting him. She didn't mind. It helped to keep things formal, like her using just his surname.

So she said, 'Goodnight,' and watched him walk away along the corridor, then turning, fit the key into the lock of the compartment and went in to bed.

She woke to the feeling that something was not as it should be.

Deacon's berth was empty. She hadn't heard him come in, but she knew from the state of his blankets he'd been there at some point. The hands of the clock at her bedside read quarter to seven. They should be getting near New York now, she thought, wrapping herself in her robe as she got up to look out the window.

It was then, when her feet touched the floor, that she knew what was different. The train had stopped moving.

Outside, the snow had settled in high drifts around the tracks. The wind sheared thin curls from the tops of the drifts and whirled them up and round and past the windows with a hollow-sounding whistle. Georgie hugged her arms against the creeping early morning cold and hurried to dress before Deacon came back.

She needn't have worried. It was another half an hour before he turned up. And he knocked.

'Good morning,' he said, as she opened the compartment

door. He came in with a tray, and cups. 'I've managed to scrounge us some tea.'

There was nothing else. The restaurant car, he told her, had been taken off at Buffalo, so there wouldn't be a breakfast till they'd reached New York, and that, the way things were going, might not be for several hours yet.

She didn't know how he had managed the tea, but she was grateful he had. Simply holding the cup in her hands made her warm. There was nowhere to sit but the edge of her berth, so she sat there, while Deacon remained by the door.

'I could try to find someone to make up the compartment,' he suggested.

'Don't be silly. Have a seat,' she told him, shifting to make room. 'We *are* supposed to be married, after all.'

Her father always said a good night's sleep made any situation better, and in fact this morning Georgie felt more positive about her new assignment, more committed to get on with it and do the best job possible. She looked up as he sat beside her. 'Can I ask you something?'

'Yes, of course.'

'Why do you need a wife?'

'I'm sorry?'

'Well, you've lived in New York. You have friends there. Why do you need me?'

He hesitated, and she said, 'If you can't tell me, that's all right. It's only that I wondered what my *purpose* was.'

Another moment passed while he considered. 'If I tell you it's important that my friends believe I'm married, would that be enough?'

It would have to be, she knew. She told him, 'Yes. But if we want to be convincing there are things I should know about you, and your family, and things you should know about me. In case somebody asks.'

He conceded the point. 'All right. Where would you like to begin?'

'With your family.'

She didn't take notes. Georgie had a good memory, and Deacon, again, had that gift of description that let her see everyone clearly: His father, the schoolmaster, getting on now, but still stern in his habits; his mother, a gentle soul, pottering round in her garden; his sister, who had married young and aged too quickly, carrying too much upon her shoulders. 'It can't be easy for her, raising the boy on her own. Not that Jamie's a difficult lad,' he said. 'Always a nice little boy, from what I remember, and I gather from her letters that he's grown into a nice young man. Nearly twelve, he'd be. I likely wouldn't know him. And I don't expect he'd much want to know me.' He gave a tight, small smile. 'Understandable, really. His father behaved like a hero, while I've lived a comfortable life over here. I'm not even in uniform.'

He said that last lightly enough, but Georgie thought she heard a harder undertone, and, curious herself, she asked, 'Why aren't you?'

'What?'

'In uniform.'

'The easy answer is I didn't have to be, and anyway, I value my own skin too much to want to go and get shot at.'

Georgie studied him. 'I don't believe that.'

'Oh? Why not?'

She didn't know why not. 'Because I don't, that's all.'

'Well then,' he said, with another small smile, 'you've a higher opinion of me than most of my family. But what about *your* family, now? What are they like?'

He'd turned the tables on purpose, she thought, but she willingly filled in her share of the blanks. 'Well, my father's a newspaperman. That's how Mother and he met – she worked as a typist, before they got married.' Her parents were well matched, in spite of their differences. 'Dad likes to travel, keep busy, while Mother would rather stay home. But they do have a few things in common. They both like to read, and go fly-fishing…'

'Fly-fishing?' Both his eyebrows rose at that.

'It's a family obsession. I'm not very good at it,' Georgie confessed. 'I don't have enough patience. My brothers are better.'

'You have more than one brother?'

'Yes,' she said, first, and then, 'No. Well, I did…my brother Mike died this past summer, in Sicily.'

'Oh. I am sorry.'

She looked away. Drank her tea. 'Yes, well. That happens in wartime, doesn't it? He was always the leader, Mike. Always the one that we followed. It's a little like losing the star that you steer by, you know, losing him. My parents feel it, too, I know. They haven't been the same. And Ronnie – that's my other brother – he'll be taking it the hardest of any of us. They were inseparable, growing up, Ronnie and Kenneth and Mike. People called them the Three Musketeers.'

'Who is Kenneth?'

She hadn't intended to talk about Ken. It wasn't a part of her life Deacon needed to know about, really, to keep up their married façade. So she said, 'Just a boy from the neighbourhood. One of my brothers' best friends.' And then, turning the tables herself, she said, 'Speaking of which, you should probably tell me a bit about *your* friends – the ones I might meet in New York.'

The tea was gone. He pulled a cigarette case from his pocket. 'Do you smoke?'

It was comfortable being with Deacon like this, in the train, with the snow piled high round the car and the buffeting wind at the window glass making her feel as though they were cut off from the rest of the world for a time. She took a cigarette and settled back.

They sat and talked and smoked until the train began to move again, an hour later. To Georgie's great relief, another restaurant car was sent to join their train at Albany, so she was able to have breakfast after all. She didn't function well without a proper breakfast.

Deacon, she noticed, ate lightly. He liked honey on his toast instead of jam. He drank his coffee black and sweet. With tea, he'd added milk. These things, and others, she made note of in her memory. It was a lot, she thought, like studying for school examinations – feeling always that she should know more; that she was unprepared.

The feeling lingered as the train began to slow, on its final approach into Grand Central Station. She looked out the window. 'Oh, well,' she said, low, to herself, 'here goes nothing.'

He had an apartment on 73rd Street – the Upper West Side, near the Park.

For such a fashionable address it was a strangely plain

123

apartment, quiet in greys and greens, with a small but modern kitchen, gleaming chrome. It looked too clean to have been shut up all the time he'd been away. There was no dust, and the bathroom smelt strongly of soap and shampoo.

As if reading her mind, he said, 'I had a friend watching the place for me, while I was gone.' And then, with a glance round, he added, 'She's a much better housekeeper than I am, I'm afraid. You probably won't see it looking this tidy, again.'

A woman friend, thought Georgie, and it struck her that, for all she'd been so focused on the inconvenience this assignment might be causing *her*, she'd never once stopped to consider what it might be costing Deacon.

Her own boyfriend, if he was even alive, was an ocean away, unaware of the role she was playing, and at any rate she only had to make believe for several days – two weeks, they'd told her, at the most – and then she'd have her life back, whereas Deacon had to move among his friends now as a married man, and, after her departure, as a man who *had* been married. There was no going back, for him. And if he'd had a girlfriend…

'You can have the bedroom,' Deacon offered. 'I'll clear you some space in the wardrobe.' He would have gone on but the phone in the living room rang, interrupting. 'Excuse me,' he said.

Georgie gave him his privacy, sauntering back through the narrow front hall for a look at the paintings that hung there. She didn't know much about art, only whether she liked it or not. These she liked. They were clean-lined and vibrant, of jazz singers, so full of life that, just standing in front of them,

Georgie could conjure the pounding piano, the smoke of the nightclub...

A knock at the door broke the mood.

Georgie turned from the paintings, not sure what to do. She could hear Deacon still in the living room, talking, which meant he either hadn't heard the door or had assumed that she would answer it. She was supposed to be his wife, and there could be no problem with his wife, she reasoned, opening the door to their apartment.

The problem lay in whom she might be opening the door to.

It might be nobody important, just a telegram delivery boy, or somebody like that. But then again, it might be one of Deacon's closest friends, the first test of her acting out the part that she'd been given. It might even be the woman who'd been living here, at Deacon's invitation, come to give him back her key.

Georgie took a steady breath and, shoulders squared, reached out to take a firm hold of the doorknob.

The man was young, a little older than herself, like Deacon; very tall and loosely jointed, with a quick, engaging smile. 'Hello,' he said. He was American. 'You must be Andrew's wife.'

It came quite naturally, in spite of all her worry, as she offered him her hand. 'Amelia Deacon, yes.'

'I'm Jim,' he introduced himself, and, holding up a paper bag, announced, 'I've brought you both some lunch.'

That was the beginning of a pattern that continued through their whole time in New York – each day, at lunchtime, Jim would arrive with a bag full of sandwiches, fresh from the drugstore on the corner, and Georgie would make coffee, and the three of them would eat together in the little kitchen.

She liked Jim. She never learnt his last name; never knew exactly who he was, or who he worked for. Being an American, he likely wouldn't be with BSC. The FBI, perhaps, or maybe even OSS. He wasn't one of Deacon's crowd – she knew that much, at least, because the first day he had come to the apartment it had been obvious, to her, the two men hadn't met before.

They talked of small things over lunch; then afterwards, the men retired to the living room while Georgie took a book into her bedroom, at the far end of the hall, and closed the door.

She couldn't hear what they were saying. Didn't want to hear. She stayed there for an hour or more, till Deacon came and knocked to let her know the coast was clear, and then the two of them would go out on their own somewhere.

He proved to be good company. She liked to walk beside him on the winter-barren paths of Central Park, or on the Boulevard, and look at all the grand expensive homes, and trade opinions of the ones they'd like to live in. Once they wandered clear across the park and came out somewhere on the Upper East Side, and he walked her past his gallery – an elegantly fronted place with large, old-fashioned windows – but he didn't take her in. 'It's still my workplace,' Deacon said, 'and I refuse to go to work when on my honeymoon.' They went other places – up the Chrysler Building, to enjoy the stunning view across Manhattan, and to the Museum of Modern Art for a new exhibition of works owned by oil tycoon

Ivan Reynolds. She found it interesting, at the museum, to see Deacon more in his element – animated, even – as he tried to show her what he thought was wonderful, or not, about the paintings. But still, she liked their walks in Central Park the best.

Evenings they went out for dinner, often to the houses of his friends. He seemed to have no shortage of them, and the ones she'd met appeared quite pleased to have him back in New York City. She was meeting them in ones and twos – a couple here, another couple there, a lone man stopping by their table at a restaurant – and so she found it not too hard to play her role convincingly, as long as she kept most of her attention on the meal and kept her mouth shut unless spoken to. It was Deacon who bore the brunt of these encounters…all the questions, and the agreed-upon explanations, how they'd met, and how long they'd been married, and why no one had heard from him in months.

He must have found it all exhausting, Georgie thought, and yet he never seemed to be as tired as she was at the evening's end, when they came back to the apartment, said goodnight, and took their places in the bedroom and the living room respectively.

The pattern changed a little, on the ninth day. After lunch she went out shopping by herself. They had a cocktail party to attend that night, and she'd been told to buy a dress – a nice dress, not too plain and not too flashy. Something elegant. She found it in the window of the second shop she went to. It fit her as though she had been the model for the dressmaker. A black dress, with a close-fitting bodice, cut low, its sweetheart neckline squared with metal clips, and on the shoulders, epaulettes of glittering jet beads all hanging down to form a fringe. She bought it on the spot.

As she rustled through the door of the apartment, with the dress bag on her arm, it surprised her to hear Jim's voice from the living room. She hadn't thought he'd still be there. 'It could be any day now,' he was saying, 'so you'll have to be prepared. It all depends on when the Clipper leaves. There may not be much warning – they'll just send me to come get you.'

'And what happens to Amelia?'

A pause, as though he hadn't thought of that; then, 'I'll take care of her, don't worry.'

This was followed by a second pause, and Georgie took advantage of the fact to shut the door behind her, loud enough for them to hear, and call out from the hall to let them know that she was back. She had never liked listening at keyholes. 'You usually hear things you don't want to hear,' so her father had told her a long time ago, and her father, as always, was right.

She didn't want to think of Deacon leaving, and that troubled her, so much so that she didn't meet his eyes when, as she passed the open doorway of the living room, he greeted her with, 'You're back early'.

'Yes, well…' She held up the dress bag. 'I found what I wanted.' She looked at Jim, instead. 'Sorry to interrupt.'

'Oh, no. I was just going,' said Jim, with a smile. He didn't say anything further, but after they had shut the door behind him Deacon glanced at Georgie, and she knew that he was wondering if she had overheard their conversation, and if so, how much she'd heard, and since there was no gentlemanly way for him to ask, she spared him the necessity by speaking first.

'You were talking,' she said honestly, 'when I came in. I heard the last few sentences.'

'I see.'

Wanting a cup of tea after her shopping, she walked into the kitchen, laid the dress across a chair, and moved to fill the kettle, while he watched her from the doorway. 'Jim mentioned the Clipper,' she said. She'd seen the Pan Am Clipper at its moorings, once – the stately seaplane that was now the only aircraft offering commercial flights across the treacherous Atlantic. 'I take it that means you'll be flying, wherever you're going?'

He couldn't tell her, anyway. She knew he couldn't tell her; that he wouldn't be allowed to give her details of his mission, but she had to ask the question.

He was silent for a moment, then he asked her, 'Would that bother you?'

She turned. It wasn't what he'd said so much as how he'd said it, almost as if he had known how she felt about airplanes and flying…as if he had known about Ken…

He was still in the doorway, unmoving. Their eyes locked. And then she knew for certain that he *did* know. He'd been told. She looked away.

She said, as lightly as she could, 'I see they've told you all about my private life.'

'I asked.' And then, to her questioning glance, he explained, 'You mentioned his name on the train. You said he was your brothers' friend. I had a sense he might be rather more than that, so I asked. I wanted to be sure he wouldn't be a complication.'

'He won't.' Her tone was curt. 'His plane went down. That

doesn't mean he's dead. And even if he is, I'm not the sort of girl who has hysterics.'

The kettle, half forgotten on the stove, came shrieking to a boil as if to punctuate her sentence.

Deacon, hands in pockets, said, 'I'm really very sorry.'

Then he gave a small, tight smile that didn't know what else to say, and turned to leave.

She instantly regretted how she'd spoken – there hadn't been any real need to be rude. In his place, she admitted, she'd likely have done the same thing. He had more of a stake in this whole masquerade; more to lose, if she made a false step.

'Wait…' She willed him to stop, and he did. 'Don't go yet. Stay and have some tea.'

He considered a moment, then stayed. 'For the record,' he said, as he fetched her the tea from the cupboard, 'I never did think you hysterical.'

'Forget it,' Georgie said. 'You had a right to ask. I should have told you myself, probably, only I didn't think it was relevant.' She settled the lid on the teapot. 'Anyway, they knew that Ken had been shot down before they put me on that train to Canada, so if they thought that it would be a problem…'

'On the contrary,' said Deacon. 'I was told that they considered it an asset.'

'Really? Why is that?'

'Because your heart and mind would be engaged elsewhere,' he told her, and the humour flashed so briefly through his blue eyes that she thought she had imagined it. 'It worried them, your living here, with me; our going out around the town as man and wife. They didn't want there to be any…well, emotional entanglements. As if that were a danger.' His smile so clearly mocked himself that Georgie didn't take offence, but found a smile herself, to share the joke.

But she was glad he hadn't pressed her for an answer as to whether it would bother her, to know that he was flying…for the truth had been a revelation, even to herself.

Which might have been why, later on, in the beaded black dress, she felt strange as she faced her reflection. She felt, for an instant, as though she were being unfaithful to Ken. She knew that was crazy, and said so out loud to the face in the mirror. 'It's business. Just business.'

The strange feeling passed. It was only herself again, there in the mirror. She leant in, adjusting an earring, and liking the way all the beads of the epaulets danced on the dress at her shoulders. She had taken more care with her hair than she usually did, and her make-up, knowing the party tonight would be larger than any event they had been to, and that her appearance would be under scrutiny by those who hadn't yet met her. She wanted to look like a woman who might hold appeal for a man who loved art.

Deacon was waiting for her in the front hall, with her coat. He turned at the sound of her footsteps, and for a long time he said nothing, only looked at her in silence, in an angle of the hallway where there wasn't light enough for her to see his eyes and know what he was thinking.

The silence made her nervous, so she asked him, 'Will I do?'

He answered quietly. 'You're lovely.'

After which there wasn't much that she could do but tell herself again that it was business, only business, as he took his hat down from the peg and offered her his arm.

It wasn't snowing, so they walked. The cocktail party was a short few blocks away, at the twin-towered San Remo apartments. Georgie had seen them before, from the park, but she'd never been inside, and the sheer luxury left her dazzled.

'Your friend must have money,' she said, without thinking, and Deacon smiled.

'She married it. I'd say she married well, except I don't believe she did. Her husband drinks.' They took the elevator up, while he explained, 'She sometimes needs to get away. That's why she had the key to my apartment,' Deacon said, 'while I was gone.'

'Oh.' So the mystery woman, Georgie thought, was someone else's wife. From what she knew of Deacon, that made it unlikely that the two of them were anything but friends. She reaffirmed this when she saw them greet each other, with a casual and easy kiss on the cheek that held as much emotion as a kiss she might have given her own brother.

Relieved, although she wouldn't have admitted why, Georgie took stock of her hostess. The woman was beautiful, dark-haired and dark-eyed, and so slender that, in her silver-toned metallic dress, she looked as insubstantial as a wraith. The hand she extended to Georgie was long-fingered, graceful, and weighted with expensive-looking rings.

'My wife, Amelia,' Deacon introduced her, and then, 'Darling, this is Sylvia.'

'A pleasure to meet you,' said Georgie, and shook the hand gently, not wanting to crush it.

'The pleasure's all mine. I'm so happy you married this dear man. He needs taking care of.' The woman named Sylvia smiled, and then held out her free hand to Deacon. 'Please, both of you, come join the party.'

Georgie had never seen so many people in one room. She found it all completely overwhelming, and was grateful for the anchoring effect of Deacon's presence at her elbow. 'What will you drink?' he asked.

'Can I just have a Coke with ice?'

'Of course. Wait here, I'll get it.'

As she watched him navigate the crush of people on his way toward the bar, she felt again that strange sensation that she'd felt in the apartment, a mingling of guilt and awareness. She watched Ken this way, in a crowd – recognising the set of his shoulders, the tilt of his head, so she picked him out easily even when all she could see was his back.

It was natural, really, with all of the time she'd been spending with Deacon, that she'd be familiar with how the man walked, but—

'So you're Mrs Deacon.' The voice interrupted her thoughts like the bang of a gavel. She wheeled, and saw no one, until she corrected her angle of vision to take in the man in the wheelchair, beside her. His wheels had slid without a sound across the thick white carpet. Georgie hadn't heard him coming.

'Yes, I am,' she said.

'You're not a Brit.'

She didn't like his tone, but she said anyway, 'I'm not, no. I'm Canadian.'

'Thank God for that. I can't stand Brits. Think they're better than we are.' He lifted his glass which, from what her nose told her, held nothing but whiskey, and twisted his mouth with contempt. He was not an attractive man – anvil-jawed and heavy, with a barrel of a chest, and arms that seemed a shade too powerful for someone so confined. 'Bunch of damned cowards,' he said, loudly enough to attract the attention of several people standing nearby. One of them, a kind-faced young man, glanced briefly at Georgie's face and, taking pity on her, joined the conversation.

'Who's that, Bill?' he asked.

'Brits. They can't even fight their own war, they need us to come finish it for them.'

Georgie wasn't a redhead for nothing. Indignant, she felt her jaw set as she told him, 'I think they've been doing all right.'

The man in the wheelchair angled a hard look up at her, as though he hadn't expected the challenge. 'Cowards,' he said, more loudly still. 'Like that husband of yours. I'd be over there fighting myself, if it wasn't for this…' One great hand slammed the arm of his wheelchair. 'What's his excuse?'

Georgie's face flushed with anger on Deacon's behalf, and she would have said something in his defence if her hostess had not, at that moment, appeared, with a faintly embarrassed look marring her beautiful face. The woman, Sylvia, smiled at Georgie, and her large eyes begged forgiveness. 'I see you've met my husband.' One diamond-ringed hand rested on the man's shoulder, not so much a gesture of affection as an attempt at restraint. 'I'm afraid he's a man of opinions.'

'Yes.' Georgie kept her voice calm for her hostess's sake. 'I did notice.'

The young man who had joined the conversation earlier tried once again to intervene to keep the peace by extending his hand in a greeting to Georgie. 'So you're Andrew's wife. Pleased to meet you. I'm—'

'Carl,' Deacon said, from behind her right shoulder. 'Good to see you.' The two men shook hands. Deacon gave a brief nod to the man in the wheelchair. 'Bill.'

The other man grunted, but Deacon was no longer looking at him. He'd turned back to the first man. 'You've met Amelia, then. Your drink, darling,' he said, and handed the cold glass of Coke to her. He wasn't drinking. Then, 'Carl's the chap who's been doing such a marvellous job of running my gallery.'

'Yeah, well,' said Carl, with a grin, 'I expect I'll be looking for work soon, though, won't I?'

Deacon felt in his pocket for his cigarette case. 'Actually, I was hoping to persuade you to stay on a little longer.' He found the case; offered the cigarettes round. 'I may be going travelling again.'

It was Sylvia who asked him, 'Where to this time?'

Georgie took a cigarette and waited to see what he'd give for an answer. He held his lighter up for her and she felt the half-quizzical brush of his gaze as he noticed her still-heightened colour, and then with his eyes squarely fixed on her own he replied, 'I've been offered a short-term position in Lisbon.'

Lisbon, she thought. Her eyes lowered. So he would be flying.

The lighter clicked shut. He went on, in his quiet and casual way, 'With Ivan Reynolds.'

That impressed those who heard it, and for a minute the talk swirled around the great reclusive millionaire and what he'd done, and what they'd *heard* he'd done, and what he might be like to work for. But Bill, in his wheelchair, ignored all the gossip and looked up at Deacon with open contempt.

'Lisbon,' he said, his loud voice breaking through all the others. 'That's Portugal, right? They've stayed out of the war, haven't they?'

Deacon said yes, they were neutral.

'Neutral.' Bill took a long drink of his whiskey. 'No chance you'll get hurt there, then, is there?'

Deacon couldn't have missed the implied insult, but he just said, very lightly, 'No. Lucky for me.' And with that he looked over the crowd and said, 'Will you excuse us a moment? There's somebody I want Amelia to meet.'

As he steered her through the crowd he said, quite low, beside her ear, 'You know, you mustn't let him bother you. He drinks. I told you earlier.' Then, as she said nothing, he added, 'I'm sorry if he was rude to you. I shan't leave you on your own again, all right?'

And he didn't. True to the role of a newlywed husband, he stayed close by her side for the rest of their time there. They didn't stay long, really. Just long enough for the word to get round of his going to Portugal, which seemed to be, Georgie decided, the main purpose of their being there this evening.

'And will you go, too?' someone asked her.

She didn't know what she should say, until Deacon cut in with, 'Oh, no, she'll stay here. I shouldn't be gone all that long, really, and it's much safer keeping to this side of the Atlantic.'

A woman shook her head. 'Oh, but you'll miss her. Won't you miss her?'

'Yes, I will,' he said convincingly. His gaze found hers and fell away. 'I'll miss her very much.'

They left soon after that. She wasn't at all sorry to leave – the room had been more crowded and more noisy and more smoke-filled than she liked, and by comparison the elevator felt quite fresh and spacious. She enjoyed the silence, too, at first. But then she cleared her throat and asked, 'Why did you tell them? About going to Lisbon, I mean.'

Her words called him out of his own thoughts. He lifted his head. 'There's nothing secret about that. They'll find out soon enough that's where I am. Ours is a rather small fraternity – news tends to travel quickly. It would seem more suspicious,' he said, 'if I went *without* telling them first.'

'But you didn't say anything before.'

'The timing wasn't set, before.'

'And now it is?'

'Yes, well, it all depends—' he started.

'On the Clipper.'

'On the Clipper, yes.'

She interlaced her hands in her soft leather gloves, pushing them more firmly onto her fingers. She didn't want to think about the Pan Am Clipper. There was a reason, she knew, why the luxury airliner didn't run scheduled flights on a publicised flight path. These days, any aircraft crossing the Atlantic was a target.

In the quiet pause that followed she could feel that he was watching her. At last he asked her, 'Are you very tired?'

'No, not really. Why?'

'Because it's early yet.' His smile was brief, but warm. 'And I do think that it would be a crime,' he said, 'to waste that dress.'

* * *

He took her to the Roosevelt Hotel, down on Madison Ave. She never did learn just how he had managed it – whether he'd made reservations in advance, or whether he'd arranged it somehow in the few telephone calls that he'd placed from the San Remo's lobby before they had left. She was beginning to believe that one should never underestimate this quiet man, who seemed so very ordinary till one focused carefully and tried to really see him.

She was seeing him tonight, and he looked anything but ordinary.

Not classically handsome, like Kenneth...he'd never be that...and he didn't have Kenneth's immediate presence, nor the easy way Ken settled into any social setting. But there was something... Georgie couldn't put her finger on it, exactly, but there was something about Deacon that attracted her, against her strength of will.

At first, she blamed it on the atmosphere – the lighted tables, intimate; the dancing, and the music of the orchestra – Guy Lombardo and the Royal Canadians, Deacon had pointed out, in case she'd been feeling a little bit homesick. He'd apologised for it not being a more lively jazz club, which he felt she would have preferred, but their BSC bosses had warned them away from such places. Presumably, Georgie thought, because the girls she worked with went to clubs like that, and they might run the risk of being seen.

They weren't too likely to be spotted at the Roosevelt Hotel. None of her room-mates could afford a night like this, she thought. In the beautiful black beaded dress, sitting here with her very first glass of champagne, she felt like she'd magically stepped into one of the movies she'd watched at the Paramount.

She blamed the champagne, too, for what she was feeling. Not that she was drunk – she'd only had a few small sips – but she found it so much simpler to blame *something* for her new, confused emotions.

Deacon glanced across the table; met her eyes. 'What are you thinking?'

'Nothing, really.' She turned her head to watch the couples dancing. 'I just…' She couldn't express it, and so she said, instead, 'I've never been anywhere like this.'

He misunderstood. 'Perhaps you would rather have stayed at the party?'

Georgie smiled at that. 'No. I would not.'

'Oh?' He seemed intrigued. 'You didn't like the company?'

'I didn't like the host.'

'I see.' He offered her a cigarette, and took one for himself. 'What did he say to you that made you so upset? Did he insult you?'

His eyes were thoughtful, and concerned, and Georgie knew she'd have to give an answer, or he'd never let it go. She shrugged one shoulder, breathing out a careful stream of smoke. 'It wasn't about me, actually.'

'Oh? What, then?'

'It was more about you.'

'About me?' He seemed faintly surprised.

'Yes. He implied that you…well, that you weren't…'

He waited, and she had to put it into words.

'He said you were a coward.'

'Ah.' Tapping ash from his cigarette, Deacon said, 'Well, most people think that, I've told you. I've long since stopped letting it bother me.'

Georgie said, 'It bothered *me*.'

He looked at her. 'Why did it?'

She could only say, in her defence, that her reaction had been completely in character. 'It would have bothered any wife, to hear someone say that about her husband.'

'Yes,' said Deacon, 'I suppose it would.' He looked at her again, and then looked down, his fingers pinching up a small fold of the tablecloth. After a moment he said conversationally, 'I had rheumatic fever as a boy. I made a good recovery, but it leaves its mark, they say, upon the heart.' He tapped his cigarette again and watched the ash fall with a hiss into the still-damp ashtray. 'When Hitler sent his troops into Poland and we declared war, I did try to sign up, but I wasn't accepted. My heart. Funny thing, really, that they won't let you go and be killed if they think you'll drop dead on the way. So they told me no, thank you. But then, one of the Embassy chaps in Brazil made it known he'd be grateful if I'd pass on anything I learnt that might be useful. A lot of fifth columnists, down there. One heard things, you know, on the street. So I kept him informed, as best I could. And that's how it began,' he told her. 'That's how I came to be here, doing this. Not the same thing, I'll grant you, as wearing a uniform, but...' He looked up, with a tight little smile. The pleat that he'd made on the tablecloth was very tidy, very crisp. '"They also serve, who only stand and wait,"' he said.

Georgie wasn't sure what astonished her more – the fact that he'd made such a long speech, or such a personal one.

'It isn't common knowledge,' he went on. 'I'm not supposed to talk about the things I do, to anyone.' He paused, and smoothed the tablecloth again with his thumb, and then he added, very calmly, 'But I didn't want you thinking Bill was right.'

She looked at him – the quiet face, his gaze deliberately angled down, away from hers – and as she looked, she felt the weight of words unspoken pull between them, binding them, connecting them as surely as if they'd been holding hands across the table. It took time to find her voice. 'I never thought he was,' she said.

He raised his head at that, and met her eyes, and smiled a little. Crushing out the cigarette, he pushed his chair back. 'Would you like to dance?'

The Royal Canadians had just begun playing a slower song, one that she recognised, one they'd made quite popular a few years back, from *Showboat*. The man who sang the words seemed to be singing straight to her, to them, the lyrics fit so perfectly with how she felt, tonight…

> *'We could make believe I love you,*
> *Only make believe that you love me.*
> *Others find peace of mind in pretending;*
> *Couldn't you? Couldn't I? Couldn't we…?'*

She stood, and took the hand that Deacon offered, and she followed where he led. She hadn't danced with anyone since coming to New York. She had forgotten how it felt to be held by a man, to feel his hand heavy at her waist, and his fingers round hers, and the warmth of his jaw a hair's-breadth from her cheek.

Time stopped. They didn't speak. The room revolved, a swirl of dresses, faces, tables, dotted here and there with lights that seemed to dance, as they were dancing, to the music of the orchestra.

His hand shifted almost imperceptibly at her back, but she felt it and moved with it, letting him draw her in closer. And then his head moved as well, lowering slightly until his cheek rested on hers, and his long, exhaled breath brushed the side of her neck.

It felt so right, she thought…so comfortable, and right. She'd almost lost track of the words of the song but she focused her mind now and listened, not wanting to lose any part of the moment, no longer resisting the surge of emotion.

The mellow-voiced singer was crooning the chorus again for the last time, the swell of the music behind him a sign he was nearing the end:

'Might as well make believe I love you,
For…'

They were no longer moving, Georgie noticed. Deacon raised his head and drew away so he could see her eyes. His own were blue in shadow; serious.

'…to tell the truth,
I do.'

The music swelled again and stopped, and the dancers around them stopped, too, some returning to the tables while others remained on the dance floor and waited.

Georgie waited, too. Deacon tightened his grip on her hand, and drew a measured breath as though he was going to say something…but whatever it might have been she never heard it, because just then she became aware of someone standing close beside them. Someone tall, and wearing a dark overcoat.

'I hate to spoil your evening,' Jim's voice said, apologetic, 'but it's time.'

Deacon dropped his hand, reluctantly, and let go of Georgie's fingers.

Jim went on, 'We have to get you to the wharf in less than half an hour. There's a car outside, and your suitcase is already in it. Frank, here, will go with you.'

She hadn't seen the second man. She barely saw him now.

'Good luck,' said Jim, and reached across her to shake Deacon's hand.

'Yes, I...thank you,' Deacon said.

She saw him collect himself, and then the keen blue eyes came round to hers and he repeated, 'Thank you.'

Georgie forced a half-smile. 'It was nothing.'

'No.' He raised a hand to touch her cheek, a gesture of farewell, and then his fingers slid beneath her hair to gently cup her neck. He leant in close. 'It wasn't nothing,' he said, just for her, and kissed her forehead. To the others, she knew, it would have looked very proper and innocent, but there was a kind of fierceness in that kiss that brought a stinging to her eyes and made her wish that...well, she wished...

'Goodbye,' he said.

'Goodbye.'

She didn't watch him go. She couldn't.

Turning, she bit her lip hard as the colours and lights blurred and ran with a warmth that spilt over her lashes and onto her cheeks. She blinked, and the rough weave of a man's dark overcoat shielded her view as the softness of a handkerchief was pressed into her hand.

'Come on,' said Jim, and he took hold of her shoulder in an understanding grasp. 'I'll take you home.'

* * *

My grandmother's clock chimed its melody into the silence.

Outside, the evening darkness settled in around the forms of trees and fences at the lane behind the house, and the window glass reflected back the warm light of the kitchen, and my grandma's face...her eyes...

You have her eyes, that's what Deacon had said to me, that morning. His last words. His last thought, maybe. I couldn't help but wonder if, when he'd stepped off that kerb, unseeing, he had been where she was now, in memory...standing on that dance floor at the Roosevelt Hotel.

My grandmother appeared to still be standing there. She wasn't back with me, yet. So I waited, and I watched her face, and marvelled at how something so familiar could be foreign to me, too. Why was it, I wondered, that we so often saw old people as simply being old? Why had I never stopped to think, before, that she had once been young, like me – had fallen in and out of love, and laughed with friends, and had her dreams and disappointments, just as I did; that she hadn't always been as she was now? Tonight, at least, the realisation hit me with the force of an epiphany.

We had much more in common than I'd known, more than just the red hair and the eyes. I'd seen some of myself in the young Georgie Murray, and I felt a new-found sense of closeness to her that I wanted to explore. There were, I thought, so many questions...

I was watching when she sighed, and blinked, returning to the present.

I asked, 'Then what happened?'

'Oh, well, that was that. He went away, and I was transferred to Washington. I didn't realise I'd been killed off,' she said, using humour, as always, to regain her footing. 'Though I suppose, now that I think of it, he couldn't have kept up the fiction of having a wife for his whole life.'

He had done exactly that, as it happened, but I didn't think raising that point would be helpful.

She said, 'You say I'm supposed to have died in New York?'

'I think so. Deacon's nephew didn't say for certain.' She had *me* calling him Deacon, now, I noticed, only for me it seemed rather more personal than less so – it was almost a term of affection.

If Grandma had noticed, she didn't say anything. 'Well, I hope they gave Amelia an exciting end. Nothing too boring.'

I tried to steer her back to the main story, which, for me, still didn't have a proper ending. 'So you never saw Deacon again? Never heard from him?'

'No. I knew he had made it to Lisbon all right,' she admitted, 'because for the first little while after he left they had me stay on in the apartment, and there was a letter that came, in his handwriting, so I knew he'd arrived there.'

'And what did he say, in the letter?'

'Oh, I wasn't allowed to read it, Katie. I wasn't even allowed to open it. I'd been given instructions to pass any letters that came on to my bosses, so I did. It wasn't meant for me,' she explained. 'I was only his cover. It would probably have been all in code, anyway – I wouldn't have been able to make sense of it.' She interlaced her fingers round her empty glass and looked at them. 'Anyway, they sent me to Washington soon after that, and I didn't hear anything more. I left BSC that summer, when my brother Ronnie died. I came back here, to help my parents. And then, of course, your grandfather came home and…well, you know what happened, after that.'

I knew. She had married my grandfather, married her Kenneth, and after years of trying they had finally had a son, who'd been my father, and in time he'd married Mother and had me. The normal chronicle of family life. But, still…

'You must have wondered…' I began, then let the sentence hang unfinished.

Grandma looked at me, and must have seen the questions still unasked, unanswered, in my eyes, because she took a moment to consider, and then said, 'Of course I did. Of course I wondered what became of him.' She frowned a little, trying to explain, so I would understand. 'I've had a happy life,' she said. 'A very happy life. I loved your grandfather, and he loved me. I don't regret a minute of the time we had together. But yes, I often thought of Deacon. He was…well, sometimes when you've put a fire out there's just a little ember burning in the ashes, still, beneath. He was like that,' she said. 'I never did forget him.'

She turned her head away and looked, unseeing, through the kitchen window to the darkness by the high back fence where she had planted the little rosebushes.

Her life, I thought, might have been different. So different. I tried to imagine her in Deacon's house in Elderwel, sitting in *his* kitchen, looking over *his* back garden. He'd had roses, too, as I remembered…lovely tea roses.

She was gone again. I saw her eyes and knew that she'd been pulled into the past again the way a floating leaf is carried further from the shore by a retreating wave. I sat there, saying nothing, only watching her reflection in the night-black glass.

And then, as from a blow, the window shattered and her image shattered with it.

Someone screamed. Her chair fell. When I dived to try to catch it, something whined mosquito-like against my ear and struck the wall behind with force enough to send a shard of plaster spiking to the floor. Again, I heard somebody scream. A chilling sound. A primal sound of shock and fear and anguish.

Then I realised it was me. My voice.

Because there wasn't anybody else.

I didn't remember too much, after that. I remembered chaos. A confusion of ambulance lights and police cars and neighbours appearing from nowhere to stand on their porches, on lawns, on the sidewalks, in little groups, watching; the house and the yard and the lane being wrapped in a tangle of yellow police tape, and officers crawling round carefully, raking the ground with the beams of their flashlights. I remembered one officer looking upset when he'd first seen my grandmother's body. I'd wanted to tell him that it was all right, that she hadn't been there when it happened – she'd been somewhere else, and in far better company...only before I could tell him, they'd ushered me out of the kitchen, and after that, things got incredibly blurry.

I had some memory of an ambulance, and someone saying 'Shock', and 'Better get her checked out, anyway', and then to my own vague surprise I had found myself taking up space in the busy Emergency room of a huge downtown hospital.

I was trying hard to focus on the frenzy of activity around me when a pair of darkly uniformed shoulders moved into my line of vision.

147

Small shoulders. A female police officer. She had a sympathetic face – I imagined that's why they had chosen her to do this kind of duty. 'You OK?' she asked.

From my slightly out-of-body vantage point, I thought that was an idiotic question. Of course I wasn't OK. I'd just seen my grandmother killed for no reason by someone who'd taken a shot at me, too. I was a long way from being OK. But I knew the policewoman was only being kind, and so I nodded.

'Good. It shouldn't take much longer.'

Her radio squawked, and she gave my arm an encouraging squeeze before turning away.

I lost sight of her in the confusion of people arriving and leaving. Another blue uniform stepped into view, but the young woman wearing it wasn't familiar – a different policewoman who, with her partner, was busy admitting a middle-aged man who appeared to be homeless, wild-haired and bare-footed in spite of the cold. A few minutes later, my gaze finally found *my* policewoman, standing just inside the big main glass doors. She was talking with two men, both fortyish, both dressed as though they'd come straight from an elegant dinner.

The policewoman said something; gestured my way, and the men looked, and nodded, and started towards me. I watched their approach with dull interest. They both walked like men of authority.

The taller one, silver-haired, spoke to me first. He had a nice voice, deep and pleasantly pitched, and my mind chose to focus on the sound of it instead of what he said. I didn't catch his name. But then he introduced the man beside him. 'Sergeant Metcalf, here, is visiting from England. He's been speaking at our conference. Now, we'll understand if you're not up to talking at the moment, but...'

It was, I thought, as though the scene from last Sunday night in London were being played again. The Englishman, all sympathy and smoothness, took a step towards me as he showed me his credentials: Sergeant Robert Metcalf, Scotland Yard. 'Miss Murray? I was wondering if I might have a word.'

Before I could frame a reply, there was a shout from the admitting desk, and everybody turned in that direction. The homeless man had pulled a knife. Hunching away from his police minders like a defensive animal, he let loose a chain of obscenities, randomly slicing the air with the weapon. They jumped him. When he struggled, my policemen – even Metcalf – sprang to help their fellow officers.

And that's when I took off.

It wasn't anything premeditated – I just wheeled and ran, on instinct, like an animal myself, in search of somewhere safe to hide.

Because the Sergeant Metcalf who'd been standing here in front of me was not the Sergeant Metcalf I had spoken to in London.

There was virtually no one around in the the *Sentinel* building at this time of night. It was past one o'clock, and the editors had all gone home, leaving only the cleaning staff and the odd dedicated reporter behind.

Our offices were spread out over two floors – arts and sports and marketing shared one level, news and business were on another, with the reference library taking up a block of space at my end. On the ground floor, at street level, was Security. I usually had to scan my photo pass to make it through. Tonight, without my pass – still back at Grandma's, in my briefcase – I'd relied on luck, persuasion, and the memory of the guard. He *had* remembered me, which, given that I hadn't been around for several weeks, was quite impressive. And although he'd hesitated, still, at length he'd let me through. So here I was, safe for the moment, in my cubicle.

I hadn't had any particular destination in mind when I had bolted from the hospital, but once I'd got outside and seen exactly where I was, my steps had turned in this direction on their own. I'd run the first two blocks, and then, to blend in better with the scattering of people, I had walked the final three, arriving pale and out of breath but full of the conviction that the office was the best place, temporarily, to go to ground.

It was. My cubicle upstairs, though not as sheltered as a rabbit hole, still shielded me from view. The cleaner had vacuumed her way past ten minutes ago without once looking up, and the only other person I could see was working clear across in Foreign, the back of his bent head barely visible above the top of his divider.

I was, for all intents and purposes, alone. Unseen.

I put my head down on my desk as though I were a child, and tried to think.

My first thought was that I had maybe made a big mistake, to run away like that. To run from the police. God only knew what they were thinking. If they questioned me right now, I didn't know what I could say in my defence, except that this, for me, was not a normal day. I wasn't thinking straight.

The shooting had reduced me to a primal, almost paranoiac state, and when I'd met the second Sergeant Metcalf all that I had registered was that something was wrong. And I'd felt frightened. I'd felt threatened.

With my eyes closed, I tried hard right now to analyse that threat.

There were, as far as I could see, two possibilities, both troubling. The man I'd met tonight might not, in fact, be Sergeant Robert Metcalf. Which wasn't good, because I couldn't think of any useful reason why he'd say he was, or why he'd want to meet me.

If he *wasn't* an imposter, but was really Sergeant Metcalf, that was worrying as well, because it meant the man I'd met in London had been lying, and again I couldn't think of why he'd do that.

All he'd said to me, that night at my hotel, was not to publish Deacon's story.

Deacon's story…

Deacon had said that himself, on the steps of St Paul's: *I have a story I could tell you…there's a murder in it…an old murder, but one still deserving of justice.* I could only assume, since he'd travelled all that way to tell it to me, that it was the same story Metcalf had meant; the same story that featured in Deacon's report.

There it was again, I thought. That damned report. If I could only read it; find out what it was the London Metcalf thought I knew…

I raised my head and, turning my computer on, began to search through telephone directories. It took a few minutes to find what I wanted. I looked at my watch as I dialled the number. Most people in England would still be in bed, at this hour of the morning. I could only hope James Cavender was an early riser.

He might not have had much of a chance yet, to search through his uncle's belongings, his papers, but then again, you never knew. He might have had some luck. The phone rang two times, then a man's voice came on. 'Hello?'

'Mr Cavender? It's Kate Murray calling. I hope I didn't wake you?'

The other voice paused, for thought. 'Oh, Miss Murray. Right. You came to Andrew's funeral. Only this isn't James, I'm afraid. It's the vicar.'

The friendly young vicar of St Stephen's Church. 'Reverend Beckett?'

'You remembered. Yes.' Another pause. 'You'll not have heard, then. About James, I mean. I'm sorry to have to tell you, but he's dead.'

I gripped the receiver, aware of its coldness. 'Dead? How?'

'Well, it was rather a sad thing. A senseless thing. We've had a run of break-ins here, these past few months, and I suppose with Andrew's cottage standing empty, and all his art inside, it made an irresistible target. And James...well, it seems he'd been having a go at Andrew's papers, and he must have surprised them, poor fellow. He didn't stand much of a chance,' said the vicar. 'There must have been a few of them. The place was an absolute shambles.'

I said, 'And he's dead?', still unable to fully accept it. It was shock on top of shock, for me. It felt as though I'd only just been speaking to him. 'When...? I mean...'

'On Sunday night. Quite late. He'd been away, that day.'

He paused, then offered, 'Was there something *I* could help you with?'

'What? Oh, no, thank you. I…no, thank you.' I was only half aware of our goodbyes, of hanging up. My rattled thoughts had focused on one small, disturbing point: It had been Sunday that James Cavender had come to my hotel; that he had waited in the Bugle Lounge to meet with me. Which meant there was a pattern of coincidence.

Two men had travelled all the way to London just to talk to me, and both of them were dead.

It might be simply that – coincidence. And yet…

My hand clutched the receiver in its cradle as my mind began to play connect-the-dots with what had happened back in London and the shooting here, tonight.

Deacon had known something that involved a murder from the past. Supposing someone didn't want that murder resurrected? What if Deacon's accidental death had been no accident? What if he'd been silenced?

Then James Cavender might also have been killed, not by an ordinary burglar, but by someone who had thought he'd known what Deacon knew.

And someone thought *I* knew, as well. The Sergeant Metcalf I had met in London had been very clear on that. I could remember, word for word, what he had told me: 'I believe you are acquainted with a Mr Andrew Deacon, and that Mr Deacon may have passed you certain information…'

Did the fact I hadn't bothered to deny it mean that I was now a target? And my grandmother – had she been killed because somebody thought I might have told her, too? My God, if that were so, then who else might now be at risk, because of me? Who else would anyone have seen me talking to?

With sudden urgency I picked up the receiver for a second time and dialled a London number. Margot. She would be in Argentina, now, but she called home to get her messages when she was on assignment. I had no idea what to say; what message I could leave...but in the end, I didn't get the chance. The line just rang and rang, without an answer.

Hanging up, I fought back my uneasiness and dialled another number. Patrick. He was probably in bed, now – or in someone else's bed – but even so...

His room-mate answered on the seventh ring, a little sleepily. 'Hello?'

'Hello, Noel, it's Kate. Is Patrick there?'

Noel was honest to a fault, if somewhat slow. 'He isn't, no, Kate.' Then, still groggy, 'Is he not with you?'

'No, Noel. I'm home, in Canada.'

'Ah, well, it must be someone else, then. I've not seen him since the weekend.' I could hear his fridge door open and the clinking of a milk bottle. 'I thought for sure that he'd gone off with you. The more fool him.'

I was feeling the first twists of actual panic, now. 'Noel?'

'Yes?'

But what could I tell him? *I think someone may have harmed Patrick because they thought he knew a secret an old man was trying to tell me...*How crazy did that sound? And so I just said, 'Nothing. Thanks.'

'Not a problem. I'll tell him you rang.'

When I put the receiver down this time the cold wasn't just on the phone, but inside me. The walls of my cubicle no longer felt like a shelter, they felt like a trap. I thought fast. I would have to get out of here. Have to get out of here *soon*. Couldn't risk being seen—

'Kate?' I jumped at the man's voice that spoke from a few feet behind me, then realised that it was familiar. It was Guy's voice. Guy Robichaud's voice. 'My God, what are you doing here?' he said. 'Are you all right?'

I knew from his reaction that he'd heard about my grandmother. And then I thought, of course he would have heard. He covered crime. He had police-band radios at home, and in his car. He would have heard the call go out. He would have been there, at the scene. I hadn't even thought to look for him.

But I was glad to see him now. I couldn't think of anyone I would have trusted more in time of crisis. He was more than just my colleague. We were friends, and fairly close ones.

His family had come from New Brunswick, Acadians, hence the French name and French looks, his brown hair almost black, like his eyes, which looked sleepy in the middle of the day or at this hour of the night and hid an intellect that could have sliced through steel.

He was beside me, now, inside my cubicle, close down where he could see my face and reassure himself I wasn't injured. 'You had me so worried. What happened?'

I told him, 'My grandmother's dead.'

'Yeah, I know. And I'm sorry. That's not what I meant. I meant, why aren't you at the hospital? They told me you took off…'

'Who did? Who told you?'

'The police. They'll be relieved to know you're here.'

155

'No.' I said that much too sharply, but I couldn't help it. 'You can't tell them.'

'Kate?'

'Please, Guy, don't tell them.' I grabbed at his arm. 'Look, I can't explain now, but I need you to promise you won't tell anyone you saw me here.'

The black eyes assessed me. 'Only if you tell me what's going on.'

'I can't. You'll think I'm crazy.'

'Try me.'

Time was running out, I knew, but Guy, when he dug in his heels, was as fixed as the Rock of Gibraltar. I cast a look around the room – the maze of darkened cubicles, the closed glass doors that led into the stairwells, and the sleeping bank of elevators. 'Look, all right, I'll tell you. But not here,' I said. 'It isn't safe.'

He stood and looked round, as though trying to see the same hazards. 'Fine, let's use the library.'

The microfilm reading room had walls, and a door. In the semi-darkness, Guy leant up against a desk, arms folded, waiting. So I told him what had happened; what I knew; what I suspected. When I'd finished, he stayed quiet for a moment, but I knew that he believed me. I could tell from his expression, just as he, too, knew me well enough to know that I was genuinely nervous.

He said, 'So what are you planning to do?'

'I don't know. For tonight, I guess get a hotel room, and stay out of sight.' I had my wallet, in the pocket of my coat. It was the only thing I'd brought with me – I'd needed my identification for the hospital – but I'd been travelling so long

I had no Canadian money left in it, only pounds and Euros. And my credit card.

Guy shook his head. 'You don't need to go to a hotel. You shouldn't be alone, not after this. You should come stay with me. I've got plenty of room.'

'No, I can't. Don't you see? It might put you in danger.'

'I'll take that risk.'

'I won't. If something happened, Guy…' I thought about my grandmother, and shook my head. 'No.'

'Well, a hotel is out of the question.'

I sighed. 'All right, then, tell me – where else can I go? There's nowhere. Nowhere I'll be safe.'

Guy turned towards me in the darkened room. 'Well, actually…' He straightened from the desk, on inspiration. 'There *is* one place.'

WEDNESDAY, SEPTEMBER 20

I couldn't get my eyes to open.

It was an unsettling sensation, to feel fully awake and aware and yet not have control of my eyelids, as if they were fastened shut. Frowning, I tried again, focusing all of my effort on that one small task.

It worked. I lay very still on my back for a moment and let my gaze wander the ceiling, the walls, not remembering where…

Then it all flooded back, and I knew where I was.

I was in Scarborough, a suburb of Toronto. Guy had brought me here early this morning, before the sun rose. I remembered a dark street of two-storey brick houses shouldered together, garages protruding in front, so alike that I'd wondered how people could ever remember which house was their own.

Like the street in *Ali Baba* where the thieves had had to mark the door with chalk so they could find their way back to it in the night.

To make quite sure that no one would be able to retrace *our* steps, Guy had made the taxi driver let us out a few streets over from the one we wanted, and I'd had to follow him along the barren, streetlit sidewalks, with my arms wrapped tightly round me as defence against the early morning cold. I'd had to hurry to keep up. His strides were long.

We hadn't spoken in the taxi. We'd both felt the need for secrecy. But I'd had questions, and with no one else around, I'd dared to ask him, 'You're sure about this?'

'Oh, yeah. Tony's OK.'

I had given him a quick and wary glance. Guy had come to the *Sentinel* two years ago after leaving the Sunday night newsmagazine of a major Canadian network. There'd been three of them doing the show, on TV – one had handled the high-profile stories, and another the glitzy stuff. Guy, in his own words, had worked as the 'sewer rat', digging down deep for the hard-hitting pieces that no one else wanted to do. The first two reporters were recognised more when they went out to restaurants; Guy's work had won awards. But he'd mixed with some pretty unsavoury characters – bikers, and convicts who'd claimed they'd been wrongly convicted, and...

I'd stopped, on the sidewalk. 'He's not one of your Mafia friends, is he?'

'Who, Tony? No. Tony's not even Italian. His last name is Shaw.'

'But you're sure that you can trust him?'

'I can trust him.' Not a hint of hesitation. 'So can you.'

The house had looked the same as all the others, ordinary. The outside light was off, as was the front hall light inside, and so I only saw a shadow when the door swung open. Someone tall. A man. A *big* man. Broad across the shoulders. Powerful.

His name might have been Irish but his accent was all English. Rough-edged, northern English. 'That was quick. You did it how I told you?'

'Yeah, we changed cabs a couple of times,' Guy had said.

'Good lad. Come in, then.' As the door had closed behind us he had flipped the front hall light on, and I'd gotten my first good look at his face. It had matched the voice, and body – craggy, hard as stone along the jawline, self-assured. He would have been my father's age, I'd thought, or maybe slightly younger, judging by the greying of his light brown hair, the lines around his eyes. 'Kate?' he'd guessed, and offered me his hand. 'I'm Tony. Welcome. You don't have a suitcase? Well, that's not a problem. We can find you what you need.'

The 'we' in this case had included his round and sympathetic wife, Marie. Between them they had found me clean pyjamas and a toothbrush, and a dozen other comforts and conveniences – a cup of tea, a pair of slippers, paperbacks to read.

I only saw the bed. Exhaustion hit me like a ton of bricks, and wrapped in all the trappings of security – a giant man to guard the door, a bedroom with a lock, and all inside a house where nobody would ever think to look for me – I gave myself to sleep.

I didn't dream.

I slept so deeply that I lost all sense of time, and my surroundings. Even now, awake, and knowing where I was, I felt disoriented still, so much so that I half suspected there'd been something in my tea besides the tea.

I closed my eyes again, and turned my face against the pillow. That was a mistake, because the images flowed up to fill the darkness – Grandma's face, and the smile I would not

160

see again. Broken glass, and the sight of her lying there dead in the kitchen.

I sat up, eyes open. The images stopped.

I wasn't aware that I'd made any sound, but I must have done, because a moment later there was a sharp knock from the hallway, and Tony's voice said, 'Kate, are you all right?'

'I'm fine,' I tried to tell him, but my voice refused to carry so I cleared my throat and tried again. 'I'm fine.' The room was light, and so I asked, 'What time is it?'

His answer surprised me. 'Two-thirty.'

Two-thirty. I'd slept through the morning and into the afternoon.

'Want me to bring you some tea?' he asked.

'Oh, you don't have to, I can get it...'

'It's no bother. Be back in a minute.'

I was up and dressed when he got back, and sitting on the bed, which was the only place to sit. He set the tray of tea and muffins on the bed beside me and then stood a little distance off, concerned, I thought, with giving me my space.

'So,' he said, 'you like the room?'

'It's beautiful.'

'My daughter's room,' he said, with pride. I'd guessed that. It was wallpapered in little blue forget-me-nots all over, on an ivory ground, with blue and pink checked curtains at the window. There were dolls, well loved, along a shelf beside the closet door, and on the dresser was a painted wind-up carousel, with pink and yellow horses. 'She doesn't live here anymore, she's all grown up,' he said, 'and on her own. She travels different places, teaching English. At the moment it's Korea.'

'Is that her?' I nodded to a photograph propped up beside the carousel – a smiling, dark-haired girl with large brown eyes.

He looked where I was looking, and then turned away and told me, 'No, that's Angie, her best friend. The two of them grew up together, thick as thieves.'

I'd raised my teacup almost to my mouth before remembering how heavily I'd slept, and my suspicions. I paused, and tried to sniff the tea without him noticing, but Tony, I was learning, didn't miss much.

With a smile he said, 'Go on, it's safe to drink. We haven't spiked it.'

Whether he and Marie had spiked the last one, he didn't say, but he put my deep sleep last night down to the room. 'It's got extra-thick walls, and the window's unbreakable. No way for noise to get in.'

It was the unbreakable window that did it. I couldn't *not* ask. 'Tony? What *do* you do?'

He said, 'Guy didn't tell you?'

'No.'

Leaning on the dresser he looked once more at the picture of the brown-eyed girl, and then, as though deciding I deserved an explanation, he said, 'Angie, there, was murdered in her final year of high school. Boyfriend did it. She had given him the boot a month before; he wasn't having it. He threatened her, she went to the police, but in the end there wasn't much that they could do. And so she died. He stabbed her.' His mouth became a grim line in his hardened face. I saw the sadness. 'Lovely girl, she was. And she'd been like a second daughter in this house. I blamed myself, for not protecting her. And so I started doing what I could to see that others didn't die as Angie did.' He folded his strong arms across his chest. 'It isn't me, alone. I'm only one link in a chain of people. Women come to us, we hide them, give them new lives, new identities, and move them to a place where they'll be safe, where they can start again.'

I understood the nature of Guy's interest in the man. It was a daring thing to do – like a privately run Witness Protection Programme. Not entirely legal, if they were actually providing false identities for people, but then in this case one could argue that the end excused the means. After all, the underground railroad hadn't been entirely legal, either, and the law, I had learnt, didn't always defend the right people.

I didn't know what he'd been told about me, but I thought that he should know, 'I'm not a battered woman.'

'Yeah, I know.' He straightened. Once again I realised just how large a man he was – he seemed to fill the room. He sauntered past me to the door, and turned. 'That doesn't mean that you don't need protecting.'

Guy was back at dinner with an update.

We were eating in the dining room. I didn't think anything of that, at first, till it struck me that this was a room not much used, and that Tony and Marie had moved the meal so that I wouldn't have to sit beside the window in their kitchen.

I'd been wondering whether Guy had filled them in on what had happened; wondering what I ought to tell them if they asked, but then, they hadn't asked me anything. But now I knew they knew at least the basics, because Guy was speaking freely about what he'd learnt today, from the police:

'So they figure the shooter was up on the roof of the neighbour's garage, at the back of the lane. They wouldn't tell me why they thought that, or what they'd found in the way of evidence, but I got the impression they hadn't found much. They're a long way from knowing who did it.'

'They probably think it was me,' I said.

'Nobody thinks it was you.'

'Guy, I ran away from them. They can't think that was normal.'

'Anyone,' he emphasised, 'would understand you running scared last night. You were tired, you were in shock, you'd just seen your grandmother murdered...and on top of all that this guy Metcalf walked in and you snapped. I can guarantee you, if you were to go to the police right now and tell them that, they'd understand.'

'I can't. I've told you. I can't trust them.'

'Are you sure? Because everything I'm getting from my sources in the department says the Metcalf who's here in Toronto right now is the real deal – a genuine Scotland Yard cop. And if all of this started in London, then maybe he can help you.'

'No.' Both hands were at my temples now, as though the touch could hold my head together. 'This thing with Deacon, it goes real high up – to Whitehall, to the government – he sent them a report. They said they didn't have it, when I called to ask. They stonewalled me. But Guy, I'm sure that they were lying. I could feel it. I...' I had some trouble putting my suspicions into words. 'Deacon used to be British Intelligence. And this story he wanted to tell, it had something to do with a murder. I don't know what I've stumbled onto here, but I do know if Whitehall's involved, then...'

'She's right,' Tony said, coming in on my side, unexpectedly. His voice was very quiet, but it carried authority. He said to Guy, 'If what she thinks is true – if the deaths of this old man in London, his nephew, her grandmother...if they weren't accidents, then she's right to think the government is probably involved. And if they are, she wants to stay away from Scotland Yard.'

Guy asked, 'But why—?'

'Because, lad, "Scotland Yard" is just a shorthand for the London Metropolitan Police, and the commissioner of the London Metropolitan Police reports directly to the Home Office. That's Whitehall, all of it – the Foreign Office, Home Office, all one great and many-headed beast.'

Guy shook his head. 'No, I meant what makes you think that the government's in on it?'

Tony leant back. 'Well, you said the old boy sent some kind of report, in the first place, to Whitehall.'

'That's right.'

'So, now, follow along with this theory these deaths were no accident. Someone was watching this Deacon bloke closely enough to know he'd talked to Kate. It'd be a fair assumption that they also knew he'd sent off this report, and where he'd sent it, which would mean they knew his story was already in the hands of the authorities.' He looked at us, to make quite sure that we'd both grasped that point. 'But they went ahead and killed him, and they've gone on killing others who they think might know this...well, this secret *thing* that the authorities already know. Now, why would they do that?'

Guy admitted that it made no sense, 'Unless they didn't know that he'd sent anything to Whitehall.'

'Yeah, that's possible. I wouldn't bet the bank on it,' said Tony, 'but it's possible. A better reason might be that they knew that Whitehall wasn't going to act on the report, that it was going to be buried. Making Deacon and the people that he told his story to the only threat.'

Guy finally saw, I think, where he was going with this logic – where my own mind had already travelled, on its own. Guy said, 'But the only way someone could know Whitehall wouldn't do anything with the report would be...'

'If they were working for Whitehall,' said Tony. 'Or if they *were* Whitehall.'

His statement was followed by silence.

We thought. Then Marie, who'd been silent till now, said, 'I think Kate's safety ought to be our first concern. I think that we should help her, like we help the other women – get her out of here, where nobody can find her.' Then she said to me, directly, 'We've got people who can change your name, your looks, and get you somewhere you'll be safer. We've even got a travel agent, brilliant lad, can get you on a flight this week to anywhere you want.'

'Oh, I don't think it's come to that, yet,' Tony said. His tone was level, quietly authoritative. 'Maybe down the road a bit, but not just yet. It's a drastic step, that, and you don't want to break the law lightly.'

Something in the way he said that struck me. My whole life was built on hunches, and I played one now. I looked at him, the big man with the rugged face, and asked him if he'd ever been a cop.

'I was, once, yeah. Long time ago.'

'In England?'

'Yeah.' He met my eyes. 'I was six years with Scotland Yard, in Special Branch. We weren't the CID, we didn't deal with crime – we did political security.'

'I see.' My guard went up.

Guy stared. 'You never told me that.'

'You never asked,' said Tony. 'Anyway, it's years ago now. Ancient history. I wouldn't know anyone there now, or else I might have been able to ask round myself for you, about this Metcalf…'

Guy said, 'Look, we're getting ahead of ourselves here. We're just working with a theory, and we may be wrong. I mean, if Whitehall were involved, why would they send that guy in London to her hotel, saying he was Metcalf, when he wasn't? Why not send the real Metcalf to talk to her?'

Nobody knew.

They didn't know, either, why Grandma's death hadn't been made to look random, like Deacon's and Cavender's. To Guy it suggested a lack of conspiracy. Tony saw something more sinister. 'They've changed locations. They may have changed killers. Who knows how many people may be in on this.'

Which wasn't reassuring, but he hadn't meant to reassure. He said things straight, and that was why, although he had a link to Scotland Yard, and logic told me there was no one I could trust, my instinct told me, on the other hand, that Tony wasn't someone I should fear.

And I had never had to trust my instinct more.

It was like being on assignment in a strange and foreign

167

landscape, with no contacts, no direction. Out of my element; over my head. There were too many questions, and not enough answers. Unless...

I tried focusing, as I'd have done in the field.

Follow the facts, I thought. Follow the story. I needed to know what was in that report.

Guy was right. We were just trading theories, without any proof, and the only way to find out who was doing this – if anyone, in fact, was doing anything – would be to find out who might have a stake in keeping Deacon silent. And to do *that*, I would have to find out what it was he'd meant to say.

I interrupted Guy and Tony, who were talking about something that I'd long since ceased to follow. 'Tony?'

'Yes, love?'

'There is one thing you could do for me.'

He raised an eyebrow. 'Name it.'

'I need access to the Internet,' I told him. 'And a telephone.'

Thursday, September 21

The vicar of St Stephen's Church, in Elderwel, was too polite to say so, but I knew he must have thought that I was odd. A normal person, after all, wouldn't have reacted as emotionally to the death of a virtual stranger as I had done two days ago, when I'd learnt of the murder of James Cavender. I tried to cover for my curious behaviour this time round, with an apology, and told him just how sorry I had been to hear the news. 'I thought he was such a nice man.'

'Yes, he was,' said the vicar. 'He was. I knew him rather well, he's been a lay reader here for a number of years, so it's been difficult this week. I'm James's executor, you see,' he said, 'and indirectly, I suppose, his beneficiary. He had no family, so he's left everything to our church.'

My mind leapt on the point, before I stopped to think how callous it might sound. 'Does that include his uncle's papers?'

'Andrew's papers? Yes, although—'

'I'm sorry,' I said, 'I know you have a lot of other things to think about just now. It's only that Mr Cavender wanted to send me a copy of something his uncle had written, and he

was going to look for it after he got home, last Sunday, but…'
I doubted that he'd had the chance to even start his search,
that night, before he had been killed. 'It may still be there,
at the house. And I wondered…I mean, if it isn't too much
trouble, could you maybe have a look for it yourself?'

'I could try. I'm not sure how much luck I'll have finding
anything, after what happened. It was—' he began, and then
cut himself short, as though trying to spare me the details.
'Well, it was a shambles, as I said. It still is. I'm going to have
quite a job on my hands, clearing Andrew's house out for the
auction. But if you'll tell me what it is I should be looking for,
I'll see what I can do.'

I had to confess that I wasn't entirely sure. 'It's a report,
I don't know how thick it would be, but he wrote it just
recently, sometime this past summer. I don't know the subject
for certain, but Mr Cavender thought it would be about
Lisbon; the time that his uncle spent working in Portugal,
during the war.'

'Did Andrew work there? I wasn't aware of that. I knew he
had travelled a good deal, but I didn't realise he actually lived
abroad.'

'He worked for Ivan Reynolds.'

'*Did* he?'

'In fact,' I told him, 'anything you find that has to do with
Ivan Reynolds, or with Lisbon, I would really like to see it.'

'Oh, of course. Of course. I don't hold out much hope,
mind, but I'll do my best.' His voice changed as though he
were shifting the receiver on his shoulder, freeing his hands.
'Just let me have your number, and I'll give you a ring if I
come across anything.'

I hesitated. For all the vicar knew, I was still in London, and it made sense to let him go on thinking that. Safer for me not to let people know where I was. 'Actually, I think it would be easier if I called you. Would the weekend be too early?'

He paused, and then, as though he had heard something in my voice I hadn't meant for him to hear, he asked, 'Is anything wrong?'

'Not a thing,' I said, striving for lightness.

'You're sure?'

I assured him I was, but he waited a moment before he said, finally, 'All right, then, I'll wait for your call at the weekend.'

Which didn't give him that much time to look for Deacon's papers, but I couldn't help the rush. I didn't have the luxury of time. Someone had tried to kill me once this week – they might be out there, right now, getting set to try again.

I didn't know how wide they'd cast their web. I'd tried again to get in touch with Margot, and with Patrick, but I'd had no luck. Which only made me worry more about their safety; made my mission feel more urgent.

I knew that, realistically, the odds were pretty long against the vicar finding anything at Deacon's house – the people who'd killed Cavender had probably been searching for that same report, and any papers that they might have found they would have taken, or destroyed. It was quite possible the only papers left were those that Cavender had brought to me in London: Deacon's letters to his sister, that he'd written while in Portugal. I didn't have them with me. They were still at Grandma's house, tucked safely in the zippered inside pocket of the briefcase that I lugged my laptop round in. I had left that briefcase sitting in the front hall, with my suitcase; hadn't thought to take it when I'd left the house. I hadn't thought of much then, I had been so deep in shock, and at the time I hadn't realised I would not be going home after the hospital.

But hindsight could be punishingly clear, and I'd have given quite a lot to have those letters with me now. I'd read them all in London, on my last day there. I'd read them again, on the plane, but I couldn't remember more than a few first names of people he had talked about, and one or two descriptive bits he'd written to his sister – his arrival in the city, a reception at the Embassy, that sort of thing. At the time, nothing had struck me as being of any significance. He hadn't really talked about his work, or Ivan Reynolds, or the intrigues that I knew must have been going on in Lisbon at that time. He'd written mostly of his meals, and of the house where he was living, and how much he missed his wife.

Of course I knew now that he hadn't had a wife, he had been speaking of my grandmother, which made me keen to read those bits again, because the emotion in them had, upon first reading, seemed so genuine.

In fact, I wanted badly to read all the letters over, in the hope of finding some small telling detail I had overlooked. If nothing else, as Cavender had pointed out to me that night in London, Deacon mentioned several people whom he worked with, and if any of them could be found, if they were still alive, they might prove helpful. Without any access to Deacon's report, I would have to try piecing together his story myself, and that meant I would have to rely on the memory of those who had known him, in hopes they'd be able to help me uncover this murder he'd wanted to tell me about.

I remembered, in his letters, he had talked about a secretary.

What had been her name? Regina something. Frowning, I half closed my eyes and tried to think...but no, the name was gone.

'Hey,' said Tony's voice, from the hall behind me.

I turned in my chair. 'Hi. Do you want to get on your computer?'

'No, no, you just stay there as long as you like, Kate. No, I've got Guy on the cell phone, here, wanting to talk to you. Is this a good time?'

Thanking him, I took the phone and held it to my ear. 'Guy?'

'Hi, Kate, I just thought—'

'You're psychic,' I told him. 'I need you to do something for me.'

Guy turned up that evening to find me still stubbornly trawling the Internet.

'Sorry,' he said, as he slumped in the chair at my side. 'I couldn't get anything out of your briefcase. I couldn't get into the house. They've got the whole place wrapped in yellow tape, you can't get through.'

'I thought you had an "in" with the police.'

'Yeah, well, I didn't know any of the guys who were on duty today. I can try again tomorrow for you. Maybe I'll have better luck. I did get these, though, like you asked.' He thumped two thick library books down beside my computer. 'They had half a shelf on Reynolds, but these are the only two books that deal with his company in the time frame you're after.'

'Thanks.'

'You finding anything online?'

I shook my head. 'Not really.' I had found a few articles about Ivan Reynolds himself – two short biographies, and his obituary in the *New York Times* – but they had told me little other than that he had died of cancer on the 6th of April, 1944, and that he'd left the bulk of his estate to a foundation he'd created in his name, for the enjoyment of the public.

There was apparently a newsreel of his funeral in the British Pathe News Archives, but I hadn't been able to access it, and most of the Internet references dealing with Reynolds in Lisbon were, predictably enough, in Portuguese.

'I need a translator,' I said to Guy.

He leant in closer, looking at the screen, and shrugged. 'I dated a Portuguese girl once. She writes for a paper in Lisbon. I still have her number. You want me to call her and see if she'd help?'

I didn't doubt she would, for him. Guy's ex-girlfriends were thick on the ground, in Toronto, and the ones I'd met had nothing but good words to say about him. It was his particular gift – likeability.

'Sure,' I said. 'That would be great.'

'All right. I'll let you know.' He stood, and smiled, and left me to it.

She said yes, of course. But by the time Guy got back to me on Friday, I had something more specific for his Portuguese ex-girlfriend to look into. In one of the library books he had brought me, I'd found a useful photograph that somebody had taken over Christmas, 1943, in Reynolds' Lisbon offices. It showed two secretaries sitting smiling at their typewriters in what appeared to be a very elegant, wood-panelled room, and underneath, the caption read: *Employees Jenny Saunders and Regina Sousa*.

There, I thought, was my Regina. Now I'd seen the last name, I remembered it from Deacon's letters. *Sousa*. She had been his secretary for the first few months, until she had left to get married.

Both the women in the picture looked quite young – the odds were good that one of them, at least, was still alive.

'This Regina, she married a Portuguese man. Deacon went to their wedding,' I told Guy. 'It was early on in 1944…I think in February, maybe. Could your friend – what's her name again?'

'Anabela.'

'Could Anabela search the local papers for that time and try to find the wedding announcement? Because if I can find Regina's married name, I might be able to find *her*, ask her some questions.'

'Do you still want all the Reynolds stuff?'

'Yes, please. And one more thing.'

'What's that?'

'Death notices. Obituaries. Anything and everything from late November '43 – that's when Deacon got there – through the spring of '44. I'm especially interested in people whose deaths weren't from natural causes.'

'In Lisbon?' said Guy, with his dark eyebrows lifting. 'In wartime? There shouldn't be more than a couple of thousand of those.'

He was right, I knew. As James Cavender had pointed out, wartime Lisbon, much like Casablanca, had been a dangerous place, filled with spies, double agents, and treachery; whispers in alleys and knives in the back. There would likely have been any number of deaths that might be termed suspicious.

But Guy sent my requests to Anabela, regardless, and she set to work at her end while I carried on digging at mine.

I was glad of the work, to be honest. The research gave me something I could cling to, pass the time with, in a week that was, without a doubt, the worst one that I'd ever spent. No fault of Tony's, or his wife's – they both did their best to make me feel at home, to cheer me, to treat me as part of the family. But I was achingly aware that I no longer had a family. I had no one. Grandma Murray had been my last surviving relative, and now, at twenty-six, I was alone.

Oh, I had friends, but that wasn't the same thing come Christmas and holidays, special days, days when you wanted the comfort of people around you who'd watched you grow up from a baby, who knew your shortcomings and loved you in spite of them; wouldn't stop loving you, no matter what.

I missed Grandma. Missed her with a pain that, in the darkness of the night, became unbearable. I only got through it by focusing hard on the hands of the clock at my bedside and counting the minutes, till sleep, at long last, surged to claim me again like a merciful tide.

My initial state of shock and disbelief had given way to a slow-burning anger, turned inwards, at first – at myself, for still being alive, and for being the reason that someone had shot at my grandmother's house to begin with. And then my anger spread, took aim at other targets – Scotland Yard, and Whitehall, and whoever else might be involved in what was going on. And there was Deacon. If it hadn't been for him, I thought, I wouldn't have a problem. If he hadn't come to speak to me… There were moments I thought he must surely have known that he'd put me in danger; other moments when I felt equally certain he must *not* have known…when I recalled the way he'd acted on the morning that we'd met, not nervous; stepping off the sidewalk without looking, not expecting any trouble…when I thought about James Cavender, and Grandma, and I knew that Deacon wouldn't have done anything to bring them harm. I knew that. But it didn't stop me cursing him from time to time, the way a man who learns he's caught a terrible disease might curse the thoughtless person who infected him.

I kept thinking of the funeral, Grandma's funeral. Guy had tried to reassure me with the promise that it wouldn't be immediate.

'They'll have to do an autopsy. They always do, for murder,' he had told me, 'so there won't be any funeral for a while yet.'

The lawyer, I knew, would arrange things. Grandma had made him joint executor. Not because she didn't trust me, but because she hadn't wanted me to deal alone with her estate, with all the hassles and the headaches and the tax returns. Besides, I travelled so much, I might not have been here when it happened. There had to be somebody else. So the lawyer would do it. He had all the details: what church to use, what readings, and what hymns. She'd left that all in writing. Still, it bothered me beyond expression that I couldn't do this one last thing for her. I couldn't even give her that.

And going to the funeral would be out of the question as well. The police were bound to be there, looking for me. And even if it wasn't the police I had to fear, I knew whoever *was* behind this would be there, as well. Unless, I thought, I managed in the meantime to uncover them. Expose them.

So I pushed on, reading every reference I could find to Ivan Reynolds' company, and Lisbon in the war years, and the British Secret Service, for whom Deacon had been working, all the while keeping my fingers tightly crossed that the Reverend Beckett would have good news for me when I phoned the vicarage that weekend.

But he didn't. As I'd feared, the thieves had ravaged Deacon's papers; there'd been nothing left for him to find. And Anabela hadn't been in touch with Guy, and Guy still hadn't been able to get near my briefcase, and I still couldn't get in touch with Margot, or with Patrick, and it seemed to me that I had reached rock bottom, that there wasn't any way things could get worse.

But I was wrong.

TUESDAY, SEPTEMBER 26

Guy came at breakfast, without any warning. He looked like he'd slept in his clothes.

I was starting to tell him as much when he cut me off.

'Someone broke into your grandmother's house,' he said.

'What?'

'Last night. You know your neighbour to the north – the old guy who's always looking out his window, never sleeps? Well, he saw someone sneaking out the back door of your grandmother's house around midnight, so he called the cops, but by the time they got there, of course, there wasn't anyone around.'

My mind was racing, making the connection to the break-in that had happened back in England, at The Laurels – Deacon's cottage – and the level of damage the vicar had hinted at.

'What did they do?' I asked. 'What did they take?'

'Not much. In fact, the officers were saying that, if it hadn't been for your neighbour, they might not have noticed anything themselves, not right away. It was only because they knew someone had been in the house that they took a look around, to see if anything was missing.'

'And?'

He sat beside me, shifting to get comfortable. 'They didn't let me in the house, you understand. I didn't get a chance to see for myself. But I was right there on the porch – I could hear the cops talking to each other, and from what they were saying, it sounded like the only rooms that really got touched were the bedrooms upstairs. It was carefully done, as though whoever it was didn't want to draw attention to the fact that they'd been there. And they left all the obvious stuff – the TV, and the DVD player.' He looked at me straight. 'But your briefcase is gone, from the hall.'

'Damn.'

'I know. Sorry, Kate. And this time, the cops *do* think it was you. They think you probably came back to pick up things you needed – clothes, and things like that. They still don't view you as a suspect in the shooting, but they're thinking maybe you know who it was, that's why you're hiding. And they're sure somebody's helping you. They asked me a whole lot of questions this morning.'

Tony, who'd listened in silence till now, spoke up. 'What did you tell them?'

Rubbing his neck with a weary hand, Guy said, 'I told them they needed to speak to her boss, on the business desk. She knows Kate better than I do, I said. We don't work much together, I said. Kate's away a lot.'

'And they believed that?' asked Tony.

'They seemed to. They're down at the *Sentinel* building right now, asking questions.' When he saw my concerned

180

frown, he said, 'Hey, don't worry. They won't find out anything except maybe that you were there that night – Security will have a record of that. But no one saw us talking, and we left the building separately.'

That wasn't what had me worried. I could think of one reason, and one reason only, why someone would risk breaking into the house just to search through a couple of rooms and make off with my briefcase: They were looking for something. For Deacon's report, or whatever it was that they thought he had given me, and, more disturbingly, maybe for clues as to where I might be. 'So, it looks like our theory was right. Someone really *is* after me.'

'Not to worry,' said Tony. 'You're safe enough here.'

'But for how long?' I asked him. 'Whoever's behind this, they're not going to stop, are they? Not until they've managed to get rid of me, to know I'm not a threat. They'll keep looking. If they've got my briefcase, they've got my address book, the names of my friends. And they've also got the letters. Deacon's letters. There were names in those, as well, of people Deacon knew in Portugal. Even if those people aren't involved, and don't know anything, the killer might assume they do.' I should have kept those letters with me, I reproved myself. I should have never been so careless. I looked away, and clenched my fingers on the table. 'Deacon's secretary, if she's still alive, would be about my grandma's age. And I'll be damned if I'll stand by and let her be a target too, because of me.'

The windows in the kitchen were all shuttered tightly – Tony and Marie's attempt to make me feel a little more secure – but I could not escape the sense of something ominous and dark approaching, seeking to get in. I said, 'It's up to me to try to end this. No one who knew Deacon will be safe unless I do. Besides, I want to make them pay, whoever did this. I want justice. For my grandmother. For Cavender. For Deacon.'

Guy said, 'Kate, you're doing all you can. And now that you've got Anabela over there to help you—'

'She's not finding anything,' I said. 'And this isn't how I work, you know that, Guy. I don't have other people do my research for me, and I don't just sit locked in a room on the Internet, either. I need to be out in the field, on the front line. I need to be talking to people.' Suddenly it all seemed very clear to me, just what to do.

I turned, and my gaze went to Tony, who sat like a rock at the head of the table, impassively taking things in. His expression barely changed, and yet I knew that he was quick enough to know what I was asking. 'Kate…'

I met his eyes. 'I need to go to Portugal.'

CHAPTER THREE

Portugal

Yet digged the mole, and lest his ways be found,
Worked under ground,

HENRY VAUGHAN, 'THE WORLD'

Friday, September 29

Halfway over the Atlantic, in the dark of night, the plane ran into turbulence. I tried hard not to take that as an omen.

For all the miles I'd travelled, I had never completely made peace with the concept of flying. I hated the feeling of takeoffs and landings, and still got a knot in my stomach whenever the ride got a little bit bumpy. And this was considerably more than a little bit bumpy. At times it felt as though the very bottom of the plane was falling out from underneath me, as though nature itself was attempting to point out how foolish I had been for leaving the security of solid ground.

I closed my eyes and put my head back, took a calming breath, and turned my mind to other things.

The memory of Guy's face at our last meeting rose accusingly. 'I'm just not sure you've thought this through,' I heard him say again.

This had been yesterday, as I had done my final round of packing before leaving for the airport. He'd been serious, very direct. 'You *are* crossing the line here. You do understand that, Kate, don't you?' he'd said. 'I mean, hiding from the police is one thing, but once you go through that airport security gate with a passport that's fake, you'll be breaking the law.'

'Yes, I know that.'

'Then why go? You don't need to. You've got Anabela to do your legwork. Look, she found the marriage all right, didn't she?'

The fax had come through just that morning – a newspaper clipping announcing the wedding of one Alvaro Marinho, a clerk at the British Embassy, to Regina Sousa. There could be no doubt. Ivan Reynolds was listed as one of the guests.

'But,' I argued, 'she hasn't found anything else.'

'Give her time.'

I didn't have time. And Anabela was already doing more than I could ask of her. She had her own job, after all; she couldn't spend her own days playing phone tag with officials at the British Embassy in Lisbon, trying to access their personnel records. As soon as I landed, I knew, I could go there in person. If I could find out where Marinho had lived when he'd married Regina…well, I'd gotten fairly accomplished at tracking down people for interviews, finding them through their addresses, their relatives. All that it took was a starting point. 'Besides,' I'd said to Guy, 'I'll get to meet your Anabela face to face.'

That was to be tonight, at my hotel. Tony's travel-agent contact, who was brilliant with last-minute deals, had found me a room at a hotel not far from the Embassy district, a good place to start my enquiries, and Anabela had agreed to meet me there for dinner.

But Guy still hadn't thought I should be going in the first place.

I'd tried explaining. 'Guy, whatever's happening, it all began in Portugal.'

And he'd said, 'You don't know that. All you know is Deacon wanted to tell you a story. You don't even know that same story was in his report.'

'But it was,' I had argued. 'It had to be. Cavender told me that Deacon was angry about Whitehall's lack of action. That was why he came to London to see me, so I'd make things public. And he sent a copy of that same report,' I'd said, 'to Portugal. Why would he do that if it didn't all tie back to when he was in Lisbon?'

He hadn't had an answer.

'Guy, it's all I have to go on. I have nothing else. I have to try. I'm running at the end of my rope here.' I'd given him a small smile. 'At the very worst, I'll get a week's vacation in the sun. I sure could use that.'

That week seemed very distant from me now. The airplane heaved and shuddered, dropping once with such a force that several people further up the cabin shrieked.

Involuntarily, my hand went to the tiny unfamiliar weight that lay against my collarbone – a little silver medal on a chain. Tony'd put it round my neck as I was leaving. 'It's St Christopher,' he'd said. 'I gave my daughter one of these when she went off to do her thing in Europe, after high school. St Christopher, he keeps her out of trouble. She comes back all right,' he'd told me. 'So will you.'

I only hoped that he was right.

Schiphol Airport, Amsterdam, was full of travellers going somewhere else. I'd passed through countless times myself, en route to various assignments, and I knew my way around.

So even though I was on a rather tight schedule to connect with my Lisbon flight, I knew that I had time enough to stop off in the ladies' room along the way, to tidy up. The long, bumpy hours I'd already spent in the air had left me feeling wilted and dishevelled. The mirror showed a stranger. I'd had two days to get used to it, but still, my new appearance caught me off my guard and made me look more closely.

Gone was the red hair my father had loved…truly gone, in the literal sense, cropped quite short, like a boy's, and dyed medium brown. Tony's wife had done quite a professional job, even tinting my eyebrows and lashes to match. I was wearing no make-up, which ought to have made me look younger, but didn't. It made me look tired.

I peered at my reflection through the glasses that were part of my disguise. Tony'd had them made with lenses that reacted to the light, becoming darker when I went outside. An added screen to hide behind. I pushed them up, now, to the top of my head, as I hoisted my carry-on onto the counter. Rummaging, I took hold of the bright blue travel wallet that held my tickets and my passport. It felt odd to have a passport in somebody else's name. Tony had managed that, of course – I didn't know the details and I didn't want to know, but I had credit cards and traveller's cheques to match the passport, in the name we'd chosen: Katherine Allen.

'You always keep your first name,' Tony'd told me. 'Makes it easier. You're less likely to slip up, that way; make a mistake.'

Setting the travel wallet carefully beside the sink, I dug deeper for my toothbrush, which had settled at the bottom of the bag. One of the stall doors behind me clanged shut, but I took no real notice, only shifted a bit to make room at the counter. A minute had passed before I became aware that I was being watched.

The woman one sink over met my eyes with recognition in the mirror; then she hesitated.

Oh, of all the luck, I thought. *Of all the rotten luck.*

Because the woman was Anne Wood, who'd sat across from me that night at Patrick's parents' house. The international lawyer, who was probably here in the Netherlands now on account of her trial at the Hague. I had long ago learnt that the world was a very small place.

Sliding my glasses back over my eyes, I gave her the brief, non-specific smile suited to meeting the gaze of a stranger, and went on with what I was doing, head down.

The water taps ran. Stopped. I glanced up again. She was still watching.

'Sorry,' she said this time. 'Only…you look so familiar.'

I forced another smile, more friendly. 'You know, a lot of people tell me that. I must just have one of those faces.'

As I quickly capped the toothpaste and tossed it back into my bag, she said, 'You're not Canadian, by any chance?'

'American.' I trusted that she, like most people, would not have an ear for the difference in accents. I saw her hesitate, and knew my looks had changed enough that, though she might wonder, she wouldn't be sure. And then, because she looked about to ask another question, I zipped up my carry-on bag and excused myself, making a getaway out of the bathroom and back into the reassuring anonymity of airport crowds. Stepping onto the conveyor-belt 'sidewalk', I settled myself with gratitude against the rail and swung my bag forward again as I felt for my passport and boarding pass.

I couldn't find them.

Damn, I thought, and hauled the bag more firmly up against my stomach, peering down inside it. All my documents and traveller's cheques and cash were in that travel wallet – brilliant blue, to make it easier to find inside my bag...except, it wasn't in my bag. I felt panic rising like bile from the pit of my stomach, and forced it down, turning my mind back to where I had last seen the wallet, and what I had done with it. Then I remembered – I'd taken it out in the bathroom, to get at my toothbrush. It must still be there, by the sink, on the counter.

It *would* still be there, I assured myself, jogging the few steps to the end of the section of moving sidewalk and heading back along the centre carpet at a run – I'd left it there less than five minutes ago.

But the bathroom was empty.

Nothing on the floors or counters; no one in the stalls.

The panic surged a second time, more powerful. Without that passport, I was trapped. In trouble. And, as Guy had warned, in trouble much more serious than I had ever known. My fingers tightened on the little medal hanging round my neck – my little image of St Christopher. But even Tony couldn't help me now, I thought. He wouldn't be able to get me new documents here. And anyway, I had no way to call him. With my wallet gone, I didn't even have a coin to use the phone.

I gave myself a stinging mental kick. How *could* I have been so stupid? After all Tony's coaching and all his hard work, his instructions on how to be careful, I'd gone and blown the whole thing before even reaching Lisbon. And in less than five minutes. It couldn't have been any longer than that since I'd stood in this bathroom with Anne Wood and...

Anne Wood. My racing mind clutched at the name. She'd been the only other person in the bathroom at the time – perhaps she'd been the one who'd picked up my travel wallet, too, and perhaps she was this minute on her way to hand it in to the appropriate authorities. She couldn't have got far, not in such a short time.

Spurred by the faint hope of catching up with her, I bolted from the bathroom, my pace growing increasingly frantic as I scanned the sea of heads and shoulders, trying without any luck to remember what colour Anne Wood had been wearing.

'Are you Miss Allen?' Asked just like that, in a light, almost cheerfully feminine voice, the question stopped me dead.

The woman who'd spoken was uniformed, very young, very blonde, driving a golf-cart-like airport convenience car. She'd been going in the opposite direction, but had braked now and was looking at me, smiling. Repeating her question, she nodded when I told her yes, I was.

'I thought so.' She reached out to hand me the bright blue travel wallet, that still bulged reassuringly. 'Another woman found this in the washroom,' she informed me, in a voice tinged with the lovely classy accent of the Dutch. 'I was taking it up to your gate, but you've saved me the trip.'

Clumsily, I hastened to undo the zipper; check the contents.

'It's a good photograph, in your passport,' the young

woman complimented me. 'I recognised you right away.'

Still feeling shaken by the whole affair, I managed to get out a 'Thank You' before the woman deftly wheeled her vehicle around and, wishing me a pleasant journey, buzzed away again along the bustling corridor.

With hands still shaking slightly from adrenalin, I sorted through the contents for a second time, to make absolutely certain. It was all there – my passport, my traveller's cheques, everything.

Stuffing the travel wallet safely in my bag again, I drew the first deep breath I'd breathed in what seemed like an age, and, boarding pass in hand, I turned and headed for the gate.

I couldn't see the runway that we landed on in Lisbon for the rain. Not that there would have been much to see – the modern airport lay, as did most airports, in an industrial area at the north edge of the city. There was no chance, from this approach, that I would see the wide impressive view of Lisbon from the harbour, with its tile-roofed buildings climbing up the terraced hills, that would have greeted Deacon, coming in by Pan Am Clipper in the final days of 1943.

I did think, though, that he might have felt as relieved as I was to have landed. I'd been reading, in my research, some accounts of the Atlantic crossings in those days, by seaplane – such a dangerous adventure, and not only because of the threat posed by enemy aircraft. The simple act of travelling by air was risky then. One of the flights not too long before Deacon's had managed to make it the whole perilous way across the Atlantic, only to crash in the harbour on landing in Lisbon, killing many of its passengers. Small wonder that my grandmother had feared for Deacon's safety.

The rain, at least, was easing by the time I caught my taxi, and the driver did his best to make up for my less than inspiring first view of Lisbon. He had a tour guide's gift for running patter, and he took me to my hotel by the scenic route, leaving behind the wider modern avenues and groomed green parks in favour of the older, crowded, climbing streets.

'We say,' he said, his English rather excellent in spite of his thick accent, 'that Lisbon is a white city, because the colour of the sun gives a lot of light, and most of the walls are in white, but also we like this pink colour, and the roofs in Portugal, the tiled roofs, they are in general red. These tiles come from the Roman times, and the mosaics of the Romans, this is what has later given us our sidewalks here in Portugal, isn't it? We have beautiful sidewalks in Lisbon.'

They *were* lovely – small even squares of stone set into intricate patterns of black, grey, and white, stunning on the larger streets and lending beauty even to the meanest of the narrow ones. I might have admired the stone patterns more had we not, at that moment, taken a stomach-dropping downward turn towards the broad blue ribbon of the river Tagus. It must, I thought, be murder to walk in a city like this.

When I said as much, the taxi driver smiled. 'The city has been built on seven hills, the legendary seven hills of Lisbon, just like Rome, isn't it? Look to the other bank of the river – you see how hilly, undulating? This is the land of this region, so you see Lisbon was constructed on hills like those, imagine.'

As we came within view of the river itself, and the harbour,

I saw a long, red bridge, like San Francisco's Golden Gate, that stretched across the strip of water to the farther shore.

'This,' my taxi driver said, 'is our most famous bridge. Till the construction of that bridge, till 1966, imagine, people had to go across the river by ferry boat. You still can do that, and it's a very pleasant trip for you to want to do one of these days, but it is better now, I think, to have this bridge. And from the bridge is one of the nicest views over the city. The best of all is from the Castelo de São Jorge, the big fort on the hill, you can see if you look out your window – is the best viewpoint of the city. But from the bridge is also very nice. From there you can see to the lighthouse that will show where finishes the river and begins the ocean.'

I couldn't see the lighthouse, but I saw the long, straight line of Lisbon's harbour wall stretched like an arrow pointing out to the Atlantic, to the whitecaps faintly visible beyond the mirror stillness of the bay. Even the clouds didn't dare venture in past that stillness. They kept farther out, like great plumes of spray tossed in the air by the ocean, enraged that it couldn't come near.

The view was a picture of postcard perfection...but I'd never much trusted perfection. Still waters ran deep, as my grandmother had liked to say, and Lisbon's glassy harbour didn't fool me. Something had happened here. Something that changed Andrew Deacon. And it *had* happened in Lisbon, I felt more sure of that than I had ever felt of anything, although I had no evidence to go on. Call it journalistic instinct. Call it Deacon's ghostly guidance – I could all but feel his presence with me in the taxi, tugging at my sleeve. *It's here*, he seemed to say, *You're close, so close...*

'So now we come to Lapa, where is your hotel,' my driver said. 'This is the part of Lisbon where the English have been living, from the times of the Crusaders, isn't it? There has for many centuries been such a great alliance with the English and the Portuguese. Our royal families married with each other, and even the mother of our famous prince, Prince Henry the Navigator, she was an English princess who became the Queen of Portugal. So always there were English people living here – the merchants, and the diplomats. And Lapa is the place, still, for the embassies, and for the residences of ambassadors. You will see many buildings of great beauty, here. The hotel where you're staying, it is beautiful as well. It was a convent once.'

Which made it as fitting a place as any, I thought, in which to seek sanctuary.

The York House Hotel wasn't the sort of a place anybody would look for me, if they were looking. Its façade fooled the eye. It appeared, from the front, to be one more ordinary building in the narrow and plain, although lyrically named, Rua das Janelas Verdes – Street of the Green Windows – just up from the harbour. The only entrance looked to be a single open doorway in the blank wall, uninviting, but by now I'd grown used to things not being what they seemed.

From the moment I stepped through that door in the wall, and was met by the young seated porter, I felt that I'd entered a world of seclusion. The porter directed me up a long flight of mosaic-tiled stairs, thick with green twisted vines that arched over the stairwell in places, creating a garden-like sense of seclusion. Already the street, and the city, felt far away, behind the thick rose-coloured stuccoed walls, and the whine of a plane overhead seemed an almost indecent intrusion.

The stairs curved up, and climbed, and curved again, and opened out into a sunny courtyard, tiled even more elaborately in a white-and-black diamond pattern and ringed on three sides by the walls of the hotel, so thickly obscured behind ivy and tropical plants and the soft drooping branches of palm trees that I might have thought there were no walls at all, had it not been for the white French doors standing open to either side, and all the multi-paned white windows set amid the green.

There were yellow-painted wooden chairs and tables in the courtyard, and a young man was busily wiping the wet of the rain from them. Seeing me, he stopped his work to come and take my single suitcase from my hand and lead me through the French door on the right.

He took his place behind the small reception desk. 'Miss Allen, yes,' he said, and found me in the register. 'We have your room. For seven nights, yes? If you would sign here, I will take you up.'

I signed, and followed him up more stairs to the second floor. The corridors twisted, grew wider in places and then closed around us again. The hotel had obviously been cobbled together from more than one building, and the corridors were sectioned, too, with narrow French doors separating them in places, and uneven steps up and steps down to negotiate. The dark red tiles on the floor were large and loose in places, so they clunked when we walked over them. We passed small window niches set with painted tiles of blue and white, with ruffled white curtains and small potted plants. There were baseboards of blue and white tiles, as well, and the white plaster walls with their curved ceilings made quite an elegant contrast to all the dark wood.

My room was equally impressive. One long window overlooked the private courtyard I had entered by. Thick rugs, like handstitched tapestries, lay on the wide-planked hardwood floor, the bathroom gleamed with mirrors, and the bed was like a canopied oasis for a queen. I'd come here with no expectations – I'd wanted a room for the week, nothing more. Evidently Tony's travel agent friend – or, more likely, Tony himself – had decided I needed to hide out in style.

'I am forgetting,' said the desk clerk, 'someone came this morning, asking for you, but I could not say when you would be arriving, so they asked me could I give you this.'

That caught me off my guard, uncomfortably. There shouldn't have been anyone, I thought, who'd know where I would be. I felt my sense of safety shatter, and my hand shook as I reached to take the envelope he offered me. Thanking him in a tight voice, I shut the door and bolted it behind him.

The curtains were open. I drew them shut, too, and retreated like a hunted creature to the deeper shadows by the bed. It took me a couple of tries to tear open the end of the envelope. It held a single sheet of handwriting. I read it…and relaxed.

Welcome to Lisbon, said the note. *I thought you might be eager to get on with things, so came to see if you were here at lunch, but I will come again at seven for our dinner, as arranged.* The signature was simply: *Anabela*. Guy's reporter friend.

I turned to check the carriage clock that faced me on the bedside table. Half past two. I still had time to kill. And as inviting as the bed was, and as tired as I might be from all the sleepless hours of travelling, I couldn't shake the little voice reminding me that someone else might already have gotten here ahead of me; that every hour wasted was an hour that I could ill afford to lose.

I closed my mind to everything except that voice, and turned my back towards the bed, and started looking for my Lisbon city map.

I couldn't find the Embassy.

I had the address, copied from the pages of the Portuguese travel guide Guy had picked up at the library for me, and the street had been only a few minutes' walk from my hotel – the Rua de São Domingos, in the heart of Lisbon's Lapa district. When Deacon had arrived here, late in 1943, this had still been the place in Lisbon where the English lived. It likely hadn't changed much since his day, I thought.

The street was cobbled, dark with dampness from the drizzling rain that came and swiftly went again with unpredictability. To either side the buildings pressed in closely, three storeys tall, or four, or sometimes five, with rows of white-framed windows and ornate old iron balconies. Despite the day's drabness, the colours of the plastered façades were marvelous – deep ochre yellow and blue-grey and rich terracotta, like weathered old brick. The buildings stood shoulder to shoulder, their tiled roofs tracing an uneven line down the steep slope of the hill, a roller-coaster drop towards a slice of pale blue water at the bottom, where the river Tagus estuary stretched to meet the darker south shore opposite.

The roller-coaster impression was strengthened by two sets of streetcar rails sunk in the cobblestones, and the cars that had been parked up on the sidewalks to each side of me closed in the space and made it feel more narrow.

Number 37 was supposed to be the Embassy, but having walked the full length of the street two times now, once on each side, I had come to the bottom again, to the place where the street narrowed too much for cars to pass through; where a tight, shadowed lane wound on downward between low, small houses, becoming the flight of stone steps that had brought me up here to begin with. I turned, at a loss.

I could see, near the top of the hill, a policeman, who'd come out from somewhere to stand at the edge of the street, and willing him to stay in just that spot till I could ask him for directions, I began the climb again, but by the time I'd reached the first main corner he had disappeared.

I stopped beneath a tangled net of intersecting streetcar cables. A woman passing briskly on the sidewalk slowed her pace, and met my eyes, and smiled. She spoke to me directly, in good English. 'Are you lost?'

I wondered how she'd known that I spoke English, till I realised that the map I held was printed in that language. Still, the average person wasn't quite so quick at observation, and while I welcomed her assistance, I was wary. 'I was looking for the Embassy,' I said. 'The British Embassy.'

'It is not here. It was for many years this building,' she said, pointing at a pale pink building further up the street, 'but it now is in the Rua de São Bernardo, in Estrela. Not in Lapa.' And she showed me on the map.

I marked the place, and thanked her, and with one more smile she carried on where she'd been going, with that same quick, certain step. I watched her out of sight, then hailed a passing taxi.

As it left the kerb, I twisted in my seat to take a good look at the massive pale pink building where the Embassy had been. It was a magnificent place, almost Georgian in its symmetry, a great block of a house with tall, multi-paned windows and giant-sized double wood doors and ornate black wrought-iron balcony railings. The roofline had large, classic dormers; more windows, more railings, and elegant, round, fluted chimneys.

There wasn't any number I could see; no sign to say that it had been the British Embassy – a role it must have given up just recently, because my guidebook hadn't been *that* out of date – but having been so long the scene of things of great importance, having heard the steps of dignitaries passing through its corridors, with whispers of affairs of state, it seemed to me this pink-walled building, growing smaller through the rain-spattered rear window of my taxi, yet retained a sense of grandeur.

So it must have looked to Deacon, too, when he'd first seen it – standing stoic on its sloped street, with the streetcar cables framing it as darkly as a spider's web.

He was tired. He'd slept little on the long flight over, despite the Clipper's comfortable cabin and the polite privacy given him by the few military men who had been his travelling companions. They'd done well to leave him be, he thought. He hadn't been in any mood for socialising.

Remembering, he moved his thumb to turn the wedding band upon his finger in a gesture that had almost grown to be part of him. And then, because that made him frown again, he turned from his study of a large oil portrait, in search of distraction.

He caught a breath of outside air, that smelt of rain-damp

earth. It came, he thought, from somewhere to his left, and so he followed it. The young man who had left him in this broad hall at the top of the sweeping main stairway hadn't told him that he couldn't move about, and since he'd already been kept waiting for the better part of half an hour, he figured they'd forgive his curiosity.

Anyone, he thought, could be forgiven curiosity in such a place as this. He hadn't been in many embassies, but Lisbon's seemed more beautiful than most. He followed the scent of fresh afternoon air through an angled glass passage that led to a great ballroom, grand with gilt mirrors. The glazed doors here stood open to a sheltered flagstone courtyard, its walls beautified by a series of blue-and-white tiles displaying varied coats of arms.

He stepped through the glass doors and into the courtyard. The change of air swept through his mind like a tonic, relaxing his frown. There were steps climbing out of the courtyard – stone steps decorated with more of the blue-and-white tiles, and shaded by the overhanging branches of a venerable pepper-tree. He had half a mind to climb them, too, and see where they would take him, but prudence kept him where he was. It was enough, for now, to be outdoors.

He was still there when they came looking for him. Without looking round, he could tell there were two of them. Their footsteps echoed plainly on the wide floor of the ballroom, one set firm and even, and the other with a slightly offset rhythm and the measured punctuation of a walking stick. He waited till they'd nearly reached the door before he turned.

The first man was the friendliest. 'Mr Deacon? My name's Evans. I'm sorry if we've kept you waiting.'

'Not at all.' He took the offered handshake, and replied to the polite enquiries as to how his flight had been, and what he thought of Lisbon, but the better part of his attention, all the while, was on the second man. He was a taller man than Evans, in his early thirties, probably, with a neatly trimmed dark moustache and an impeccably tailored suit. The walking stick was his – from necessity, rather than affectation, judging by the way he held it – but his handshake was decisive, brisk, with no hint of infirmity.

Evans, thought Deacon, was clearly the diplomat, the Embassy man, while the other, though he didn't have the aura of officialdom, was something more important.

'JL Cayton-Wood,' was Evans's introduction. 'He runs things for us, here in Lisbon.'

'Call me Jack.' The man stood back, head angled as he took a look around the little courtyard. 'I see you've managed to find one of the nicest spots in the Embassy.'

Deacon nodded. 'Yes. I've been admiring the *azulejos*,' he said, using the proper name for the Portuguese blue-and-white tiles.

'Ah, you know what they are, then,' said Evans. 'Yes, they are remarkable. Each tile bears the arms, crest and name of a past minister or ambassador. A chronicle, if you like, of British diplomats in Lisbon.'

JL Cayton-Wood cut in, 'I'm told you're fond of gardens, Mr Deacon.'

'Yes.'

'Then come, let's take a stroll.' He glanced pointedly back at the wide-open doors of the ballroom. 'These walls are a little too close for my liking.'

Evans led the way up the stone steps overhung by the pepper-tree's branches, with Deacon behind him and Cayton-Wood labouring last, with his walking stick. The man's frustration with the weakness of his body, with his limp, was nearly palpable, and from it Deacon guessed that it was not an ancient injury, but one he was still learning to adapt to.

The steps came up onto a broad lawn, with beautifully kept gardens bordering the green and shade trees scattered round for elegance. It was unexpectedly large for what was, essentially, a private townhouse garden in a crowded street, and Deacon paused in silent admiration of the aspect.

Cayton-Wood sent him a brief look, but his next comment passed over the subject of gardens and came to the point. 'You'll have been briefed on Ivan Reynolds.'

'Yes,' said Deacon.

'Tell me what you've learnt.'

He'd always done quite well at school, reciting facts. Putting his hands in his pockets, he answered, 'His mother was Russian, his father American. They sent him to Paris for schooling; he chucked that and went out to Persia, to work in the oil fields. Came back a year later with shares in the company that would eventually make him his millions. He married,' – he felt his own ring, without meaning to – 'married a Spanish woman, who died in a fall from her horse a year later. Since then he's had two mistresses; no children.'

'Three mistresses, in point of fact. The third one isn't common knowledge. Not that it's a vital point. Go on.'

'In 1936 he came to Lisbon, liked it, settled here, and since the war began has been an instrument in keeping our side well supplied with oil. He has also,' Deacon said, 'become a passionate collector of fine art, which is, I gather, why you've brought me into this.'

'Correct,' said Cayton-Wood. The effort of walking showed plainly on his face now, and he pointed to a stone seat by the parapet. 'Let's sit.'

There wasn't room for three men on the seat. Cayton-Wood sat, taking a slender cigar from his pocket and lighting it, while Deacon accepted the offer of a cigarette from Evans, who elected to stay standing.

Cayton-Wood said, 'He has been a problem for us, Ivan Reynolds. In the first place, he's American; a friend of their Ambassador, which makes our operation rather delicate. And he moves in the highest of social circles. His money' – Deacon thought that word was spoken with an emphasis that marked the condescension of a true-born member of the upper class for those who'd earned their wealth and rank more recently –'his money buys him influence with people, and admits him to the confidence of several of our side's top men.'

Deacon said, 'And you believe he's passing on our secrets?'

'There are indicators. We keep a close watch on radio transmissions coming out of Spain. Franco may have kept his country officially neutral, but he's a Fascist through and through, and it's no secret where his sentiments lie. He'd be part of the Axis himself if it weren't for the fact he's just finished his own Civil War – fighting communists left his finances too weak to support another military action, but still he's been doing his part from the sidelines, and giving what comfort he can to our enemies. Recently, his agents have been sending out more information than they ought to know.

One particular detail I know was discussed in Reynolds's presence. In fact, there were only three men in the room at the time: myself, the Ambassador, and Mr Reynolds. Myself I can vouch for, and I shouldn't think it likely the Ambassador would be involved in treason. Reynolds, on the other hand, still has connections with Madrid. One of his brothers-in-law has a position of some influence in Franco's government.'

'I see.'

Evans, blowing smoke, remarked, 'It's purely circumstantial, of course. But we do think it merits us keeping a rather close eye on him.'

'It's my understanding,' said Deacon, 'you already have someone inside the company.'

Cayton-Wood answered that. 'Only a girl. She's not technically one of our own – she's engaged to a Portuguese chap on the Embassy staff. She can keep us informed, in a general sense, as to Reynolds's meetings, and his correspondence, but we needed someone on a higher level, someone who could go behind closed doors with Reynolds, move within his sphere. You had the right credentials for our purpose.'

'But I wasn't married.'

'Yes, well they took care of that for you in New York, I understand. Found you a suitable girl, did they?'

'Yes,' he said, careful not to let his face or voice betray his feelings. He focused instead on the handle of Cayton-Wood's walking stick, leaning beside him. A carved ivory dragon's head handle, with red eyes that watched him back. Taking a hard pull on his cigarette, he asked in casual tones, 'Why will Reynolds not hire an unmarried man?'

'I don't know,' replied Cayton-Wood.

Deacon lifted his gaze.

Evans said, 'He's a rather eccentric man, Reynolds. And notoriously stubborn. You may find working for him difficult.'

'You'll have help,' Cayton-Wood said, turning in his seat to face the sound of footsteps coming up into the garden from the courtyard. 'Ah, here he is. I wondered where he'd got to. This young man is Alvaro Marinho. He's the chap whose fiancée has been our eyes and ears, so far, in Reynolds's offices. He's going to drive you to the flat where you'll be living. I've no doubt you'd like a chance to settle in, and have a rest before you start.'

Deacon rose, hand extended, to greet Alvaro Marinho, but he found that, as before, the better part of his attention remained fixed upon the tall man who stayed seated at his side. And he found that he was wondering why Cayton-Wood had felt the need to answer his last question with a lie.

'Alvaro Marinho,' I said the name over, when asked. 'He worked for you in 1944.'

The Embassy's procedure for enquiries was distinctly British – fill out a form in reception, telling them the nature of your question; take a number; have a seat inside a smaller room, and wait your turn to talk in person to the two employees standing patiently, politely, behind glass, like tellers in a bank. Behind them, a tidy compact office space contained a few desks and computers at which three more people were typing.

The whole set-up, small as it was, worked precisely, efficiently...one applicant up, the next down, one departing, and one coming in through the silent glass door, while the two front-line staff in their neatly pressed shirts gave their answers through small speaker-windows set into the glass.

My question was, apparently, the one that clogged the works.

The young woman staffing my window said 'Ah', bent her head, and looked thoughtful. 'You see, this is a problem. This man that you are looking for, you say he worked here very long ago. We wouldn't have those records. You would have to try the Foreign Office, maybe, in London, and I'm not sure even they would know...' She paused, and frowned, considering. 'Will you excuse me for a moment, please? I'll ask my colleague.'

I waited while she walked my query back to a middle-aged man sitting at one of the desks. He stopped working, listened, then he too shook his head and, rising, came across to speak to me in person.

This was apparently an unusual enough occurrence to draw a few curious looks from the other three people at work in the office, including the young man in charge of the next window over, who glanced up once or twice from his paperwork, as though he, too, was interested in what the older man might say.

The speech, when it came, was disappointing. 'I'm very sorry,' he said, 'but there were a lot of people working for the Embassy during the Second World War, and many more rendering service who didn't actually work here. This man, by his name, he was Portuguese, yes? A locally engaged member of the staff?' He shook his head, as though that clinched the matter. 'Nobody kept records of such things, you understand. There would be no way of knowing where he came from, where he went.'

My heart sank. I hadn't expected this. My own experience with the British was that they kept quite meticulous records of *everything*, and I would have thought that someplace as official as an Embassy would—

'I am very sorry that we cannot be of help.' Returning my request form through the stainless-steel pass-through tray set in the counter, beneath the protective glass, the man sent me a courteous, dismissive smile intended to remind me of the other people waiting in the rows of seats behind me. But I could feel, without his help, the press of time. It was already nearly four o'clock – I only had, at best, an hour, before things started closing.

Running into one wall made me seek another avenue. I held my ground a moment as I forced myself to think.

The problem was, I knew virtually nothing else about the man who'd worked here but his name, and that he'd married Deacon's secretary. There'd been nothing in the newspaper announcement Anabela had found as to where the newlywed Marinhos might have lived, but perhaps, I thought, in the official Marriage Register...

I was about to ask where I might find Birth, Marriage and Death Registers from 1944, when the young man at work in the next window, having dealt with his customer, glanced over once again, his eyebrow arched.

'There is a man who keeps the gate,' he told me, 'at the English Church. He had a job here, in the war. He might have known this man that you are searching for.'

I looked at him with gratitude. 'And where,' I asked him, 'is the English Church?'

* * *

The door looked less than promising. A double metal door, ornately barred and painted forest green, the only bit of colour in the long grey stretch of high stone wall, if you didn't count the scrawls of red graffiti. Still, someone had taken the trouble to sweep the sidewalk where I stood – a tidy mound of leaves lay heaped against a curved place in the wall, where rain had puddled on the cobblestones...though cobblestones, I thought, was surely not the right word, conjuring, as it did, something large and rough-set. These were small stones, square-edged, smooth like marble and set with precision, like ancient mosaics. Above the heap of leaves, a thickly growing patch of vine with small white flowers tumbled down the wall to soften the graffiti and the bleak grey stone.

A smallish silver plaque fixed to the door proclaimed, in stamped Art Deco lettering, that I had found the English Church and Cemetery. Beneath the plaque, an intercom and button sat in open invitation.

I only had to push it once. Behind the door, I heard light steps on stone; heard the turn of a key in the lock. It was a woman, not a man, who swung the door back to admit me. An older woman, short and round and smiling, dressed in black, and carrying an umbrella, though the rain had tapered off now to a manageable drizzle. With the hood of my jacket pulled up, I was scarcely aware of the wet, myself.

Neither were the birds, it seemed. The birdsong was the first thing that I noticed, once inside. The wall behind me blocked the sound of passing traffic from the street, and gave me the sensation I had stepped into a secret garden, sheltered and secluded. This was a place, I thought, much more alive than dead – richly green and private, with all manner of hedges and lush trees and flowering vines, and tree trunks softly furred with green, and twisted branches tangling overhead.

The woman made a gesture to the sky and said something in Portuguese that might have either been an apology for the weather or a protest that I couldn't have a proper look around when it was raining; but I only smiled back and said, in English, 'Please, I'm looking for Joaquim.' I carefully pronounced the name, 'Jo-ah-KING', as I had learnt it from the young man at the Embassy.

The woman's gesture, this time, was broader. She said something very quickly that I didn't have a hope of understanding, though I caught the word *'Igreja'*, which I knew meant 'church', so I pointed in the direction that I thought she had been pointing and I said, myself, *'Igreja?'* and she answered back and nodded. Then, having shown me how to lock the door as I was leaving, she trundled off towards a little mausoleum tucked to one side of the cemetery, just inside the wall.

I went straight on, and took the main path, also paved with small square cobbles, edged with low box hedges underneath the arching cypress trees, and small green clearings either side that sheltered leaning tombstones. There were more stones crowded thick along the other paths that ran off left and right, and left and right again a little further up. It wouldn't be a bad place to be buried, I decided, in this garden of a graveyard with the songbirds singing endlessly, unseen, from every corner.

There seemed to be no uniformity to the stones, apart from their grey and white colours – plain, upright crosses stood alongside recumbent great monuments, cracking with age. It gave the place a warmly communal feel, actually…people who had likely been from different walks of life and different classes, sharing ground now in this little consecrated bit of England in a foreign land, united by a language and a faith.

According to the young man at the Embassy, this graveyard had for three centuries now been the final resting place of choice for Protestants who died in Lisbon, including, he had said, the famous author Henry Fielding, who had come here in an effort to regain his health, without success.

Had I been here on a holiday, I likely would have tried to find his tomb – I'd enjoyed reading *Tom Jones* at school – but I did not have time, today, to be diverted. The path by now had brought me to St George's Church, a pink-walled building traced with lovely grey stone arches, and a large rose window rising over everything like some enormous rolling wheel whose motion had been stilled.

There was nobody here, at this end of the church, and any doors that I could find were firmly locked. One of those doors, in a little side porch, looked as though it hadn't been opened in a hundred years. It was a massive thing, of solid wood with elaborately wrought-iron hinges, and cold iron rings for handles – the sort of a door you expected to find in a medieval castle. I tried it, all the same, and knocked, and the sound echoed round in the small, cloistered space. There were windows here, but even they had a medieval feel – high and arching between carved stone columns, with small diamond panes of opaque, sea-green glass that let light come through softly. The columns were carved at the bottom to look like the waves of the sea, and their tops were wound round with stone thistles and roses and leaves. The walls had been plastered calm aquamarine, and combined with the pale greenish light from the tall leaded windows the total effect was of quiet, and stillness.

I could hear the rain pattering down on the leaves and the stone of the walkway outside, just behind me, but here in the porch I felt totally cut off, secluded.

It was a jolt when, unexpectedly, the door before me opened with a creak of ancient hinges and a man stepped out…an older man, in working clothes. He looked me up and down and, with the sharpness of the woman in the Rua de São Domingos, pegged me as a tourist. 'Yes?'

I cleared my throat. 'Joaquim?'

'Yes, I am Joaquim.'

'I was sent here by somebody at the Embassy,' I said. 'The British Embassy. I understand you worked there in the war.'

He looked at me more closely. 'Yes.'

'I'm looking for a man who worked there, too. You might remember him.'

When I mentioned the name, Joaquim stepped fully through the door and swung it closed behind him with a clang. He was a tall man, though his shoulders had begun to stoop with age, and in his weathered face I thought I read a keen intelligence. 'Marinho,' he repeated, faintly frowning. 'I don't know…'

'He married a woman by the name of Regina Sousa. She worked for Ivan Reynolds.'

At first I'd thought he might be having trouble with my speaking English, but his pause had been merely for thought. His use of the language, in actual fact, was quite effortless, as might be expected of someone who'd worked at the Embassy. 'Yes, I remember him now, this Marinho of yours. I remember his wife. She was very pretty, very nice. The rest of us were envious.'

My pulse gave an expectant leap. 'Do you know what became of them? Do they still live in Lisbon?'

'No. No, they left here not long after they were married. Moved away.'

'You wouldn't know to where?'

Again I felt the sharp look; the assessment. 'She was, perhaps, a relative of yours, the wife?'

I suppose I could have told him yes; invented some relationship, but I wasn't altogether sure a lie would make it past those eyes. I settled on a partial truth. 'I'm looking her up on behalf of a friend of hers – someone she worked with. My grandfather, actually.' That wasn't bad. Deacon had been, however unofficially, my Grandma Murray's 'husband'.

It seemed to satisfy Joaquim. He raised his eyebrows. 'Ah. Because there is a person who might know, who might have kept in touch with them. I could ask him.'

'Oh, would you?' I hadn't meant it to come out on such a note of neediness, but it did, and he reacted with a purposeful glance at his watch.

'He won't be at home until later this evening,' he said, 'but if you leave me your name and a number where you can be reached…'

I was already scrambling for pen and paper. Tearing a page from the small notebook I'd brought, I pressed it smooth against the window ledge and wrote. 'I'm here for a week, at the York House Hotel.' As I passed him the details, I said, 'If you can find out anything at all, I really would appreciate it.'

He took the page and folded it in careful quarters. 'Your

grandfather, he worked for Ivan Reynolds, did you say? It is only that the company was small, and I knew many of the people there.'

I gave myself a mental kick, embarrassed by the oversight. Here I was, supposedly a journalist, and I'd completely failed to realise that Joaquim, who had moved and worked among the British during the Second World War, might be a source of more than just the secretary's address.

'I would be curious,' he said, 'to know the name.'

And so I told him. 'Andrew Deacon.'

'Deacon.' Once again, he tried the name himself, and shook his head. 'I'm afraid I don't remember him.' He gave a small shrug and half turned to look out at the weather; the rain coursing down from the leaves of a green and brown palm tree that grew just outside the arched door of the porch.

But I had seen the fleeting light of recognition, and was not convinced. Watching his face carefully, I said, 'He was in charge of Mr Reynolds's art collection, for a time. Mrs Marinho was his secretary.'

'Ah.' He nodded. Looked at me again. 'I don't remember him.'

'Oh, well, he was only here for a short time, a few months really, towards the end of the war. He doesn't talk about it much,' I ventured. 'I gather there was some unpleasantness. A death.'

'There were so many deaths, in those days,' was his rather vague reply. But I hadn't been mistaken about the intelligence – I sensed it again in the small silent moment before he closed our conversation with, 'I will be sure to let you know if I learn anything of interest from my friend.'

I knew dismissal when I heard it. 'I'd appreciate that, really. Thank you.'

Nodding an acknowledgement, he pulled the big door open to the church. It creaked protestingly. 'Safe journey, menina,' he said. Then he stepped inside, the door slammed shut, and that was that.

I was thinking, with my head down, as I stepped out round the corner of the porch into the rain, and straight into the path of a man coming round in the other direction. We collided, and the impact knocked my glasses to the unforgiving asphalt.

'Hey, I'm sorry,' he said, bending to retrieve them. 'Are you OK?'

My first thought, when he straightened, was that he must be from Boston, by his accent. And my second was that, Patrick notwithstanding, he was one of the best-looking men I'd seen. He was fairly young – my side of thirty-five, probably – average height, average build, but with the kind of a face that was hard to forget. Not a pretty-boy face, but a harder one, masculine, strong, like the hand he held out to me now.

He was holding my glasses. Both lenses were cracked.

'Sorry,' he said again. 'Look, let me pay for these.' Then, because I'd taken so long to answer, he asked, in a slower voice, 'Do you speak English?'

I actually blushed. 'Yes. I…sorry, it's just been a very long day.' Taking the ruined glasses from his hand I said, 'It's all right, you don't need to pay for anything. It was an accident, and anyway, I've got a spare pair back at my hotel.'

'You're sure?'

'Very sure.'

'Then at least let me buy you a coffee.' His voice was persuasive, and in different circumstances I might well have given in to it. But not now. This was not why I had come to Lisbon.

'Thanks, but no.'

'I'm harmless.' And he smiled. It was a great smile, but I held to my resolve.

I flattered myself that I felt his eyes watching me as I walked all the way back down the rain-slicked path, between the dripping trees. But both times that I glanced behind he wasn't watching me at all. The first time he was standing where I'd left him, on the path, head bent to read a leaning tombstone in the softly falling rain. And the second time he wasn't there, he'd gone.

My footsteps, so intrusive in the little English Cemetery's garden-like tranquillity, were swallowed the minute I stepped through the heavy green door in the wall, by the purposeful swish of the traffic along the wet street.

The light had flattened, here, and evening had begun to settle in. I couldn't do much more today, I thought, in terms of searching, and for all the running round I'd done I wasn't any closer to my goal.

I'd had such high hopes for the Embassy, but I salved my disappointment with the hope that Anabela would have more to tell me when we met tonight.

With that in mind, I started looking for a cab to take me back to my hotel. It wasn't easy, with the rain. Most taxis passing me were full already, moving by so quickly that I doubted if their drivers would have noticed me at all. I'd walked some distance on my own before I saw an empty cab approaching.

As I stepped out to wave down the driver, a gunmetal-grey hatchback slid to a stop at the kerb just in front of me, blocking my view, but the taxi had, luckily, seen me. The driver stopped, casting a clear arc of rainwater onto the roadway as, ducking round the rear of the hatchback, I pulled my collar up and made a run for it.

The restaurant, like the rest of my hotel, was classy – quiet and exclusive, sectioned into separate rooms. I'd come down fifteen minutes early, so I'd have a chance to choose a table that would give some privacy for me to talk with Anabela. Nobody was sitting in the first small section I walked into, but the tables there were open to each other, and unshielded, so I turned my eye instead towards the section on my left, built long and narrow like a cloister, with a low, wood-beamed ceiling, the beautiful blue-and-white Portuguese tiles forming baseboard and wainscoting, expertly set in the rough-plastered white walls above floors of polished white marble.

This, I thought, would be the better place to talk. Each little window alcove in the long row sheltered a small table so discreetly that I'd walked past two and noticed nothing till the woman spoke. 'You're Katherine.' She said it with certainty; smiled when I turned. 'Guy is good with descriptions.'

He'd described her to me, too, of course, though he needn't have bothered. He had a predictable taste in his women – I'd known she'd be striking, with dark hair, worn long and unbound past her shoulders. The cigarette was a bit of a surprise, because he didn't ordinarily go for smokers, but maybe Anabela had had other charms to compensate.

We shook hands, and I sat.

The window alcove had been meant for two. She had a wall at her back, I had one at mine. Our knees were almost meeting underneath the table. In between us was a long white window tilted partly open to the courtyard, letting in a cool, pervasive breeze that stirred the curtains, patterned blue and white to match the tiles. The tablecloth was pure white linen, very fine, and set with ivory plates and sparkling wine and water glasses, silver cutlery, and one small glass of dainty yellow flowers, just like daisies, with black centres. Black hearts, I thought, set at the centre of innocence.

She said, 'You got my message, did you, earlier?'

'I did, yes, thanks.'

'I thought you might have come in on a morning flight. Guy wouldn't tell me when you were arriving.'

'Probably,' I said, 'he was just being cautious.'

She tapped ash from her cigarette and exhaled rather thoughtfully, her eyebrows raised a fraction. 'So then it's true…there's something in this business that requires caution?' Sitting back, she said, 'I wasn't sure. Guy can be so James Bond sometimes, you know?'

I did know, but I didn't really blame him, in this instance. Since the shooting in Toronto, I too had developed all the instincts of a secret service agent – always wary, always watching, lest the shadow of an enemy should cross my path. It wasn't anything I could control. I had been changed. My senses were so heightened by the constant threat of danger that, just sitting here, I felt aware of everything – the sound of other voices conversing at tables in the next secluded section of the restaurant; the clink of glasses and cutlery; the quick steps of the waitress on the marble floor, approaching us; the furtive rush of the breeze over the window ledge, lifting the curtains at my shoulder; the slam of a door at the back.

There was music playing quietly from somewhere – soft guitars behind a plaintive female voice singing songs that were almost like Renaissance airs, a fitting background for a menu that offered such uncommon delicacies as 'stewed wild pigeon with ham'. I'd never had pigeon before, so I ordered it; then, settling back, said: 'I really appreciate all of the time you've put into this.'

Anabela shrugged. 'It was nothing. I'm happy to do it.' And not only for Guy's sake, I decided. She impressed me as a woman who would go to any lengths to help a colleague.

It was good to feel a part of my old world again, however briefly. The ground was familiar and firm – we were journalists, having a meal, talking shop, sharing research.

Anabela told me, 'I have copies of the records that you wanted, of the deaths. November 1943 to April 1944.' She balanced her cigarette end on the ashtray and bent to her briefcase, retrieving a thick manila envelope that thumped between us on the little table. 'There are many. And you wanted to know news of Ivan Reynolds also, yes? I had success there, too. The newspapers, I don't think that they very much approved of Ivan Reynolds. Which is quite good for us, because, you know, they wrote about him constantly.'

I had the envelope open, now, and was leafing through the pages as she pointed to them. 'There, I found you many articles about the man, his company, the projects they were working on that year. Most I found in Portuguese, and so I made you my translations.'

'Why didn't they approve of him?'

She paused to give the question some consideration. 'I couldn't tell you that. Perhaps his wealth, his attitudes – he was a most neurotic man – but no one ever comes right out and says that this is why they don't like Ivan Reynolds. No, it's more subtle. It's a thing you sense, when reading all these articles – how often these reporters choose to write about him; what they write; their tone. I don't know why he wasn't liked,' she said. 'You maybe would have had to know the man himself, to answer that.'

I'd come across a photograph, and studied it a moment. I'd seen dozens of such photographs, of course, in my own reading, but I hadn't yet seen one like this, that showed him as he would have looked when Deacon first arrived in Lisbon. Reynolds would have been in his late fifties, then – a powerfully built man with a broad and slightly heavy face, and deeply set, distrustful eyes.

The young girl beside him looked vaguely familiar.

'Who's this?' I asked.

Anabela took a look. 'Oh, that's his mistress. Jenny Saunders.'

Jenny Saunders. I knew that name, too. Then I placed it. Recalling the book I had read in Toronto, with the picture of Reynolds's office, I said, 'She was one of his secretaries.'

'Yes. You've been doing your homework as well, I see.' Anabela smiled. 'She was eighteen, I think, or seventeen. Too young for such a man. But when he died, he left her almost all his money. I have tried to find what happened to her, but it is

220

quite difficult. She seems to simply disappear.'

Our food came – first a starter of pâté on a tiny dry bread square, with a scattering of cut chives and a minuscule half-tomato, then a fresh tomato soup, scalding hot and delicately seasoned.

'The other secretary, too,' said Anabela, 'you already have the clipping that I sent you, from the wedding, with translation, so you know her husband worked in Lisbon, for the British Embassy.'

'Yes, thanks, I—'

'But she doesn't live in Lisbon now. I had some difficulty tracing her, but in the end I used a friend of mine, with the police. He owes me favours.' Pushing back her empty plate, she smiled, and it occurred to me that most men likely didn't mind much, being in her debt. 'He gave me her address. She lives in Evora. You know where this town is?'

'I'll look it up.'

'It is the finest of our walled towns, in the Alentejo, to the east, towards the Spanish border.' She described it for me, while the waitress took my empty soup bowl and replaced it with the 'stewed wild pigeon with ham', which looked, uncomfortably, just like a pigeon that someone had stepped on by accident, wings stretched out flat on the plate. I covered a forkful of meat in ham, gravy and green beans, disguising it.

Anabela wasn't talking anymore. When I glanced up, I found her watching me and frowning slightly, but it wasn't because of my meal. She was thinking. Then she said, 'You need to know that you are not the only person who is looking for this woman.'

I forgot about my fork, half raised. 'I'm sorry?'

'My friend from the police, he telephoned me yesterday to say that he'd been asked to look the address up again, for someone else.'

'I see.' I felt a tingle in the region of my stomach. 'Did he say for whom?'

'Officially, for one of his superiors. But there was someone else's name, as well, on the request. He told me what it was – I wrote it down. A Polish name,' she said. 'Jankowski. M Jankowski. Do you know this person?'

'No.' I frowned. 'Is it a man, or a woman?'

'I don't know. I only thought,' she said, 'you'd want to be aware of it, especially since Guy…well, he did make this sound quite cloak and dagger, honestly.'

I didn't comment. I was thinking.

This other person who, like me, was looking for Regina Marinho, could, of course, be unconnected to my own concerns; coincidental. There were any number of legal and personal reasons why someone might want to want to find somebody else, and M Jankowski's motives might be innocent. But instinct told me otherwise.

On a purely gut level, I knew what I'd suspected since the shooting in Toronto to be true – that whomever I was up against was also on the trail of Deacon's past.

But maybe I was not as far behind as I had feared. In fact, I might now have a chance to get a half a step ahead, because my adversary wasn't faceless any more – I had a name. The fox, I thought, might finally have a chance to double back behind the hounds and do some hunting of her own.

I looked at Anabela. 'Could you find out any more for me about this M Jankowski?'

'I can try.' She reached a hand towards her cigarettes and lighter, then appeared to reconsider, glancing back towards the restrooms. 'You'll excuse me for a minute, I just have to… you know.' Standing, with her purse in hand, she promised, 'I will not be long.'

My appetite had vanished, but I managed, in her absence, to get enough of my stewed pigeon put away so that I could pile the rest to one side of the plate, chasing the last tough bite down with a long drink of water that tasted unexpectedly of melon. I let the waitress take my plate, and ordered tea, for warmth.

Not that the restaurant's temperature had changed, but still, the night felt somehow chillier; the table more exposed. I hugged my arms and looked round at the other diners, those that I could see: Two children, sitting with their parents, looking tired; a couple, middle-aged, heads bent in conversation of a quieter kind; a younger woman, eating on her own, lost in a paperback romance that she was holding in her free hand, turning pages at a leisured speed. There wasn't one face that appeared to be suspicious, out of place. But then, I told myself, there wouldn't be.

It wasn't me I worried for, as much as Anabela. Information had a tendency to flow both ways, in my experience, and if she had been able to find out that someone else – this M Jankowski person – had been looking for the secretary, then it was a fair bet someone else knew Anabela had been asking questions, too. Which meant she wasn't safe.

I felt sure she'd already sensed that, somewhat, on her

own, but she deserved to know the whole of it: the incidents in London, and the shooting of my grandmother. I owed her that, at least. I'd have to tell her.

I was working out exactly what to say, where to start, when a man's voice called, 'Kate!' and I glanced up from habit... then kicked myself for so soon forgetting Tony's warnings about always thinking, always being on my guard. The man, of course, hadn't been calling to me. It was the father at the nearby table, chastening his daughter who had stooped to pick up something from the floor. The little girl stopped short and climbed back to her seat while I looked down again, still frowning at my lapse of judgement.

I heard footsteps on the marble floor and raised my head expectantly. It wasn't Anabela. Just the waitress, with a message.

'Your friend asked me to apologise, but she has had a call from work, and had to leave. She said to please forgive her. She has paid the bill.' The waitress smiled, and warmed my tea, and left me sitting on my own.

I thought it strange that Anabela would have sent someone to tell me she had left, instead of telling me herself. However urgent the call – and I realised, in our business, some calls could be pretty urgent – she should have been able to spare thirty seconds to tell me goodbye.

My frown deepened. I was electrically aware of my surroundings, now. I didn't want to be here. I'd feel safer in my room upstairs, where I at least could lock the door to give me the illusion of security.

I stood. In my imagination, all eyes watched me as I walked toward the exit, my shoes loud against the marble. In my hurry to get out, I pulled the door too quickly and its swing threw me off balance. I would have fallen if the man just coming through the door had not been quick enough to catch my elbows; hold me steady.

'Careful,' he said.

Something warned me, as I raised my head to thank him. Some prescient tingle, that might have been simply the voice, or the height that the voice had been speaking from, led me to know I'd be facing a person who wasn't a stranger.

His eyes were brown. That registered. I hadn't really seen them, in the rain outside the English Church. They laughed at me. He said, unable to resist the line, 'We have to stop running into each other like this.'

'Sorry.' I straightened.

'No problem. No harm done. I see your glasses survived this time.'

Instinctively, I raised one hand to make sure I still had them on. It wasn't often that I found myself unsure of what to say, and the moment of silence stretched awkwardly.

Finally, I asked him inanely, 'You're staying here too, are you?'

'Yes,' he said, letting go my elbows. His quick downward glance held amusement. 'Small world.'

'Yes.' My world seemed increasingly small these days.

Stepping aside, he said, 'My offer to buy you a coffee still stands, by the way. If you feel like it later, I'll be in the bar.'

And then, with a nod, he politely moved past me and into the restaurant, and waited for someone to seat him. At least, I thought, he wasn't being pushy. I met all types, when I travelled, and the pushy ones were worst of all.

I fought the urge to glance behind me as I went upstairs. The twisting corridors felt claustrophobic, and unsafe. It was a huge relief to reach my room, and turn the key behind me.

Up-ending the manila envelope that Anabela had given me onto the bed, I shuffled the papers and clippings in search of Regina Marinho's address. With that in hand, I tried to dial directory assistance, looking for her number. But I had no luck. It wasn't listed.

Heavy-shouldered with defeat, I crossed to tug the curtains tighter shut across the window. From the courtyard, I heard music, faintly, and the sounds of voices drifting over from the bar.

I wondered, vaguely, whether the American would actually be looking for me, later on tonight. It didn't matter – I would not be there. I'd had a long day, an exhausting day; I didn't need to waste time drinking coffee with a stranger in a hotel bar. His being handsome didn't enter into it. Or maybe, to be fair, it did.

I'd had my share, already, of unwanted complications.

So instead I took a bath, and went to bed, and slept so soundly that I didn't hear the footsteps coming softly down the hall, or hear them stop outside my room, or hear the rasp of paper being pushed beneath my door.

SATURDAY, SEPTEMBER 30

The envelope was lying on the floor inside the door when I woke up next morning.

At first I thought it might have been a note from Anabela, to explain why she had taken off so suddenly. But when I had the single page unfolded, I could see it was a fax. It hadn't come from Anabela. It was from Joaquim, my English Cemetery man.

He'd spoken to his friend, it seemed. His fax was brief – a name and address, little more. I was surprised he'd followed through. I hadn't thought he would. It didn't matter that I'd already been given the address, by Anabela. It was always good to have a second source, and this confirmed that Regina Marinho in fact lived in Evora. And there was more: he had sent me her phone number.

Not a bad way to begin my day, I thought.

The woman who picked up the phone at the other end when I called through spoke good English, like everyone else I had met here in Portugal. Only she wasn't the woman I wanted. Not Regina Marinho. Her housekeeper, maybe. Regina Marinho was out.

I asked, 'Can you tell me when she *might* be home?'

'I do not know.' Coldly, unhelpful, as though she suspected I wanted to come and break into the house later.

'No, I mean…this afternoon,' I said. 'Would she be home this afternoon?'

'I do not know.'

'May I leave a message?'

'If you like.'

'My name is Katherine Allen. I'm in Lisbon, and I'd really like to speak to her. If she could call me back, at my hotel…' And I read her the number, although from the silence I had no great faith she was writing it down.

'Does she know you?' the voice asked, protectively.

'No.' And then, the half-truth that had worked for me so far: 'She knows my grandfather. His name is Andrew Deacon.'

'Ah.'

'She will remember him, I'm sure. They used to work together.'

'Yes, I will give her your message, when she comes,' the voice replied, but in a tone that made no promises. Dismissing me, she said goodbye and hung up the receiver.

But I didn't leave it there. I hadn't travelled all this way to be put off so easily. Regina Marinho might have someone screening her calls, but she couldn't screen *me* if I turned up in person and knocked at the door.

It was time for a road trip.

I wasn't as keen on the prospect as I would have been a day ago – not because of Anabela's telling me that someone else was also on the hunt for Deacon's secretary, but because my self-protective instincts had been strengthened by my realisation, at the English Cemetery, that Joaquim had not been wholly truthful with me. He *had* known Deacon – at the very least, he'd recognised the name, I'd seen it in his eyes – but he'd denied it.

Up till then, I had been thinking all of Deacon's friends and colleagues were my allies in this business, and that finding them would be my only challenge. Having met Joaquim, I now thought differently. I knew there was a chance that Deacon's secretary might not be all I'd assumed. It stood to reason, after all, that just as anyone who'd known Deacon in his Lisbon days might also know about the murder, so, too, any of them might have been involved.

They might not all be glad to see me.

And I wouldn't know, until I'd met them, which of them to trust.

Finding a rental car company hadn't been difficult.

Finding my way out of Lisbon was trickier. Once I got clear of the small streets and onto the highways that carried me south and then east, I breathed easier. Until I caught sight of the car, in my mirror.

A gunmetal-grey hatchback, keeping its distance. I changed lanes and passed a few cars, to be certain, and for a few minutes I nearly believed I had only imagined it. But then the grey car settled behind me again, with a steady but menacing purpose.

Something uncomfortable stirred in my memory – the car that had swished to a stop at the kerb as I'd flagged down a cab near the old English Cemetery. It, too, had been grey, and a hatchback. I hadn't thought much of it, at the time. I'd just assumed that somebody was stopping to drop someone off, but now another possible scenario, more sinister, occurred to me. I couldn't help wondering what might have happened if I hadn't run for that taxi.

I glanced in the side mirror. The sun was high and over us, reflecting on the windshield so I couldn't see the driver, just the car, and that was staying far enough back that I couldn't tell its make, or read the licence plate. I slowed a bit, but it slowed, too, and when I sped up again it matched my pace exactly.

My mouth dried. I felt the sudden fear, the pure adrenalin surge of a lone swimmer spotting a shark in her wake. Because I *was* alone. This was a busy stretch of highway, but if I pulled off and stopped, no one would notice my distress – especially not when they saw the grey car stopping, too, to 'assist' me.

Tony hadn't coached me, in Toronto, on what I should do if I were being followed on the highway. On foot, yes. He'd covered that. On foot, I was supposed to find a busy place – a restaurant, maybe, or a market, packed with people – and seek shelter there. Safety in numbers, he'd told me. My odds for survival were better as part of a crowd.

It was all the advice that I had now, to go on. My eyes searched the road ahead, desperate, and saw in the distance a rest stop, with gas pumps. The rental car shuddered and leapt as I floored the accelerator, rocketing between the cars ahead of me with reckless disconcern. When I'd put three cars and a tour bus between me and my pursuer, I glanced at the mirror. The grey hatchback was nosing out impatiently behind the line of cars, but it was blocked.

I grabbed my chance, and took the exit.

It was sheer luck that the tour bus came off with me, like a shield that kept me safely out of view. I saw the grey car shoot straight past on the highway as I pulled around behind the flat-roofed restaurant building with the bus, and eased into a parking space.

My hands were clenched so tightly round the steering wheel I had to consciously release my grip. And then the shaking started. It took hold of me so violently I nearly didn't have the strength to stand, to leave the car, and yet I knew I had to manage it. The tour group had begun to disembark beside me, streaming from the bus doors in a cheerful, noisy, brightly coloured flood of human chaos. There was not much time.

I stopped the shaking with an effort, making tight fists with my hands, and pushed my door open. For a minute, on the asphalt, I felt vulnerable. A target. Then the people from the tour group, without meaning to, enveloped me, and like a cork on water I was carried in their current to the restaurant, through the swinging doors.

It was a cafeteria. I bought a cup of coffee and a roll, and found a seat in the middle of the crowding tables, facing the front windows but well back from them, where I could see the road.

It wasn't till some fifteen minutes later, when I'd started to relax a little, that the grey hatchback came smoothly down the exit ramp, into the parking lot.

Whoever was behind the wheel had seen through my manoeuvre, and had doubled back.

I didn't breathe. I knew nobody looking in could see me,

but I shrank against my chair, as if that futile act could hide me. I wanted to bolt, make a run for it, but I could hear Tony's voice, in my head, saying: 'Stay with the group,' so I stayed with the group, still not breathing, and willed the grey car to pass by.

A grey Renault Clio – I saw what it was, now. It crawled past the windows, the sun still reflecting too brightly for me to see who was inside. And then it vanished, and I knew that it had gone behind the building. Where my car was parked, in plain view, by the tour bus. The waiting was an agony. My heartbeats shook my ribcage, painful, pounding in my ears. And then, just when I thought I couldn't bear the tension any more, the grey hatchback slid by, and turned, and sped back up the ramp onto the highway, heading east, to Evora.

I exhaled, on a shaky sigh. My coffee had grown cold, the cream congealing on its surface, but I sat there several minutes longer, sipping it, until the tour group's members started clearing off their tables, standing, gathering around their guide. I stood, too, and moved in among them, using them as camouflage to cross the parking lot again and slide into my rental car.

I made sure that I got back on the highway well before their bus did, though. I didn't want anything blocking my view of what might be behind me. Or what might be waiting ahead.

The landscape changed.

Wide, empty stretches of harvested grain fields, and scrub brush and parched-looking pines and cork trees with their blood-red trunks. An arid place, watchful and silent, where the frames of a few of the low whitewashed houses were still painted blue, in the Moorish tradition, to protect against bad spirits, and the evil eye.

The evil eye, I thought now, could have seen a long way, here.

Last night, at dinner, Anabela had described to me this region. 'It is called the Alentejo – means "beyond the Tejo", our name for the river that you call the Tagus. In the Alentejo there are not so many rivers as there are when one goes north, and there are not so many people, and the people who do live there have known suffering, throughout our history. This was the land for the battles, in Portugal. For the invasions. So in the Alentejo most of the villages and towns they are surrounded by the walls of a castle, and most famous of these is the regional capital, Evora. It is considered our museum town, our jewel. And it's a fascinating place, like in the old days – all whitewashed inside, with its wrought-iron balconies, and with the lamps, and with small streets, surrounded by walls that were built by the Romans.'

In my mind, from her description, I expected a medieval apparition, a walled fortress like you sometimes saw in movies, rising stalwart from the landscape of pine-covered hills, but of course it wasn't anything like that. The town of Evora had long since grown beyond its ancient walls, and had spilt outwards in an orderly array of white-walled buildings, some quite modern, topped with red-tiled roofs and edged with ochre-yellow paint.

I chose a hotel from the several clustered just outside the high town walls, to the south-west, and parked the car at the back. I hadn't caught sight of the gunmetal-grey Renault Clio since I'd left the rest stop, but I didn't want to take chances. I didn't want *my* car to lead anyone to Regina Marinho's front door. Besides which, I'd feel safer on the sidewalks, with the other tourists. I would walk from here.

There weren't too many cars, as it turned out, within the old town walls. I noticed them when they went by, the sound a rude disturbance of the more congenial human noises – lively voices, laughter, passing footfalls on the cobblestones, the noises which had doubtless filled these narrow streets a thousand years ago; before that, even, when the Romans had first come to build their walls and settle here.

It was after I'd crossed a large square with a fountain that I first heard someone behind me. Firm steps, with no owner – an echo that followed when I turned a corner, and stopped when I stopped to look over my shoulder. I saw no one there. Quickening my pace, I turned in to a narrow street, with pretty balconies of old wrought iron, and shutters that rolled down to hide every window. The cobblestones beneath my feet were granite, hard and ringing, softened only by a long cascade of flowered vine that tumbled down one house's wall to puddle on the pavement.

Still the footsteps came, and then another sound, that I heard only very faintly, to begin with – the melodic, lively twittering of songbirds.

Looking up, I saw the source. Beside two windows on the upper storey of the nearest house, someone had fastened several birdcages against the outside wall, their wires dark against the whitewashed plaster, bright colours flashing through them as the birds within the cages fluttered, hopped, and sang.

A voice spoke, behind me – a pleasant voice, speaking in accented English. 'They are beautiful, do you not think?'

Wheeling round, I saw a woman standing several yards

away. She had a striking face, high-cheekboned, stoic in a way that made it hard to guess her age. Her accent, too, was not the easiest to place. It sounded Eastern European. Russian, possibly. Or Polish.

My first reaction was relief. I'd feared the worst, when I had heard those footsteps, and it made me feel much better to find out my fears had only been imagined.

Still looking at the birds, she said, 'It must be a hard life for them, being out here every day where they can see the sky, and yet not fly where they would go. Like little prisoners.'

I was about to agree when her gaze came down, meeting mine. Something behind her eyes made me uncomfortable. 'Then again,' she said, 'they might not care. They might not even know that they've been caught.' Her smile was almost imperceptible. 'Some creatures don't.'

The unease I'd felt earlier resurfaced with a rush.

She took a step towards me, and the hand that had been in her pocket started to move, also, but a burst of laughter interrupted from around the corner, and a clattering of people surged into the street, dividing us. A tour group – very possibly the same one that had been my saviours earlier. I didn't stop to reason, then. I tore my feet from where they had been rooted on the cobblestones, and fell in with the crowd. I looked back once, and saw the woman standing where I'd left her, making no attempt to follow, but that didn't reassure me.

And the minute I had turned the corner, out of sight, I ran.

I made certain I was all alone, that nobody was watching, before I approached the house.

It looked like nothing from the street. It was, in actual fact, rather ugly – a plain, flat-walled, two-storey slab with three iron-grilled windows, two up and one down, rimmed round with the same mustard-yellow paint that traced the frame and the foundation line. The whitewash was peeling in places and hadn't been able to cover the horizontal line of power cables that ran straight across the building and connected with the next adjoining housefront. I might have made the mistake of thinking this was a poor neighbourhood, if it hadn't been for the fact that the green iron gates to the garage-like opening in that plain wall had been left to stand open, allowing me to see not just the tidy black sedan that had been parked upon the intricate mosaic-patterned cobblestones, but the whole of what appeared to be a sheltered courtyard, thick with potted trees and plants, with delicately worked wrought-iron balconies in front of long french windows, and the lovely Portuguese blue tiles known as *azulejos* set around at intervals to beautify the space.

I didn't go into the courtyard at first. There was an intercom button beside the street entrance, and that's what I pushed. It took a long time before somebody answered. The housekeeper again, I guessed, and knowing she spoke English I identified myself and said, 'I telephoned earlier.'

'Yes, for Senhora Marinho. A moment.'

I waited. As I stepped forward, under cover of the big garage-like doorway, the second door within the courtyard opened and a woman moved to stand within the frame.

Not the housekeeper, I thought. An older woman, close to Grandma Murray's age, with pale hair neatly pulled back from a face with quite extraordinary cheekbones. Her English was flawless. 'Miss Allen?' she said. 'Do come in.'

It was gorgeous inside, lots of dark wood and warm light and elegant carpets, but I didn't register much of the detail. I paused in the entryway, feeling myself under scrutiny.

'I would have known you at once. You look quite like your grandmother,' Regina Marinho said. 'It's years ago now, of course, but I did see her every day at work. The wedding portrait,' she explained, and smiled. 'Mr Deacon kept it on his desk. He liked to look at it. I think he missed her terribly. But then, he always said that she was safer in New York.'

Which answered at least one of my wonderings. She hadn't been completely in his confidence. She couldn't have been, if she'd believed his sham marriage to my grandmother to be real. But she was sharp. And not just in spotting the way I resembled my grandmother, either.

Her pleasant blue gaze brushed my hand, my left hand, as she led me along to a quiet back sitting room, more like a study, with needlepoint chairs and a fire burning warm in the dark-mantled fireplace. 'You're not married, my dear? So then Allen's your maiden name? That would mean you're Mr Deacon's daughter's daughter, is that right? I am glad that he had children – he so wanted them. Please, sit, I'll have some tea brought in.'

She offered me an armchair by the fire and chose one closer to the doorway for herself. I didn't know whether that was because she wanted me to have the warmth, or because from her own seat, with the tall lamp at her shoulder, she could see my face in full light while her own was half in shadow, far more difficult to read.

'It's not usually so chilly yet, this time of year,' she said. 'I can't recall the last time that I had to light the fires in

September. Are you warm enough? Would you like tea, or coffee?'

'I'll drink either.'

Beside her chair, a little round-topped table held a telephone. She lifted the receiver and, pushing what must have been an intercom button, spoke a brief Portuguese phrase to whomever had picked up at the other end; then, veined hands folded calmly in her lap, she gave me back her full attention. 'So. Is Mr Deacon still alive?'

I hadn't expected the question to come quite so soon, or so bluntly. I paused before answering, and it appeared that my pause was an answer enough.

'No, I thought not,' she said. 'There aren't many of us left from the old days. Your grandmother, too? Well, at least they're together. My doctors tell me it will likely be a few years yet before I can be with my own dear husband, rest his soul. The curse of health.' Her smile was only faintly visible, in shadow. 'Did Mr Deacon keep his health, then, till the end? He was always so fit when I knew him, I'm afraid I can't imagine him any other way.'

I thought of the old man I'd met that day; how he had creaked to his feet...

'Yes, he stayed very healthy.'

'I did wonder. It has been so many years.' She turned to me and took the reins in hand. 'So. Is there something that you'd like to ask me? Something that you wish to know?'

A sharp woman indeed. But not, I thought, a woman I should fear. I had a feeling, based on nothing more than instinct, she was someone I could trust.

I took a leap of faith, and said, 'He died last month, in

238

London. I was with him. It was meant to be a hit-and-run, but I don't really think it was an accident. I think somebody killed him.'

'Ah.' She looked completely unsurprised, as though it somehow fit with her long-held image of Deacon that he could not have been felled by any force except by one that wasn't natural.

I said, 'I think that he was killed because of what he knew, and that whoever killed him is now trying to get rid of anybody who might share that knowledge. There have been other deaths.' I drew a breath, and then went on, 'Your life might be in danger. There's a chance that I was followed here today.'

'I see. And so that's why you've come, to warn me?'

'That's part of the reason.'

'Why else, then?'

I met her intelligent gaze. 'I believe this has to do with something that happened when he worked for Ivan Reynolds. I was hoping I could ask you a few questions.'

She considered this. A moment passed. 'How much did he tell you of what he was doing in Lisbon, with Reynolds?'

I couldn't clearly read her eyes, but something told me I was being tested, so I opted for the path of partial honesty. 'I know he was placed there by British Intelligence.'

'Then you know more than you ought to.'

'He mentioned a murder. An old one, he told me, but one still deserving of justice.'

She softened. 'Yes, that sounds like something he'd say. He was always a great one for justice. In Biblical terms, if need be.'

I pressed ahead, to take advantage of her contemplative mood. Taking out my palm-sized tape recorder, I set it in plain view, awaiting her permission. 'I just thought, if you could tell me some of what was going on back then, when you were working with him, then I might be able to piece together what he might have known that someone cared enough to kill him for. He tried to tell me what it was,' I said, 'but I...I didn't take the time, you know, to listen.'

It was the right approach to take. She held her silence for a moment longer. Then, 'It's all such a long time ago, my dear. I don't know what help I can be to you. But yes, for Mr Deacon's sake,' she said, 'for his sake, I will try.'

And for an instant, when she turned her head, the light that filtered through the lampshade showed a younger face, as she began to speak.

She'd been twenty in the year that Deacon came to work for Reynolds.

She'd been working there herself two years already, as a secretary. Not to Ivan Reynolds himself – he had his own private assistant – but to the other men who had the offices below him, on the first floor, men who came and went with frequency, according to the volatile moods of their employer. In December 1943, there were, by her count, three, who shared her equally: Reynolds's personal aide, Roger Selkirk; a Spaniard named Manuel Garcia, who kept the accounts; and Vivian Spivey, the man who looked after the firm's shipping business.

She liked Roger Selkirk immensely, as did everyone. He was a witty and affable young man, always ready with a joke and quick to laugh, and with an inborn generosity. He often arrived at work in the morning short of pocket money or cigarettes because he'd given them to someone in the street. Regina found his cheerfulness infectious, like a smile so broad one couldn't help returning it.

The Spaniard, Garcia, was more of a closed book. Friendly enough in his own way, he nonetheless kept himself very much to himself, leaving on time every evening, retreating alone to the one-bedroom flat that he shared with his equally taciturn wife. Not so easy to know, but Regina still liked him.

She didn't like Spivey.

From the beginning, there'd been something in his face she didn't trust. His eyes, she thought. They rarely met her own directly, and she felt a bit uneasy when they did. He was lean and round-shouldered, which made all his suits look ill-fitting, and his smile, when he smiled, never seemed to be with you, but at your expense. It was almost a smirk.

She was not at all sorry when Spivey was taken away from her, then, that December, and given instead to the newest girl, young Jenny Saunders. Regina had been grateful for the decrease in her workload, though she knew it wouldn't last. A new employee was arriving, and she knew she'd be assigned to him – that's why they'd shifted Spivey, to make room.

Thus far the office rumour mill knew little about Andrew Deacon except for his name, that he came from New York, and of course that he was married. Reynolds wouldn't hire anybody now who wasn't married, not since that young American a few months back had tried to get too close to Jenny Saunders. Reynolds was protective of his property. He'd sacked the young American, and cleared the office of all single men who might attempt the same transgression.

Spivey and Garcia had escaped the purge – they both had wives. And Roger…well, it wasn't any secret Roger's interests didn't run to women, and so he, too, had survived. But others hadn't been so lucky, and among them had been the curator of the ever-growing private Reynolds art collection, leaving vacant the position Andrew Deacon would be coming now to fill.

Regina knew a little more about him than the others did, though no one in the office knew she knew. No one – not even Ivan Reynolds – knew the double role she played within the company, nor that she had been placed there with a purpose by the British Secret Service. She'd been volunteered, to start with, by her father, who with several other businessmen, pro-British like himself, had formed a Vigilance Committee to inform on any enemy activity in Lisbon that might come to their attention.

It had been through her father, too, that she had first met Alvaro Marinho. She had fallen for him instantly, and would have married him a year ago had it not been for his insistence that she was still needed where she was. And Ivan Reynolds, while he only hired married men, demanded that the women he employed all be *un*married.

So Regina had kept to her post. Her job, for the British, involved mostly watching the mail, intercepting particular letters coming in and going out, and seeing that they got to Alvaro so he in turn could pass them on to be examined – opened expertly and then resealed without a trace, returned to her as though they'd never left her desk. She kept a careful log of Reynolds's visitors; from time to time she listened in on phone calls, but she couldn't get within his private circle. She'd tried getting close to Roger, but for all his friendly nature he had proved to be too circumspect, and so now they were bringing Andrew Deacon over.

She remembered the day he arrived at the offices.

Monday, it was, and a dreary grey day that was playing on everyone's nerves. Even Roger had come in unsmiling. Garcia had been called upstairs to answer some question or other about the accounts, while Spivey, skulking at his desk, grew by the minute more intolerable.

Jenny Saunders stepped out of Spivey's office with a face that looked distinctly unimpressed. 'I'm getting coffee,' she announced, and her normally pleasant American voice had an edge. 'Would you like a cup?'

'No, thanks,' Regina said. 'I've just had one.'

'I might be a while.' The door closed behind her with a force that fell just short of an actual slam, and Regina, with a smile of understanding, turned her own attention to the filing cabinet.

Nothing moved in the office. It wasn't until she turned back to her desk that she saw him, and his presence caught her so off guard she nearly dropped the file she was holding.

'Oh,' she said. And then, recovering, 'You must be Mr Deacon.'

She had no idea when he had come in, or how long he'd been standing there, but she didn't think it had been very long – he didn't strike her as the sort of man who'd be so unmannerly as to just stand there and watch without letting her know he was there in the room. She was good at reading people; she could always spot a gentleman.

He said, 'I am, yes. Sorry if I startled you.'

'I didn't hear you come in, that's all.'

'Yes, well, I'll try not to do it again.' He had quite lovely eyes, she thought. Blue and alive, in his otherwise ordinary face. He was dressed well without being flashy – grey suit, white shirt, navy-blue tie, and a grey hat that he'd taken off and was holding in one hand, politely.

A gentleman, Regina thought again, and she was glad that she had been assigned to work for him. She told him, 'I'm Regina Sousa. You can call me Regina, it's what everybody does. I'll be your secretary. Let me show you where your office is.'

It was the largest office, last one down the passage, in a corner of the building with tall windows on two walls, and an impressive desk of polished rosewood. Deacon didn't seem to take much notice of the windows or the desk, but looked, she noticed, at the paintings on the walls.

'It's very nice,' he said.

'I'm glad you like it. Mr Reynolds wants to meet with you for lunch. He said he'd come down here himself and fetch you later.'

'Fine.' He'd only brought a briefcase, and he set it down now on the desk and asked her, 'Are you very busy at the moment?'

'Not really, no. I have two letters Mr Selkirk wanted typed by noon, but—'

'Then perhaps when you've done those, if you have time,' he said, 'you'd bring us both some coffee, and we'll talk.'

'All right.'

When she came back, he looked more settled at his desk.

She had expected that the room would look too large for him; she hadn't thought that such a quiet man could fill the space, and yet somehow he did, and did it in a way that made the room seem it had always been his own. This was remarkable, to her, because as far as she could see he'd added nothing to the room except two items that he must have carried with him in his briefcase. She saw them as she came around to set the cup of coffee on his desk: a modern novel, and a photograph.

The novel was *The Robe*, by Lloyd C Douglas, this year's winner of the Pulitzer. She had a copy of the book herself, at home, and owned it for the reason Andrew Deacon did – because it was the codebook. He would use it for the messages that he'd be sending out, through her, to Alvaro, and for deciphering the notes that came back in reply. Like her, he'd write the coded messages in ink that turned invisible, on otherwise innocent letters of business. The code, even if it were detected, was useless to anyone who didn't know the codebook, consisting as it did of strings of numbers – 0512217 being the fifth word in the twelfth line of the two hundred and seventeenth page.

Because they shared a codebook, he'd be able to send messages to her, as well, and she to him, in secret, if the need arose.

She shifted focus from the novel to the photograph. It sat inside a handsome leather folding frame he'd angled round to see while he was working; not for other people's eyes.

He saw Regina looking, and he said, 'My wife, Amelia.'

'Oh.' It was a coloured photograph. She looked at the softly red hair of the woman; the laughing green eyes and the plain ivory folds of the wedding dress. 'She's very beautiful.'

'Yes,' he said, glancing away. 'Yes, she is.'

'You must miss her.'

'I should miss her more if something were to happen to her. She's safer to stay in New York, while this war's on.' He swivelled his chair and reached out for his coffee cup. 'Thank you for this. Please, sit down.'

It took her less than half an hour to tell him what she knew about the people working there. He took no notes, but paid careful attention, and when she was done he seemed satisfied.

Thanking her, he smiled. 'You're a very keen observer, Miss Sousa.'

'Regina.'

'Regina, then. You seem to have this business well in hand. I can't think why I've been brought over.'

'Because I can't go where Reynolds goes. The dinners, and the gatherings. You can. You're on his level.'

'Yes, well, that rather depends on how well he and I get on, doesn't it? We shall see.'

She could have told him that he needn't worry. She'd worked for Ivan Reynolds long enough to know that Andrew Deacon was exactly the sort of a man he would like. And indeed, she could tell from the moment that Reynolds stepped into the office, at lunchtime, that she had been right.

It always interested her to see the reaction of people meeting Reynolds for the first time. He was not what most expected – neither tall nor swaggering, looking a little untidy as though he had dressed in a hurry, his grizzled dark hair never totally tamed by the comb. Yet whereas Deacon's office would have looked too large for many men, it looked too small for Reynolds. He commanded every room that he walked into, and he did it with an energy she'd never seen in any other man.

Deacon didn't really react one way or another; he simply stood and offered his hand in introduction, and Reynolds's features relaxed into something approaching a smile.

'Glad to have you,' he told Deacon. 'You came highly recommended. Has Regina here been showing you the ropes?'

'She has, yes.'

'Well, that's good. That's very good.' The handshake over, Reynolds coughed and looked around, his shrewd eyes taking in the wedding portrait on the desk before they moved on. 'What do you think of your view?'

Deacon, his back to the window, said, 'I like it very much.' He nodded at one of the paintings that hung on the nearest wall. 'The Kandinsky is especially fine.'

The painter's name meant nothing to Regina, who knew little about art, but Reynolds seemed to be well pleased. He said to Deacon, 'I can see we're going to have a lot to talk about, at lunch. You'd better get your hat.'

They stayed out a considerable time. They weren't back when Regina returned from her own lunch, to find Roger Selkirk making himself comfortable at her desk, tipped back in the chair with his arms folded, talking to Jenny.

'Hullo,' he said, as she came in. 'I like that scarf. It suits you.'

She shrugged her coat off, hung it on its peg, and smiled. 'All right, what are you after?'

'My dear girl, why would you think I'm after anything?'

'You aren't here to compliment my fashion sense.'

Jenny, looking happier again, said, 'He's been dying to ask you about Mr Deacon.'

'Hardly dying,' Roger said. 'I'm merely curious.'

Shooing him out of her chair with a good-natured wave of her hand, Regina sat. 'I'm surprised you weren't down here this morning.'

'Yes, well.' He shifted position to lean on the edge of her desk, instead. 'One doesn't want to appear *too* intrusive. Besides, I was wanted upstairs. Quite a scandal, we had. I was just telling Jenny. But come, first things first – what's this Deacon chap like?'

'Very nice. Very pleasant. A gentleman.'

'Ah, then he'll be odd man out here,' Roger said. He grinned. 'What else?'

'I don't know anything else. He's only just arrived. I haven't had much time to analyse his character.'

'No need to be sarcastic.'

Jenny, from her desk across the office, said, 'Well, I'll trade you your new man for Spivey, Regina.'

'No, thank you. I've had him.'

'How on earth could you stand it?' the girl asked.

'I couldn't.' Calmly sorting through the morning's mail, she said to Roger, quite as if she didn't care, 'What sort of a scandal did you have upstairs, then?'

'Ah.' Roger didn't often gossip. For him to be doing it now meant the news must be something uncommonly interesting. 'Well,' he said, settling in, looking round to make sure that they couldn't be heard, 'the old man nearly gave poor Garcia the sack. It seems there's something of a shortage in the petty cash. The old man was reviewing the books at the weekend and found things were short by a few hundred pounds. That's why he had Garcia up this morning, called him on the carpet. And Garcia said he knew about the shortage; that he'd noticed it some months ago and watched it growing larger, but that he couldn't account for it being there. Which of course was an unlikely story, but the more the old man raged and shouted, the more Garcia held his ground, and they had it out in Spanish, and at last the old man told him, fine, they'd start again from scratch, but if the money should fall short again, then,' he slashed his throat from ear to ear with one neat finger. 'Anyhow, Garcia demanded a new petty-cash box, with new keys, so I'd imagine that will end his troubles.'

Jenny asked him, 'You don't think he did it?'

'My darling girl, if an accountant wants to rob his company, he'd be far more creative about it, and he'd likely steal more than a few hundred quid.'

Regina agreed. 'Who, then?'

She already had her suspicions, but she wanted to see whether Roger might share them. He did. With a quirk of one eyebrow, he asked them, as teacher to pupils, 'Well, who kept the petty cash before Garcia?'

Jenny said, 'Mr Emmerson, wasn't it? I know he left not long after I started, but—'

'And who did Mr Emmerson – and his keys, presumably – go home with every Friday night, for dinner?'

'Who?' Jenny asked.

Roger looked at Regina. She said, 'Have you said anything to Mr Reynolds?'

'Heavens, no. No, I dislike Spivey as much as the next person, but I know better than to cross him, or accuse him without evidence. He's slippery – he can slide around the issue and come out unscathed, and next you know, *your* head is on the chopping block, instead of his. Just look what became of our poor young American friend.'

Jenny lowered her head, and Roger, as though suddenly realising what he'd said, turned and started to say something to her, but just then the outer door opened and closed with a wind-driven bang, and the inner door opened and they were no longer alone.

Roger cheerfully greeted the man who came in. 'Ah, Vivian. Just the man I was looking for.'

Vivian Spivey hunched out of his overcoat, shaking the remnants of rain from its folds as he hung it on the rack beside the door. 'Oh? Why is that?' He took his hat off with one long, thin, hand – an undertaker's hand, Regina thought – and turned his long, thin face to Roger for an answer. His eyes were cold and empty of emotion.

Roger straightened from Regina's desk. 'Mr Reynolds had some questions about the number of barrels coming over on the next shipment. Do you have a moment to go over the manifests?'

'Yes, all right, then. Come on through,' Spivey told him, impatient.

The office seemed more airless without Roger to enliven it. Regina glanced over at Jenny, who was silently cranking a fresh sheet of paper into her typewriter, and she wondered if she ought to say something herself, as Roger had intended to, to comfort the younger girl, but in the end she thought it best to let the matter lie.

It was none of her business. Not that Roger wasn't right

– Spivey probably had been at the bottom of the young American's fall from grace. It hadn't been a secret that the two men had disliked each other, and she'd witnessed more than one occasion on which Spivey had manoeuvred to have somebody he didn't like removed from their position.

She was glad he hadn't managed to remove Manuel Garcia. But she knew the Spaniard wasn't in the clear, just yet. He'd have to watch his back. And so, she thought, would Andrew Deacon.

There was a sense, that New Year, of a turning of the tide; a sense the war might soon be over, and the world restored to… well, if not to normal, then to something rather better than it was at present. The optimism caught, and spread. The first few weeks of January, nearly all the talk around the office was about the much-anticipated Allied landings – when they'd likely come, and where.

'Perhaps Spain,' Spivey said, and his glance at Garcia was pure condescension. 'They wouldn't meet with much resistance there, I'm sure.'

Garcia, without looking up, reminded everybody in the room that Spain was neutral. 'We do not fight this war.'

'No, but you're in it, just the same. There's no such thing as being neutral,' Spivey said. 'Everyone, in time, comes down on one side or the other.'

Garcia raised his head. 'We have had our own years of war, in Spain. I fought then. I fought my countrymen, my brothers, and I learnt it is not always so easy to distinguish these "sides", as you call them, from one another, or to know which one is right.'

Deacon, watching silently as always, made no comment, but Regina thought that in his eyes she saw a new respect and liking for Garcia. After that, she noticed Deacon always stopped to say good morning to Garcia, and to exchange a few words, from politeness. That was how the two men each discovered that they shared a love of gardening. Regina overheard them once discussing some elusive wildflower by its Latin name.

'But yes, I know where this is growing,' Garcia was saying. 'Not far to the north, I will show you. I go there on Sundays, to paint.'

Deacon's eyebrows rose in interest. 'You're a painter?'

'Not a good one. It is only, how do you say it, my hobby. My wife would say I use it to escape the house, and her.' He smiled.

Regina hadn't seen Garcia smile much. It made him look a very different person; not so driven.

Deacon's smile was not so great a transformation, but she liked it, all the same. She found that she looked forward to it every morning, just as she looked forward to his quiet, undemanding presence, calming at the centre of her day.

Reynolds, also, appeared quite approving of Deacon. Three times now he'd had him to parties, and once to an Embassy lunch, introducing him round. And on one remarkable occasion he'd asked Deacon if he'd mind escorting Jenny to the theatre. *That* had caused some tongues to wag around the office. Reynolds had never asked anyone other than Roger Selkirk to stand in for him with Jenny, and the fact that he'd asked Deacon showed a great degree of trust.

It was clear that the significance of this had not escaped

their higher-ups. The messages for Deacon came more thickly now, and then one Friday afternoon word came that he should clear his next day's calendar, as JL Cayton-Wood would send a car for him at breakfast. Regina knew this because, when he got the message, Deacon called her to his office.

He looked thoughtful. 'Are you busy at the moment?' That was what he always said when she came in, no matter how pressing his own concerns might be, as though he didn't want to cause her inconvenience.

She assured him no, she wasn't.

'Good. Please, do sit down. I wondered, could you tell me what you know about Jack Cayton-Wood?'

She sat, and frowned a little. 'Well, I haven't met him often. I know my father does do business with him, now and then. Nearly everyone dealing with exports and imports in Lisbon must do business, at some time, with Mr Cayton-Wood. He virtually controls the harbour here – there is not much that can happen at the docks without his knowing and approving.'

'And how long has he been doing this?'

'A year, perhaps a little more. The man who held that job before him died, you see, quite suddenly, and Cayton-Wood had friends in the right places, so I understand. He is quite young, some think, to have such power, but before this he already was a military officer. He fought under Montgomery in North Africa. El Alamein.'

'Is that how he injured his leg?'

'Yes. It will never heal, I'm told. So he was discharged, and came here, to Lisbon.'

Deacon took this in, and then he asked her, 'Do you like him?'

'He is very well respected.'

'That's not what I asked.'

She said, honestly, 'No, I don't like him. I don't know why I don't, but there it is.' She wouldn't have spoken so plainly to anyone else, but with Deacon it seemed that he truly did want her opinion. In this instance, she couldn't help thinking he shared it.

She never did know where he went with Cayton-Wood, that Saturday, or what the men discussed. Her Alvaro, who was with them, said only that they'd spent the afternoon just north of Lisbon, in the spa town of Caldas da Rainha, where the hot sulphur springs had for centuries soothed, even healed, those in need. Cayton-Wood, Alvaro told her, took the waters for his leg. But Alvaro said little else, and Deacon, when she saw him in his office Monday morning, said less still.

He looked as though his thoughts were troubled. He'd turned his chair so that his gaze fell full upon his wedding photograph, and he was sitting there in silence, staring, so absorbed he didn't seem to hear Regina coming in. She set his coffee quietly beside him, on the desk.

She asked, 'Is everything all right?'

He didn't answer right away, but as she watched, his eyes turned with an effort from the portrait and he smiled shortly. 'Thank you for the coffee.'

He was thinking of his wife, she knew. But there was in his eyes a certain sadness that she didn't understand.

He said, 'I'm told that you're engaged to Alvaro Marinho, from the Embassy.'

'That's right.'

'He seems a very nice young man. A good man.'

'Yes, he is.'

'When will you marry?'

'We do not yet know. This war...'

'Ah, yes. This war.' He turned his face away, to look once again at the leather-framed portrait. 'What our lives might have been, were it not for this war.'

She followed his gaze, to the lively green eyes of his red-headed wife, and she couldn't help asking, 'Are you sure she wouldn't be happier here?'

He said gently, 'It isn't a question of happiness. She's much better off where she is. No, we must think first of those whom we love, not ourselves, and try always to do what is best for them.'

Saying the words aloud seemed to resolve something for him. Taking a sheet of stationery from his desk drawer he wrote four brief lines across it in his neatly slanting script, and signed it. Then he folded it and slipped it in an envelope. 'Here,' he said, writing a name on the envelope, 'could you please see that this gets delivered to the Hotel Rosa, in Caldas da Rainha?'

Regina glanced at the name on the envelope as he handed it over; it meant nothing to her. 'Of course.'

She knew she should have mentioned that delivery, and the name of the man whom the message had gone to, when she made her weekly report...but she didn't. It didn't seem right, somehow, spying on Deacon. Passing along things that Roger and Spivey and Manuel Garcia said, well, that was one thing. But Deacon was in the same business that she was – invading his privacy just seemed improper.

And so, the next week, when she learnt he'd been invited

to Garcia's home for dinner, she didn't put that detail in her report either.

She was, though, like everyone else at the office, amazed. Roger, stopping by her desk the next day after lunch, to chat, was keen for information. 'Did he tell you what the wife was like? I've never so much as glimpsed Manuel's wife, myself. I'm not even sure she exists.'

'She exists.' Regina smiled. 'She telephones him now and then.'

'Ah, so you've never seen her either? How very interesting.' He looked towards Deacon's office. 'He's not in, is he?'

'Mr Deacon? No, he's gone to see a painting.'

'Well, that's inconvenient.' Roger's eyes danced mischief. 'I shall have to have him round to *my* house for dinner, I suppose, if I want to learn anything.'

'Wouldn't it be simpler to invite Mr Garcia?'

'I have, darling. He didn't accept. I don't remember the excuse he used. The problem is, you see, he's Spanish, and the Spanish and we English have a thing. I don't know that they've ever really forgiven us for that Armada business.' He leant on her desk, arms folded. 'And now, of course, it's wolfram, and this Monreale affair.'

Regina stopped her filing for a moment to look up at him. 'What's that?'

'Monreale, my dear. He's Consul for the new Fascist republic the Italians have set up for themselves, at Salo. Franco's allowed him to open an office in Madrid, for passports, and the Allies are protesting. And last week in the House of Commons Eden said he'd warned the Spanish government to stop supplying wolfram to the Axis...'

'What is wolfram?'

'Tungsten, some call it. A black ore that's used as an alloy to harden steel – that makes it a strategic export, in a war. Anyhow, the Spanish have apparently been warned there might be quite grave consequences if they keep up the supply. Needless to say, they're not terribly fond of us, just at the moment. So I don't imagine Garcia would want to come over for dinner,' he said, summing up. 'No, I'm better off trying your nice Mr Deacon.'

That afternoon, Regina said to Deacon, 'Roger's going to ask you to dinner.'

'Oh, yes? Why is that?'

She smiled. 'I gather he's planning to pump you for information on Mr Garcia. He's like an old woman, he likes to know everyone's business.'

'It's a wonder no one tried persuading *him* to work intelligence,' said Deacon. 'It would have saved them the bother of bringing me over, not to mention the expense.'

'It was considered once.'

'But?'

'They didn't think him suitable.'

'Not because he was a homosexual, surely? It's common knowledge, isn't it? That would make him immune to blackmail.'

'No, it wasn't that. He drinks,' she said. 'Sometimes too much. And he's been known to use cocaine. He is a good man, but his habits make him vulnerable.'

'I see.' He thought a moment, then he asked, 'What does he drink?'

'Scottish whiskey.'

'Then I shall enjoy having dinner with Roger,' said Deacon, head bending again to his work. 'One couldn't get whiskey at all in New York.'

Regina Marinho smiled now, in remembrance. Pouring out a second cup of tea for each of us, she said, 'I did so like him. He was like a breath of clean air, in those offices. Really, I'd have worked for him for ever, if they'd let me. But of course, they didn't let me.'

She had never been to Deacon's flat. She'd never had a reason to, but Alvaro was ill today, and it was Saturday, and there had been a message from New York, and she'd been ordered to deliver it.

The house was in the Lapa district, not far from the Embassy, along a narrow sidestreet that fell steeply to the harbour. Deacon had the third-floor flat. His windows had a dizzy view across the jumbled red-tiled roofs that hugged the hill below. To the east a wall of dark cloud rose above the water, but the sun was bright against it, and the specks of wheeling seabirds were a blinding white.

Regina watched the birds and waited patiently while Deacon decoded the message, in case he should need to send back a reply. This was a different code, not meant for her eyes, nor for anyone else at the Embassy. Deacon had gone to the next room to do the decoding; she didn't know what key he used.

It wasn't her concern. She only knew what she was meant to know, and nothing more. But she could not resist, this first time being here in Deacon's flat, the urge to wander round and see what details of his life she might discover.

The flat had come furnished, she knew, and the sofas and tables and curtains were simple and spare. One armchair had been moved from its deeply indented place on the carpet to a new spot near the window, and the smoking-table at its side was weighted by a stack of books – the one on top a novel by the author Nevil Shute, the next below it a collection of the poems of Rupert Brooke.

She was looking to see what the other ones were when a knock at the door interrupted.

Deacon heard it too. He came through from the back room and warned her to silence, then motioned for her to change places with him, ushering her into the back room and closing the door between them as he went to find out who had knocked.

Regina saw the single bed, the chest of drawers, and realised that the only thing more damning to her character than being found in Andrew Deacon's flat would be to be found in his bedroom. With that in mind, she kept close to the door, so that if it were suddenly opened she could at least try to stay hidden behind it.

She heard a man's voice, angry. Cayton-Wood. His walking stick stabbed at the floor with each step as he entered the sitting room. '...shockingly poor judgement,' he was saying.

Deacon's voice calmly replied, 'I was told I might use my discretion.'

'Discretion!'

'Garcia invited me. I saw no harm in accepting.'

'You ought to have cleared it with us first. With me.'

'Why?'

'Because Manuel Garcia is a Spanish agent!'

'Yes, I knew that.'

'What?'

'He's not a very good one,' Deacon said. 'I'd say he transmits once a week, from somewhere not far north of here, by radio. I doubt he'd be the person passing on high-level secrets – he'd have no way to access them, really – but from time to time I've seen him looking round in Spivey's office, so perhaps he keeps Madrid informed of our oil shipments.'

Regina heard a match strike, and Cayton-Wood's next words were faintly muffled as though he were speaking while lighting his pipe. 'Figured this out on your own, did you?'

'It wasn't difficult. I should imagine you saw it yourself, quite some time ago. How did you manage to turn him?'

A pause, then again the imperious, 'What?'

'He does work for us, as well, doesn't he?'

The open annoyance in Cayton-Wood's voice was tempered by a grudging admiration. 'It appears, Mr Deacon, that I may have underestimated you.'

Deacon said nothing.

Cayton-Wood said, 'He came to us, Garcia did. His wife's health is poor, and he needed the money. He was already transmitting each week to Madrid, so we kept to that schedule, but under our own supervision. He sends them what we tell him to send – a little truth, a little fiction. Keeps the fish firmly on the hook, you might say.' A longer pause, and then, almost carelessly, 'How did you know he transmitted by radio?'

'We've talked a few times about radios; it's clear he knows his way around the equipment, but there was nothing at his house. I looked.'

'And why did you assume that his transmission point was somewhere to the north?'

'Something he said to me once.'

'Ah.' When no further explanation came, Cayton-Wood said simply, 'Well, just see you keep away from him, in future. All agents can be dangerous, and a turned agent is the least trustworthy of all.'

'Don't worry,' Deacon said. 'I'll watch my step.'

Regina, standing on her side of the closed door, couldn't see the look that passed between the two men, but she felt it. It was tangible, electric in the room.

'You do that,' Cayton-Wood said, almost as a challenge. Then the heavy rhythmic tapping of the walking stick recrossed the floor; the front door opened, closed, and he was gone.

The next week, on the 28th of January, Britain and America cut off their oil supplies to Spain to punish Franco for his staunch refusal to stop selling wolfram to the Axis powers.

The offices at Reynolds were in chaos. One of their tankers, en route to a Spanish port, had to be diverted to the docks at Lisbon. Letters and cables from Reynolds's brother-in-law in Madrid came so thickly that Regina had a hard time keeping pace with them. The letters all sang the same song – was there not some way Reynolds could help lift the oil embargo? And Reynolds would always reply, in his various wordings, that no, he could not. But because Regina didn't know if some more subtle message might be hiding in between those lines, she intercepted all the letters anyway, and the Embassy's experts were forced to work full speed to open and reseal each one before it could be missed.

She didn't see much of Deacon. He kept busy, these days, cataloguing works of art that Reynolds bought at auction, searching out the works that Reynolds ought to buy, appraising others. He spent hours in the storage vaults upstairs, or on the telephone with dealers and restorers, and whatever time was left he seemed to spend with Ivan Reynolds. But he still made a point, every day on arriving, of saying good morning to her, and to Jenny, and of stopping by Manuel Garcia's desk to say hello.

Regina didn't know, herself, how she should be now, with Garcia. She was not supposed to know he was a spy, and so she did her best to act the way she always had around him, but she found it very difficult, with what she knew, to not pay more attention to his actions. She'd never noticed him before, as Deacon had, in Spivey's office, but a few times these past weeks she'd seen him just outside the door, while Spivey was at lunch. She mentioned this in her reports, and left the matter there.

One morning, as she walked to work, a car drew up beside her. An expensive car – a long, black Humber limousine. She'd seen it several times before; she knew it would be Cayton-Wood in the back, before he'd cranked the window down. He wished her good morning, and smiled, and said, 'Do let me give you a lift.'

'That's very kind, but I don't mind the walk.'

'My dear, I must insist. It's only business, don't be nervous.'

She wasn't nervous, getting in the car; but she was watchful. She knew he was high up in British Intelligence – that put them on the same side, but she still kept an eye on the streets they were driving through, wanting to be very sure they weren't making a detour.

He asked, 'How's your father this morning? All right?'

The way he asked that brought a faint frown to her forehead. She had not seen her father for two days, which wasn't that unusual, except, 'Why would he not be?'

'It's only that I wondered, after last night...'

She was worried, now. 'What happened last night?'

'You haven't heard? The Vigilance Committee, they were raided at their meeting by the local police. I'm not certain what the charges were, but I believe things did get rather nasty.' He glanced up from tamping fresh tobacco into his pipe. 'It won't happen again, though. I've told them they'll be under my protection from now on.' He struck a match into the silence between them, and puffed out the smoke without asking her whether she minded. 'That's not what I wanted to tell you, though. No, I've got good news, for you and your young man. You're free to get married.'

She stared at him. 'Sorry, I'm...what?'

'As of next week, we no longer need you at Reynolds. We appreciate your having stayed this long, of course, and the personal sacrifices that you've made on our behalf, but happily that's finished now. You're free to get on with your life.'

She hadn't expected that. For a few moments, she didn't know how to react. 'But,' she argued slowly, 'Mr Deacon... that is, surely *he* still needs me there.'

'Don't worry about Mr Deacon.'

She did worry, though. All through the following week, as she made preparations to leave; made excuses to Reynolds, to Jenny, to everyone else, she was worrying, still, about Deacon. With her gone, he'd be on his own. He'd relied on her this far, for so many things, for so many small details, and errands, and now…it was almost as if they were *wanting* to take away all his support; leave him stranded. She'd said so to Alvaro. She'd said, 'This doesn't feel right. I shouldn't be leaving him now, not like this.'

Alvaro had simply shrugged and said, 'You cannot fight a man like JL Cayton-Wood, Regina. You must do as he decides. And anyway,' – he'd held her face in both his hands and smiled – 'we can be married now.'

Deacon himself had been decent about it. He'd given her a little silver brooch for a going-away gift, and he'd done his best to reassure her he'd be fine.

'You'll have to be careful,' she'd said, 'around Spivey.'

'I will be.'

And when she had looked at him, still unconvinced, he had told her, 'It's all right. To every thing there is a season, don't forget. Your war is over now, Regina. You have earned your time of peace. Go and be happy.'

She'd nodded, and her gaze had for the last time fallen on the coloured photograph of Deacon and his wife. She'd asked, 'You will come to the wedding?'

'Yes, of course.'

And he had come. He'd stood at the back of the church, half in shadow, through the ceremony, and when she and Alvaro had turned to face their guests she'd seen him smiling. But later, when she'd looked for him outside, he wasn't there. He'd slipped away, unnoticed in the crowd.

'That was in March.' She looked at me and smiled, a shade regretfully. 'I didn't see him after that. I didn't make it to the funeral, Mr Reynolds's funeral, sadly. I was ill.'

I was thinking. 'Ivan Reynolds' death…you're sure that it was natural? I mean, it wasn't—'

'Murder? No, my dear, that one I'm sure of. He had cancer of the pancreas. It took him rather swiftly, so he hadn't long to suffer, poor man. No, he wasn't murdered. I've been trying,' she confessed, 'to think whom Mr Deacon might have meant. It *was* wartime, of course, and Lisbon was a place of danger. There were many deaths.' Her forehead creased a little, trying to recall. 'Roger would know more than I would about things like that.'

She had said that in the tones of someone speaking of a mutual acquaintance, as though she took it for granted I'd be speaking to this Roger. 'Roger Selkirk?' I asked, sorting through the names of all the people in her narrative.

'That's right. Did you ask him about murders when you met him?'

I was confused now. 'I've never met him.'

'Oh, but, I assumed… I'm sorry, dear, but it was Roger who first rang to let me know that you were here, and that you'd like to come to see me, and could he please give you my address and number, so I naturally assumed you'd been to talk to him.'

He must have been the source, I thought, to whom Joaquim, my English Cemetery man, had gone – the person whom Joaquim had thought might still know where to find Regina. Had I known, I might have met with him before I'd come to Evora. Frustration at the missed opportunity coloured my voice as I said, 'No, I got your address from someone else. I never met Roger Selkirk. Does he still live in Lisbon?'

'Oh, yes, and of course you must speak to him. Roger's a

character. And he'll appreciate having a pretty young girl to tell stories to. Here, let me get his address for you.' Standing, she crossed to a small roll-top writing desk in the far corner and opened a drawer to explore among the envelopes and papers.

Journalism, I thought, was all about asking the right questions, at the right time. I asked carefully, 'Is there anyone else I should speak to?'

She tipped her head, thinking. 'Well, Jenny, of course. Jenny Saunders that was, Jenny Augustine, now.'

'Reynolds's mistress?'

'Oh, my dear,' she said gently, as one who knows better, 'she wasn't his mistress. No, she was his daughter.'

That floored me. 'His *daughter*?'

'That's right.'

'But…the biographies, the articles…well, no one ever mentions he had children.'

'No one knew, outside the company. Inside, there were a few of us, but Mr Reynolds was a careful man. He'd known the Lindberghs, you see, when their baby was kidnapped and killed, and it had quite a lasting effect on him. He was terribly paranoid; always concerned someone might try to do harm to Jenny, if they knew that she was his daughter. So he let her mother raise her, in America.' She added, '*She* was kept a secret, too, the mother. Almost no one knew about her. An actress, I think she was. Quite independent. But Jenny herself was a bit of a handful; she had a strong mind of her own, and when she finished school she was bound and determined to live with her father, so he brought her over to Lisbon.'

'But didn't she mind…I mean, the rumours about them…'

'Oh, Jenny didn't care what people thought, and Mr Reynolds didn't, either. They were exactly like each other, in that way, although at times I think that she was more than even *he* could handle. Still, she was great fun.' She closed one drawer; opened another. 'I'm sure she'll be able to help you. There wasn't much that went on in those days that she wasn't aware of. She was quite a bit sharper than most people realised, you know…she still is.' Finding the envelope she wanted, she reached for a notepad and started to write. 'I don't know if she's still at this address, mind. We used to have a card at Christmas, but it's been a few years. She was living in Washington. Georgetown. A lovely old house. She's alone now, and doesn't see visitors often.' She gave me the address, and added, with certainty, 'But she'll see you. She had rather a thing for your grandfather, Jenny did. Thought he was wonderful.' Looking back down, she said, 'All of us did.'

It was hard for me to reconcile her statement with the colourless old man I'd met in London, whose face I couldn't even bring to mind. Ask the right question, I thought again, at the right moment: 'You wouldn't happen to have any photographs of him?'

'Your grandfather? Yes, I should think so.' Another desk drawer opened, protesting. 'It would be here, if I had one. A bit of a jumble, I'm afraid. I never was much good at putting things in proper albums. My husband always said…ah, here we are. That's your grandfather, third from the right.'

I took the photo from her hand with great anticipation. It had been taken out of doors, against a high hedge – several people standing smiling in a row, the men in dapper suits and hats that made them look not unlike gangsters, and the women neatly packed into the slender hourglass dresses of the Forties, some with gloves. They would be very old now, all of them, I thought. Quite old, or dead. And yet their faces, frozen laughing in the snapshot, were as youthful as my own.

I counted the heads from the right…one, two, three…

He was average height, neither the tallest man there, nor the shortest; his build neither heavy nor slight. And he'd turned, at the moment the camera had snapped, to the woman beside him, to listen or speak, so his features had blurred from the motion. I couldn't make anything out but the fact he was clean-shaven. Maybe, I thought, if you already knew what he looked like, it would have been easy to tell who he was. But for me, with no image to work from, he might have been faceless. Invisible.

'He was very nice-looking,' said Regina Marinho. 'Not flashy, but nice-looking.'

'Yes,' I agreed. For, what else could I say?

'I always distrusted the flashy ones. Cayton-Wood, he was a handsome man, terribly handsome, but not the same league as your grandfather. Not someone you could depend on. That's him, on the left, with the moustache.'

A tall man, and notably good-looking, as she'd said, with his dark hair and Douglas Fairbanks grin. I wouldn't trust him either, I decided.

'He's dead, too,' she said. 'Though that's no loss. He went back to England before the war's end, and he died there. He drowned, I believe, while out sailing.'

She was waiting for the photograph. I handed it back, not

bothering to ask if I could keep it. I could tell from simply looking at her face she wasn't one to part with memories. But she gave me, in its place, another tidy piece of notepaper with Roger Selkirk's Lisbon address written on it. I copied both addresses – Roger's and Jenny's – with care in my notebook, and tucked the originals safely away.

'You'll enjoy Roger, I think,' she said. 'He's a far better teller of stories than I am.'

Which was her polite and gentle way, I knew, of saying she was growing tired; that it was time to end our interview. Not that I could blame her – even without looking at my watch, I could tell from the change in the light outside the window that the afternoon was giving way to evening. I had taken up enough of her time.

Switching off my tape recorder, I pocketed the small machine and stood. 'You did a wonderful job, really. Thank you so much.'

'If it helped at all, my dear, then you're quite welcome.' Smiling, she shook my hand. Then, almost in the manner of an afterthought, she said, 'You mentioned danger.'

'Pardon?'

'You said earlier my life might be in danger. Could you tell me how?'

It surprised me to discover I'd forgotten, clean forgotten, in the course of actually meeting Regina Marinho and hearing her talk, that I'd come here not only to learn what she knew, but to warn her. I said, 'I'm so sorry. I should have told you right at the beginning, you should know.'

I didn't tell her all of it. I didn't mention Grandma Murray's death, or what had happened in Toronto, because telling her all that would mean I'd have to blow my cover and reveal my true connection to the story. But I *did* tell her my theory that somebody else was on the same path I was, and I told her all about the grey car this morning, and the woman who had spoken to me in the street, and what I'd learnt from Anabela, last night over dinner.

'I see.' She took it all in, unperturbed. 'And this Jankowski person, then, is...?'

'I don't know, exactly. But I know that he – or she – was also looking for your address. M Jankowski, was the name. It might be nothing...' But I didn't think, myself, that it was nothing. I remembered Anabela pointing out that M Jankowski was a Polish name. The woman here in Evora who'd faced me in the shuttered street had spoken with an Eastern European accent.

'On the other hand,' I said, 'I'd feel much better if I knew that you'd be careful.'

'My dear, you needn't worry. I'll take care. And I have others who'll take care of me.' She smiled, and raised her gaze again to mine, and then, 'You have her eyes,' she said, on a note of discovery. 'Your grandmother's eyes. Oh, that must have pleased Mr Deacon. He loved her so much.'

My mind travelled back to a day in September, to an old grey man who'd looked into my face the way Regina Marinho was looking right this minute, and who'd said 'You have her eyes,' but in a different sort of voice, and who had walked off lost in thoughts – or maybe memories – so deep he'd failed to notice the approaching car, the danger...

'Yes,' I told her quietly, 'I do believe he did.'

* * *

270

I stopped in the Cathedral square.

My mind had been preoccupied, for several minutes now, with the unsettling thought that I had missed something this afternoon; had seen it and had let it pass without an understanding of its true importance. The feeling was so strong I nearly turned round to go back to Regina Marinho's, then held myself in check with a reminder that I didn't know if it was something I had seen or something I had heard, and either way the moment was now lost. I couldn't get it back. The best that I could do now was to focus my subconscious in the hope that I'd eventually remember.

So I stopped in the Cathedral square, and tried to think. It was a contemplative place, not large, with lovely older buildings all around a quiet stand of mottled plane trees and some other lace-like trees whose name I didn't know. And, framed by these, at the square's farther end, there rose a ruined Roman temple.

It was an unexpected sight. The great Cathedral, with its towers and its turrets and its deeply carved front entrance, had been built to impress; to dominate the square, but the little Roman temple, with its fallen, broken columns, stole the eye, and the imagination.

It drew me to it, making me forget, for just that moment, why I'd come here, and the weariness I felt, and all my troubles.

I had always had a love of ancient history – of heroic deeds and tales of war and gods of old mythology – and I felt like a child, filled with wonder and awe, as I tipped my head back... far, far back, to stare upwards.

The temple soared above me, high on its stone podium,

its fluted columns standing like a skeleton against the early evening sky. The south colonnade was entirely gone, but the three sides remaining were remarkably untouched, the long flat fascia stones still resting on the fancy upturned capitals. I only had to squint, and I could picture it intact. In this light, I could even imagine the ghosts of the Romans who'd worshipped there, moving among the long shadows.

And then, in one breath of the breeze, the ghosts vanished, chased off by the modern-day sounds of more people approaching. Another tour group – Evora appeared to be a magnet for them – poured into the little square and gathered at the temple's base expectantly, their faces upturned, as was mine, with obvious appreciation.

A good-looking young man with very tight trousers pushed through to the front of the group, where he turned to address them. 'OK, everyone, I'm going to ask you please to come closer, otherwise I'll be shouting. Now, we are standing at the main religious centre of Evora, from the Roman times till nowadays. Behind me what you have now is the Roman temple, called sometimes the Temple of Diana. We are lucky to have such a temple here, is very rare, because the Roman temples often disappear. This is a small one, from the first century before Christ, and was saved because they used it from the late years of the thirteenth century till the nineteenth century, it was used as a slaughterhouse, so it was entirely covered with walls, with mortar and brick walls. Then came the nineteenth century, and it was a very romantic time, you know, when people were dreaming of the old civilisations like Greece and Rome, and they had just discovered a short time ago the ruins of Pompeii, and they were so enthusiastic with that, they started to imitate the old styles of art. The same movement in Portugal, and we paid more attention to these ruins, and so it was discovered that we had this precious monument beneath the bricks.'

Which only went to show, again, I thought, that things weren't always what they seemed to be.

I was listening to the young guide explaining the finer points of Roman temple architecture, pointing out how granite had been used to build the lower parts, the columns, while the finer, more delicate detailing on the Corinthian capitals had been done in marble, when I spotted, with surprise, a now-familiar face among the tourists.

He had seen me, too. His brown eyes smiled at me above the crowd, as though he found the constant crossing of our paths amusing.

When the tour group shuffled off to the Cathedral, the American stayed put.

'Hello,' he said, as if our meeting here were natural. He was reaching for his camera, with his eyes fixed on the temple, but he stopped me when I would have moved. 'No, stay,' he said. 'If you don't mind. It helps to give a sense of scale.' He took the shot, and, lowering the camera, closed the space between us, coming over. 'Look, if we're going to keep this up, we should probably introduce ourselves. I'm Matt.'

I hesitated. Shook the hand he offered. 'Katherine.'

'Katherine. Hi.' He wasn't really flirting. It was friendliness, I thought, and nothing more. It was one of the truisms of travel that people on vacation in a foreign land would always tend to bond with the familiar.

I felt something of the same bond, too. I'd been so on edge

all day, between the drive down and my sense of being followed in the streets and that strange woman who had spoken to me – everything had left me feeling painfully aware of how alone I was, how isolated; so there was a definite appeal in standing here, now, in the company of somebody I recognised, whose eyes held no agenda.

I felt safe. And I was in no rush to lose that feeling, so instead of pointing out that his tour group was now nearly at the Cathedral, I asked, 'So, what brings you to Evora?'

'Romans. I can't resist places like this.' He pushed his hands deep in his pockets and nodded upwards at the ruined temple. 'You?'

'Oh, just a day trip.'

'Then you're heading back to Lisbon? When, tonight?'

I shook my head. 'Tomorrow.' I'd intended, when I'd first set out this morning, to just come here, do my interview, and turn around as quickly as I could, but that had been before my close encounter with the Renault Clio. I had taken a hotel because there wasn't any force that would have driven me back out onto that highway, after dark. I'd wait until the morning. Wait for light.

He said, 'Then let me buy you dinner. If you don't have any plans, that is.' I hadn't expected the smile. I hadn't thought that he would look at me that way, not in my current incarnation, with my mouse-brown hair and glasses and my ordinary clothes. My disguise had been designed to not attract attention, after all, and I'd have thought that, to a man like Matt, I'd scarcely register.

'Don't you eat with your group?' I asked.

'What? Oh, them.' He looked, as I was looking, at the

people who were clustered now around their guide outside the steps of the Cathedral. 'No, I'm not with them. I'm here on my own. They were just standing here when I came out, you know, so I thought I'd stay and listen.'

I glanced around. 'When you came out of where?'

'I'm staying right here, at the *pousada* – like a state-run bed and breakfast, in the old monastery.' He pointed to the long white building stretching low behind him. 'I've got a great view of this temple from my window.' Then he asked, 'What about you? Where are you staying?'

'Nowhere like this. Just a hotel.' I considered his offer as I took a long look round the emptying square. The tour group was moving into the Cathedral. That left just a few people wandering round, and in the waning light the place had taken on a sense of loneliness. I couldn't shake the memory of those footsteps, sure and certain, coming after me this afternoon, through narrow winding streets, and of the woman who had told me that some creatures didn't know when they'd been caught.

I hadn't seen her since, though I'd been searching every sidewalk for her face. But that meant nothing. She might well be watching me, and waiting for another opportunity to get me on my own.

I looked at Matt, and borrowed courage from his air of rugged capability. 'I don't have any plans,' I said. 'I'd love to go for dinner.'

'Great. I saw this little place around the corner, it's not far.'

Walking beside him, I knew I had chosen my bodyguard wisely. He walked on the street side, to guard me from traffic.

I couldn't remember the last time a man under fifty had done that. Later, I knew, when our dinner was done, he would likely be one of those men who would walk me back down to my hotel, with no expectations. And if anybody *did* step from a shadowy corner, he looked like he could handle it.

I never would remember, after, much about the restaurant that he took me to, except that it was small, and very crowded, and alive with conversation. I felt warm. There were warm smells of food around me, and warm light reflecting through glasses of red wine, and warm bodies packed to the rough-plastered walls. And there was a piano. An older piano, a small one, that seemed to be there for the ambiance. No one was playing. I noticed it only because it was near us, and because I had such trouble holding Matt's gaze while we talked – I needed something else to focus on, to help me keep my balance.

He spoke Portuguese, and read it well enough to tell me what was on the menu, and to carry on an easy conversation with the waiter, when we ordered.

So I asked him, 'Have you been to Portugal before?'

'No,' he said. 'This is a first for me.'

'Oh. I thought maybe you had family here.'

'Because I speak the language, you mean? No, I don't know anybody, here. All my family connections outside of the States are in South America. My mother's from Brazil,' he said. 'That's how I learnt my Portuguese.'

'And you're from…where? From Boston?'

'Near there.' His slanted a look at me. 'Accent gave me away, did it? I get ribbed about it at work, a lot. People tell me I sound like a Kennedy.'

I smiled. 'You don't work in Boston, then?'

'No.' I caught the flash of humour in his eyes, and realised I was asking questions in the same efficient way I ran an interview. I couldn't help it. That was how I'd learnt to interact with people, working at the *Sentinel*. Besides, I'd spent this afternoon exploring Deacon's past, and I was still in journalistic mode. Except, nobody was supposed to know I was a journalist.

I reached for my water glass, glancing around at the tables close by us. Nobody looked threatening, though there was one middle-aged woman two tables over with whom I would not have enjoyed crossing swords. She was sitting with an older couple – her parents, I presumed, from her resemblance to the man. They looked, all three of them, a little out of sorts, as though they'd only just been arguing.

Matt was asking, 'So what about you? Where are you from? Your accent's Canadian, isn't it?'

I brought my attention back. 'Yes.'

'I knew a guy in college, came from Canada. From Renfrew, Ontario. Do you know where that is?'

'No,' I lied. 'I'm from Vancouver.'

'Oh. And what do you do?'

I was ready for that. Tony'd coached me very well, and I had chosen as my cover occupation something I'd spent several summers doing – working at the checkout of a grocery store. It might not be too glamorous, but nobody could trip me up on the details. And I'd travelled enough on the West Coast to answer any question he might ask about Vancouver with authority.

I found it a relief, though, when the talk swung back around to him.

Matt proved to be good company, and good at conversation. I learnt he was a lawyer, never married, with no children; that he owned an Airedale terrier named Reuben, who was staying with the neighbours; that he was an only child. His parents lived in Arizona.

'I find they're getting crankier with age,' he said, and grinned. 'Are yours like that?'

'No.' I looked again towards the little family group two tables over. The older of the two women, the mother, would have been about my Grandma Murray's age, and with that realisation I felt, suddenly, the crushing weight of what I'd lost. Felt the urge, too, to go tell the grumpy daughter not to waste her time in petty quarrels. Life was never long enough.

The old man at that table stood, and, heedless of the protests of the women, made his way to the piano, where he sat, and set his shoulders, and began to play. He played quite well, from memory.

Matt was watching too. 'He's very good.'

I nodded. I could not have done more then, than nod, because I'd recognised the song. It had been Grandma Murray's favourite: 'Make Believe'.

Had I been a person of more faith, I might have thought that she was trying to communicate, to comfort me. But even though I didn't, in my heart, believe that possible, and even though I knew that I was utterly alone, I closed my eyes and felt her spirit with me, briefly, in this far-off, foreign place.

Deacon couldn't see the soldier playing the piano on account of all the girls who'd gathered round the young man, laughing, pressing closer, each one urging him to play a tune especially for them.

Across the table, Cayton-Wood, filling his pipe, said, 'He's good, isn't he? Came in last Saturday week. I'm debriefing him. Tea?'

Deacon accepted the offer, and settled himself in his chair, waiting. He hadn't been keen to come back here, to Caldas da Rainha, any more than he had wanted to have lunch with Cayton-Wood, but the request had been official.

He had thought, at first, that he was being set up for a reprimand, but Cayton-Wood was acting in an unexpected manner. If Deacon hadn't known any better, he'd have said the other man was getting ready to apologise.

The tea came, and was poured, and Cayton-Wood glanced over. 'Look,' he said, 'I may have been a little heavy-handed, when I ordered you to stay clear of Garcia. You were using your best judgement, as you said.'

Deacon, hiding his surprise, said nothing.

Cayton-Wood went on, 'In fact, given our latest position with Spain, it appears to me your friendship with Garcia could be useful.'

'Oh? How so? I thought he'd already been turned.'

'He has been. But this situation with our cutting off petroleum supplies, it's having a tremendously destabilising effect in Spain. Franco won't say it, of course, but his people are suffering great deprivation. He's desperate for petroleum, from any source, at any price. We've noticed no fewer than three Spanish agents, new agents, in Lisbon.' His empty teacup rattled in the saucer as he set it down. 'Garcia's not a bad man, and he's helped us willingly enough, but there will be new pressure on him now, from Madrid, and I'm not sure how he will weather it.'

Deacon acknowledged this. 'And I'm to do what, exactly?'

'Observe him. Just that. Take your drives in the country, the way you were doing. Have dinner at his house, invite him to yours. Be as sociable as you like with the Garcias, provided you keep your eyes open. Let us know who comes and goes, and what his state of mind is. We need to be certain he's still on our side.'

'Understood.' Deacon's own tea had grown cold in the cup. He looked toward the corner, where the young soldier playing piano was still holding court with his girlish admirers.

Cayton-Wood followed his gaze. 'I rather think the uniform is much of the attraction.' He spoke lightly, but the slight edge to his voice reminded Deacon that Cayton-Wood had worn a uniform himself once, and would still be in one now if fate had not decided otherwise. The dragon's-head walking stick stabbed at the floor as he stood. 'I'll go see what's become of our driver. Wait here.'

Deacon sat for a moment in silence, then reached for his cigarette case. Catching the eye of the waitress, he motioned her over. 'That chap at the piano, does he take requests?'

She shrugged. 'I can ask him. What song would you like?'

Deacon told her.

He watched her approach the young soldier, and ask. The music stopped a moment, then the soldier raised his head and gave a friendly nod to Deacon, and began to play.

It sounded no less beautiful in this small, rustic room than it had sounded in New York:

We could make believe I love you,
Only make believe that you love me.
Others find peace of mind in pretending;
Couldn't I? Couldn't you? Couldn't we…?

Deacon might have closed his eyes if he had been alone, but he was not. Instead he looked towards the window without seeing it, and lit his cigarette.

Evora felt different in the dark.

Within the walls, the town took on a cloistered feel, medieval – yellow lights from tavern doorways slanting out across the rough-edged granite cobblestones; little huddled groups of people clopping past us down a narrow curve of street, beneath the tightly shuttered windows of the silent, sleeping houses. Again, if I just squinted, I could half believe I'd been transported back in time, expecting to hear wagon wheels creak by instead of, every now and then, the quiet thrumming of a car that made us press against the buildings as it slowly slipped on past.

Matt walked again on the outside, to shield me. His shoulder almost brushed mine with each step. I was aware of him, and fighting the sensation.

We had reached the small Cathedral square. The Temple of Diana rose majestically in floodlights, soaring high on its stone podium, its fluted columns standing like a skeleton beneath the cloud-chased moon.

The moon was perfect – pale and full, and great black sections of the clearing sky were deep with stars. As settings went, it was incredibly Romantic, in the true sense of the word. I could easily imagine some great poet – Byron, maybe – sitting musing in the ruins, and I felt a primal pull to do the same.

Matt must have felt it too. 'You want to have a closer look?'

'All right.' I made my own way up, climbing the uneven, crumbling edge of the podium, scrambling over the great blocks of granite, finding my footholds with care in the stone, and enjoying the view that I gained over Evora, little lights spreading out far and below me, and close in the foreground the huge rounded columns, half shadow, half bright in the wash of the floodlights. Nearby a section of column had toppled to lie on its side like a giant stone log, and I perched on it, soaking up atmosphere, while Matt explored.

Even derelict, this ancient spot felt sacred, and protective. Surely nothing could come near me here, to do me harm. I felt removed from danger.

So it gave me an unpleasant jolt to hear the footsteps coming through the square towards the temple, sure and certain. Some startled creature – a bat or a nightbird – shot suddenly out of the temple above me, in panic. I stood up myself, and turned.

Nothing was there. Only the empty square, with its tall army of rustling trees, and the watchful Cathedral.

'It's quite a place, isn't it?' Matt stepped clear of the columns and into the glare of the floodlights, that cast him in shadow, enormous, against the pale stone. Then he looked at me properly. 'Are you OK?'

I was more relieved to see him than I would have cared to say. Relieved to not be on my own. 'I heard footsteps.' I glanced behind a second time, to make sure that the square was truly empty.

'They must have been mine. An echo, or something.' He grinned. 'Or a ghost.'

'I don't believe in ghosts,' I said. 'Do you?'

He shrugged. 'It's hard to spend any time in a place like this, and not believe in ghosts.'

I didn't disagree. I only said, 'It's getting cold.' The peace of my surroundings had been spoilt for me, and it was time to leave.

I would have found my own way down, but Matt was there already, offering his hand to help me balance on the steep descent. It wasn't the first time we'd touched. Only this time the contact was different – it lingered, even after I'd been solidly delivered to the ground. And when he finally took his hand away, I missed it.

He was watching me. I felt the angle of his gaze and raised my chin to meet it, and we stood a moment looking at each other in the shadow of the temple. The *pousada*, and the room where he was staying, were just steps away, but he made no attempt to use the moonlight, or the moment, to his own advantage.

When he spoke, he only said, 'You're shivering. Come on, I'll get the car, and take you back to your hotel. You'll be warmer if we drive.'

I didn't say much in the car. The drive was a short one, and I spent it mostly reminding myself that this wasn't the place or the time.

If I'd met Matt a month ago… But I had been a different person then.

And this was not a man like Patrick, not a man – or so I sensed – who saw relationships as games; who cast them off without a care. To be involved with Matt would be to be *involved*, and on a level that I couldn't reach, just now. Not when my energies were focused so consumingly on searching for the truth, and on survival.

And that passing thought of Patrick helped me find and keep my level. Patrick might be dead now, on account of me. I had no way of knowing. Guy was keeping up enquiries at his end, but I'd been warned I shouldn't try to call, myself. You never knew who might be listening.

But as of Thursday evening, when I'd left, I'd had no word of Patrick, or of Margot. So however tempting it might be – and it *was* very tempting – to stay close to Matt, to go on feeling safe, and keep the comfort of his company, I knew I shouldn't do it. I'd been wrong to bring him into this at all. I didn't want anyone else that I knew getting hurt, and even the armour of a white knight was no shield against the aim of an assassin.

I looked at him more closely, at the slightly rugged features and the laugh-lines at the corners of his eyes, and wished again it could have been another time, not this – a time when we could both have met as simple tourists.

He, of course, blocked from the tangle of my thoughts, continued on as if we were exactly that – two people on a holiday, connecting. As we pulled up at the front of my hotel, he said, 'So you'll be going back to Lisbon in the morning?'

'Yes.'

'I was wondering…' He paused, and killed the engine. 'I'll be back there myself, in a couple of days, and I wondered if you'd maybe like to have dinner.'

It took me a minute to sort through my answer, to find the words to turn him down politely, and in the end he must have mistaken my silence for indecision.

'Think it over,' he said. 'Let me know. I'll be back Monday night. Not at the York House, though. I needed something closer to the airport. Here, let me give you the number.' He took a pen from one of his coat pockets and dug into the other with a frown. 'Damn, I don't have anything to write on. Do you have a piece of paper?'

My tidy speech of refusal wouldn't have the same effect now, I decided, so the least offensive thing to do would be to take his number, and say thank you, and just leave it at that. I'd failed to show up once already, for that coffee in the hotel bar – I doubted he'd be shattered if I didn't call, this time.

I rummaged in my own pockets, in search of a suitable scrap of paper, and found my rental car receipt. 'Here,' I said, but when I tried to draw it out, my hand dislodged another, smaller paper from my pocket, and Matt caught that as it fluttered to the seat.

'Thanks. That'll do.' There was writing already on one side, so he flipped it over, scrawling down a few lines in a firm, decisive hand. 'There you go,' he said, handing it back to me.

'Thank you.' I took it without looking at it, trying to say thank you in the larger sense, for everything. There wasn't any way, I knew, that he could understand. No way for him to know the value of the role he'd played, as bodyguard, this evening.

He turned his head, and held my gaze a fraction of a second, and he smiled. 'Anytime.'

I'd known he wouldn't try to kiss me, just as I'd known that he'd get out before me to come round and open my door. While I waited in my seat, I looked down at the paper I held in my hand and tried to read what he had written, by the half-light of the streetlamps. He had given me the name of the hotel where he'd be staying, and the phone number. But all I really noticed was his name. His full name.

Matt Jankowski.

He was at my door. He opened it, and cold night air rushed round me with a paralysing force. I counted two heartbeats, then three, before I pushed myself to move, to stand, to step clear of the car.

The car...

I hadn't paid too much attention, before, to what I'd been riding in. Now, from the sidewalk, I turned to look down at the gunmetal-grey Renault Clio.

Matt slammed my door shut and stepped onto the sidewalk beside me, his presence no longer a comfort, but something else. 'You want me to walk you to the door?' he asked.

My fist clenched round the paper with his name and number on it and I thrust it deep into my pocket, so he wouldn't see the shaking of my hand. I fought to keep my voice unchanged. 'No, thanks. I'm fine from here.'

'All right.' He smiled. 'Goodnight, then.'

I had never felt the urge to run as strongly as I felt it at that moment, and it took all my control to turn my back on him and calmly walk the twenty yards or so across the street to my hotel's bright entrance.

Matt stayed standing where he was and watched me, all the way. I know he did, because when I'd passed through the doors I glanced behind and saw him there, arms folded, leaning on his car.

I knew he wouldn't follow any further. Not tonight.

But I felt anything but safe.

It was cold on the balcony.

I had angled my chair on the hard floor tiles so I could sit with my back to the sliding glass door and have a view over the street and the sheltered outdoor café near the hotel's covered entrance. Here I saw everyone, coming and going.

Two balconies over, and one floor below me, a woman came out, smoked a cigarette, went back inside. I heard laughter. It seemed very far from my world.

My world, now, was reduced to one name: M Jankowski.

It wasn't an everyday name, and it wasn't very likely there'd be two of them touring round Portugal at the same time. And the grey Renault Clio was more than coincidence. It had undoubtedly been Matt who'd pulled up to the kerb in the rain yesterday, when I'd flagged down my taxi. He'd been there, at the cemetery, close enough to follow me; it would have been easy for him to have followed my cab to the York House Hotel. As easy as it would have been for him to follow me today, to Evora.

He hadn't needed to use Anabela's police friend to track down Regina Marinho's address – I had led him straight to her front door.

I'd tried phoning to warn her, just now, but the voice that had answered had been a new one – neither hers, nor the housekeeper's. A man's voice, middle-aged, and having trouble speaking English.

'No, she is not here,' he'd said. 'Is gone.'

I'd shifted the receiver. 'When will she be back?'

'*Not* here,' was all he would tell me, before hanging up.

That had worried me. Matt had been with me all evening, true enough, but he might not be working on his own. As Tony had once pointed out, who knew how many people might be in on this? Perhaps the woman who had spoken to me in the street this afternoon…perhaps a stranger, faceless, blending with the crowd. And while Matt had been keeping me occupied, someone else could have been killing Regina Marinho.

Maybe she'd taken my warning to heart, I thought. Maybe, being ex-Intelligence herself, she'd recognised the danger and had gone to ground somewhere where she'd be safe. I hoped she had. But still, I couldn't shake my sense of paranoia.

The wind bit chill. I drew my knees up to my chest and hugged them, tightly. I'd been certain all along, of course, that those who'd murdered Deacon, and his nephew, and my grandmother, would send someone to Portugal, to track and kill the few remaining witnesses who might lend their support to Deacon's story. And if Matt was among the assassins they'd sent, then so be it.

How he'd known who I was, I could only guess. Maybe, despite Tony's caution, my cover had been blown in Toronto, and my enemies had known exactly where to find me, where I'd be. Or it might have simply been back luck, that Matt had overheard me talking to Joaquim in the church porch at the English Cemetery. I had mentioned Deacon, and Regina – it would not have taken more to make him wonder who I was. A disguise like the one that I wore – just the glasses, and haircut and colour – would not, I thought, hold up to really close scrutiny. And he'd seen me not wearing my glasses.

His interest in me made more sense, then. By making me think that he found me attractive, he doubtless was hoping to lower my guard. He could turn up whenever he liked, and I wouldn't ask questions. He could follow behind while I led him, unwittingly, straight to the people who might know what Deacon had known – the people whom he had been sent here to silence. And then, with my usefulness over, he'd just have to smile and persuade me to meet him as I'd done before, just the two of us, on our own. And he would strike.

I didn't know how much was real, of what I'd just imagined, but I knew it didn't matter. If I was to stay alive, and do the work I had to do – find justice for the murders, past and present, and reclaim my life – I couldn't let my feelings cloud my judgement. It was difficult, admittedly, to picture Matt Jankowski as a killer. But why couldn't it be him, as well as anyone? I couldn't forget Deacon saying, about the little man who'd been the subject of the trial I'd been covering in London: *He doesn't look the type, but then they don't, always.*

The chill I felt when thinking that felt colder than the breeze upon the balcony, but still I didn't leave my chair to go inside. I sat there till well after midnight, unnoticed; keeping watch, all the while, on the brightly lit front of the hotel. I counted some twenty-eight cars pulling up the long curve of the drive, but no gunmetal-grey Renault Clio.

That should have reassured me; but it didn't.

SUNDAY, OCTOBER 1

First light found me on the highway, heading back to Lisbon.

If my theory was right – that Matt was using me to lead him to the few surviving witnesses, my only consolation was the almost certain knowledge that he didn't know I knew. For the moment, that gave me an edge, and I meant to exploit it.

He thought that I was heading back to my hotel. He wouldn't be expecting me to go to ground. To keep one step ahead of him, I only had to make it back to Lisbon before he did, and then do my best to disappear.

I only had one person left to see in Lisbon, anyway – I wouldn't need much time. I'd tried to call ahead to Roger Selkirk, let him know that I was coming, but his answering machine had been switched on. That hadn't worried me, considering the early hour, but still, I knew the sooner I could make it back to speak with him, the better.

The traffic wasn't heavy, and my confidence was rising, when the grey hatchback slid like a predator into my rearview and settled itself three cars back.

Damn, I thought. I tried pushing my own car a little bit faster. I shouldn't have. Something clunked warningly under the hood, and the engine stalled. Quickly, I steered to the side of the road. The car behind me had to veer out sharply to miss hitting me. It didn't stop. The next car did though, pulling in to offer me assistance.

As it did, the Renault Clio shot past like a bullet.

While I watched it out of sight, I heard a knocking at my window. 'You all right?' A woman's voice, a British voice, and speaking in the loud, slow way that people did when they weren't sure that they'd be understood. 'Do you need help?'

I rolled my window down.

In keeping with the smallness of my world these days, I found myself confronted by the woman who'd been eating with the older couple last night, at the restaurant, and whose father – I assumed it was her father – had been playing the piano.

She looked fiftyish, herself. Her hair was blonde enough to mask the grey, clipped short to frame a firm-jawed face without a hint of make-up. Her figure, too, was lean and tough. A woman not to mess with.

Staying safely in my car, I said, 'No, thanks. I've only stalled. I'm sure I can get it restarted.'

But when, after several minutes of trying, it became obvious that I couldn't, she said, 'Might as well give up. We'll take you to a telephone, so you can call out the Automobile Association, or whatever people do here for breakdowns.'

I hesitated. It seemed a bit coincidental, that the woman who should stop and offer help to me should be a woman I'd already seen, of all the tourists who were roaming round in

Portugal. I didn't trust coincidences. But I also knew that they could happen sometimes, and it seemed unlikely that a paid assassin would have brought her ageing parents on the job – I saw them clearly in my rearview mirror, waiting in the car.

In the end, it was their presence that decided it. I climbed out, pocketing my keys. 'All right. Thanks.'

'Wendy Taply,' was her brusque self-introduction, but her handshake was friendly. 'Don't worry, I'm a very safe driver, though my dad will tell you otherwise. He'll tell you lots of things, no doubt. He likes to talk.' Walking me back to her car, she pulled open the door and announced, in a raised voice, 'We're going to give her a lift to a phone.'

Her father, in the front seat, turned. 'No need to shout.' He had a strong voice himself, for an elderly man, and a decidedly belligerent chin. No doubt Wendy Taply got her firmness from him. 'I'm not deaf.'

'No one said you were, Dad.' Then, to me, 'My parents, Len and Ivy.'

Ivy Taply, soft in every aspect, shared her daughter's English accent, but her husband, Len, spoke with a different cadence that I couldn't place, until I'd introduced myself and he, repeating my name back, pronounced it 'Ketherine'. Then I pegged it.

Smiling, I said, 'You must be South African.'

'That's right.' He seemed quite pleased. 'From Cape Town. Do you know it?'

'No. I worked with a South African,' I said. 'I've never been there.'

'You should go. There's no place like it. I remember, when I was a boy, I'd go out on my dad's farm and pitch a tent under the stars and the animals, all the wild animals, they'd be around you so close you could—'

'Not now, Dad,' Wendy said. Strapping herself into the driver's seat, she looked me up and down, her eyes assessing. 'Are you travelling alone, then?' There was something in her voice, I thought, that sounded rather envious.

I replied that yes, I was.

Len Taply said, 'A risky business, these days, travelling alone, when you're a woman.'

He had no idea, I thought in silence, as we pulled back out onto the highway.

Wendy bristled. 'Women *are* allowed to travel, Dad.'

'I didn't say they weren't. I meant it's harder for them, that's all.'

Any doubts I might have had about my safety with the Taplys disappeared. This wasn't put on for my benefit – the bickering was real. They were exactly what they seemed to be: a family on a holiday.

Len Taply looked at me. His eyebrows had the white and wiry overgrown appearance some men's eyebrows got with age. They made him look quite wise and knowing. 'You're American,' he said, and because he seemed so certain and he seemed to get his way so little with his wife and daughter, I said, 'Yes, I am.'

'My best friend, Jack, he married an American. They live in Cleveland. We go a good ways back,' he told me, 'Jack and I…'

Beside me in the back seat Ivy warned, 'Now, Len,' but he paid no attention.

'Joined up on the same day, so we did. They sent us to

293

North Africa. Oh, I could tell you stories…'

'There's a restaurant,' Wendy cut him off. 'They're bound to have a telephone.' She looked at me. 'You've had a near escape, you know. His stories last for days.'

I glanced at Len Taply. His head had lowered slightly, and he'd sunk back into silence. Looking at him now I thought of Deacon, and my grandmother, and all the nameless others who'd had stories of their own to tell, to whom I'd never listened.

'Oh, that's all right,' I said. 'I only wish I had the time to hear them.'

I had time, as it turned out, to hear a few of them. Having put my call through to the emergency number listed on my car rental contract, I let the Taplys drive me back again to where my car sat stranded. And because they wouldn't hear of leaving me alone to wait, I stayed where I was sitting, in the back seat of their car, and let Len Taply talk.

He told a lot of tales about the years that he'd spent farming in South Africa – tales of coming face to face with lions and with rhinos, and he seemed to enjoy telling them so much that I kept listening, encouraging him to go on when his daughter would have stopped him.

Then the tow truck came, and I got out to deal with it. The serviceman from the rental company seemed to take my car's refusal to start as a personal challenge. He spent several minutes beneath the hood, stubbornly searching for what had gone wrong. I waited with growing impatience, my eyes on the highway, aware of each car that was passing. I felt too exposed.

At last the serviceman stepped back, and let the hood slam

down, and talked at some length on his two-way radio. And then he said, to me, 'This will not start. Our closest office is in Evora, so I will take you there now, and we can give you a new car. There may be a little wait, because this is an automatic, and they do not have an automatic there, so they will have to find one from somewhere else, but we will hope to have you on the road again before too long.'

'There's no way you can just take me to Lisbon?'

'No, because we are now very close to Evora. We have an office there, and it is very clear, our policy, to use the closest office. I am sorry.'

Wendy Taply wandered up to join me. 'Something wrong?'

The serviceman explained, again.

Wendy asked him, 'Would they have an automatic at your Lisbon office?'

'At the airport, yes, but—'

'Well, then.' Taking charge, she told me, 'We can run you up to Lisbon, if you like. We're going there ourselves. We're making one small detour to the north, at Dad's request, but we should be in Lisbon shortly after lunch, if that suits you, and we can drop you at the airport, if they'll have your new car ready for you then.'

I glanced again towards the traffic, growing heavier, behind her. Matt hadn't circled back yet, but I knew that, if he didn't, someone would. Besides, if I'd been followed from Lisbon, they'd have known where I'd rented my car – they'd be able to track me down, now, to the office in Evora; pick up my trail again. They'd have a harder time finding me, I thought, if I were travelling in someone else's car – especially if I were coming into Lisbon from the north, and not from the direction they expected.

'Actually,' I said, 'if you can take me to Lisbon, I won't need another car. I can get by on foot, once I'm there.'

The serviceman spoke to the rental car company at length again, on his radio, but finally things were settled, and I cleared my few belongings from the car. There wasn't much: a pair of sunglasses, two pens, and the manila envelope that Anabela had prepared for me.

'No luggage?' Wendy asked.

My suitcase was, of course, still back in Lisbon, at the York House. I hadn't planned on staying overnight in Evora, but, as with the night I'd stayed over at Patrick's parents' house, I'd made do with little more than my trusty toothbrush. With my job, I had grown used to doing that, from time to time, but I realised how strange it must look to a woman like Wendy, and I wished I had a better excuse to offer her than simply that I'd left my things in Lisbon.

She was going to ask something else, but I jumped in first. 'Thank you for doing this. It's very nice of you.'

'Not a problem. Dad will enjoy having the audience.'

He clearly did. He rattled on for half the morning, stopping only when a wave of drowsiness appeared to overcome him, and he fell asleep mid-sentence.

'Not to worry,' Wendy said. 'He always does that. It's his medication.' Glancing round to make sure that her mother, who'd been dozing for some time, was still asleep as well, she said, to me, 'You know, you really needn't humour him. He's not so hard done by. We do let him off his lead, once in a while.'

'I didn't...'

'No, but that's what you're thinking, I know. "Poor old man," you're thinking, "with those bloody women bullying him." Truth is, Dad's not someone you can bully,' she informed me, a note of fondness creeping into her gruff voice. 'He's all right, my dad. It's just that when you've heard those stories told a hundred times, you don't need to have them told again. Besides, he never tells the really meaty ones. He was shot down in the war, my dad was. He was on a reconnaissance flight in the Mediterranean, flying Mosquitoes. Had to ditch over the Vichy French coast, but he didn't get caught. Made his way through the mountains – God only knows how, as he didn't speak Spanish or French – and then here, into Portugal, right down to Lisbon. They got him a flight to Morocco from there, and then back to his base. But he never tells *those* stories. Too close to truth, they are.'

He was, in that way, like my Grandpa Murray, who had also been shot down in France, and had somehow escaped, and had managed, with what I could only assume was a great deal of difficulty, to find his way through enemy terrain to safety.

He had never talked about it, either. Not to me.

Wendy said, 'This is the first time he's ever been back. He and Mum have a friend with a flat in the Algarve, that's what got him down here, but it's taken him about a week to work up to Lisbon. It's really a bit of a pilgrimage for him – that's why he's insisting we come from the north, through the town where he was billeted when he first made it into Portugal. It's a spa town, he says, with hot springs, but in those days it was full of refugees, and those who'd escaped out of occupied Europe. Like Dad.'

A spa town, with hot springs. I felt the hair prick at the back of my neck. 'What's it called, this town?'

'Caldas da Rainha.'

The same town that Deacon had gone to, that Saturday so long ago, with Jack Cayton-Wood and Alvaro Marinho. I had the fact fresh in my memory. I could still hear Regina Marinho's voice saying how sad she thought Deacon had looked on the following Monday, and how he'd sent a message to someone at one of the hotels in Caldas da Rainha.

I'd been right, I thought, not to discourage Len Taply from telling his stories. He might yet have something of interest to tell me. Not that I expected he'd known Deacon – it would have been too much of a coincidence to think the two of them had ever met – but his knowledge of the town itself, and what had happened there, might be of use to me.

The trick would be to find a way to make him talk about the war. Like Grandpa Murray, he appeared to hold those memories private. So much so that, as we neared the town, he seemed to change his mind.

'Stop here,' he said to Wendy.

Wendy stopped.

He didn't leave the car. He sat for several moments looking out the window at what little we could see, and then he roused himself, and said a quiet, 'That's enough. We can go now.'

They must have been strong memories indeed, for him to want to touch them only through a pane of glass.

Not wanting to miss the chance to see the town with someone who had been there in the Forties, I tried to think of some way to persuade him not to leave.

'Why don't you let me treat you all to lunch?' I offered, but before I could go on to say that there must be a restaurant or two that would suit us in Caldas da Rainha, Len Taply spoke up.

'You're our guest,' he said. 'We'll buy *your* lunch. As I recall, there's quite a lovely town just south of here, called Obidos. A little town, with walls all round, and rather picturesque. We could stop there.'

Which wasn't what I'd wanted. But my disappointment faded when we pulled into the parking lot outside the walls of Obidos. The Taply women were talking as we got out of the car, but I only half listened, staring upwards instead at the small grassy hill that rose behind them, maybe twenty yards away.

Len Taply came up close behind me – looking up, too, at the hill…and what was on it. He said, 'It's been a good many years since I've seen one of those.'

I'd seen several, in my travels – different shapes and different sizes. But I hadn't thought I'd see one here, in Portugal. It was a windmill, squat and round, with whitewashed stucco and a blue stripe painted round both base and top. It looked, in shape and colouring, exactly like the windmill in the painting I had seen in Deacon's house; though, in that painting and his photograph, the windmill's canvas sails had been in use, spread fully on the large revolving frame of ropes and wood.

This windmill's sails were tightly rolled and tied along their spokes, the frame unmoving. It looked sadder that way, as though it had outlived its usefulness and been forgotten.

At my shoulder, Len Taply said, 'Shall we go take a closer look?'

Wendy glanced over. 'Up there? You must be joking.' She stayed in the parking lot, with Ivy, but I went with Len.

It took a few minutes to find the path up, in the tangle of brambles and trees that had covered the hillside. Then we climbed. Len went first, with surprising agility. I scrambled after him, holding at times with my hands to small rocks, clumps of grass, anything I could find. I was warm when I got to the top, breathing hard. I paused to catch my breath.

I wasn't altogether sure Len even knew that I was there. He had the contemplative look of someone dealing with a memory – not a sad one, but a memory. And perhaps because he'd done so much remembering today, the private wall that had been holding in his wartime stories seemed to crack from all the strain, and as the thoughts spilt over, it appeared to me he felt a sudden urge to talk.

'I saw inside a windmill once,' he said. 'Might even have been this one, though I don't recall a town close by.' He looked around, as if to judge the landmarks. 'Still, it might have been. I wonder if there's some way we could have a look inside.'

As if in answer, an old woman trundled past us, leisurely, in a black dress and headscarf, and took up position outside the locked door of the windmill. Turning towards us, she smiled, her face wrinkling more with the change of expression, and silently held out one hand, palm turned upwards, expectant.

The coins Len Taply offered to the woman seemed to satisfy her, because she took an old plain metal key from her pocket and unlocked the door, motioning us to go in, still with that unspeaking smile.

Inside, the windmill was quiet, and filled with the scent of old sawdust. A flight of open wooden stairs wound up along one wall into the loft, where at the centre of the bare swept floor the round stone millwheel lay unmoving, a few grains of corn still caught rough in its edges. There was a small round window up here, to let in light, and tools hung round the walls – a coil of rope, a metal-handled rake – but all of it looked old, as though it had been quite some time since anyone other than tourists had been in here.

Standing in the loft, Len looked around the cramped and tidy space, and shook his head. 'No, this isn't the same one. I'd know. I'd remember. Rather exciting, it was, when I went. Very secret. I wasn't allowed to tell anyone. Likely I shouldn't be telling you, either,' he said, with a wink, 'but then, the war's long over. Can't hurt anybody now, I shouldn't think.'

He paused, as though he wanted prompting, so I asked, 'What were you doing?'

'I was sent to fix a radio. They'd rigged one of these windmills up, you know, to make transmissions from. I don't remember, as I say, exactly where it was. He drove me to it in the dead of night, this chap. Said here, fix this radio. That's what I did, you see. That was my job. Not my job in the Air Force, but that's what I worked at before I joined up. I loved radios. This chap who drove me, he'd found all that out, when he'd talked to me first. That was *his* job, to debrief all of us who came down out of France, to find out what we'd heard, what we'd seen, what we knew. Just a young man himself, not that much older than most of the boys, and an officer, but he'd been wounded at El Alamein. Had a gimpy leg.'

Cayton-Wood, I thought, and felt a small thrill of excitement that the stories were connecting up in ways I'd never hoped they would. So Len had met with Cayton-Wood. At least, I thought he had, and then I knew it for a fact when he went on,

'I don't recall his name. He looked a bit like Douglas Fairbanks. And he drove a big, black Humber limousine. Very posh. Where he was transmitting to, I didn't know. I didn't ask. I only did the job, and that was that. It wasn't much, but being in the night-time, and so secret…well, I thought it was exciting.'

There were a hundred questions I wanted to ask him, about his time in Caldas da Rainha, and when exactly he had been there, and if there was anything else he remembered about Cayton-Wood, but they weren't easy questions to work into plain conversation, so I took a more general approach. 'I expect there were lots of exciting things going on, so close to Lisbon, you know – foreign spies, and intrigues; bodies turning up in alleys…'

'Oh, I heard some stories, yes. But none that would be fit to tell a nice young lady like yourself.'

He drew himself up gallantly, regaining his control, and I could almost hear the door slam shut again against that section of his past. He told me, 'Anyway, we ought to go back down and join my wife, and Wendy. Go for lunch. There's nothing here to see.'

The old woman, still standing at the open door, stepped back to let us out.

As she was locking up, I paused and turned back for another

last look at the squat little windmill, standing forlorn on the rock-strewn hilltop, and once again I had that bothersome feeling, the same as I'd had after leaving Regina Marinho's. Well, maybe, I thought, not *exactly* the same, because then I had felt that I'd overlooked something important, while now I felt more as though something important was missing.

And then, in an instant, the two feelings melded in one, and I knew what it was. I could see in my mind the old photo she'd shown me of Deacon, with Cayton-Wood standing a few faces over, a tall figure leaning his weight on a walking stick. And over that image James Cavender's voice, like a ghost in my memory, repeated the story of how he'd discovered his uncle, despondent and drinking alone, after spending the day up in London. '… *it seemed to me that he was staring at one photograph, specifically.*' The photo of the windmill, like the one that rose now from the hill in front of me. '*And when my uncle told me, "He's not dead",*' the voice went on, '*I rather fancied he was speaking of the man who's in that photograph. A tall man with a walking stick – the outline of the figure's fairly clear.*'

That solitary figure was the thing my mind had missed, just now, when I'd looked at the windmill. From my own imagination I could conjure it, no longer just a shadow. I could see the face, the features – see the man about whom Deacon had been speaking when he'd said, half to himself, half to his nephew: 'He's not dead. He should be dead.'

I saw Jack Cayton-Wood.

Deacon looked to the windmill again, judging distance, then back to his camera, adjusting the settings to make the best use of the late morning light.

He'd chosen a slightly different angle than the one that Garcia was painting from. Garcia, with an eye to colour and texture, showed more of the trees in the landscape behind, whereas Deacon preferred the uncluttered, clean lines of the far-distant hills and the ocean beyond.

The Spaniard looked up from his easel and smiled. 'You take as long to make your photograph as I take with my painting.'

Deacon admitted it. 'But I rather doubt my end result will be as good.'

'You flatter me.'

'I don't. I tell the truth.' He did, at that. 'You ought to sell your paintings, Manuel. You could make your living at it.'

But Garcia, mixing colours on his palette, only shrugged. 'I do not think my wife would be so happy with an artist's pay. She likes too much the money that I earn from Mr Reynolds.'

'Sell your paintings on the side, then.'

Once again the shrug. 'Perhaps, someday.' He was back at work now, concentrating.

Deacon liked to watch Garcia paint. It was one of the rare pleasures of his week to take a Sunday drive into the countryside and pass a few hours in Garcia's quiet company, sharing the capture of beauty on canvas and talking of things that had nothing to do with the war.

It gave him hope to know that all the ugliness and hatred of these times had not yet managed to destroy completely that which was, to him, the very essence of humanity: the simple need for people of like minds to make connections; the capacity for friendship.

He was mindful, naturally, of what Garcia was, and mindful, too, of his own orders, his own loyalties. But still, he couldn't help but like the Spaniard.

Without looking up this time, Garcia dryly said, 'It is supposed to be the quicker way, you know, to use the camera. We have been here twenty minutes, and you have not moved.'

'I'm waiting for that cloud to pass.'

There wasn't much wind to help matters along, but at length the long cloud drifted clear of the frame, and Deacon, his eye to the viewfinder, prepared to take his shot. He hadn't expected the door of the windmill to open.

The man who came out didn't see them, at first. He locked the door after him, took a few paces away from the windmill and paused, a tall figure against the expanse of blank sky. Deacon, watching him still through the camera lens, wasn't aware that his own hand had moved till the shutter clicked.

It was the tiniest of sounds. He doubted whether even Garcia, behind him, had heard it, and Garcia was a good deal closer to him than the man beside the windmill, but instinct advised him to lower the camera as Cayton-Wood turned.

Garcia had stopped painting, in surprise.

Deacon couldn't be sure, but he thought he saw Cayton-Wood cast a quick glance at the door of the windmill before starting down the small path towards them. By the time he'd reached the halfway point, his smile was in place.

He greeted them both, took a moment to admire Garcia's artwork, then, as though it were quite normal that the three of them should run into each other in a setting so remote, he squinted skyward and remarked that they had picked a lovely

305

day for it. And then he dropped his gaze to Deacon's camera. 'I'm sorry,' he said, 'if I spoilt your shot.'

And with that he excused himself, nodded, and left them, retreating along the steep path through the trees, leaving Deacon to wonder.

Not only had Cayton-Wood not told them why he had come there, or what he'd been doing alone in the windmill, but he'd also shown the physical reactions – the faint flush, and the adrenalin-fuelled eye movements – of a man caught unawares; a man who hadn't wanted to be seen.

That Deacon hadn't seen the Humber parked below seemed further evidence of Cayton-Wood's attempts at self-concealment.

Curious, he looked towards the windmill. He'd already formed a theory as to what might be inside it, based on the fact that, of all the windmills scattered through the countryside surrounding Lisbon, Garcia had chosen *this* windmill; had driven straight to it, had known the way, had seemed very familiar with where he should park and which path he should take. It would be a good spot for a transmitter, Deacon thought – far enough out that one wouldn't be noticed, and common enough to blend in with the landscape.

But that did nothing to explain why Cayton-Wood would come up here alone.

Or why Garcia, head bent, frowning, to his painting, should look suddenly so thoughtful, and so worried.

Manuel Garcia.

There it was, in black and white. It hadn't meant a thing to me the first time I had read it. He'd been one name among the many in the list that Anabela had prepared, at my request – the list of those who'd died between November 1943 and April 1944.

He'd made it nearly to the end. He'd died on April 6th. I felt a small surge of excitement as I read the name again. Perhaps *he* was the murder victim Deacon had wanted to tell me about. There was no cause of death recorded on the list – it was a simple register of names, and dates. But still, I thought it promising.

Which meant there were two obituaries that I needed to look up now, or have Anabela find for me: Manuel Garcia's, here in Lisbon, and JL Cayton-Wood's, in England. Cayton-Wood's would be more difficult. I didn't have a date, or an exact location, and only Regina Marinho's word that he had died at all, but I was hoping Roger Selkirk might be able to supply me with more details when I met with him.

He would know about Garcia's death, as well. It was strange that Regina Marinho had not.

Of course, I reasoned, it was possible she'd never heard. She'd left the company in March, she'd said. But if she'd kept in touch with Roger Selkirk all these years, and if he was as up on things as she said he was, it seemed unlikely she would never have been told about the Spaniard's death. Unlikely, too, that such a thing would simply slip her mind, when she was talking to me, given that her memory of events had seemed so crystal clear.

Wendy, from the driver's seat, asked, 'Mum still sleeping?'

'Yes, she is,' I said.

'It was all that lunch, I expect.' She glanced back. 'Do you always bring your work with you, on holiday?'

'It isn't really work.' I packed the pages back into their

envelope, and set it to one side. 'Just reading.'

We were coming into Lisbon.

Wendy asked, 'Where would you like to be let off?'

I wasn't entirely sure. I couldn't go back to the York House just yet – Matt would know where I was, then. He likely had somebody watching the door. I'd considered bunking in with Anabela, then abandoned the idea. Someone might have seen me eating dinner with her, Friday night – they might know who she was, and where she lived. And while I would have liked to stay at the hotel where Wendy Taply and her parents were, to have a bit more time to talk to Len, I knew I couldn't risk that, either. I had no idea who might have been watching, on the highway, when I'd gotten in their car, and just because I didn't think that we'd been followed, that didn't mean I was safe.

My best bet was to try to disappear; to take a room at some small pension, where no one would think of looking for me.

I told Wendy, 'Any big intersection will do. I'll take a cab or the subway from there.'

They dropped me at the Sete Rios subway stop, across from the Zoological Gardens. There was a hasty exchange of handshakes, and good wishes, but my 'thank you' seemed inadequate, for all that they had done.

I felt a momentary pang of deprivation when they'd left me, but that was quickly replaced by a sense of release. Like an animal loosed from its tether, I turned and plunged into the thick of the crowd.

The room I found was basic, even threadbare, but it had a private telephone.

There was nobody answering, now, at Regina Marinho's.

I had better luck with the next number I tried. Anabela sounded almost pleased to hear from me. 'I tried to call you yesterday, and then again this morning. You had asked me, when we met, if I could find out something more for you about this M Jankowski? Well, I asked my friend with the police, and yesterday he sent an email, with a bit more information. M Jankowski is a man – his name is Matthew James Jankowski, an American, and my friend thinks he may have some connection to the government. I'm not sure why, but I think it has something to do with the level at which he was making requests. Does this help?'

I wasn't sure exactly what it did, except to make me feel that the water in which I was swimming had just gotten deeper. I already suspected Whitehall was responsible for Deacon's death – the thought that the American government might be involved, as well, was information that I could have done without just then.

But still, I thanked her. 'Look, could I ask one more favour?'

'Yes, of course.'

'I need to find a Portuguese obituary.' I told her for whom, and the date of the death. 'I'm going to try to have a look myself, tomorrow, at the library, but just in case…'

'Oh yes, I understand. It is no problem.'

'And I'm at a different number now.' I told her what it was.

She wrote it down, and paused. 'Is everything all right?'

'It's fine. I'm fine,' I reassured her, but I wasn't sure that I'd succeeded.

'I will be in touch,' she promised, as she said goodbye.

I had one final call to make.

The phone rang five times before Roger Selkirk picked it up. He had a nice voice. Very English. 'My dear girl,' he said, 'it's no bother at all. No, I love having visitors. When would you like to come?'

'Would tonight be too early?'

'Ah. Tonight's rather tricky, I'm afraid. I play bridge on Sunday nights. Would tomorrow suit you? In the morning?'

It would only mean a few more hours, I told myself. And Roger Selkirk should be safe enough. Matt had already been in Lisbon – if he'd known of Roger Selkirk, he'd have dealt with him then, before I'd even entered the picture. Which meant Roger wasn't on Matt's hit list. Not yet.

'Tomorrow,' I said, 'would be fine.'

'Good. Shall we say ten o'clock, then? That should give me time to make myself presentable.' His tone grew mildly curious. 'Was there something in particular you wanted to discuss about your grandfather?'

'Whatever you can tell me.' I avoided the specifics. Roger Selkirk, like everyone else, was an unknown quantity – as with Regina Marinho, I wouldn't know until I'd met him whether he was someone I could trust.

Tomorrow, I thought, I could ask him my questions.

And first among those would be whether Manuel Garcia, in fact, had been murdered.

MONDAY, OCTOBER 2

Roger Selkirk's house was small.

It had no garden at the front; the door sat nearly on the sidewalk, with black wrought-iron grilles across the windows to each side. The walls were stuccoed, painted a deep yellow that had weathered to a duller amber, but the door was brightly red.

Just two doors further on, the narrow cobbled street became a flight of worn stone steps that steeply fell downhill, towards the harbour. I could catch the scent of sea air on the breeze that chilled my cheeks, and hear the crying of the gulls. —

I was alone. No one had followed me, I'd made quite sure of that. Remembering my early morning trip with Guy to Tony's, in Toronto, I had taken two buses and three separate taxis to make absolutely sure no one would follow, and then I had come the last few blocks on foot.

Behind me, up the incline, I could see the red-tiled roof of what had once been the old Ivan Reynolds offices, around the corner. I'd passed that building by on my way here; I'd stopped to look at it, but time had taken all its charm and left a modern-looking shell – a dress shop on the ground floor with apartments overhead that didn't look as though they harboured any ghosts.

My hopes were all with Roger Selkirk now.

I drew a breath, and knocked.

I didn't worry when he didn't answer right away. He would be, after all, an old man, Deacon's age, or more. I gave him what I thought was time enough, then knocked again. There was no bell.

It wasn't till I'd knocked the third time that I started to suspect he wasn't there. 'Mr Selkirk?' I called loudly, as I pounded once again. I got no answer.

There were curtains at the windows – plain lace curtains that, at night, and with a light on in the house, would be quite easy to see through, but in the daytime they veiled every detail of the darkened rooms inside, and I saw nothing.

It was past ten o'clock now, the hour we'd set for our meeting. At a loss, I crossed over the street to the house of a neighbour, whose windows stood open. The woman there didn't speak English. I knew she didn't understand what I was asking her, though when I mentioned Roger Selkirk's name she nodded and said something in reply, her one arm gesturing towards the road.

'He's gone out?' I asked. 'Do you know where?'

She looked blank, and I tried to recall what the Portuguese word was for 'where'. I ventured, *'Onde?'* I pronounced it 'ON-day', hoping that was right.

Her face cleared. *'Cemitério dos Ingleses,'* she said distinctly.

That, I understood.

The English Cemetery.

* * *

Joaquim was busy pruning back a vine that grew among a stand of headstones. Though it had been a few days since I had talked to him, he recognised me right away.

'Yes, yes,' he said. 'You wanted the Marinhos. I remember. Did you get my message?'

'Yes, thank you.'

'And did you get to speak with her?'

'I did, yes.'

'Good,' he told me, rustling, head bent, among the vines. 'That's good.'

'She said I ought to talk to Roger Selkirk, so I called him, and we were supposed to meet at ten, this morning...but he wasn't at his house. His neighbour told me I might find him here.'

Joaquim straightened then, and looked at me. I'd forgotten how sharply assessing his eyes were. He said, 'You will, in three days. He was found dead this morning.'

I felt a turning in my stomach.

'It was not unexpected,' Joaquim said. 'He was quite old, you understand. He had, how would you say it? A good innings.'

It was devastating news. Roger Selkirk had been my last link, here in Portugal, to Deacon, and I'd had such great hopes...

'How did he die?' I asked.

Joaquim said, rather carefully, 'He fell, I'm told. He was not good with stairs.'

I didn't buy that. And I wasn't entirely convinced that Joaquim did either.

'I'm very sorry,' Joaquim said, 'that I am not more help

313

to you this time. He was a good man, Roger. He would have enjoyed to meet you.'

Salt in the wound. Trying to salvage something, anything, from my deep pit of disappointment, I asked, 'Is there anybody else you know who worked for Ivan Reynolds? Anyone that I can talk to?'

He considered this. Then, 'No one, no. They are all gone, now. Roger was the last of them. They are all gone.' And with a sigh, he bent back to his pruning.

I nearly turned away, before remembering that he himself had been here at the time, among the English. I hadn't pressed him, earlier. Perhaps I should have done. I said, 'My grandfather once spoke about a murder at the company.'

I was watching him; I saw the pause in movement, small but telling. The sound of his shears bit the silence. 'I would not know anything about that.'

It wasn't the first time he'd told me a lie. He'd told me before that he hadn't known Deacon, and I hadn't believed him then, either. I could have demanded he tell me the truth, but it wouldn't have been any use – he was someone who played his cards close to his chest. And, in honesty, I couldn't blame him. He had no more reason to trust me than I had to trust him, and maybe, in the circumstances, even less.

And then, on impulse, I made a decision.

I said, 'There's an American, named Matt Jankowski. You may remember him, if you see him – he was here on Friday, the same time I was. In his thirties, brown hair, brown eyes, and he can speak Portuguese.' I drew breath. 'I don't know whether he's already spoken to you. I don't know whether you gave him the same information you gave

314

me. But if he comes back, you might want to be careful.'

I waited a moment. He didn't look up.

I felt suddenly foolish for trying to warn him. A man like Joaquim didn't need any warning. If someone tried to deal with him the way they'd dealt with Deacon, and with Cavender, and Grandma, and now with Roger Selkirk, maybe – if somebody tried the same thing with Joaquim, I had a feeling that the odds were in his favour.

He was not about to talk to me, that much was plainly evident, and so I turned on the path to leave.

I'd gone three steps when he said casually, 'So now you will go back home, to America?'

I stopped. Turned back, to look behind. 'Yes.'

He never stopped pruning. The sound of the shears went on, hard and methodical, cutting away the loose parts of the vine, the dead wood, all the pieces that cluttered and choked. 'Talk to Jenny,' he said. 'Jenny Saunders. Her last name now is Augustine. She has a house in Washington, DC, a place called Georgetown. She will have the answers you are looking for.' He glanced up, and our eyes met, very briefly. 'If you know the questions.'

Jenny Augustine's telephone number was unlisted.

Hanging up the payphone, I leant my shoulders on the glass and watched the cars pass by and felt, in that one moment, like a distance runner reaching breaking point, exhausted. The finish line I'd hoped to reach this morning had been moved beyond my range of sight, across another ocean. There was no one left to talk to, here in Portugal. Regina Marinho, like Margot and Patrick, was missing. Joaquim wasn't talking. And Roger was dead.

315

All I had, now, was Jenny. *She'll see you*, Regina Marinho had said, and I hoped that was right, but I couldn't make the same mistake with Jenny that I'd made with Roger Selkirk. I should have talked to Roger on the phone last night, before he'd gone out for his evening of bridge. I shouldn't have waited. I wouldn't, with Jenny. I only hoped no one else got to her first.

Filled with new determination, I dialled information for a second time and got the local number for my airline.

The young woman at the airline desk was courteous and helpful. Yes, she said, it would be possible, she'd only need my ticket information and a credit card. I found both in the pocket of my jacket. As I pulled them out, another paper drifted to the dirty pavement at my feet, and after reading out my numbers to the woman on the phone, I bent to pick it up.

It was the paper Matt had written his hotel's phone number on, but it had fallen face down, so when I picked it up the first thing that I saw was what was written on the other side.

My heart dropped.

The woman on the phone was talking, asking me a question.

'Yes,' I said. 'That's fine.' She read me the details again but I only half heard them, then, 'Thank you,' I said, and hung up, with my eyes still on the paper.

It was Roger Selkirk's name, and home address.

The address that Regina Marinho had copied out for me, in Evora. I had copied it again into the notebook that I carried with me everywhere, from habit, and I'd used my notebook for direction, when I'd gone to Roger's house. I'd forgotten I was carrying this piece of paper still.

I thought of Matt, in Evora; how casually he'd glanced at what was written on this paper when he'd caught it as it fell out of my pocket. After all the effort I had gone through this morning – the buses, and taxis, and trying to cover my tracks so that no one would follow me – after all that, to find out Matt had actually *seen* Roger's address; that I'd all but handed it to him...I felt almost physically sick.

Smoothing the folds in the paper, I turned it and read once again the few lines Matt had written, fighting back a surge of anger. He had played a game with me – a coward's game – and he had won. I wouldn't let him win again.

The next move would be mine.

I took the telephone in hand, and firmly dialled the hotel's number.

'Yes,' I told the front desk, 'I would like to leave a message for a guest of yours.'

The bar at the York House Hotel was an elegant, gentleman's room, with warm, wood-panelled walls and cane-backed chairs with deep gold cushioned seats. The polished serving counter lay beneath a barrel-vaulted ceiling lit with recessed lights that shone down on a silver tray of brandies set beside a silver cooler of champagne, topped by a crisp white linen napkin. The bartender, formal in white dinner jacket, black trousers and tie, got me a drink and then left me to sit while he crossed the small courtyard and went through the other French doors, to the main hotel.

Nobody here, so it seemed, had taken notice of the fact that I'd been gone for nearly three days. When I'd arrived back a few hours ago, the desk clerk had done nothing more than smile and say good evening. I had been relieved. I hadn't wanted to explain my absence.

I'd showered, and changed my clothes, selecting what to wear with the detached precision of a soldier changing into battledress.

And then I'd come down here, to wait.

I'd turned my chair so I could see the open doorway. I had purposely sat close to other people – to one side of me, a couple, young, my age, were drinking wine, and not far off three men in business suits were gathered at a table, speaking earnestly in French.

I knew I was protected. Still, the moment Matt walked through the door, I had to fight the traitorous adrenalin surge that wanted me to run. I couldn't let it show. I couldn't let him see my fear. My life, and Jenny Augustine's, depended on my staying calm; on doing what I had to do.

He smiled, from the door, and came across to join me. 'Hi.'

'Hello.' I put everything into the smile I returned to him. 'You got my message, then.'

'I did. I'm glad you called.' He didn't say he hadn't thought I would, but there was something in his tone – a certain trace of satisfaction, or…relief? No, surely not, I thought. It must be satisfaction, that I'd done what he'd intended me to do. I understood why he might not have been too sure I would. I'd stood him up, before, and from his viewpoint, I supposed, I had been sending out mixed signals. Tonight, I'd have to try to keep my energy consistent. I wanted him to think he'd been successful, that he'd fooled me into thinking he was just a charming tourist, and I wanted him to think that I had made this date because I liked him.

'Well,' I said, with what I hoped would pass for shyness, 'I didn't want to leave Lisbon without thanking you for Saturday. I really had a nice time.'

'So did I.' He sat, and settled himself comfortably, and took the bait. 'You're leaving? When?'

'Tomorrow morning. I would have liked to have stayed longer, but something came up, and I have to go back.'

'Nothing serious, I hope?' He was better at acting than I was. He sounded sincere.

'No, it's just…' I broke off. Paused, as I'd rehearsed, to let him think that I was groping for the words. 'There's a person I promised to meet in Toronto, and tomorrow night's the only time that he can see me. It's important.'

'"He"?'

'It's not like that. He's over eighty.' Purposely, I left it there. I knew he'd taken note of it, as I had hoped he would. I had him thinking now.

If he thought I had already led him to everyone of value, then I wasn't any use to him, and I could be disposed of. But if I could make him think I wasn't finished yet, it bought me time. To be of any help to Jenny Augustine, I had to stay alive.

The waiter had returned. Matt hailed him. 'Will you have some wine with me?' he asked. He hadn't missed the fact that I was only drinking sparkling water.

I'd been avoiding alcohol since I'd arrived in Portugal. I'd feared that even small amounts might blur my thinking, make me sloppy, apt to make mistakes. But tonight, I had to do what any woman who was meeting with a man she was attracted to would do; I had to keep my actions normal.

That was more difficult, this time, with Roger Selkirk's death still freshly on my mind – it took more concentration.

Roger's death had stirred unwanted memories for me – I'd remembered Deacon stepping off the kerb that day in London; I'd seen Grandma Murray falling as her kitchen window shattered, and I'd felt again the horror of those moments; felt the closeness of the danger.

I felt it now, this near to Matt. I needed to relax. So I said yes to wine, and took a sip. It helped.

He asked me, 'What have you been up to, here in Lisbon?'

'Oh, nothing much.' I shrugged, and kept it light and friendly. 'Sightseeing. What about you? You were going someplace after Evora, weren't you? Where did you go?'

He had to think about it. Only for an instant, but I noticed. 'Tomar,' he said, 'and then Coimbra, so that I could see the Roman ruins at Conimbriga.'

It wasn't the truth, I suspected, but lacking any first-hand knowledge of those towns myself, I couldn't test him. 'What makes you so interested in Romans?'

'That's my mother's fault,' he said, and grinned. The hardness left his features when he talked about his childhood, and the myths his mother read to him as bedtime stories, and how his own fascination with the long-dead Empire had evolved to match her own. 'I went out trick-or-treating as a Roman once, with the sheet and everything. My dad went insane. He's a man's man, my dad, and he hated the thought of his son going all over town in a dress, as he called it.'

My father would have never known what I wore out for Hallowe'en. It had been Grandpa Murray who had walked me round the block, and made a great admiring fuss about my costumes. I asked, 'What does your father do?'

'For a living, you mean? He's a butcher.'

Like father, like son, I thought harshly. I took a slightly larger drink of wine than I had meant to. 'What made you want to be a lawyer?'

The wine warmed me while he talked, and made the whole encounter easier. The conversation flowed as well as it had done in Evora, or so it seemed to me. This time I noticed, though, that Matt spoke very freely of his past, and of his parents, but grew tighter with the details of his present. I heard stories of his college days, but nothing of his workplace. And although he told me several tales that featured his dog Reuben, I learnt nothing of his friends. Perhaps he didn't have any. A job like his, I reasoned, wouldn't lend itself to sociability.

Yet he seemed sociable enough, with me. That made him dangerous, because he had a way of asking questions that was almost incidental, so you didn't see the trap until you'd started to reply.

After finishing one of the funnier stories about his dog, he asked, 'Do you have pets?'

'No.'

'Not a dog person?'

'No, it's not that. I love dogs. But I travel too much, and that wouldn't be fair to an animal.' And then I stopped, because I realised what I'd said. Not that it mattered. He knew who I was, I was sure of that, and so it was of no importance if my cover story cracked a little here and there. Still, I'd told him I worked in a grocery store – not the sort of occupation where a person had much cause to travel.

I didn't want him scoring points, however minor they might be. I set my wineglass down, and tried to think a step ahead for the remainder of our talk. When he started saying something about Canada again, I knew that he was leading up to asking more about my meeting with my non-existent old man in Toronto. I was ready, and I kept my answers vague. And when he asked about the scheduling of my flights, although he did it very neatly, I was ready for that, too.

He said, 'You'll have to get up pretty early, then. Are you driving yourself to the airport?'

I shook my head. 'No, I got rid of my rental car. It was giving me trouble, yesterday, on the drive home from Evora' – he already knew this – 'so I let the company take it back.'

'Didn't they give you a new one?'

'I didn't want a new one. I've seen what the streets are like here in Lisbon. I'm not brave enough to tackle them. I'm not that skilled a driver.'

'Aren't you?' His tone was dry, or so I imagined, but when I raised my head his eyes were neutral. 'I can drive you to the airport, if you like.'

I hadn't seen *that* coming, but I dodged it handily. 'Thanks, that's really nice of you, but I've already got a taxi booked. Besides, it's way too early in the morning.'

'I should let you get some sleep, then.'

I had been wondering how I would bring the conversation to a close. The fact he'd done it for me left me so relieved I quickly looked around the bar, because I didn't want him seeing the emotion in my eyes.

'I've enjoyed this,' I lied. 'Thanks for coming.'

'You're welcome. Maybe we can try it again sometime.'

A bigger lie: 'I'd like that.'

'Then here, take this.' He handed me his business card. 'You can call me next time you get down to the States.'

I bent my head to read it. Cleared my throat, which had gone dry. 'You live in Washington.'

'That's right. Have you ever been there?'

I'd been there several times for work, and knew it well. The address for his office was on F Street, downtown, a short walk from the White House. 'No,' I said, 'I've never been.'

'Well, then, you'll have to make a point of it. I can show you the sights.'

'Sounds fun.' I pocketed the card, and found a smile to show him.

Matt smiled back, his quick and boyish smile, the one that looked so genuine, the one that made his brown eyes warm. It was the wine, I knew, but for that one small moment I could almost wish that things weren't what they were. But then the spectres of my grandmother, and Cavender, and Deacon, rose between us, and my mind grew hard again.

Matt paid the bill, and walked me out.

I was relaxing slightly now – the meeting over, and the time of danger past – and I think something of that must have made my smile a little brighter as we said goodbye, because he kept my hand a little longer than he needed to, and then, without a warning, leant in close and kissed my cheek.

'Take care,' he said.

I had a long time, after he had gone, to wonder why he would have said that, and to wonder if he'd feel regret, when it came time to kill me.

TUESDAY, OCTOBER 3

There were only a handful of passengers on the flight from Lisbon up to Amsterdam. None of them looked threatening, but that meant nothing. I'd looked for Matt outside the airport – I'd been looking for his car – and though I hadn't seen him, I'd felt sure someone had watched me, maybe followed, when I'd walked into the terminal. And while I'd known that *he* would not be on my plane, I knew that someone might.

They wouldn't be too fond of me. My flight left at the less-than-godly hour of six a.m., and no one on the plane looked properly awake.

Including me. I hadn't slept well. I had dreamt unsettling dreams that left me so on edge that, in the end, I'd turned on all the lights and spent the last few hours of the night curled in an armchair in a corner of my room, rereading every note I'd made, and every bit of information Anabela had passed on to me.

I'd spoken to her yesterday, before I'd met with Matt. She'd searched the whole of April, and of May, and there was no obituary for Manuel Garcia. She'd been apologetic. 'I am so sorry,' she had said, 'that I could not do more.'

'You've done so much. I don't know how to thank you.'

'There is no need. Just be careful.'

'Oh, don't worry,' I had told her. 'If things go well, then I'll have bought myself some time. They won't be keen to hurt me.'

But they meant, I knew, to follow me. I couldn't let them do that.

In Amsterdam, while making my connection, I was vigilant. I had a lot of time to kill. The flight bound for Toronto didn't leave till after one o'clock. I ate an early lunch, and sat in plain view, reading, for a while, before I made my way towards the gate and took a seat within the waiting area. Time went by; the small space filled. I didn't look around because, again, there was no point. I wouldn't recognise the face. But I felt certain, even if there had been no one on this morning's flight from Lisbon, there'd be someone on *this* plane. They wouldn't want to run the risk of losing sight of me.

At one o'clock I stood, and stretched, and headed for the washroom on the far side of the hall. I gambled that no one would bother getting up to follow me in there – the one door in and out was in full view of everybody in the waiting area.

At the sink, I washed my face and took a silent look at my reflection, just as unfamiliar to me now as it had been four days ago, in this same airport. Mindful of my near-disaster then, I checked my bag with care to make quite sure my travel wallet, with my passport, was still in it, before shouldering the strap. A group of women had come in, laughing and talking to one another, taking turns at the sinks while they freshened their make-up. Waiting, I put on my jacket and buttoned it carefully, changing my look, and then took the silk scarf that I'd stuffed in my pocket and tied it around my head, Grace Kelly-style. When the women began to leave, I left as well, blending in to the group, letting them be my shield as I whipped round the corner, away from the gate.

Thirty seconds later I was safely out of view, lost in the crowds of Schiphol Airport. Five more minutes and a smiling young attendant reached his hand to take my boarding pass, as I stood, out of breath from running, at another gate.

'You are for Washington?'

I nodded.

'We were just about to give the final boarding call,' he said. He bent his head to read my pass, and in my paranoiac state I thought he took too long to do it, but at last he waved me through. 'Enjoy your flight, Miss Allen.'

Safely in my window seat, I took my scarf off; turned my head against the cushion; closed my eyes.

The engines surged. I felt the motion, knew the moment when we left the ground, but these things only touched the edges of my consciousness. My fingers found the little medal on its chain around my neck, my parting gift from Tony in Toronto, and again I made a silent prayer – but not for my own safety.

Please, I asked St Christopher, the patron saint of travellers, *Please let me be in time.*

CHAPTER FOUR

Washington

Nothing but danger about me,
Danger behind and before,

ROBERT LOUIS STEVENSON, 'TICONDEROGA'

STILL TUESDAY, OCTOBER 3

Washington, DC, took on a look of clean austerity in autumn.

I criss-crossed the city in taxis for half an hour, covering my tracks, watching through windows the stark, passing beauty set off by the strong, angled sunlight of late afternoon: holly hedges bright with small red berries; some trees naked, others gold and fluttering; grass littered with leaves; people jogging, in pairs and alone; the Potomac River a bright slash of blue with a few white boats dotting its surface; the white of the Washington Monument, and the gold gleam, slightly tarnished, of the giant figures looming at the end of the bridge as we crossed back again out of Arlington.

It was past five o'clock when the final taxi dropped me off at M Street and Wisconsin, in the heart of Georgetown. If the driver later saw my picture featured in a paper or the nightly news, he wouldn't know exactly where I'd gone – a lot of tourists liked to be let off at M Street and Wisconsin, it was central and convenient to the upscale shops, the restaurants and boutiques, the rows of eighteenth-century townhouses that had stood here since George Washington had first begun to build his capital along the banks of the Potomac, and the even more exclusive streets where one might spot the wealthy or the famous; all the things that made this area of Washington a Mecca for so many people. Even at this hour of the evening, with the streetlights full on and the deep blue sky flattening into darkness, the brick sidewalks seemed barely to contain the flood of life, the jostling of humanity that moved against the constant sounds of traffic, squealing brakes, and slamming car doors. A bright red Gray Line trolley car came labouring uphill as I crossed over Wisconsin and wove myself as quickly as I could into the tapestry of people heading west on M Street.

Jenny Augustine lived on Potomac Street – not a long walk, but a world from the bustle of M and Wisconsin. There was here some measure of peace, that began with the silent cars lining both sides of the street, parked and idle. And over them, the ginkgo trees, tall trees, venerable, clinging to their golden, fan-shaped leaves in staunch defiance of the season. The scattering of leaves they had allowed to drop lay thinly, green and gold, across the worn brick sidewalk underneath, concealing in some places the uneven, crumbled spots that caught my heels.

The houses, too, gave the impression they'd been here forever. They were joined together, federal, lovely, some with Mansard rooflines, brick walls painted soft dove grey or yellowed cream or simply left the natural deep red. All up the street I saw front-door lights gleaming on black wooden shutters, and black iron railings, and black painted doors with brass numbers and knockers and letter slots, softened at times by small shrubs planted close to the walls at the edge of the sidewalk.

The Augustine house had black bars on the street-level windows as well, and a lion's-head door knocker that looked as if its role was to intimidate. Inside the house, a dog barked when I knocked, but its barking was silenced. I waited.

When I knocked the second time the dog again barked, and again fell silent suddenly, as though someone had stilled it with a firm command. I couldn't hear a human voice, but after a moment I heard the dog snuffling, close by the base of the door, and I knew that its owner could not be far off; that he or she was, in all likelihood, standing right there in the front hall, a few feet away from me, listening. Waiting. As I was.

I could have said something out loud, but the street was so quiet, and I would have had to raise my voice to be heard through the solid wooden door, and I didn't know for certain that the area was safe. Instead I took my notebook from my bag, and wrote a name across one page, then tore it off and slipped it face-up through the letter box.

It was the longest minute I had ever stood on somebody's front step.

And then, in the silence, a lock clicked, and another, and the door swung slowly inward on its hinges.

It struck me, as we looked at one another, that the image I had formed of Jenny Reynolds in my mind had been of someone young – as young and vital as she'd been in all the photographs I'd seen, and in the tales that had been told to me. It took some doing to reconcile that image with the woman I saw now, so old, so plain, her shoulders stooped as though the burden of the years had just become too much to carry. For a moment I rejected the idea, even though I knew it must be her, it had to be. She had her father's facial lines, his nose, his cheekbones.

She held the piece of paper up, the one on which I'd written 'Andrew Deacon'. In a quiet yet commanding voice, she asked me, 'What is *your* name?'

I'd grown almost used to being Katherine Allen, but this was, I thought, my final port of call – there wasn't anybody left to talk to, after this. It didn't matter any longer who I was, and so I simply said, 'Kate Murray.'

She looked me up and down, and finally nodded satisfaction. 'Then,' she told me, in decided tones, 'you may come in.'

The dog was a Boston bull terrier, small and suspicious. It circled behind as I entered the house.

'He isn't used to strangers,' I was told. 'But he doesn't usually bite.'

Which was all the reassurance that I got before she turned and led me down the hall. I'd expected the inside of the house to look like something from the pages of a decorating magazine, one of those ones that showed rooms I could never afford, filled with fine art and mirrors and flower arrangements. The hall, at least, was none of that. It was, like the owner herself, quite surprisingly plain – a coat rack, an umbrella stand, a row of family photos, and an oriental runner that had worn at its centre till the pattern of the carpet had begun to disappear.

She was talking. 'Andrew told me to expect you; to be nice to you. I must say, you've taken your time, though, in—'

'Not here.' I stopped at the door of the room she had entered, refusing to follow. This kitchen, like my grandmother's, was cosy, warm, inviting, with a scrubbed pine table set beneath a window, overlooking the back yard. 'We can't talk here. Is there another room?'

She turned, surprised at first, and then she looked me up and down a second time, with growing shrewdness. 'I think, Kate Murray, that you'd better tell me just exactly what is going on.'

'And so,' I finished off, 'that's why I came to you; that's why I'm here.'

She lit her third cigarette, exhaling into the already smoky small room that her husband had used as a reading-room, windowless, lined round with glass-fronted barristers' bookshelves that caught the reflection of lamplight and cast it back to us from all four walls. The chairs wrapped round you, sagging at their centres where the springs had worn, a comfy spot to sit and talk, and I'd already talked too much.

I'd left nothing out, from my first meeting Deacon to my turning up this evening on her doorstep, and through it all she'd sat and smoked in silence. Not a single interruption. I admired that in people – the ability to sit and listen quietly, without interjecting their own thoughts and opinions – mostly because I was incapable of doing it myself. But in this instance I'd have rather had her interrupt. The story, told unbroken, sounded just like that: a story. Hardly plausible.

She drew on the cigarette, thinking. 'I knew he was dead,' she said finally. 'No one got in touch to say so, but I knew. He said he'd call, you see. He said he'd call again, and when he didn't...' A small movement of her shoulder, like a shrug. 'He was always a man of his word. So I knew.'

She had taken it matter-of-factly, I thought, just as Regina

Marinho had, but with the same thread of wistful regret, as though something had passed from the world that would not be replaced. It wasn't love, not love, not in the same way that my grandmother had felt it; yet these women had felt *something*, had esteemed the man so highly that the knowledge of his death somehow diminished them.

'When,' I asked her, 'did you talk to him?'

'The last time? Oh, back at the beginning of September.'

'And he mentioned my name to you?'

'Yes, several times. He made me write it down. He didn't trust my memory, I suppose, even though he had ten years on me. Men can be like that. Unreasonable. Anyhow, he told me you'd be calling on me soon, and that I ought to let you in and be nice to you — his exact words. I don't expect he trusted me with that, either. I've never had a reputation, really, for being nice.' The willful Reynolds jaw was very much in evidence as she angled her head to tap ash from the cigarette.

Into the pause, I said, 'Did he say why I'd be coming to see you?'

'He said you'd fill in the details.'

'Oh. I see.'

'I gather, from what you've just been telling me, that you can't do that.'

'No.'

She echoed, 'No.'

I took my tape recorder out and showed it to her. 'Do you mind if I use this?'

She shook her head. 'You're sure he mentioned murder?'

'Yes.' I paused a moment, thinking, and then asked, straight out, 'How did Manuel Garcia die?'

'Garcia?'

'Yes. He died on April 6th.'

'Oh, I remember the day well enough. But that wasn't a murder. It wasn't a nice death,' she said, 'but it wasn't a murder.'

'You're certain of that?'

She nodded, drawing deeply on her cigarette. Her gaze began to drift and lose its focus in a way that I now found familiar. Quietly, she said, 'I'm very certain. I was there.'

The day had got off to a promising start. She'd arrived at the office to find out that Vivian Spivey was ill, and would not be at work. That, for her, was as good as a holiday. Like Regina, Jenny had no use for Spivey, and lately her already poor opinion of the man had darkened to something approaching real hatred.

It had started the previous autumn, when she had been seeing a young man who worked in the legal department. James Iveson was from New York, like Jenny. He blew through the office that fall like a breath of fresh air, irresistibly fun, and of course, for Jenny, he had the added appeal of being somebody she had to keep secret.

It wasn't that her father didn't like James – quite the contrary – but Reynolds was increasingly upset about the rumours that marked Jenny as his mistress, and, protectively, he tried now to discourage any actions that might hurt her reputation. Life was dull for her, and sneaking out with James to go to nightclubs, or the movies, gave her something to look forward to; a temporary thrill.

And then one night, somebody took her father's car and

left it parked in front of James's house till dawn, right on the street, where everyone could see it. Her father, when he found out, hit the ceiling. James was fired, and Reynolds purged the whole office of unmarried men.

She tried protesting, arguing, telling her father it hadn't been her; that she'd been in her own bed all night, but the evidence was damning, and the word of her accuser more reliable.

The person who'd accused her had been Spivey. She suspected from the start that he had been involved, because he disliked James. She didn't know the details, only that the air grew chilly in the office when the two men faced each other, and that Spivey resented the favour that James had been gaining with Reynolds. Suspicion had turned to certainty after she'd talked to her driver, Joaquim. He'd been off that one night, or else she would have had his word to back her up, but he—

'Joaquim?' I couldn't help the interruption. 'Your driver's name was Joaquim?'

'That's right. Why?'

'I think I might have met him, when I was in Portugal. Did he also do work for the British Embassy, do you know?'

'I honestly couldn't tell you. He wasn't exactly a talkative person, Joaquim. He didn't say much, about himself or anyone else. He overheard a lot of conversations, in the car, but I think he'd have stood up to torture before he repeated so much as a word.'

Yes, I thought, that sounded like the man I'd met in Lisbon.

Anyhow, she told me, picking up the thread of narrative,

Joaquim had made a point of speaking to her, a thing that ran contrary to his character. He'd said that he'd seen Spivey at the garage on the afternoon before the car was taken to be parked at James's house. There would have been no reason, so Joaquim had said, for Spivey to be at the garage, but the keys to both cars were kept there, in plain view. There would be no point in accusing Spivey, Joaquim had said, on such speculative evidence, and even less to gain by confronting him, since Spivey's ill graces, once gained, could be poisonous. But Joaquim had thought Jenny should know, for her own sake. Before returning to his normal, tight-lipped self, he'd offered the advice that, 'It is good, in a garden, to know where the snakes lie, so one can step carefully.'

Her personal opinion was that, if a snake were dangerous, one ought to take its head off with a shovel, but she knew Joaquim was right. Her father trusted Spivey, and that made a shield so strong that any arrows aimed at Spivey were deflected back upon the one who'd fired them. She'd have needed the Biblical David's skill with a slingshot to topple the man from his pedestal. So she'd stepped carefully.

Even when she'd been assigned to Spivey as his secretary, later in the year, she had kept her complaints to a minimum, though working in close confines with the man had galled her terribly.

He'd known it too. She'd seen it in the way he smiled when she was in his office, a sadist's smile that took its pleasure from another's impotence. And there'd been little she could do but bite her tongue and tough it out.

Till Deacon came.

She hadn't known, when she'd first seen her father's new

337

curator, that this quiet-spoken Englishman would change her life so greatly. She'd thought him rather dull, in the beginning; but that hadn't stopped her envying Regina, who, with Roger Selkirk, and now Deacon, claimed the two best-mannered men to work for in the office.

In fact, Jenny had never thought that anyone could be as nice as Roger, but while Roger was a sympathising confidant, a shoulder she could lean on, who could cheer her and give good advice, he wasn't one to intervene between her father and herself – he trod a neutral path.

Deacon, who had less to say, was more inclined to act.

One day, after taking dictation from Spivey, she'd been attacking her typewriter in a black mood when she'd become aware of Deacon, by Regina's desk, observing her. He'd looked away again, not saying anything, but later on that afternoon she'd had an unexpected summons from her father.

Her father hadn't been the sort of man to sit at desks. Upstairs, in his wood-panelled office, she'd found him pacing like a restless animal between the two long windows. When she'd entered, he had stopped and turned to face her, strong arms folded. 'Mr Deacon has asked for assistance, a few hours a week, cataloguing the paintings. Regina can't do it, she's buried with work as it is, but we thought, since you've only got Spivey to worry about, that you might have the time.'

It had not been exactly a question, but Jenny had answered it anyway, feeling like a prisoner being granted an early parole. 'Yes, I'd be glad to help.'

And so each week she'd spent a few hours working side by side with Deacon in the storage room, among the artworks, putting numbers on the canvases and writing down the details of each piece. The work was easy, and she knew he hadn't really needed her at all, to help him. She had told him so, one afternoon.

'Perhaps not,' he had said.

'So why request me, then?'

He'd shrugged, not looking up from the small statue he was numbering, and in his quiet voice he'd made the comment, 'Mr Spivey's not an easy man to work for, I'd imagine.'

'No,' she'd answered, wondering why he had changed the subject, till she realised that he hadn't changed it. Then more slowly, with new understanding, she'd said, 'No, he's not.'

'Well, then.' Glancing up, he'd nodded at the page that she was writing. 'Just keep on with that. And take your time.'

He hadn't always kept her working in the storage room. He sometimes took her with him when he went to meet with dealers, or appraise a private painting Reynolds wanted to acquire. 'A change is as good as a rest,' he would say, and it was.

To counter Spivey's protests, Deacon had often remarked to her father how impressed he was with Jenny's eye for art, and with her eagerness to learn about the subject. It wasn't true – she hadn't known a good work from a bad one – but, for Deacon, she had tried.

It had felt good to be rewarded with her father's warm approval, and his pride. Being able to sit with her father and look at a painting and speak, at least, in the same technical language, had finally given her the kind of connection she'd wanted with him all her life.

She'd had Deacon to thank for that, as she'd had Deacon to thank for the freedom her father increasingly gave her, beginning the night when her father, attacked by a stomach complaint, had told Jenny they wouldn't be able to go to the theatre. Deacon, silent till then, at the storage-room table, had spoken up out of the blue: 'I could take her.'

She'd known what her father would answer. He'd never allowed someone else to escort her – only Roger, and Roger was busy that night. She'd been turning away, disappointed, when he'd unexpectedly said, 'Yes, all right.'

So she'd gone to the play after all, and from that evening on she'd adored Andrew Deacon.

She smiled through the memories, now, sitting with me in the windowless room of her Washington house, while her cigarette, forgotten, burnt to ash between her fingers.

She said, 'I don't know why he bothered with me, really. I mean, I was young then, and pretty, and used to men paying attention to me, but Andrew was different. He didn't want *that*.' Her smile deepened. 'I know, because I made a pass at him once. He was a perfect gentleman about it, very polite, but he wasn't the slightest bit tempted. I ought to have known. He was too much in love with his wife.'

She noticed the state of her cigarette, and reached to gently tamp it out.

'Amelia, her name was. She died, did you know that? A week or so after my father.'

'Died how?' I was curious, wanting to know what the story had been.

'She was walking, I think, in a park, and a strong wind blew down a great branch from a tree, and it hit her.'

That would have pleased my grandmother, who had

340

wanted Amelia to have an exciting end; nothing too boring.

'It was an awful month, for deaths. Garcia, and my father, and then Andrew's wife…it absolutely crushed him, when he got the news. He went back to England soon after. I don't know,' she said, 'that he ever recovered from losing Amelia. I mean, he went on with his life, and he travelled a lot, but he never remarried; he never had children. I always thought that was a shame. He'd have made a good father. Look how he took it on his shoulders to watch over me, all these years, as though I were his responsibility. He never missed a birthday, or a Christmas, or—' She paused, as though acknowledging that all of that was past; that Deacon wouldn't be there anymore. A match scraped in the silence of the moment as she lit another cigarette. The small flame flared, and danced, and died within one breath. 'But I've gotten off topic,' she said. 'You were asking me about the day Manuel Garcia died.'

The first part of the morning had passed quietly; happily, even, with Spivey not there. Jenny had typed a few letters for Roger. The new secretary, Miss Bryce – who wore her hair back in a no-nonsense bun and insisted on being called *Miss* Bryce, no Christian names, thank you – was struggling, still, with Regina's old workload, and Roger was fussy about how his letters were typed.

He'd been grateful.

'Thanks, darling,' he'd said, as he half leant, half sat at the edge of her desk while he proofread the pages. 'I'll have a few more, but they won't be till later. Your father wants me over there this afternoon, to take dictation.'

'Over there' was the house where Reynolds was impatiently

341

confined to bed, recovering from surgery. His doctors had wanted to keep him in the hospital, but he had argued, 'Hospitals are where you go to die,' and he had said it with such force, with such defiance, that in that moment Jenny had believed that he might truly win the battle with his illness. She'd been told the odds weren't good. The stomach troubles that had plagued him for the past few months had worsened to the point where he'd had difficulty keeping down his food, and when he'd finally called his doctors in, the verdict had been grim: it was a pancreatic cancer. Not survivable. The surgery might help him live a few more weeks; a month, perhaps, but medically, they could do nothing more.

Jenny hadn't accepted the news. She'd just begun to get to know her father; she was not prepared to lose him. And besides, it was impossible to think that Ivan Reynolds could be felled by such a little thing as cancer. Even with all the weight loss, and lines plainly drawn on his face by the pain, he looked larger than life; indestructible. That gave her hope.

He'd looked better, she'd thought, when she'd seen him that morning. He'd been sitting up, giving the poor private nurse he had hired proper hell for the strength of his tea.

She warned Roger about this, now. 'Watch out. He's more like himself today.'

'Well, that's good news, then, isn't it?' Gathering his letters, he nodded towards Spivey's office. 'Vivian's not in today, I see.'

'He's ill.'

'Something serious, I hope?'

She smiled. 'I don't know.'

'Ah, well. Bit of a break for you, anyway, having him out of

342

the office.' He grinned. 'You can take a long lunch.'

She hadn't thought of that, but he was right, she could. And so she did, returning well past one o'clock. Miss Bryce was there to meet her at the door, concerned.

Miss Bryce said, in a disapproving whisper, 'There's a man in Mr Spivey's office.'

Jenny shrugged her coat off, frowning. 'What man?'

'He didn't give his name. I told him Mr Spivey wasn't in, and he should wait for you, but he said never mind, he knew what he was looking for, he'd only take a moment.'

'Is that so?' She hung up her coat on its peg, and trained her gaze on Spivey's door. 'All right, thank you, Miss Bryce. I'll take care of it.'

She was braced for a confrontation when she entered Spivey's office, but the man who stood behind the desk was not a stranger. He glanced up as she came in, and smiled. 'Miss Saunders. Good. You're back.'

She relaxed. 'Mr Cayton-Wood. How can I help you?'

JL Cayton-Wood met Spivey every month, to keep abreast of Reynolds's oil shipments passing through the harbour. He was a charmer, not the sort of man a woman should take seriously, but he was *so* handsome that, at times, she could forget.

She said, 'Miss Bryce said you were looking for something?'

He'd spread out some files from the tray on the desk and was searching through papers. Ships' manifests mostly, from what she could see.

'Yes. Mr Spivey was compiling a report for me, on what was shipped last autumn…'

'Well, you won't find it there,' she said, coming around the desk, businesslike. 'Those are the ships that are on their way now, or already in harbour.'

'Ah, yes. The *Hernando*.' He stepped aside, reading the name on the top of the files as she stacked them. 'That's the one that was headed for Spain, was it not, just before the embargo? I'm surprised that Mr Reynolds hasn't already diverted that petroleum somewhere else.'

'I'd imagine he's had other things on his mind.'

'Yes, of course. Do forgive me. How is he? I heard he had surgery.'

'Yes. He's recovering well, thank you.' She checked the drawers of Spivey's desk and came up empty. 'I don't know where else to look for that report. I know I haven't typed one, so it wouldn't be in our front office. If you like, I could call Mr Spivey at home.'

'No, don't bother the poor man. I'll make do without.'

'But—'

'It's not that important.'

Which didn't explain why he'd come here in person to look for it, Jenny thought, but she said nothing.

Garcia was in the front office when they came out, having a word with Miss Bryce. He looked taken aback to see Cayton-Wood there, but the two men exchanged civil greetings. Then Jenny introduced Miss Bryce to Cayton-Wood, who chatted some few minutes before putting on his hat.

Garcia watched him leave, and frowned, and with a curt, 'You will excuse me,' to the ladies, went out after him.

Jenny sat back at her desk. Through the window, she watched the little pantomime unfolding; saw Garcia call to

Cayton-Wood, and stop him on the sidewalk; saw the two men talking, Cayton-Wood's face shielded by his hat, Garcia's guarded.

'What a very charming man,' Miss Bryce said.

'Yes,' said Jenny, watching still. Garcia was alone, now, on the sidewalk. Cayton-Wood was walking off. The Spaniard stood a moment, head bent, then he turned and came inside. The office door swung open. Closed.

Garcia paused, his head still down, and told Miss Bryce, 'I do not wish to be disturbed.'

And then he went into his office, and he shut the door.

The tape in my recorder whirred through to its end, and clicked. I changed it over, trying not to make much noise, but Jenny Augustine seemed not to mind the interruption. In the room the lamps seemed very bright all of a sudden, as she shifted in her chair so she no longer faced her own reflection in the glass front of the bookcase opposite.

Quietly, she said, 'He shot himself. At two-fifteen, exactly. I was looking at the clock. I'd never heard a gun go off before – I thought a gas pipe had exploded. So I went to see.'

She let her eyes close for a moment, as though closing them could wipe the memory from her mind. It didn't.

She could hear the others coming up behind her, but she couldn't seem to look away from the horrific scene. Someone's hands closed gently round her shoulders; turned her; drew her close against a man's starched shirtfront. 'It's all right,' said Deacon, in his quiet voice. 'It's over. No, don't look.'

Miss Bryce, behind them, looked, and screamed, a shrill,

unnerving sound in that small space. She might have gone hysterical if Deacon hadn't taken charge.

'Miss Bryce,' he told her firmly, 'could you please call Mr Selkirk down.'

He had to say it twice before she heard him. Then she nodded, gathering her wits. A woman like Miss Bryce could cope with any crisis if she had a task to do.

'And when you've done that,' Deacon said, 'please put the kettle on, for tea. I think we'll all be needing some.'

He would have sent Jenny off too, but she stayed. She'd had a bad shock, and she wanted the comfort of Deacon's calm strength. But she stood to one side of the door, where he told her to stand, out of view of the room and the damage inside, while he went in and took a closer look.

She'd thought Roger would be with her father by now, but he hadn't left yet. He came running. 'What's happened? Miss Bryce said that…God.' He stopped dead, at the door to the office. 'Oh, God.' He raised a stricken face to Deacon. 'I just saw him at lunch. He was fine. Why on earth…?'

'Jenny, dear,' Deacon said, coming out of the room, 'was there anyone with him, this afternoon?'

'No.' She was shaking. She folded her arms, but she couldn't control it. 'No, he was alone. He stepped outside to have a word with Mr Cayton-Wood a while ago, but only for a moment; after that he didn't want to be disturbed. But there was no one else here with him. I'd have seen them coming in.'

'Well, that settles that,' said Roger. 'And besides, it looks as though he's left a note.'

'Yes, to his wife. There was this, as well,' Deacon said,

taking another long envelope out of his pocket. He gave it to Roger. 'It's for Mr Reynolds.'

'Oughtn't we to leave that where it was, till the police have been?'

But Deacon's eyes insisted. 'Better you deliver it yourself, I think. We wouldn't want it getting...lost.'

Even in her shocked state, Jenny felt that she was missing something, some small understanding that had passed between the men.

'Right,' said Roger, as he pocketed the letter. 'Right. I'm off to see the old man, anyway. I'll break the news.' He took one final, disbelieving look into the room, as though his mind could not accept what it had seen there. 'Poor Manuel.' And then, more practically, 'This won't do the company any good either, you know.'

Jenny Augustine smiled very faintly. She said, 'That was Roger. For a man so addicted to gossip, he always did try to steer clear of a scandal. He needn't have worried, though. None of the papers took notice of Garcia's suicide – they had a more important death to write about.'

And I remembered, then, why April 6th had seemed such a familiar date. 'Your father's.'

'Yes. He died that night. When I got home that evening, I could see that he was getting worse. His lungs were filling up with fluid, and the nurse was wanting him to go back in the hospital, but he was stubborn.' Lifting the chin that was so like her father's, she said, 'So he died in his bed, in his sleep, like he wanted to die. And everyone forgot about Garcia. Everyone, that is, except Andrew. It troubled him, I know, because the two of them were friends. I think he felt that he could somehow have prevented it. And then, of course, his wife died, and that really did him in; so he went home.'

I asked her, 'What happened to Cayton-Wood?'

The question appeared to surprise her a little. 'Oh, he went home, too, back to England, but not till the summer. After the Allies had landed in Normandy. I heard he was killed in an accident – sailing, or something like that. Men that handsome seem to bring bad luck upon themselves,' she said.

She would said more, I felt sure, but the dog barked. Not a single bark, but the sharp burst of high-pitched yelps that signalled an intrusion. Jenny Augustine reached down and laid her hand firmly on the terrier's head. 'Quiet.' Into the silence we both sat and listened.

The knock came again, clearly audible this time, and once again the dog replied.

'Were you expecting anyone?' I asked.

She shook her head.

There were no windows in the room that we were in, but in the darkened front room, down the hall, I found that I could edge the blind away from the window frame just enough to see a thin slice of the street and the black-railinged steps leading up to the door. There were cars in the street – I saw one, double-parked, with a driver inside, headlights on, engine idling. And on the steps a man was standing on his own. I couldn't really see his face, until he moved to knock again. The lamplight caught the light brown hair; the harder lines of nose and jaw.

A face I knew.

I eased the blind back into place with care. Jenny Augustine was sitting where I'd left her in the other room, the dog curled like a wire spring between her feet. The years had settled round her once again with unforgiving firmness. She looked old, just as my grandmother had looked that afternoon, when…

'I don't think that we should stay here,' I said, taking charge. 'Is there a back way out?'

I only hoped the people at the front door didn't know about the lane. I wouldn't have known that it was there, myself – there wasn't any indication from the street that any lane or alleyway ran up behind the houses, and at any rate, it didn't run the full length of the block, but dead-ended at the high wood fence surrounding Jenny Augustine's back yard. It was a narrow, almost squalid, little lane, with solid wooden fences rising close at either side to block the light that angled downwards from all but the highest house windows, and the air hanging thick with the smells of bare dirt and bagged garbage.

It was dark, and I was trying to be quiet, but the uneven ground wasn't easy to walk on. Now and then I hit a patch of brick, or stone, that made me stumble. It must have been even more difficult for an elderly woman. And she'd brought the dog, impatient on its leash, which didn't help.

The dog's paws scrabbled in the dirt, its snuffing nose and panting breath so loud to my own ears that I felt sure we'd be discovered. Then it stopped, and crouched, and all the hair stood stiffly up along its backbone as it growled.

Ahead of us, against the iron gate that marked the lane's far end, a man stood out in silhouette.

I'd already pushed Jenny Augustine into the shadows, flat

up to the fence, with myself pressed close beside her, when the gate creaked open, slowly, and the man came through. The dog growled again, low. I willed it to silence.

The man moved towards us, but cautiously; half blind, as we were, in the dark.

I held my breath. My heart thumped at my ribcage and my legs ached to move, but I stayed like a statue until I felt I'd have to either scream or run as a release – and then the man suddenly stopped, and half turned to the wall. Metal scraped on metal, and a garden door swung open, and the man was gone.

A neighbour. Not a threat. And anyway, he hadn't seen us.

I counted to ten, to be safe, and was about to leave the wall when I heard noises, soft and furtive, overhead. Looking up, I saw the ragged outline of an overhang of shingles on the roof of someone's shed, butting up against the fence's other side. I froze, in fear. I remembered Guy telling me what the police knew about Grandma's murder – 'They figure the shooter was up on the roof of the neighbour's garage, at the back of the lane.'

Jenny Augustine moved at my side, and I stretched out my arm to hold her still. Looking up, I waited, while the noises came again, more marked, this time: a stronger thump, a scuffing sound, and, suddenly, the short-lived, banshee shriek of fighting cats. The sound, so close above me, made my heart bolt upwards, even while it calmed my fears.

And then the dog barked, and I snapped back into motion, coming free of the wall and guiding Jenny Augustine behind me down the lane, before all the noise gave away our position.

We stopped a minute on the dark side of the iron gate that opened onto Prospect Street, halfway between 33rd and Potomac. I peered out, making certain there was no one standing waiting at the corner, before cautiously pushing against the black bars. The gate squeaked on its hinges, I couldn't help that, but I caught it before it clanged back into place, and I eased it gently shut.

Our escape plan was hazy, at best. I just wanted to get us away from the quiet streets, back to the busy ones, and so I let Jenny Augustine lead me away from Potomac. We circled round, back down to M Street. There were definitely more people here, walking round us on the sidewalk, talking, laughing – but I still felt too exposed. Every set of approaching headlights, every car that passed us by, seemed somehow sinister.

I wanted to get indoors, out of sight of searching eyes, but we had the dog.

'Max!' Jenny Augustine said, on a note of frustration. I turned. She was tugging the leash of the dog, who'd dug in with all fours on the red-bricked paved sidewalk, refusing to budge. To me, she explained, 'When my husband was alive, he used to stop here for a coffee, on their morning walk. It's remarkable what animals remember. Max, come *on*.'

I looked around, taking notice for the first time of exactly where we were.

A gap between the buildings on the sidewalk opened here into an upscale pedestrian alley, with what appeared to be a long arcade of shops along one side, warmly lit bow windows jutting out from dark brick walls, and columns, fancied up by hedges and a row of the old-fashioned-looking lampposts that were such a feature of Georgetown.

This, I knew, was more than what it looked to be – it was, in fact, an entrance to the giant and expensive three-floor mall of Georgetown Park. Inside, we would have been able to find some measure of anonymity, and safety…if we hadn't had the dog.

But still, I conceded, the dog hadn't done badly, stopping us here. Because facing the row of shop windows, along the little alley, were the rounded green awnings of Dean and Deluca's, the gourmet food and coffee shop. And down the alley's centre was a row of outside tables for those customers who liked to drink their coffee out of doors.

Safety in numbers, I thought. We could make ourselves part of the crowd, less conspicuous.

We found a table in the middle of the open alley, not too close to any of the lampposts, so it fell more in shadow than light, partly screened by a square-trimmed yew hedge in a planter behind. My chair faced the main part of Dean and Deluca's, a long, glassed-in gallery, like a greenhouse, built on the side of the red-brick main building, with cane chairs and marble-topped tables and slowly revolving fans moving the air above tables of people, not one of whom took any notice of us. Even the table of women directly beside us seemed far too involved in their own conversation to even be aware that we were there.

The dog settled down with a stretch and a yawn at his mistress's feet. She asked, 'What now?'

'I don't know.'

We sat for some minutes in silence, both thinking.

A man came and sat at the next table over, in my line of vision. An old man, about Deacon's age, very tall and loose-jointed, and wearing the same kind of overcoat Deacon had worn. I made a point of looking at his face, the way I should have done with Deacon – really looking, at the kindness of his features, and the downturned eyes beneath the winging eyebrows, and the still-full head of thick white hair. I knew that I would never see this man again, and yet I went on looking at his face, as though by doing that, I somehow could atone for what I'd failed to do with Deacon.

I said quietly, 'I'm sorry, Mrs Augustine, for getting you into all this.'

'Don't be silly.' She drew her coat closer around her, to keep out the cold. 'This is the most excitement I've had in years.' Her smile was dry, and brief, as though she'd fallen out of practice. She looked me over. 'Seems to me that Andrew knew what he was doing, when he got in touch with you.'

'What makes you say that?'

'You're a fighter. After everything that's happened, you're still here, still trying to get to the truth.'

'It's my job.' But I knew, in this case, it was more than that. So did she.

She asked, 'What will you do with the truth, when you find it?'

'I really haven't thought that far ahead. His nephew—'

'James?'

'Yes. He thought Deacon got in touch with me so I'd bring the story out into the open. You know, make it public.'

'A book, then.' She nodded. 'Well, when the time comes, you make sure you come see me. I have some connections in publishing.'

It was touching, I thought, that she had so much faith in

me. I hadn't even gotten to the end of Deacon's story, yet. I'd never tried to write a book. And frankly, it remained to be seen whether I'd be able to get us through tonight alive.

We'd have to start, I thought, by getting coffee. We couldn't sit here any length of time without at least an empty cup in front of us, it wouldn't look right. I took out my wallet and counted the change.

Jenny Augustine asked, 'What's that for?'

'We need coffee.' I explained why; then I stood. 'I'll be as quick as I can. Will you be all right out here, alone?'

'I have Max,' she said, patting the dog at her feet. 'Don't worry. No one is going to molest an old woman in a place like this.'

Behind her, the elderly man at the next table over was turning a page of his newspaper, and the four women beside us were still busy talking and laughing. It looked like a safe enough place, for the moment.

The line at the counter was short, and I kept a watchful eye on Jenny Augustine the whole time I was waiting, only turning my back for the minute it took me to pay the cashier. But a minute was all that it took. When I turned back to look, she was gone.

Panicked, I pressed my way back through the tight maze of tables and chairs to the place where I'd left her. The coffee from one of the cups I was holding sloshed scaldingly over my wrist, but I paid no attention. I looked towards M Street, my frantic gaze searching the faces of strangers.

And then the familiar voice suddenly spoke, at my shoulder. 'Here, let me help you with those.' Matt Jankowski reached over to take the two coffee cups from me. 'Is this where you're sitting?'

I don't believe I even felt surprised that he was there, and not in Portugal. In a fatalistic kind of way, it almost seemed inevitable.

I faced him, and in a calm voice that sounded nothing like my own, asked, 'Where is she?'

Matt said, 'She's with a friend of mine. A friend of hers, too, as it happens. You don't need to worry.' He pulled out a chair for me; set down the cups. 'Here, drink your coffee. You look cold.'

I felt cold. I crossed my arms over my chest, tightly, tucking my hands under, close to my body, so Matt wouldn't see they were shaking. But I didn't sit.

'Look,' he said, 'if you're *that* cold, we don't have to stay out here, you know. There's a restaurant a few blocks away where they make a great steak. Have you eaten yet?'

That did it. Here I was, practically frozen with fear for my life and the life of the woman I'd failed to protect, and he had the audacity to stand there speaking normally, as if we were old friends and there was nothing wrong. It was too much to bear in silence.

'If you think I'm going anywhere with you,' I told him evenly, 'you're crazy. I'm not moving. I'll stand here all night, if I have to, so whatever you're supposed to try to do to me, you'll have to do it here. And I can tell you now, I'm going to scream. I'm going to make the biggest scene I can, if you so much as touch me.'

And after this brave speech, I stopped for breath, and waited.

It was the expression on his face, really, that made me start to doubt myself. He looked as if I'd hit him with a hammer.

'Christ,' he said at last, and sat, and drank his coffee back as though he wished it were a double Scotch. 'Is that what you've been thinking? All the time we spent together, you've been thinking I'm a murderer?'

I didn't answer, but I took a chair, as well – still wary, and still watching him, but needing the support.

Tight-lipped, he exhaled and looked aside…searching, I think, for the words to convince me. Finally, he said, 'Kate, I haven't been trying to hurt you. That's not why I'm here. I was asked to protect you.'

'Protect me? I don't understand.'

So he tried to explain.

Matt Jankowski could remember, to the day, the first time he had heard of Andrew Deacon. It had been September 20th, a Wednesday. He'd been having lunch, at a small coffee shop just down the street from where he worked. He liked to eat alone. It was an hour of peace in what was usually, for him, a hectic workweek, serving corporate clients.

He'd been sitting in a booth, as was his custom, with the high backs of the bench seats blocking out the noise and bustle of the coffee shop, when the old man had approached him.

Matt had recognised him, naturally. He'd seen him many times at work, this senior partner who still kept a corner office in the building, even though he had officially retired some years before.

He was a legend in the firm. He'd been in the FBI's Special Intelligence Service in Latin America during the war, and lectured, still, at Georgetown University. An unassuming-looking man, with friendly eyes that took a person's measure at a glance. He'd said hello to Matt from time to time, when they had passed each other in the hall, or shared the elevator, but they'd never really spoken.

Till today.

Today he introduced himself, and shook Matt's hand, and took the seat across from him, depositing his briefcase at his side. And then he said, straight off, 'I'm told that you speak Portuguese.'

Matt thought that an odd way to begin a conversation, but he nodded. 'Yes, I do.'

'I'd like to ask a favour. Do you have a minute?'

'Yes.'

'I have a friend,' the old man said, and stopped. Then, quietly, 'I *had* a friend. He passed away, last week.'

'I'm sorry.'

'So am I. We had a long association. We were colleagues, in a way, except of course he wasn't FBI. He worked for the British. A good man. An honest man. Rare, in these times.' He paused, then, as though thinking of how to proceed. 'Before he died, he sent me a document – details of a murder that happened in Portugal, years ago. My friend was there; he knew the murderer. Afterward, he tried to bring the man to justice, but…well, it gets complicated. Recently, he raised the case again, but the authorities in Portugal aren't too keen to investigate. The case,' he said, 'is old, and cold, and based on one man's recollections. Still, I feel I have a certain, shall we say, responsibility. My friend sent that report to me, and now it's mine to run with. The problem is, it all comes down to just his word, his version of events. *I* know he's credible, but if I'm to present his case, I'll have to establish, beyond any doubt, that he's telling the truth.'

Matt admitted that would be a challenge, and the old man nodded.

'Yes. The murderer confessed to him in private, no one else was there. But in my friend's report he mentions several other incidents and conflicts that took place, and my thought is that if I could find the people who were there when *those* things happened, and have them back his stories with their own – if I can show that every other thing he says in his report is gospel truth, then…well, it's simple probability,' he said. 'If someone tells you XYZ, and you know X is fact, and Y is fact, it stands to reason Z is likely fact, as well.' He settled back. 'I've done some digging, and I know of seven people, still alive, who might be helpful. And there's one more woman I'm not sure of – I don't know if she's still living; I can't trace her married name. One of the seven lives right here, in Georgetown. The rest, though, they all live in Portugal. And at least three of them don't speak much English.'

'I see. So you want me to help you with the phone calls? Be your translator?'

'No, son. I want you to go there.' He smiled. 'Be my legs. I'm not young anymore. I'm not up to the trip. I need someone to go and find these people for me; take their depositions.'

'But…'

'It wouldn't take more than a couple of weeks, and you wouldn't be all on your own. The Legat' – he pronounced it LEE-gat—'at our Lisbon Embassy is a nice kid. He can't help

358

in any official sense, obviously, but he'll be able to point you in the direction of people who can.'

'Legat?' Matt repeated, as he tried to take this in.

'Oh, sorry. Legal Attaché. It's what we call the FBI man at an Embassy abroad.'

'I thought the FBI was only involved in domestic operations, here on American soil.'

'No, most of our Embassies have a Legat. Sometimes a domestic case spreads overseas, and then the Legat takes it up, among other things.'

'So if you have a guy in Lisbon, on the ground already, why do you need me?'

'He isn't mine. He's FBI, and this is not an FBI investigation. He would lose his job if he went off and interviewed these people for me, even if he did it on his own time. No, this is my own operation – it's personal.' The tightening along his jaw was slight; Matt almost missed it. 'Like I said, nobody else wants to pursue this. There are people in high places, even today, who would rather my friend had stayed silent.'

Matt asked him, 'Why *did* he stay silent so long?'

'He had his reasons. He explains them all in here.' The old man clicked his briefcase open and drew out a thick manila folder, sliding it to Matt across the table. 'You can read it for yourself. You'll need to read it, anyway, before you go.'

'I haven't said I will go yet.'

'I know you haven't.'

Matt dropped his gaze from those confident eyes that belonged in a much younger face, and began to read.

Time passed.

The world of the coffee shop seemed to recede, growing

more insubstantial. He didn't hear the clinking of the dishes any longer, or the hum of conversation – he was sixty years removed from it, in Portugal, with Deacon. He could see the people moving through the offices at Reynolds like the players on a stage. He saw their faces, heard their voices, felt he knew the details of their lives, and the moment of the murder was as real to him as if he'd been a witness to it. He, too, felt the deep sting of injustice when he read about the murderer, and what had happened afterward, and he felt Deacon's conflict in the bitter years of silence that had followed. But he understood the reasons.

When he'd finished, he looked up, to meet the old man's waiting gaze.

Matt said, 'If what he says is true…'

'It is.'

'Then your people in high places have a right to be afraid. I can't imagine that they'll just stand by and let this all come out.'

'They won't. In fact, I believe they're already trying to prevent it.'

'How?'

The old man's eyes were very level, very calm. 'My friend was killed – a hit-and-run. The driver and the car have not been found. A few days after that, the only family he had left, his nephew, was found murdered. A burglary, they're calling it, though nothing much was stolen, really. Just the private papers of my friend.' He paused, to let Matt fully grasp the implications. 'There may be other deaths. Perhaps my own,' he said. 'It's not without its dangers, what I'm asking you to do.'

Matt didn't reply for a long minute. Frowning, he ran his thumb along the folder's open edge, in front of him. 'I'm busy this weekend,' he said, after thought. 'And I promised a client I'd meet him on Monday.' He raised his head, and met the old man's eyes. 'But then I'm free.'

He had landed in Lisbon on Tuesday, the 26th of September.

He'd picked up his rental car, taken a room at an airport hotel, and got straight down to business.

The first of the names on his list had belonged to a man – in a nursing home, now – who'd been a member of the Vigilance Committee during the war. The man had told Matt what he could, which wasn't much. Matt hadn't gotten too much, either, from his second witness, a former shipyard worker who now lived just south of Lisbon, in the fishing town of Setúbal. But the next day he'd taken a run up to Caldas da Rainha and talked to a woman who'd once run a small hotel there. *She'd* remembered the details; her mind had been sharp. And she'd been able to recall Regina's married name – if not the town she'd moved to.

With this new information in hand, Matt had paid his first call to the American Embassy, and had found the FBI man there, the Legat, just as helpful as the old man who had sent him had predicted. The Legat had put Matt in touch with the local police, who had helped him to locate Regina Marinho.

Matt had phoned through to Evora and, finding that Regina was away and wouldn't be at home till Saturday, had gone back to his list of names, and started searching for the next one down: Joaquim.

It took a little time to find him, he was such a private man, but by the Friday afternoon, Matt's search had ended at the English Cemetery.

'The problem was,' he said, 'you beat me to it. I was nearly at the church when I heard you two talking, in the porch. You mentioned Regina Marinho, and so I stopped, and listened. It seemed a bit more than coincidence, for you to be asking one of the people I'd been sent to talk to about *another* of the people I'd been sent to talk to. And you mentioned Andrew Deacon.' He looked curious. 'Why did you tell Joaquim that Andrew Deacon was your grandfather?'

'I didn't think he'd want to help me otherwise.'

'Anyway, when you said you were the granddaughter, that rang a warning bell, because I was pretty sure that Andrew Deacon didn't have a family. So I thought I'd better find out who you were.'

He had put aside his plan to talk to Joaquim, for the moment, and had followed me. He'd planned to offer me a ride, but when that hadn't worked, he'd tailed my taxi back to the hotel.

He'd had a strong gut feeling I'd turn out to be important; so, although he had a perfectly good hotel room himself, near the airport, he'd taken a second room down at the York House, to keep a close eye on me till he could find out just how I connected with Deacon.

Meantime, he'd put through a call to Washington. The old man in the corner office had been most intrigued. He'd taken my description, and assured Matt he would find out what he could at his end.

Matt had gone down to look for me that evening, in the hotel's restaurant. I'd already been sitting with Anabela, so he'd taken a table in one of the neighbouring sections, effectively screened from my view. He could see us, himself, but not hear. He could tell it was not just a personal meeting – he had seen her pass over the envelope. Curious, he'd followed Anabela out, and overheard her phone call; watched her leave. He had been coming back in hopes of catching me alone, when we had literally bumped into one another, at the door.

All he could think of was to offer once again to buy me coffee, and to hope I'd take him up on it.

He'd waited in the hotel bar till closing time. It hadn't been a wasted evening, though. From where he'd sat, he had been able to see both the window of my room, that faced onto the courtyard, and the French door leading to the hotel's lobby. He could tell I hadn't left; that I was still inside.

And on his way back to his room, he found there'd been a fax for him, from Washington: a photograph, a little grainy, taken from a newspaper, and under it the written question, *Could this be the woman?*

Matt had studied it, and though he hadn't been exactly sure, he'd seen enough of a resemblance to reply that yes, it could.

And that, he told me, had changed everything.

There wasn't anybody sitting near us, now. The closest people I could see were several tables over.

We were set apart, unnoticed.

Matt looked down, and drew a pattern on the table with his coffee mug. 'I heard a story, then, about a woman named

363

Kate Murray. A reporter, pretty gutsy, pretty good at what she does. It turns out Andrew Deacon knew of her. He met with her in London – she was listed as a witness to his accident. The statement that she gave to the police said that the two of them were talking just before he died. Then, a week or so later, she goes back to Canada, back to Toronto, and that very same night someone fires a shot through her window.'

I said very quietly, 'Two shots.'

'Two shots. Now her grandmother's dead. And Kate runs. It's a strange thing to do, but she's read the report,' – I saw no real need to correct him on that point, not yet – 'she's a very smart woman, and maybe she figures she can't really trust the authorities, not when she knows who she's up against. So she just runs. Disappears. No one knows where she is. No one knows if she's even alive.'

Matt had heard this story late on Friday night, and when the old man in the corner office had finished telling it, he had asked Matt, with an urgency that transmitted itself through the telephone lines, 'Where is she now?'

'She's here. At my hotel.'

'You make damn sure you don't let her out of your sight. And Matt? Get me a photograph, if you can manage it. I'd like to see for myself if it's Kate.'

So Matt had followed me to Evora.

Or tried to. He had lost me on the road, but having reasoned that my purpose in going to Evora would be to try to see Regina – whose address he also had – he'd carried on, and set up watch near the Marinho house.

He hadn't known he'd be ahead of me. He'd somehow

364

missed seeing my car near the tour bus, when he'd circled back round the rest stop, and so he had thought I would be at Regina's already. He hadn't expected to see me arrive, and go in. And he hadn't expected to find that he wasn't the only one watching.

I couldn't help breaking his narrative. 'Was it a woman?'

'A man. At the end of the street. He didn't notice me, but I saw him.' He'd followed me, apparently, when I had left Regina's. Matt had followed, too, and when I'd stopped to look up at the old Roman temple, he'd quickly slipped into the tour group beside me, and that had been that.

All the time that I'd thought I'd been using him to be my bodyguard, he had been volunteering. He'd done it, to begin with, out of duty to the man who'd sent him, but as the night had worn on, that had changed.

Matt said, 'Up to then, you were like an assignment. One more thing for me to investigate.' I felt the brief touch of his glance. He looked away. Most lawyers I knew didn't have a problem finding words, but even without them, I knew what he wanted to say. I had felt it myself, at the time.

I asked him, 'Did you really have a room at the *pousada*?'

'No.'

'Where did you sleep, then?'

'I didn't.'

He'd stayed in his car. After dropping me off, he had gone round the block and parked well in the shadows, from where he could just see the hotel's front entrance. He'd tried, as it happened, to speak to Regina – he'd called from his cell phone, and given his name. He'd been told that she wasn't at home; that she wouldn't be home for a good many days. He'd been concerned, as I had been, and so he'd stayed awake. He'd watched me when I went out on my balcony, he'd watched me while I sat there, and when I had gone inside he went on watching, through the night, to see I didn't come to harm.

The next day, he'd been following me back to Lisbon when I'd had my breakdown. He had managed to come back around in time to see the tow truck, and to guess my rental company would take me back to Evora to get me a replacement. Thinking he would find me there, he'd hunted down the local office of the company. My car had turned up, sure enough, but I had not been with it.

He had panicked for a moment, then. The thoughts that he'd been thinking on his breakneck drive to Lisbon weren't thoughts that he really wanted to remember. And of course, I hadn't been at my hotel that night.

'I thought the worst,' he told me.

Still, first thing Monday morning he had gone to see his young FBI friend at the Embassy, and the digital pictures he'd taken of me Saturday, standing in the ruins of the Temple of Diana, had found their way by email back to Washington. Within the hour he'd had another phone call from his old man in the corner office.

'That's Kate.' He'd paused, and Matt had all but seen the clenching of the old man's jaw, a half a world away. 'You keep your eyes wide open. Don't let anybody hurt that girl. Her safety's more important to me now, than all the rest of it. You understand, son?'

Matt had understood. He hadn't had the heart to tell the old man that he didn't have a clue where I was at that moment. All morning, and all afternoon, he'd searched for me. And then, defeated, he'd gone back to his hotel. And found I'd left a message.

That, I thought, explained what I'd seen in his eyes, and hadn't understood, when we'd met at the hotel bar – relief. Relief I wasn't dead; that he still had a chance to keep me safe.

He'd planned, last night, to lay his cards out on the table, tell me everything. Well, possibly not *everything*. Enough, at least, to prove to me that we were on the same team, and to let me know that he was there to help.

He'd worked it all out, what he wanted to say, and the best way to say it…

And then I had told him, the very first thing, that I'd be flying to Toronto in the morning. He had known he wouldn't see me after that.

So Matt had let it go.

He'd let me go, too. Someone else had already been lined up to take on the role of my guardian angel when I arrived back in Toronto, so Matt's job, in that respect, had ended when, this morning, he had watched my plane take off.

Then he had driven back downtown, and had some breakfast, and tried to come up with a plan for his day. 'I still had three names on my list, for Portugal: Roger Selkirk, Joaquim, and a woman who'd worked as an Embassy code clerk. Joaquim's name came first, so I started with him.'

But Joaquim hadn't been at the cemetery. Nobody had known where he might be, or when he might return. Irritated by the inconvenience, Matt had moved on to Roger Selkirk's house. The neighbour I'd talked to had been outside, this time. She'd told Matt what she'd told me…except Matt had, of course, understood. And when, gripped by a growing sense of urgency, he'd gone to try to find the former code clerk, her home, too, had been deserted.

He'd had a sense, unsettling, that he was running second in a race. For all he knew, he might already have been beaten.

He'd wasted no more time. He'd put one last call through to Washington, and then had gone directly to the airport. The only flight they'd been able to get him on at such late notice had been routed through Frankfurt, arriving in Washington nearly an hour and a half after mine.

He'd been met by a car at the airport, and driven to Georgetown, to talk to the last person left on his list.

'Jenny Augustine,' I said.

'That's right.' Matt sat back, in a way that implied he was nearing the end of his tale. 'But again, you were already there.'

He'd known, before he'd even knocked at Jenny's door, that I was in the house. There had been someone watching the Augustine house all that day, and they'd seen me arrive. He'd also been informed that we were definitely in the house; that nobody had left. But then, of course, they hadn't known about the lane.

He might have gone on standing on the front step, thinking we were in there and not answering, if he hadn't received a call on his cell phone from the man who'd been watching the house all day, and who'd just left Matt a moment before.

'He'd been sitting all day in his car,' Matt explained. 'He'd been dying to stretch his legs, grab a quick coffee. So he came down here. And lo and behold, there the two of you were. He thought I might be interested to know that. And I was.' He lifted his own mug again, more for something to do than for anything else, I decided, because his coffee must have been as cold and unappealing now as mine. 'So that's the story. Any questions?'

I had several, actually, but only one that really mattered. 'How can I be sure that Mrs Augustine is all right?'

'You just have to trust me, on that. Take my word.'

I said nothing, and he looked at me with understanding.

'Kate, I'm not the enemy.'

'I don't know that.'

'Yes, you do.'

I looked away. His eyes were too compelling when they watched my face like that. He was right – I *did* know that he'd told me the truth, but these past weeks had changed me so deeply, I'd had my emotions and thoughts under guard for so long, that I couldn't just switch it all off, not at once.

I said, 'And this is what you meant to tell me yesterday, I take it?'

'More or less.'

'I see.'

'I thought,' he said, 'that we'd get farther if we worked together, if we pooled our information. You talked to Regina Marinho; I didn't. You talked to Andrew Deacon.'

Again, I didn't see the need to tell him that he'd got it wrong – that Deacon and I hadn't really discussed much of anything, and that I'd never received his report.

Matt must have been getting used to speaking through my silences. He said, 'Look, Kate, you have to trust me. I'm on your side. If there's anything you've learnt, anything you've been told, that can help us build a stronger case against this guy, we need to know.' His voice grew more persuasive. He reminded me, 'This isn't easy, what we're trying to do here.'

And he told me why. He told me that, unless we proved, beyond all doubt, that Deacon's accusations had been true, we'd never convince the authorities that the man Deacon had named in his report might also be linked to the present-day murders. We'd never get justice for Deacon, or Cavender, or for my grandmother. The murderer would win again. 'He'll walk,' said Matt. 'Because even with the testimonials I've got to back it up, the report on its own isn't going to be enough, I don't think – not given this guy's connections. He'd laugh at us. And I don't think he's about to confess.'

He was right – he had made a strong argument. But he had made one mistake. He'd assumed that I, too, had read Deacon's report, so he'd mentioned the murderer's name. Not the name that he'd gone by in Portugal, years ago, but the name he went by now.

Matt sensed the change in me, I think. 'Kate?'

'Yes?'

'You're tired, I know. Why don't we leave this till tomorrow? Let me come and get you after breakfast, you can meet my friend...'

I said, 'Your old man in the corner office?'

'Yes. I know he wants to talk to you.'

No doubt he did, I thought, but I was still a bit preoccupied. My newly focused mind had travelled backwards, and I felt like I was standing once again beside the grave at Deacon's funeral, with the young priest Thomas Beckett reading from

Ecclesiastes, underneath the sun: *For God shall bring every work into judgement, with every secret thing...*

Every secret thing...

I looked at Matt. 'All right,' I said. 'Tomorrow.'

And I smiled, so he'd believe me.

Chapter Five

England Again

I pass, like night, from land to land;...
The moment that his face I see,
I know the man that must hear me:

COLERIDGE, 'THE RIME OF THE ANCIENT MARINER'

WEDNESDAY, OCTOBER 4

Later on, when I looked back on it, the only explanation I could give for what I did next was that, at the time, I saw no other way.

My life, as I was living now, was not a life. To be in fear, to be in hiding, using someone else's name – this wasn't how I wanted to go on. And it would never stop, so long as both the murderer and I were still alive. My only thought on that long morning flight to London was that, one way or another, I would see it end, today.

I'd left a note for Matt, at my hotel: just an apology for missing our appointment, nothing more, but I had felt I'd owed him that, at least, for all that he had done. I hadn't said where I was going, or what I'd resolved to do, because he would have tried to stop me. And I wasn't letting anybody stop me. This was my fight now, to finish.

'Purpose of your trip?' the customs agent asked me, as I stood before him with my single suitcase.

'Business.' For, although I couldn't tell the truth, that answer came the closest.

It was raining when I came out of the terminal. I had lost a day through travelling – already it was night here, and the rain fell cold and unrelenting from the strangely glowing sky that seemed to hover, eerily, a step from total darkness.

I said nothing in the taxi; only watched the water chasing down the window glass in rivulets, until I recognised the lights and streets of Shepherd's Bush. 'Turn here,' I said.

There was no sign of life from Margot's flat. I hadn't thought there would be, really, but a part of me had hoped. I paid the driver, set my suitcase on the step, and bent to feel beneath the iron railing for the key she always kept there. I'd expected she'd stop doing that last year, when her neighbour in the flat next door had woken in the middle of the night to find a man beside her bed, a living nightmare. The woman's screams had sent the man running, but all the tenants on the street had been uneasy afterwards. One had moved, and one had bought a dog, and one had put in an alarm. But Margot, who'd fearlessly travelled all parts of the world on her own, and who liked to meet danger head on, had gone a different route: she'd left her spare key in its place, and got a gun.

It wasn't legal. How she'd come by it, I didn't know, but Margot often played outside the rules. She had shown it to me once – a deadly thing, so cold and heavy in my hand. I had been glad to pass it back to her.

'I couldn't ever shoot a gun,' I'd told her.

That was then.

I found the key, and got the front door open, locking it behind me as I stepped into the narrow hallway. I left the lights off – there was no point alarming the already vigilant neighbours, I thought, as I felt my way through to the back of the flat, and the bedroom. The gun, I hoped, would still be in her bedside table, where I'd seen it last.

Had I not been so focused, I might well have caught the warning signs: the waiting silence of the rooms; the bedroom door conveniently ajar. But as it was, the rough male hands that grabbed me took me wholly by surprise.

I struggled. I couldn't call out – his arm pressed my throat in a choke-hold. In panic, I tried to gulp air and discovered I couldn't do that, either. Bright spots of light exploded in my head, behind my eyes, and blood roared upwards to my ears.

A blinding flash, as though someone had hit the wall switch for the lights, and I was turned, and then I heard the man say, 'Jesus!'

And he let me go.

Without his arm to hold me up I landed heavy on my knees, bent forward, gasping. He came with me, leaning down so his concerned face hovered inches from my own. 'You all right?'

It was Margot's friend, Nick, the security expert, who'd been such good company on my flight home to Toronto, three weeks ago. He'd done well to recognise me, after only one meeting and with my new hair colour, but clearly he knew who I was.

'I didn't realise it was you,' he said. Twisting round, he called back to the darkness of the bedroom, 'It's your friend. The one from Canada.'

And the next thing I knew, there stood Margot herself, in the doorway. She looked as surprised as I felt. *'Kate?'* Her gaze raked my face, to be sure. 'What on earth…?'

I found something resembling my voice. 'You're alive.'

'Well, of course I'm alive.' She was already at my side, kneeling to get to my level, her eyes a mixture of confusion and concern. 'Did Nick hurt you? We heard the noise, you see,' she started to explain, as I began to notice how the two of them were dressed – or not dressed. That explained, I thought, why there had been no lights on in the flat, although it was still relatively early in the evening.

Nick stood, and stretched, and defended his actions. 'Yeah, well, it's a good thing I *was* here, or she'd have met with you and that damned gun.'

Margot ignored him. She was looking at my hair again... my face. 'What *have* you done to yourself?'

I said, 'You haven't heard?' But it was obvious she didn't have a clue about the shooting in Toronto, or the fact that I'd been on the run.

'Heard what? I've been away. I just flew back this morning; haven't even rung the office.' She sat back on her heels, her eyes expectant. 'What the hell have I been missing?'

'Idiot,' said Margot, but she meant it fondly. She leant to pour the dregs of our second bottle of Bordeaux into my glass. 'So you were just going to march in here, take my gun, and...then what? Face the lion in his den, and shoot him?'

'Yes.' The small word had a stubborn edge. I hadn't changed my point of view.

'It wouldn't work. Nick, talk to her.'

Nick, who'd just speared a new bottle of wine with the corkscrew, looked up. 'It would work, all right.'

'Nick!'

'But it's not very smart. You'd get caught,' he assured me.

'It's difficult to get away with murder.'

'He did,' I said. 'He got away with it in Lisbon, all those years ago, and he's getting away with it now. He's untouchable.'

Margot said, 'No one's untouchable.' Leaning back in her warmly lit sitting-room chair, with the strange wooden carvings and tapestries everywhere round her, she looked like some tribal wise woman preparing to give her advice. 'There must be some other way we can get him.'

The 'we' came so easily to her, that for the first time since I'd left Tony's house in Toronto, I felt that I wasn't alone.

Nick had bested the cork. It came clear with the sound of a shot. 'I can think of a way.'

Thursday, October 5

Nick steered the van to a spot by the five-barred gate, just off the edge of the road, and killed the engine. Margot's car lights, pulling in behind us, lingered on a second longer; then they, too, died and left us in darkness. The sky here was truly dark, not like in London. I saw cold stars shine past the black blowing shapes of the trees.

Margot's car door opened. Closed. I heard her walking forward, and I rolled my window down. She said, 'I've changed my mind. You shouldn't do this. It's too dangerous.'

'I'm safe enough. You're here. Nick's here. If anything happens—'

'We'll never get up there in time. You'll be dead.'

'But you'll have it on tape. You'll have everything on tape. He won't be able to escape that.'

'Yes, well,' said Margot, fidgeting against the cold, 'you will forgive me, won't you, if I don't find that to be much consolation.'

Nick spoke up. 'Don't worry. He's not going to harm her. If he threatens her, she only has to show him this.' He held up an end of the wire I was wearing, and tucked it back into place, making sure everything was properly secured and out of sight. 'Right then,' he told me, 'when you're ready. Let me have a final sound check when you're in the car.'

I had expected to feel nervous when this moment finally came, but as I stepped out of the van my nerves were steady. I felt calm.

Margot passed her car keys to me. 'Kate,' was all she said, but I understood.

'I'll be all right. I have to do this.'

In the car, I locked the door and clicked my seatbelt safely shut, as though that could protect me from what I would soon be facing. Then I said, out loud, so Nick could have his sound check: 'Ready. Wish me luck.'

I waited till Nick pushed his driver's door open a fraction and gave me the 'thumbs-up' sign. Then, with a deep breath, I started the car.

The great house rose out of the landscape to greet me as though it had stood there forever, a sprawling thing, solid, a looming black shape with the night sky behind it. The approach from the gate, up the long gravelled drive with the pond to one side, offered none of the welcoming views that I'd had on my first visit. The gabled wings, the angled chimneys, and the rows of stone-silled windows with their small glass panes were all in darkness now, save for two windows high up and three others on the ground floor.

I turned the car onto the broad gravel curve to the east of the main door and crunched to a stop.

He wouldn't be expecting me to do this – I had that, at

least, in my favour. Surprise, I'd been taught, was a powerful weapon, when one was behind in the odds.

The woman who answered my knock at the door still looked, to me, as carefully preserved and polished as some of the decorative objects that lined the front entrance hall – the carved wooden mirror with its hooks for hanging coats on, and the marble-topped table beneath it, and the large Japanese-looking blue and white porcelain floor vase that held an assortment of canes and umbrellas. I'd missed the significance of those canes the first time I'd seen them. I noticed them, now. I noticed, in particular, the cane with the ivory white dragon's-head handle, its red eyes glaring at me from the middle of the jumble.

Patrick's mother frowned faintly, attempting to place me. 'Yes?'

'I've come to see the Colonel.'

'Well, I'm afraid he's not…that is, it's rather late, and—'

'Let her in,' a voice behind her interrupted. Neither one of us, it seemed, had heard the wheelchair. Patrick's mother, turning, looked as surprised as I was by the presence of her husband in the shadowed hall behind her.

'Darling…'

'It's all right,' he told her. 'Let her in.' And then he turned as well, his wheels a whisper on the carpet as he led the way into the room beyond.

It was the study I had so admired on my first visit – a man's room, wine-red wallpaper washed with quiet light from fabric-covered floor lamps, and lithographed prints of a fox-hunt in frames chasing round the four walls, leaping draperies and bookshelves. He'd been reading. A paperback thriller sat open, face down, on an inlaid octagonal table, the book's spine strained with the fat curve of still-unread pages. Beside the book, a small cut-crystal goblet with a trace of something deep red at its bottom caught the room's soft light, expensively.

Patrick's mother hovered in the doorway.

'Darling, we'll be fine,' the Colonel said. 'You needn't worry.' And the smile he sent his wife was a dismissal.

As she left, he wheeled himself towards the table and his book, retrieving, as he went, a glass decanter from a nearby shelf. 'You've changed your hair,' he said. 'I can't say I approve. I'm rather fond of red hair on a woman.' The decanter, like his nearly empty glass, held dark red liquid. 'Port,' he told me, with another smile. 'A particular weakness of mine, I'm afraid. I always did like a nice glass of port of an evening. Would you care to join me?'

Ever the charmer, I thought. Only now, I was immune. All I saw was a man who'd done murder; who'd ordered my grandmother's murder, and Deacon's; who'd stolen my own life as surely as if he had killed me, as well. It was all I could do to control my emotions – to stand there without giving vent to my rage. But I knew that my only hope now of defeating the man was to make him feel comfortable; get him to talk. To confess.

I accepted the wine he held out, though I had no intention of drinking it.

Standing, I watched him refilling his glass; watched his face. He hadn't changed much from his photographs. Men didn't change much, as a rule. And yet I'd failed to see it. As with Deacon, when I'd met the Colonel weeks ago, I'd seen an old man, nothing more.

Now it was obvious, even without the moustache, who he was.

'I must say, I expected you sooner,' he said, settling back in his wheelchair, the glass in one hand. 'I told the others. They underestimated you rather badly, I believe.'

'But you didn't?'

'Well, perhaps just a little.' The smile had retreated to his eyes. 'I should imagine you have questions. Do sit down.'

'I'd rather stand, thanks.'

'I'm an old man, in a wheelchair. Hardly a danger.'

I couldn't let that pass. 'Tell my grandmother.'

He'd been about to drink, but he lowered his glass. 'Ah, your grandmother. Yes, that was unavoidable. They thought she was too great a risk.'

'"They"?'

His eyes indulged me. 'I'm an old man, in a wheelchair,' he repeated. 'What I did, I did a long, long time ago, when I was young. I couldn't do it now. You surely don't believe that I could kill a man with these?' He held his hands towards me, veined and frail.

I didn't answer. But I'd learnt to never underestimate the elderly. Age and frailness notwithstanding, I would not have turned my back to him.

'Besides,' he said, 'It was different then. One had ideals, you see. Time steals those from us, one by one – you'll find that out yourself, when you get old, like me. You'll find that the things you once held to be truths will seem ridiculous, unworthy…but in those days…' He broke off, and paused. 'Your generation's never been to war. You couldn't hope to understand.'

'I understand the difference between killing someone in a war, in combat, and cold-blooded murder.'

'Do you, now? I wonder.' Looking down, he tilted his glass so that the port inside it caught the light, a clear, deep red, like blood. 'Would you care to hear my version of the story?'

I'd been counting on the offer. Moving as close as I dared, I selected an armchair that backed onto the bookcases, facing both him and the door. As I sat, I felt the thin line of wire press into my skin, and I hoped they were hearing this, down in Nick's van, at the foot of the drive. 'Yes, I would,' I said.

John Lawrence Cayton-Wood – 'JL' to acquaintances and 'Jack' to friends and family – had been born into that elevated level of society where everything he would become was already decided. He'd obediently followed on the path his parents set for him – first boarding school, then Eton; then, because he was a second son, and by tradition in his family second sons took a commission in the army, he had finished off his schooling at the Royal Military College, Sandhurst. Coming out an officer, he'd found himself, a few years later, fighting in North Africa. El Alamein had ended his career.

He'd refused, out of pride, to return home a cripple. And since the wound in his leg had stubbornly resisted proper healing, he had looked around for prospects outside England. An old friend of the family had put him in touch with the man who had, at that time, wielded the greatest influence over all business done at the harbour in Lisbon, and Cayton-Wood, offered a job, had accepted, though his sights had been set, even then, on the highest position. He'd turned the whole of his intellect to that task, and after three months of plotting and intriguing he had managed to disgrace, and then displace, the man who'd hired him.

Settled in the top office, he'd soon developed a comfortable lifestyle, moving freely among the elite men and women of Lisbon society; dances and parties and Embassy functions and glittering nights at the local casinos. It had been at an Embassy luncheon, in fact, when he'd first been asked whether he'd be interested in doing secret work to help his country. His connections, he'd been told, were unmatched; his background impeccable; his abilities obvious.

Faced with such flattery, he had said yes. At the time that he had been recruited into it, the British Secret Intelligence Service, or SIS, had been focusing resources on Spain and Portugal. The SIS – also widely known as MI6 – was in charge of all British intelligence work done on non-British soil. It had several branches, and one – Section V, as in 'Victor' – was dedicated to counter-espionage, meaning that it gathered information on all secret foreign operations being planned against the British. Portugal and Spain were fertile hotbeds of such plans, in those years. Lisbon, in particular, with all its foreign agents moving openly amongst each other, lent itself to careful observation.

Cayton-Wood began by finding and recruiting, on his own, a web of sub-agents, almost all of them Portuguese nationals, all of them strategically located, who could keep him well informed. Some he found in the households of foreign ambassadors; some in the better hotels. And of course, he had Vivian Spivey. He'd met Spivey one day by chance, at the harbour, and though they were not of the same social class, he'd been aware of what he'd gain by being friendly to the man. Spivey worked for Reynolds.

Ivan Reynolds didn't like Jack Cayton-Wood. He'd said so to his face, and to as many other people who would listen. Not that it did Cayton-Wood any harm, because Reynolds himself wasn't really well liked, but it did create difficulties from an intelligence perspective. Reynolds's oil was a vital resource for the British, though his loyalties were suspect. Spivey could keep Cayton-Wood informed of shipping movements, but his snooping round the offices was limited by co-workers. Even Regina, with her greater access to Reynolds's mail and his phone calls, could not get as close to the man as the SIS wanted. So, since Reynolds snubbed Cayton-Wood socially, no course was left but to bring in a new man; a new agent.

Deacon.

From the start, Cayton-Wood didn't care for him. He favoured men with weaknesses; with vices he could turn to his advantage. A man who liked drink, or young women, or boys, could be bribed along, or threatened with exposure. Andrew Deacon was, in Cayton-Wood's opinion, quite the worst sort of a man to have to work with: He was honest.

Worse still, he was observant, and intelligent – both qualities that made him rather dangerous to Cayton-Wood. Because, for several months now, Cayton-Wood had been discreetly sharing information with the Spanish. Nothing vital, in his view. But, having long shared Winston Churchill's own opinion of the Soviet regime, that it was a disease bent on spreading like cancer across the whole world, Cayton-Wood had thought it unforgivable that certain facts should not be shared with Franco, who'd made such a valiant stand against the communists. That Franco's sympathies lay with the Axis hardly mattered, not when one took in the broader picture, because when this current war was over, with the British and Americans triumphant, it was obvious their guns would then be turned towards what Churchill called the 'poison peril' in the East – and Spain, in that fight, would be once again their ally.

Cayton-Wood's conviction that the Spanish ought to be informed of certain British plans that might affect them might have remained only that – a conviction – had it not been for Manuel Garcia, who'd walked into the British Embassy one morning with an offer to turn double agent if he and his wife could be promised safe passage to England, to start a new life, at the war's end.

Garcia was not the first enemy agent to offer his services. By that late stage of the war, when it seemed almost certain the Allies would win, a great many foreign agents had left their sinking ships and were already 'doubled', sending useless information back to their home countries under tight British control.

For someone like Manuel Garcia, who transmitted his reports each week by radio, the usual procedure was for Cayton-Wood to choose a lesser agent, fluent in Morse code, who'd act as the controller; who'd accompany Garcia every week to the transmission site and sit beside him, making sure he said what he'd been told to say – a mix of truths and half-truths and straight lies, designed to misinform the enemy and steer his forces in the wrong direction.

But Cayton-Wood hadn't let anyone else be Garcia's control. He had done it himself. He'd been able, that way, to send any and all information he thought should be sent. He'd thought it one of the more amusing ironies of his business that Garcia, who considered himself a traitor to Spain, was in fact being one of its most useful agents.

There were a few bumps, of course. Someone – he didn't know who – had got wind of the leak, and was trying to trace it. But Cayton-Wood managed to steer the suspicion to Reynolds.

A neat trick…except it brought Deacon, now, into the picture. And Deacon, disturbingly, chose to make friends with Garcia.

While Garcia didn't know that his reports to Spain were full of truths and not misinformation, Cayton-Wood knew Deacon wouldn't be so easy to deceive. One stray comment from Garcia would be all that it might take, and Deacon's too-sharp brain would do the rest. He'd be on to the game in a heartbeat.

The solution, of course, would have been to have Deacon shipped back to New York, and given Cayton-Wood's ruthless expertise in all things underhand, it should have been a simple thing to do, but Deacon proved to be a harder person to get rid of than the other men he'd targeted.

And then had come the 28th of January, and the cutting off of Allied oil supplies to Spain. And Cayton-Wood had seen, almost immediately, how he could, with one move, help the Spanish *and* dispose of Deacon.

The idea of an oil embargo was, to him, ridiculous, and reckless. Franco's forces were already doing all they could to hold a brave line against the communists, but the danger remained. Taking away the country's oil would hurt the common people, bring them hardship, make them suffer.

They would protest, and the communists would use that to their own advantage, seeking to destabilise the government.

That had to be prevented, at all costs.

Cayton-Wood knew, thanks to Spivey, that one of Reynolds's tankers, the *Hernando*, was already in the mid-Atlantic, having just received instructions to change course from Spain to Lisbon. Soon it would be in the harbour, under his control. And if the oil went missing while the ship was at its berth, and somehow found its way to Spain, well…such things happened, in a war.

It would be easy enough to put the blame on Reynolds, with his family connections in Franco's government, and the daily cables that he'd been receiving from Madrid, begging him to help lift the embargo. Not to mention the fact that he had a Spanish secret agent working on his staff – Manuel Garcia, who had access to a transmitter.

That it would be Cayton-Wood, alone, who used the transmitter to send the needed information to Madrid would never cross the mind of anyone in SIS. Garcia could deny he'd been involved, but he would never be believed. He'd be discredited, and lose his chance to live his dream of starting a new life in England. Unless – and here, thought Cayton-Wood, lay the true stroke of brilliance – unless Garcia wanted to do Cayton-Wood a favour, in return for having everything put right with SIS.

All that Garcia would have to do – and Cayton-Wood had no doubt he would do it – would be to say, on the record, that Deacon had also been part of the scheme to ship oil to the Spanish; that Deacon and Reynolds had planned the whole thing, and had tricked him into helping them by making him believe that they were doing it for Britain.

Exit Deacon. And, since the question of Reynolds's loyalty would have been answered, the SIS wouldn't bother sending a new agent to take Deacon's place. Garcia would stay on, and would continue to perform his useful functions, more firmly than ever under Cayton-Wood's thumb.

As plans went, it came close to perfection.

Putting it in action was an easy thing to do.

He began by taking Deacon out for tea. Across the table, he apologised. 'I may have been a little heavy-handed when I ordered you to stay clear of Garcia. You were using your best judgement, as you said. In fact, given our latest position with Spain, it appears to me your friendship with Garcia could be useful.' And he told him why.

Deacon listened quietly, his gaze from time to time drifting around the small restaurant as though he were looking for someone. 'And I'm to do what, exactly?'

'Observe him. Just that. Take your drives in the country, the way you were doing. Have dinner at his house, invite him to yours. Be as sociable as you like with the Garcias, provided you keep your eyes open.'

The damnable thing about Deacon, thought Cayton-Wood, was that his eyes always seemed to be too fully open; that all of the effort one put into fooling the man was for naught. Deacon's answer, 'Understood,' left Cayton-Wood with the uneasy sense that he *did* understand.

Still, Deacon did as he was told. He met Garcia frequently enough that Cayton-Wood's spies could assemble a decent-sized file, filled with dates, times, and places, and photographs, all of which would, later on, be used to back Garcia's false 'confession' about Deacon's role in working with the enemy.

Then, when the *Hernando* finally entered Lisbon's harbour, Cayton-Wood took the next step of contacting Madrid. That, too, was simple. He'd mastered Morse code as a boy, and he had babysat Garcia long enough to learn the Spaniard's 'fist' – his own peculiar way of tapping out the chain of dots and dashes that made letters in the code. Whoever got the message at the other end would think it came straight from Garcia. Cayton-Wood knew this because he had, in fact, transmitted twice on his own, in the past. He didn't like doing it – he did it only when the information he was sending was so clearly sensitive that even Garcia would have known that it should not be shared with Spain; but he didn't like making the trek to the transmitter all on his own, in case somebody saw him. Far better to speak through Garcia where possible, safe in the shadows behind him, than risk getting caught.

If he'd needed reminding of that, he got it when he left the windmill after his transmission, to find Deacon and Garcia standing further down the hill, in plain view. He made a dignified retreat, but felt the weight of Deacon's damned observant eyes. If only he himself had eyes like that, he thought, he'd be invincible.

But in the end, the person to confront him wasn't Deacon, but Garcia.

It turned out, as luck would have it, that another Spanish agent who had been assigned to Lisbon had dropped in to see Garcia, and had mentioned how impressed the higher-ups were with his facts on the *Hernando*.

Cayton-Wood hadn't expected this turn of events. He thought he'd allowed for every possible contingency in his carefully structured plan, but twice now, in this same afternoon, he'd been thrown off by people getting in his way. First it had been that young chit of a girl, Jenny Saunders, who'd stopped him from getting the papers he'd needed from Spivey's desk. Now here was Garcia coming after him, in public – on a sidewalk, of all places, just outside the Reynolds offices – demanding he explain what he was up to.

It was too like a badly staged play to be real, in Cayton-Wood's opinion – the Spaniard might as well have slapped a gauntlet down upon the pavement.

Cayton-Wood considered his options. It wasn't the most convenient of times for him to deal with the problem. He was due across town for a meeting in half an hour. But this was something he'd known he would have to do, sooner or later. He stood, calm, while Garcia accused him:

'You used the transmitter. Alone. You used my name. And what you have arranged would not, I think, have the approval of the others at the Embassy.'

'I shouldn't bother them, if I were you.'

'And why is that?'

'Because, Manuel, it might appear to them that *you* made those arrangements, and that would undoubtedly cause you some trouble.'

'I will tell them. I will tell them that it was not me.'

'Ah, yes,' he said, 'but which of us would be believed? I wonder.' He could see some of the righteousness ebb from Garcia's face. 'No, I'm afraid, Manuel, that when my colleagues learn of this affair – that is to say, when I inform them the petroleum is gone from the *Hernando* – I'm afraid things will look rather black, for you.' He paused, for full effect. And then, when he was very sure the implications had struck home, he added casually, 'Unless, of course, somebody put a good word in. Convinced them it wasn't your fault.'

'Yes?' Garcia asked blackly. 'And who would do this?'

'I might.'

'For what price?'

'You insult me.' He smiled. 'For a very small favour, no more.' And he said what it was.

Garcia listened. Shook his head. 'I cannot do this. Not to Mr Reynolds. Not to Deacon.'

'Oh, I think you can. I think you will. You really have no choice, not if you want to get to England, as you'd planned. Of course, you could go back to Spain, I suppose, when the war's over, but that might be rather risky for you and your wife, if it were to come out you'd been working for our side. Who knows? With all of Franco's agents round about these days, you might not even make it back to Spain.' He smiled again, and left it there, and went to keep his meeting.

It was late when he got back to his own office. Nearly dinnertime. His secretary, a self-martyring girl with a joyless expression, was putting on her coat when the telephone rang.

'Not to worry, I'll get it myself,' he said, waving her on. He wasn't meaning to be nice. Truth was, he'd simply reached the point where other people were an irritation, and he wanted to be rid of her. He wouldn't know, till afterwards, how fortunate an impulse it had been.

The telephone kept ringing, an annoyance in itself. He picked it up, his tone impatient.

It was Ivan Reynolds calling. Not the smoothly condescending voice of his assistant, but the man himself, abrasive, demanding that Cayton-Wood come to the house. It was not a request, but a summons.

Cayton-Wood kept his temper with an effort. He was tired. He'd had a long and trying day, and clashing swords with Ivan Reynolds wasn't how he cared to end it. 'I'm afraid that's quite impossible.'

'The side door. After nine o'clock,' was Reynolds's answer, and the line went rudely dead.

He had a mind to go straight home, but he was frankly curious why someone who so publicly despised him should be asking for a meeting. So, of course, he went.

He'd been to Reynolds's great house on the hill once before, and he knew of the existence of the side door, though he'd never had the privilege of using it. It was the unofficial entrance, unattended, used by close friends and, presumably, the mistresses. A person given access to the side door didn't have to ring the bell, or knock; he simply let himself in, like a member of the household. Cayton-Wood thought it decidedly odd that he should have been asked to go in by that door. He went in with his guard up.

Inside, it appeared there was only one direction for the visitor to go, and that was upwards. A set of broad stairs, soft with carpet, climbed and turned and climbed again towards a spacious landing. Here again, there was no choice – just one great set of double doors of panelled oak set in the wall ahead.

Cayton-Wood waited a moment, leaning his weight on his walking stick while he recovered from the stairs. He wasn't about to show weakness to Reynolds. The man was beneath him in every respect, and would need a reminder of that.

With his breath back to normal, he knocked at the doors.
'Come in.'

The room, which seemed to function as a bedroom and a sitting room, was very large, and furnished all in browns and golds and varnished woods, a masculine domain. A Tiffany lamp by the four-poster bed cast a dragonfly pattern of amber and red on the wall, falling short of the shadows that lay in the corners.

Cayton-Wood hadn't seen Reynolds since the surgery, and it surprised him to see how thoroughly the cancer had consumed the older man. The fiery American, who once had ruled a room by simply standing in it, now seemed smaller, withered, insubstantial, as though part of him had already begun to cross the grey divide between the living and the dead.

Death was not unfamiliar to Cayton-Wood. He'd seen it often enough, in North Africa; but it had always been quick death, in battle, and nothing like this. This repulsed him, and yet he found it gruesomely intriguing.

'Taking good care of you, are they?' he asked, looking round. 'I thought you had a nurse.'

'I gave her the night off.'

'I see. Was that wise?'

'It was necessary.' Settling back on his pillows, Reynolds folded his arms in an attitude that suggested his old, imperious self. His features, tightened as they were with pain, were openly contemptuous. 'I have to say, I didn't think you'd have the guts to come.'

'How could I not? Your invitation was so charming.' He had not been asked to sit, but his leg was throbbing wickedly, and since there was no one to stop him doing so, he took a chair and swung it round to face the bed, and sat. There was no one to stop him lighting a cigar, either, so he did that too, and blew a careless stream of smoke towards the ceiling. 'What is on your mind?'

'Manuel Garcia.'

Cayton-Wood purposely didn't react. 'What about him?'

'He's dead. He shot himself this afternoon.'

He hadn't seen *that* coming – it had not been in his plan, and it would complicate things. *Damn*, he thought. 'I didn't know.'

'Of course you didn't,' Reynolds said. 'Spivey wasn't on the job today, was he, so he couldn't tell you, and no one outside of the company knows, yet. Just the Coroner, and I don't think he's on your payroll, is he?'

Cayton-Wood smiled a tiny, cold smile that stopped short of his eyes. 'Not yet, no.'

'You haven't asked me why Garcia killed himself.'

'I can't say I'm much interested.'

Reynolds's smile was rather different. It was predatory, satisfied – the smile of a cat that's backed a mouse into a corner. 'He explained it all in here,' he said, and reaching to the table at his bedside he held up an empty envelope. 'Oh, I don't have the letter anymore,' he said, as Cayton-Wood leant forward. 'I had Roger pass it on to your Ambassador. I thought that he might want to know what you've been up to.'

Cayton-Wood sat back. The smoke from his cigar wreathed upward, and he narrowed his eyes against it, trying to look unconcerned. 'I rather think my word might have more weight with the Ambassador than that of a damned Spanish spy.'

'Maybe. But I'll make sure that people get to hear about it. That's all you have to do in this town to ruin a man – start a rumour, raise suspicion. You know all about that, don't you?' The wily eyes were fixed on his in steady accusation. 'Now you'll know how it feels. I don't think you'll be welcome in Lisbon too long. You're about to become an embarrassment.'

Cayton-Wood knew he was right. Whether the British believed what Garcia had written or not, the suspicion itself would be Cayton-Wood's undoing. He'd no longer be of use to them. His careful plans, his careful life, were set to crumble round him like a child's house of blocks, and all because Garcia had gone noble on him, bloody fool. He cursed the Spaniard silently.

Reynolds watched him, gloating. 'Need a drink? There's brandy in that bookcase, just behind you. You could bring me one, too, while you're at it. I'm in a mood to celebrate.'

Cayton-Wood rose, taking advantage of the opportunity to turn his back and hide his expression from Reynolds. Pouring the brandy, he focused his mind, keeping calm. If Garcia had been able to find a way, however final, out of *his* dilemma, surely there was some way out of this, if one could only find the path.

'I've got you,' said Reynolds. 'It took me some time, but I've finally got you, you bastard.' His words held no violence, and yet there was hatred enough to make plain why he'd called Cayton-Wood here tonight. It hadn't been enough that he should pass Garcia's letter on and know that punishment would follow; he had wanted to deliver the *coup de grâce* himself – to look his adversary in the eye and feel the satisfaction of that victory, before death could come and take that from him, too. He said, 'Your connections won't help you this time. There's nothing you can do to make those friends of yours support you, in the face of treason.'

Cayton-Wood set down his brandy. With the other glass in hand, he turned, advancing on the bed, his thinking done. He passed the glass to Reynolds. 'Actually,' he said, 'there *is* one thing.'

It was so simple, he thought afterwards, to take the pillow, press it to the ill man's face, and hold it through the moment of weak struggle.

On the table by the bed there was a telephone. He picked it up, and calmly dialled a number. 'It's Jack Cayton-Wood. I'm sorry to disturb you, but I've got a situation here. I'm going to need your help.'

He'd stopped now, and was watching me. The ageing eyes were shrewd. 'You didn't know,' he said. 'You didn't know that it was Reynolds.'

When I didn't answer, he went on, 'At any rate, that was the beauty of it all, you see. To kill a dying man. There's no suspicion, then, of murder. We were on our own, the two of us. No witnesses.'

'And Whitehall backed you up.'

'Of course. They had no choice. An SIS man killing Ivan Reynolds? At the least, it would have caused a dreadful row with the Americans.'

It struck me cold how casually he spoke about it. He had calculated all this in the time it took to pour a glass of brandy, back in Ivan Reynolds's bedroom. He'd known that, by committing such a crime – one that could cause a minor nightmare for his government, in terms of its relations with America – he had guaranteed the SIS would shield him, in its own self-interest. And it had.

He told me how. 'They fixed the whole scene beautifully. You never would have known that I was there. There was some plan, I believe, to buy the doctor off, but in the end that proved unnecessary. He took the death for what it seemed to be, and looked no further.'

'And Roger Selkirk? He'd seen the letter Garcia left, hadn't he? At least, he'd delivered it to the Ambassador.'

'Yes, well, Roger was a different matter. *He* was bought. Or rather, we persuaded him that speaking out would not be wise.'

'You blackmailed him.'

'A nasty word. But yes, if you prefer to call it that.'

I frowned. 'But how? I mean, everybody knew he was a homosexual, from what I'm told. That couldn't have possibly hurt him, to have that come out.'

'No, you're quite right. It couldn't. But the gentleman with whom he was consorting at the time was, shall we say, not open with his preferences. A private man, a family man, a man of some importance. It would have been disastrous for him if certain facts had been made public.'

I know my face reflected what I thought of him. 'Why didn't you kill Roger at the time, if he was such a threat?'

'It wasn't my decision.' He reflected a moment, then said, 'I'll tell you, the person I ought to have killed was your Deacon. They wouldn't let me do that, either, but they didn't know what a colossal pain he would become. *I* knew. I knew the morning of the funeral, when he came to see me.'

* * *

His secretary, looking mournful, hovered in the doorway of his office.

'Yes?' he snapped, not looking up. 'What is it?'

'Mr Deacon's in the waiting room. He's wondering if he might have a word.'

'Yes, all right, send him in.' Shutting his ledger with a frown of impatience, he pushed it to one side and glanced at the clock. It was less than an hour till the funeral, and he had been told to be there at the start of the service. 'I don't have much time,' was his greeting to Deacon, 'so what's on your mind?'

'Murder,' Deacon replied, in a mild voice that didn't quite balance the chill of his eyes.

'I'm sorry?'

'No, I don't believe that you're the least bit sorry, that's the problem. You've got used to doing what you want, to whom you want, and damn the consequences. Well, I'm here to hold you to account.' He hadn't moved, yet it felt like he'd somehow advanced upon Cayton-Wood.

'What *are* you talking about?'

'I don't know what it was you told Garcia, what you said to him, but I do know your hand was on that trigger every bit as much as his was. You're responsible.'

Cayton-Wood lifted his eyebrows, looking at Deacon in much the same way that a man eyes a bug he's preparing to squash. His smile was a reflex action, meaningless. 'Actually, if you must know the truth, the blame lies more with you. It was Garcia's rather touching, if misguided, sense of loyalty to you that made him choose to blow his brains out.' Then, because that gave him the advantage, he pushed back his chair and stood, preparing for an exit before Deacon could come back at him with questions. 'You know, much as I'd like to continue this, Andrew, the fact is I don't have the time. So if you'll kindly step aside...'

'Make no mistake, I will report you. I will tell all I know about this game that you've been playing with the Spanish – and I know a great deal more than you might think.'

Cayton-Wood was nearly at the door. He could have walked away, and held his tongue; but, goaded by the thought that Deacon had the gall to talk to him – to *him* – in such a tone, he turned. 'Don't you dare try to threaten me. You'll find you're playing far out of your league. No one threatens me, understand? Ask Ivan Reynolds.'

He saw that strike home. Then he pushed through the doorway and out of the office and slammed the door, hard, at his back.

'I shouldn't have said that, of course,' he admitted to me. 'It amounted, I suppose, to a confession, and it caused no end of trouble for the higher-ups at Whitehall. Deacon wrote to them, soon after. He reported me.' The fact seemed to amuse him, briefly. 'They promised him a full investigation, then they reassigned him back to England. Reynolds, after all, was dead; there wasn't any purpose left for Deacon at the company. The story given out was that his wife had died, quite suddenly, and he was going home because of that. I went home, too, but not till summer's end, and at my own request. There was an opening in London that I fancied, and I'd grown rather tired of life abroad. Deacon was being kept out of the way, but he still was a bit of a nuisance. I paid him a visit to try to convince him to stop.'

'At Southampton,' I said. 'At the docks.' The scene James Cavender had witnessed as a boy, and had remembered. 'I gather it was you who ruined the shipment of his household goods?'

'You know about that, do you? It was just a little parting gift, arranged before the ship left Lisbon harbour. Quite a simple thing, to pay a chap to soak a crate with water. And it did have a spectacular effect. I thought it might help,' he said, 'frighten him off. But he was like a bulldog with a bone. He simply wouldn't let it drop.'

Deacon had petitioned Whitehall, sending letter after letter telling what he knew, demanding Cayton-Wood be brought to justice.

Whitehall had continued to put Deacon off with promises – they'd hold internal inquiries, they'd said. They would investigate. 'Truth was,' the Colonel said, 'they rather hoped he'd go away. But then he wrote to the Prime Minister, and once he'd done that, well, they had to take action. So someone decided the simplest thing was to kill me.'

His 'death', conveniently at sea, had been carefully faked, right down to the formal death announcement in *The Times*, and the funeral at St Martin-in-the-Fields. And Deacon had been taken to that funeral, and then afterwards, in offices at Whitehall, he'd been asked, in patriotic terms, to keep his mouth shut. Nothing good could come of it, not now, they'd said – not now that Cayton-Wood was dead. It would do damage, on a diplomatic level.

'They had him pegged,' the Colonel said. 'He was an

honourable man. Presumably he didn't want to see his country pay the debt for one man's sins. For my sins. It was me that he was after, and if I were dead, in his mind, that was justice of a sort. And I did suffer,' he assured me. 'It wasn't easy, being dead. I had to sever contacts, leave the country altogether.'

He had gone to Kenya, started a new life in business there, choosing the Damien-Pryce name by cobbling together the surnames of two of his ancestors. He'd done well in his business, and better with his women. He had married twice. 'Outlived them both,' he said, 'which left me rather nicely situated. I'd have likely stayed in Kenya, if it hadn't been for Patrick's mother.' She'd been over on holiday, visiting friends, when he'd met her. He'd been doubly seduced, by her prettiness and by her money, and when he had learnt that her aunt was a powerful Member of Parliament, he had proposed on the spot.

'So I came back to England,' he said. 'Not a problem, by that time. The war had been over for twenty-five years. There wasn't really anyone at Whitehall who remembered me, or why I had been exiled. My parents were gone. True, my brother and his wife were still on the family estate up in Derbyshire, but that was miles from my wife's home, down here, and the odds of my ever meeting up with anybody who had known me were even slimmer than the odds that they might recognise me. I've often thought that ageing is the best disguise of all. Nobody notices one's face, when one grows old.'

'But Deacon noticed,' I reminded him. 'He saw you at the Chelsea Flower Show.'

'That was unfortunate.' The Colonel filled his port glass for a third time. 'I'd never been to the damned thing before.

Not my idea of fun, you see. Only this year Venetia'd got tickets and my wife was quite keen and the both of them thought I could do with the outing, and a man like me stands very little chance,' he said, 'when the women around him decide he could do with an outing.' There was the charm again, effortless.

Ignoring it, I asked him, 'Did you know that he had seen you?'

'Oh, yes. Heavens, yes. I don't know which of us was more affected by it, him or me. I knew I'd made a terrible mistake, you understand. If I'd been on my own, it might have been all right, but being in Venetia's company...she's highly recognisable. I knew that Deacon wouldn't have much trouble finding out my name, the name that I'd been using since the war, and then...' He shrugged. 'I knew he wouldn't let it go, a second time. I knew he'd give me trouble.' He paused, and drank, and then he said, 'It wasn't that I thought that he'd have better luck, this time around, with Whitehall – it was still in their best interest to make sure the truth of Reynolds's dying didn't come to light. I knew that, if he went to them, they'd bury his report. But life, if nothing else, has taught me to expect the unexpected. So I hired a man to watch him; let me know what he got up to.' There'd been nothing, in the summer, to be much cause for alarm. Then, 'One day I got a call to say that Deacon had gone up to London. Sat in on a trial at the Old Bailey, of all things. At first I thought he'd gone to get a look at Patrick, but it wasn't Patrick's trial. And my man said that Deacon hadn't seemed to be at all interested in the proceedings; he had spent the whole time watching a young woman, with red hair, and when she'd left, he'd tailed this same young woman back to her hotel. It made me curious. So, just for one day, I had my man follow you, instead of Deacon. That,' he said, 'is how I learnt your name.' He set the port glass down, with care. 'Your occupation.'

A clock was ticking somewhere in a corner of the room. It sounded loud, suddenly, marking the passing of time. He said, 'I never had much use for Ivan Reynolds, as I said, but he was right about one thing. He told me all one had to do to ruin a man was start a rumour – the suspicion was enough to do the rest. And he was right.' His smile was practical. 'I couldn't let Deacon sit down with a journalist; tell what he knew. I'd given up a good life once already for the man, and I was damned if I was going to see him ruin the life that I've got now. I built this life. It's mine.'

It wasn't only how he said the words; it was the look behind his eyes that made the coldness start to clutch at my insides. I had been right to fear this man. He might be old, and frail, and sitting in a wheelchair, but the truth was he was just as evil now as he had ever been, and every bit as dangerous.

He said, 'I had to know how much you knew. The fact that my man hadn't seen Deacon speak to you didn't mean you hadn't talked on the phone, or that Deacon hadn't written to you earlier. And if you knew the story, then there might be others…people you had talked to. The only way to know for sure was to arrange for someone to get close to you.'

I knew, already, who he'd sent to do the job, but since I wanted it on tape, I said it: 'Patrick.'

'Yes.' The Colonel smiled. 'I don't believe he minded the assignment. I didn't tell him everything, mind you – only that Deacon knew certain details of my past that could cause problems for me, and, indeed, for Patrick. The sins of the fathers, and all that, you know. That was all Patrick needed to hear.' His smile deepened. 'Patrick, for his faults, does have a marvellously developed instinct for self-preservation. He was only too keen to help, if it meant keeping out of the tabloids, but of course, even when the boy helps, he's about as much use as a gun with no bullets. He couldn't tell me anything, and in the end, there was nothing for it but to invite you down for dinner, so that I could talk to you myself. And then Patrick, in typical fashion, did something quite foolish. He was on his way to Chambers, so he told me, and he saw you on the steps outside St Paul's, with Deacon, talking, and the only thing that he could think to do was run him down. And with my wife's car, more's the pity. I adored that car. It cost me quite a lot to have to sink it in the pond.' His face was honestly regretful; more upset about the losing of the car than Deacon's death. 'So then my wife knew something odd was going on, and when my wife's alarmed, she calls her Aunt Venetia.'

I could tell from his tone that he hadn't been pleased. I couldn't imagine a sharp and powerful woman like Venetia Radburn being satisfied with anything less than the whole story, any more than I could imagine a man like the Colonel being anything but loathe to share the strings with a competing puppeteer.

'Ironic, really, that I'd been using her for bait to get you down here for dinner, and in the end she took control of that event.'

Ah yes, I thought. The dinner. All those seemingly innocent questions about the accident I'd witnessed, and what the old man might have said. About my grandmother. Venetia

Radburn, smiling as she'd poured my wine. And afterwards, when I'd gone up to bed, the sounds of everybody talking in the sitting room below.

'I felt certain, at the time,' the Colonel said, 'that you knew nothing. If you had read Deacon's report, you'd have known who I was, and you wouldn't have been so relaxed. No one's that good an actress. But Venetia wanted convincing, so I arranged one final test. Someone official, this time. Someone you might feel compelled to talk to.'

'You mean Metcalf.'

'Who?'

'The man at my hotel,' I said.

'Was that the name he went by? I didn't know. I told him to choose someone very official, a real Scotland Yard man, in case you should check the credentials. I'd hoped, you see, that even if he weren't able to find out what you knew, he might be able to persuade you to let Deacon's story drop, for fear of prosecution. But that didn't work, of course.' His mouth quirked. 'I was told you didn't take too well to his suggestions. And he also said he was quite sure he'd seen Cavender passing you something, that night in the bar. The very fact that you were *meeting* with Cavender, let alone accepting documents from him, seemed evidence enough that not only did you know of Deacon's story, you were working on it, actively, and I'm afraid that rather sealed your fate, my dear. And Cavender's.' I'd never known a person speak so casually of murder. For although he hadn't gone himself to Deacon's house in Elderwel, to strike the coward's blow that killed James Cavender, he'd sent the men who'd done it. It had been his plan. His murder. 'I did think it better to be safe,' he said, 'than sorry.'

Better to be safe than sorry. So my grandmother had died. I forced back my anger enough to ask, 'Why didn't you just kill me when you had me here, in London?'

The Colonel said, 'Because I'd complicated things, you see, by bringing Patrick into play, with you. Venetia wouldn't hear of doing anything to you while you were in England, for fear it might somehow touch Patrick. You must understand, my dear, that Venetia's had a grand design for both my boys since they were in their prams, and when young John died, well, it all fell onto Patrick. Number 10 Downing Street, that's what she chose for him, steered him towards. Any scandal that might jeopardise his chances, well, she simply wouldn't hear of it. As the man you'd been seeing, he might have been questioned had anything untoward happened to you. It was safer to wait, we decided, until you went home. Will you have another glass of port?' He held up the decanter, as an offering. 'No? Anyhow, we weren't successful, were we? Killing you, I mean. And then you disappeared...*that* gave me a few bad moments, I can tell you.'

'But you found me.'

'Yes, that was a stroke of luck. Anne Wood had been in Amsterdam, and seen someone who looked like you. She mentioned to Venetia, when they talked, how much this woman looked like you. She'd thought it odd, too, that the woman would say that she wasn't Canadian, when she was holding a passport from Canada. She'd read your name, and your plane ticket. So we found out you were headed for Portugal.' He'd known that I'd be going there to speak to living witnesses, and so he had arranged to have Regina watched, and Roger. When I'd turned up at Regina's house, they'd followed me from there. 'You gave them quite a time, I'm told. Who was the young man, with you?'

When I didn't answer him, he smiled. 'No matter. Good for you, though. You were always too intelligent for Patrick.'

Coldly, I asked, 'Where has Patrick been? I would have thought that you'd send *him* to Portugal, to tie up your loose ends for you.'

'Good Lord, no. I could never trust Patrick with something like that. No, I brought the professionals in, for all that. I sent Patrick on holiday. Greece. Kept him out of the way for a while, and gave him a chance to calm down. He was too unpredictable. Still is. I can't say he'll be pleased to find out you've returned.'

'I'll be sure to watch my step, crossing the street.'

That amused him. 'A wise policy.' Setting down his glass, he searched for something in his pocket. 'You'll want to watch your step regardless, I'm afraid, my dear. Oh, you've nothing to fear, here, tonight,' he said, seeing how my wary gaze had followed his movements. He pulled his hand free of his pocket to show me he held nothing more than a packet of matches. But he knew what I'd been thinking.

He said, 'When I was out in Africa, some of the chaps used to set bait for lion, and hide there and wait till the beasts came in close enough to make a kill. No sport in that. I always liked to do my hunting in the open, where the lion had a decent chance.'

His eyes, on mine, were condescending, making very sure I got his meaning. He was letting me know I was safe, for the moment, because I had come to him here, but that once

410

I went out of this house, went back into the open, the game would be on.

He took a cigar from a box on the table beside him, and lit it, and shook out the match. 'I shall miss you, Miss Murray. I mean that. You've been a delightful opponent.'

I'd had all that I could stomach of his company. I'd gotten what I came for. 'Oh, don't worry, Colonel Cayton-Wood,' I said, and stood. 'I have every intention of being the last person standing. I'll see myself out.' And though I'd said I'd never turn my back on him, I held my fear in check and did it now, and walked – although I felt like running – out of the room to the echoing entry hall, where, from its shadowy corner, the dragon's-head walking stick reared up to watch me with evil red eyes as I passed through the front door and slammed it behind me.

Friday, October 6

There were benches set along the Thames embankment, in the shadow of Westminster Bridge, but I stayed standing. I set my back to the river, so that I could see both the traffic that rushed past in an unceasing current of its own along the busy street beyond the footpath, and the people strolling past Westminster Pier, where I was standing. They were mostly people on their way to work, or tourists checking the times of the boats to the Tower of London, Kew Gardens, or Greenwich.

There were just enough people about so that I could feel safe, without feeling myself overwhelmed. And two benches downstream, Nick and Margot were sitting, pretending an interest in feeding the pigeons and reading the paper, respectively.

The autumn morning air was cool and damp, and rich with car exhaust, and diesel from the river boats, and the decaying scent of fallen leaves on pavement. The forecast called for rain, and I could smell that coming, too, and see the gathering of grey cloud further east, above the river.

Clear and ringing, loud above the noise of traffic, Big Ben

chimed the quarter hour and left the last note hanging, pure, reverberating in the air. I heard the hard, approaching sound of footsteps, and I turned my head.

I recognised him right away. He seemed to have more difficulty spotting me. I'd given up on my disguise – I wasn't wearing glasses any longer, and I'd chopped my hair last night, myself, with scissors, so the red roots would show through. If Colonel Cayton-Wood enjoyed the sport of hunting, I'd decided, he would get no joy from me. I'd stand and face him in the open; take his victory from him. I refused to be a fugitive for ever.

I'd given my description on the phone, to Sergeant Metcalf, but he sounded less than sure. 'Miss Murray?'

I nodded, accepting the handshake. 'Sergeant Metcalf. Thanks for coming.'

Cautious habit made me pull back, keep my distance. I was taking a risk, I knew, meeting him, even in public. Instinct told me he was what he said he was – an uninvolved policeman. And from what the Colonel had told me last night, the real Metcalf – this man standing next to me now – was an innocent victim of stolen identity. But I knew full well I couldn't believe all the Colonel had told me last night. He was good at deception. And I didn't know, for certain, Sergeant Metcalf wasn't on the Colonel's payroll.

If he was, then what I was about to do was meaningless.

Even if he wasn't, it was very likely meaningless as well, although at least, then, whoever the Colonel had hired to follow me, watch me, would see what I did here this morning, and with whom. That might, if I was lucky, make the Colonel stay his hand.

At any rate, I had to meet with Metcalf, and accept the risk.

And Metcalf, to his credit, didn't look the least bit threatening. He was a large man, broad-shouldered, broad-faced, with patient eyes, set deep, surrounded by creases. He looked like a big country farmer, plain-dealing, good-humoured, instead of a policeman. It was probably, I decided, an impression he'd have cultivated, making people feel at ease enough to open up to him. In interrogations, he'd have been the one who got to play the good cop.

He'd put his hands back in his pockets, respecting my withdrawal, and the glance he angled down at me showed genuine concern. 'You're not too cold out here? My office isn't far.'

'I'm fine, thanks.'

Nodding once to show he understood, he asked me, 'Have you been in London long?'

'Not really, no.'

'I must say, I was quite surprised to hear from you. Not at all the way I'd thought to end my week.' He smiled. 'I'm glad to see you're well. We've all been worried.'

'"We?"'

'The Toronto police, and myself. They've kept me informed, as a courtesy, because of my...well, my involvement, if you like. Although I'm still not certain how I got involved.' His smile made deeper creases round his eyes. 'I suppose it began with that message you left on my voicemail. Yours was the second message I'd received that day, from someone whom I'd never met, who talked as though we'd spoken. The first was from some chap who said he'd just remembered one more detail of the accident he'd witnessed, that I'd questioned him about. He didn't leave his name – just said the driver of the car must have been tall, because the seat was quite far back. And that was that. I hadn't a clue what he was on about. Then you called, apologising, and again, I knew we'd never talked. You left a name, at least, though. And a number. In Toronto, where I'd just arrived, myself; so I decided that I'd better try to find out what the hell was going on.' He paused, and then concluded with, 'Except I never got the chance to ask you.'

A boat chugged behind us, its bow turned upstream. Metcalf watched it for a moment, and then asked me, 'I assume you'd met with someone else, who said that he was me?'

'Yes.'

'When was this?'

I told him, giving him the details I remembered.

He took it in, frowning. 'I see.'

'So when you turned up at the hospital in Toronto,' I finished, 'and somebody mentioned your name, all I knew was that you weren't the man I had talked to in London.'

'And that's why you ran. You thought *I* was the one who was playing a part.'

'I didn't know what to think. I was in shock, still. I just knew that something was wrong.'

With another nod, he said, 'That was a queer chain of events, that night. I was having drinks with my Canadian counterpart, talking over my presentation, when I overheard the call come in and recognised the address. So I asked if I could see you. If I'd known that I would frighten you, I would have stayed away.'

'No, it was good that you came to the hospital, really.' If I hadn't seen him and realised that something was rotten, I wouldn't have gone into hiding, wouldn't have changed my identity, wouldn't have been on my guard. I'd have stayed where I was, in the open, a nice easy target for Cayton-Wood's killers. 'I'd be dead, if you hadn't,' I said to him bluntly, and tried to explain.

It took time.

When I'd finished, he looked past my shoulder to the looming outline of the Houses of Parliament, rising on the far side of Westminster Bridge. Thoughtfully, he chewed his lip. And then he said, 'It won't be easy, mind, to bring a charge against a woman like Venetia Radburn.'

'No. I don't imagine that it will be.'

'But you've got it on tape, you say? This man's confession?'

'Yes.' I closed my fingers round the hard case of the tape, and pulled it from my pocket. Held it out. 'It's just a copy. I've made others.'

He folded the tape into his large hand, and smiled. 'You're a very resourceful young woman, Miss Murray.'

'I've had to be.'

'Trust no one, is that it? Well, not to worry. You've had a hard few weeks, but it's all over now. Just leave it in our hands, and we'll take care of things.'

I didn't share his confidence.

He said, 'This chap who said that he was me, the one you met when you were here in London, can you tell me what he looked like?'

'I don't know…middle-aged, average height, sort of bland.'

'Would you know him again?'

'I doubt he'd look the same again.' That would be my greatest problem, I imagined, in this game that Colonel Cayton-Wood was playing: I'd never know who he might send against me.

Metcalf, mindful of my wariness, said, 'Well, perhaps when you're back in Toronto, you might spend a bit of time working with one of the police sketch artists, to draw me a face. Give me something to go on.' He added, 'I shouldn't imagine the Toronto police will give you any trouble now.'

'No.'

There was nothing more to say. He wished me luck, then, and I shook the hand he offered me, and said goodbye, and watched him walk away. He vanished with the crowd into the dark mouth of the underpass that crossed beneath the busy street. I stood, my back still to the river, till Big Ben had chimed another quarter hour, before I turned and slowly walked towards the bench where Nick and Margot sat.

'That's done, then,' Margot said, as she looked up at me. 'Do you think he'll do anything with what you've given him?'

'No,' I said honestly. Scotland Yard was, after all, a part of Whitehall, and even if Metcalf were on my side, I had no faith in his being able to take the case against Cayton-Wood any farther than it had been taken over half a century ago. Some things, I reasoned, didn't change. The players might be different, but all governments were dinosaurs, resisting evolution.

It was a good thing, I thought, that Metcalf was not my only hope.

Nick stood, stretching. 'So it's back to Shepherd's Bush, then, is it?'

'No,' I said. 'There's one more stop I have to make.'

The rectory at Elderwel stood silent, its shuttered windows watching as we parked in the shade of the steeple of St Stephen's Church. Nick didn't get out of the van, but he watched in his turn as I walked the short distance to let myself in through the lychgate.

There was no wren in the yew tree today; no sign of life within the quiet churchyard. I passed a freshly mounded grave, as yet unmarked, on which the flowered offerings had already begun to fade and wither, and I stood and looked at them a moment before wandering on through the wind-feathered grass to a lonelier spot in the churchyard's north corner.

Andrew Deacon didn't have a headstone either, yet. Maybe he'd never have one, now, I thought. His nephew, the last of his family, was no longer around to arrange things. I supposed that it didn't much matter, in the greater scheme of things, whether you had a headstone or not – when you were dead, you were dead. But still, it didn't seem quite right for someone to have lived a life and then to…well, just disappear, with nothing left to show where they had been.

I thought I was alone, until a man's voice asked, behind me, 'Can I help you?'

The vicar of St Stephen's was in gardening gloves this afternoon, a San Francisco 49ers baseball cap pulled low to shade his eyes. He'd been pruning a shrub or a hedge, something spiny, and carried a bunch of the branches in one hand, the shears in the other. He looked at my face as I turned, and I saw his polite friendliness give way to recognition. 'It's Miss Murray, isn't it? Sorry,' he said. 'I've been battling a hedge at the back of the church. Not my thing, really, gardening. I've a friend who's an absolute wizard at it – born with green fingers, he was. I just dabble.' He set down the branches and stripped off one glove, looking pleased. 'Well, this is quite a lucky meeting. I had hoped you'd come back. I've been having a devil of a time trying to find your address, you know. Your newspaper said they weren't sure where you were…'

'I've been travelling,' I said, and would have asked him why that mattered when he cheerfully cut in, 'A good thing that I didn't post that package to you, then. Can you wait here a minute? I'll just run across and fetch it.' And then, in case I thought him rude, 'I'd ask you to the house for tea, only my wife's having one of her meetings, and they can get rather fierce. I stay well clear of them, myself.' He smiled, not looking the slightest bit clerical. 'Won't be a minute.'

He took a bit longer than that, but not much. 'Here you are,' he said, holding out an old-fashioned document storage box, its corners reinforced with yellowed tape. 'I know I wasn't any help to you in finding that report that you were after, or anything having to do with Ivan Reynolds, but after we spoke on the phone last I *did* find this. Most of Andrew's things were sold at auction, you understand, but my wife had her eye on this rather nice night-table – mahogany…she's partial to mahogany – and so she managed to persuade the auctioneer to let her have it, straight out of the house, for a price. It had three drawers, all full. This,' he said, and handed me the box, 'was in the bottom one.'

I held the box and frowned. 'What's in it?'

'Newspaper cuttings, mostly. Some photographs. My wife and I, we thought that it should properly belong to you.'

'To me?'

'It's yours by rights.'

I didn't understand. I dropped my gaze to Deacon's grave. 'I don't have any claim, you know, to anything he owned. We only met the once.'

He was looking at me curiously, quiet. Then he said, 'Sometimes the once is all it takes.'

I raised my head.

He smiled. 'I believe there are no random meetings in our lives – that everyone we touch, who touches us, has been put in our path for a reason. The briefest encounter can open a door, or heal a wound, or close a circle that was started long before your birth…you never know.' He gave a small shrug, bending to retrieve his armful of branches and the garden shears. 'You'll understand,' he promised, 'when you've had a chance to go through that.'

I looked where he had nodded, at the box held in my hands, but as tempted as I was to lift the lid, I knew that this was not the time or place. Not here, with Nick still sitting watching from the van, outside the churchyard. So I told the vicar, 'Thank you. It was kind of you to keep this for me.' Then I asked, 'Did all his art collection sell at auction, too?'

'Yes, I sent all the paintings up to Sotheby's, you see, because I knew Andrew had dealt in art for years, and I have no idea, myself, of value. Couldn't tell a Rembrandt from a reproduction, if my life depended on it. One of the paintings, I'm told, sold for quite an outrageous amount, to an American, bidding by telephone. Andrew,' he concluded, 'must have had an expert eye for art.'

Oh, well, I thought. So much for my idea of buying the windmill painting. It would have been nice to have owned it, a kind of connection with Deacon, and all that I'd learnt about what had gone on, but the painting was no longer here, to be bought.

Looking down, I asked, to change the subject, 'Will he have a headstone?'

'Andrew? Strange as it may sound, he didn't want one. Left express instructions, in his will. He never was the sort to call attention to himself.'

And so in death, as in his life, I mused, the man remained invisible.

The vicar, watching my reaction, said, 'I don't suppose he thought there'd be too many people coming here to look for him, with all his family gone. He'd have been pleased, I think, to know that he was wrong, to see you standing here.' And then, as if remembering he still had work to do, he smiled again and asked me to excuse him. 'Good luck to you, Miss Murray,' was the way he chose to say goodbye. 'Take care.'

The churchyard felt a colder place when he had gone. I hugged my arms around the box he'd given me, and, looking down one final time at Andrew Deacon's grave, I turned and slowly made my way between the silent headstones to the lychgate, and the waiting van.

I was alone when I opened the box.

I don't know what I had expected I would find. Newspaper clippings, the vicar had said, and some photographs. My mind, I supposed, had been stuck in one track for so long it had simply assumed that it would all be somehow linked to what had happened all those years ago in Portugal. So when I finally lifted up the lid and saw what actually was in there, I was not at all prepared.

The clippings – photocopies of clippings, actually, with the stamped name of a clipping service marked in every corner – had been stacked in reverse chronological order, so the first one, on top, had the most recent date. It also had my byline – the first piece I'd written on the trial from London, in September. Beneath it was another of my articles, from Paris, and another, and another... Not, by any means, the comprehensive body of my work, but a pretty fair sampling.

It felt strange, to be leafing through the clippings, and to know that Andrew Deacon had been following my progress since I'd started with the *Sentinel*; that he'd actually paid a service to keep track of my articles, and copy them, and send them to him.

And it had gone beyond my own work, my own newspaper. Descending through the stack, I found the notice of my college graduation, from a different paper, and my father's death; my mother's death, my birth, my parent's marriage – the entire history of my life, played briefly, in reverse. But it was not my life, alone. Here was my grandfather's obituary, and my father's birth announcement, and, at last, on genuine newsprint, flaking and yellowed, the marriage of my grandparents.

Beneath that, in a jumble, were mementos.

A programme from the Broadway musical *Oklahoma!*; the ticket stubs from that performance; the paper menu from a restaurant; matchboxes; a handkerchief, that smelt of roses, faintly, when I raised it to my face.

And then, as promised by the vicar, photographs.

The prints were small, the kind that people used to take with those little Brownie box cameras, but each, to me, was like a jewel. My grandmother, in New York City – young, and laughing, arms outstretched against the New York skyline in a wide embrace of life. She was alone in all the pictures. Deacon must have been behind the camera, playing the infatuated honeymooning husband, taking snapshots of his bride in front of all the major city sights, like any other tourist.

These would doubtless, with the Broadway programme and the other keepsakes, have been part of Deacon's cover; something to keep with him in case anybody searched his things in Lisbon.

And yet, I thought, he'd kept them all these years, long after they could be of any use. It wasn't just a question of remembering my grandmother; he'd kept these bits of her preserved as though their marriage had been real, as though the family he'd kept track of in the newspapers, year after year, with all those careful clippings laid aside, had been his own.

I took the final item from the box – a folded leather picture frame, the kind meant to stand freely on a tabletop or desk, with a solid book-like cover that flipped open to reveal the photo mounted on the inside. Something warned me, as my fingers raised the cover, what the photograph would be, but even so it stole my breath.

The wedding photograph. My grandmother and Deacon. And so, at last, the shadow at my shoulder had a face. Not the face as I had seen it in September, but the youthful one by which, perhaps, a person ought most properly to be remembered. My grandmother had said he was an ordinary-looking man until one saw his eyes, and I agreed. His eyes were pale, intelligent, his best and strongest feature. For a long time I sat silently, intent on studying the image that for so long had eluded me, determined to commit to memory everything about him: how his hair waved, and the way he smiled; the angle of his chin.

And then my eyes came back to his, and stayed there.

'Hello, Mr Deacon,' I said quietly. 'I'm very pleased to meet you.'

It was closure, of a kind. But still, I knew the journey wasn't over yet.

I set the photograph beside my bed, that night. They'd come this far with me, my grandmother and Deacon. I could only hope they'd give me strength to do what I knew needed to be done.

CHAPTER SIX

Home

The night is gone;
And with the morn those angel faces smile
Which I have loved long since, and lost awhile.

JOHN NEWMAN, 'LEAD, KINDLY LIGHT'

SATURDAY, NOVEMBER 11

There was very little left to mark the site. In fact, as I took the turning south towards the lake and found myself surrounded on all sides by low stretching industrial buildings, I nearly thought I'd got it wrong...and then, beyond the buildings to my right, I saw the flags – four flags, unfurled against a sky that had been growing greyer as I'd travelled eastward.

This was it, I thought. I slowed the car.

The road curved, and the buildings on my right gave way to open space – a small green rise of hill, and on its top a low-walled concrete monument, not large, that held the four tall flagpoles with their emblems of the Province of Ontario, and Canada, and Britain, and the States, all set at half-mast. I was very near the water now. I could tell from the strength of the wind as it slapped the flags around and rippled up the grassy hill to where a sign, in plain black letters, read 'Intrepid Park'.

It didn't look like much of a park – only the unassuming monument, and a few young maple trees with trunks so slender they seemed scarcely able to withstand the bursts of wind that shook the leaves like something wild.

But I wasn't the only pilgrim. A Canadian Forces bus had blocked the driveway of one of the industrial buildings, and mine was the last in a long line of cars that had parked at the edge of the road. Still, the little assembly of people beneath the four flags looked quite small, I thought. More like a gathering of family than a formal Remembrance Day ceremony. I felt conspicuous as, head bent to the driving wind, I climbed the gently rising hill towards the monument.

No one paid me any real attention. Most of the people were busy talking amongst themselves, some obviously politicians, working the crowd with their handshakes and smiles. There seemed to be a scarcity of old men, and old women – that struck me straight away. I counted only a scattered handful of them, most wearing uniforms and ribboned bands of medals, sitting quietly on metal folding chairs that had been set in rows for those who found it difficult to stand. The people around them were younger, respectful in dark coats with red plastic poppies pinned through their lapels, or dressed in military uniform, without a coat, and shivering against the cold.

There was no shelter on the hill. The modest monument's low wall had been shaped as a long open crescent, like arms spread to embrace the slate-blue water of Lake Ontario that stretched away unbroken to the stormy grey horizon.

Just a half-hour's drive to the west lay Toronto. There, the lake was more civilised, reflecting back the bright lights of the cultured city skyline, with the small bit of well-controlled green that was Toronto Island lying just off shore. But here, at the southernmost boundary of Whitby, the lake had no such pretensions. It looked icy and forbidding, chopped up by the wind into frothy white waves over which seagulls dipped and hung, shrieking.

The landscape looked forbidding, too. Where the little park ended at the bottom of the hill, the rough ground began – dead brown grass tipped with gold and the odd tenacious patch of green, split by a narrow bicycle path that came from the fields ringed by woods to the right. Beyond the bicycle path there was nothing but scrub brush that fell off abruptly as though there were bluffs or a cliff at the lake's edge.

It was a lonely place. And yet today, Remembrance Day, these people round me had all made the journey, as I had, to stand here in this spot above a long-abandoned site, now turned to blowing field.

There was movement from the monument. The soldiers of the vigil were about to take up their position. Soberly, they stepped forward from the ranks, two of them, each moving to one end of the curved monument. A few sharp, barked commands, and measured motions made in unison, and both were soon like statues, heads bent, rifle barrels resting on their polished boots. They'd stay like that, I knew, the whole length of the ceremony. Motionless.

Between them, I could see a plaque set in the centre of the wall. I couldn't read the words from where I stood, but then I didn't need to. I'd already done my research. I knew what was written there. It read:

CAMP X

1941–1946

ON THIS SITE BRITISH SECURITY COORDINATION
OPERATED SPECIAL TRAINING SCHOOL NO. 103 AND
HYDRA. S.T.S. 103 TRAINED ALLIED AGENTS IN THE
TECHNIQUES OF SECRET WARFARE FOR THE SPECIAL
OPERATIONS EXECUTIVE (S.O.E.) BRANCH OF THE
BRITISH INTELLIGENCE SERVICE.

HYDRA NETWORK COMMUNICATED VITAL MESSAGES
BETWEEN CANADA, THE UNITED STATES, AND GREAT
BRITAIN.

THIS COMMEMORATION IS DEDICATED TO THE SERVICE
OF THE MEN AND WOMEN WHO TOOK PART IN THESE
OPERATIONS.

I turned again, letting my gaze travel out across the windy, unkempt field to where the line of dark trees rose to block the view across the lake. Somewhere down there, in a building long gone, in this place full of silence and secrets, my grandmother had first met Andrew Deacon.

Now there was nothing, just the shadows of dark snow clouds chasing over empty space, and overhead a single gull with black-tipped wings that rose and wheeled and headed out across the lake like an escaping spirit.

The flags above my head flapped noisily, their cords and metallic rings striking the tall flagpoles with the hollow clinking sound of cold aluminum. The sound wrenched me back to the present.

The service began.

It was simple, short on speeches, just the solitary bugle and a reading from the military pastor, who had chosen as his text a passage I had never heard, from the Apocrypha, beginning '*Let us now praise famous men.*' The words were fitting, bittersweet: '*And some there are who left a name behind, to be commemorated in story. And there are others who are unremembered; they are dead, and it is as though they never did exist...*'

I thought of Deacon, in his grave without a headstone; of his grey and faceless presence that had haunted me so long. Not faceless now, I thought. Deliberately, I closed my eyes to conjure up his image from the photograph, his smile, his eyes.

And then, as if in answer to my effort and my mood, the reading changed. Another voice, the younger voice of one of the cadets, read out the words of Binyon's proud 'Prayer for the Fallen':

'*They shall not grow old, as we that are left grow old. Age shall not weary them, nor the years condemn. At the going down of the sun, and in the morning, we will remember them.*'

I opened my eyes. The sun, on cue, broke through the clouds at just that moment, falling warm upon my frozen back like a comforting hand, and casting long shadows across the dead grass at the feet of the uniformed young men and women standing still, in ranks, before the monument. And for one brief minute, to my eyes, those shadows made a second army – ghosts who stood at fixed attention in between the living bodies, silent and aware.

I hadn't been to a Remembrance Day service since I was a child. I didn't know that Binyon's poem called for a response;

so it surprised me when it came, from those few older men and women in the crowd, from those old soldiers, standing straighter now than anyone around them, their scattered voices finding strength: *'We will remember them.'*

I very nearly said, 'Amen.' But I stayed silent, while the clouds came back. The shadows melted on the ground. The soldiers of the vigil stirred, becoming human once again. The people round me stirred, as well, and broke off into small groups, chatting, huddled in the cold.

I looked across the empty, blowing field, and tried again to see it as my Grandma Murray had described it: the gate, and the checkpoint; the transmitter tower; the huts and the buildings; the commandant's comfortable office. But even my imagination couldn't fill the gaps. It was a field, and nothing more. I remembered her saying, 'I've never been back. Never even had a look at it. It wouldn't be the same.'

I understood.

It didn't matter, though, I thought, if there was nothing left to see. I hadn't really thought there would be. And, besides, I had another purpose.

The little banquet hall was filled with people come for the reception. Nothing fancy – tea and sandwiches, to warm those who'd been standing in the cold wind for the service at the monument.

Not everyone had come here, from the look of it, but I was reassured to see at least a handful of the older men in uniform relaxing at the tightly clustered tables.

One of the women serving coffee helped me locate the President of the Camp X Historical Society. He was young, with a friendly face. 'Right, I remember,' he said, when I told him who I was. 'We spoke on the phone. You wanted to interview some of the veterans who trained at Camp X, didn't you? Come on, I'll introduce you to a few of our more interesting alumni.'

They were all nice, every one of them, and eager to be helpful, though I had a sense that they'd been asked these questions many times before by young reporters, not unlike myself, in search of human interest pieces for Remembrance Day. I talked to them in turn, using my tape recorder and notebook to capture their reminiscences; their anecdotes. And at the end of every chat, I finished with a question that I felt sure they had *not* been asked before: 'Do you, by any chance, remember an instructor by the name of Andrew Deacon?'

Of course they all said no, as I'd expected that they would, but still, I'd thought it worth a try.

Finally, the young President of the Camp X Historical Society looked round the room and said, 'I think that's all of them. There are fewer and fewer every year, you know? It's sad.' He brought his gaze around to me. 'Which paper are you with, again?'

I told him, and he promised to keep an eye out for my article, and shook my hand, and wished me well, and left me on my own.

I was packing up my notebook and my tape recorder when an old man stopped beside my table.

'I remember him,' he said.

I looked up. He was very tall, and loose-limbed, with a quick, engaging smile.

I asked him, 'Pardon?'

'Andrew Deacon. I remember him. I knew him pretty well, in fact. May I join you?'

'Please.' He must, I thought, have been sitting somewhere close enough to have overheard my last interview, although I couldn't recall seeing him at any of the nearby tables, or, for that matter, at the outdoor service earlier. He wasn't in uniform; just in a plain shirt and trousers, with jacket and tie, and he hadn't been pointed out to me as one of the Camp X alumni. Still, his face, for some strange reason, rang a chord within my memory, and I felt I *should* remember him from somewhere. I held my hand out. 'I'm Kate Murray, Mr...?'

'Iveson.'

Iveson. That seemed familiar, too. I put my tape recorder back where it had been, in the middle of the table, and asked, 'Do you mind being taped?'

'Not at all.'

'So,' I began, 'was Andrew Deacon one of your instructors, then, when you were at Camp X?'

'Oh, I was never up here, at the camp. No, I knew Andrew in New York,' he said, and met my eyes, and smiled. 'When he was living with your grandmother.'

Surprised, I let the tape run on in silence for at least a half a minute. 'Mr Iveson...'

'It's James,' he introduced himself. 'But you can call me Jim.'

My second cup of coffee was noticeably stronger than the first, and I was glad of it. I hadn't fully grasped the fact that I was sitting with the same man whom my grandmother had talked about – the Jim who had turned up on Deacon's doorstep in

434

New York, their first day there, with lunch in hand; who'd turned up every day thereafter, for his private talks with Deacon.

'You were briefing him, I take it, for his assignment in Lisbon?' I asked.

'Well, I had certain inside information when it came to Ivan Reynolds and his company. I'd worked for him myself, see.'

And at that, my memory cleared and all the pieces snapped in place with the precision of a Chinese puzzle. Iveson. James Iveson. That's where I'd heard his name before: The young man from New York, who'd gone to work for Ivan Reynolds, and had taken Jenny out to nightclubs on the sly, until he had been set upon by Cayton-Wood, and neatly framed, and fired.

He told me the story in summary, from his perspective, and it was essentially the same thing that I'd heard from Jenny Augustine in Washington, except he knew exactly why he had been made a target.

He'd been working for the FBI, back then. Portugal had been, technically, outside the FBI's area of operations, but the FBI's director, J Edgar Hoover, had a personal relationship with Reynolds, and when questions were raised about Reynolds's loyalty, Hoover had said he'd be damned if he'd stand back and let his rival, 'Wild Bill' Donovan of the OSS – Office of Strategic Services – have a free hand with the investigation.

The OSS, to Hoover, was an upstart organisation, created during the war to carry out espionage and counter-espionage abroad. Like the members of its British counterpart, the SIS, or

MI6, OSS agents worked outside the law, and could assassinate their enemies. The FBI had been reduced, for the most part, to a domestic police force, confined to American soil.

Portugal should have been Donovan's patch, then, but Hoover had gone straight to see the President. Ivan Reynolds, Hoover had argued, was an American, and that made the soil that his company sat on American soil, no matter what damned country it was in, which put it squarely in the FBI's domain.

No one knew if Roosevelt had been convinced by Hoover's argument, or if he'd even authorised the FBI to send a man to Lisbon, but a man was sent to Lisbon, notwithstanding.

Jim had sensed from the beginning there was something crooked going on with Cayton-Wood and Spivey. But he'd nosed around too openly, and Cayton-Wood had pegged him as an agent, and a threat. Jim hadn't stood a chance.

'I didn't see it coming,' he admitted to me now. 'I was too young. Too inexperienced. But I could sure let the next man know what to expect, and who to keep an eye on.'

I said, 'And the next man was Deacon.'

'That's right. We'd had our crack at it; the British wanted their turn. He was perfect for it, really. I was just a lowly lawyer, but he had the knowledge of art, the experience, that gave him a good chance at getting much closer to Reynolds than I could have done. So I briefed him, and helped get him ready to go.'

He'd gone to the apartment with an image in his mind. They'd only told him Andrew Deacon was an Englishman who dealt in art, so Jim had pictured someone very witty and flamboyant

– not the quiet, down-to-earth man he had found. The wife, too, had been a surprise. She was not at all glamorous, and more attractive, in Jim's eyes, because of it.

He'd developed a great fondness for Amelia Deacon as the days had passed.

If she hadn't been a married woman, he might well have tried to make a play for her himself. She was so lively, and so young. She lit the room when she walked in. When they ate lunch, the three of them together in the small apartment kitchen, Jim always tried to make her laugh so he could hear the sound – her laughter was infectious. It even made her husband smile, and that was an accomplishment.

It wasn't that Andrew Deacon was humourless. Far from it. The man had a very dry wit, and a drier delivery. But he was the quietest man Jim had met. Sometimes, when Jim and Amelia were talking and laughing together, it seemed as though they were in one world while her husband sat back and looked on from another, as though he wasn't sure himself just how to bridge the gap and join them.

But Amelia Deacon bridged it for him. If he sat too long in silence, she would twist the conversation round to bring him in. 'Tell Jim about the time...' she'd start, and he'd be with them once again, not on the sidelines anymore, but in the game.

Small wonder Andrew Deacon loved his wife. And she loved him. Jim saw it clearly, in the way they interacted; in the way they smiled, and touched, and in the way they watched each other when they thought the other person wasn't looking.

Jim would have given a lot to have somebody love him like that.

'Do you have a girl, Jim?' she asked one day, as she handed him his tea.

'No. Too much work,' he said, and grinned. 'You have to take them dancing, buy them flowers.'

'I love flowers,' she admitted. 'Roses, most of all. Except, of course, the yellow ones.'

Jim raised an eyebrow, curious. 'What's wrong with the yellow ones?'

'They have an ugly meaning. Every flower has a meaning, don't you know? My grandmother had this old book, a Victorian book, called *The Language of Flowers*, and it listed all of the meanings, so lovers could send secret messages in their bouquets. It all sounded very romantic.'

Jim thought it sounded very complicated. 'What do yellow roses mean?'

The answer came from Andrew Deacon, sitting in his corner. 'They mean jealousy.' Then, to his wife's surprised look, he explained with a half-smile, 'We had the same book in our house, when I was a boy.'

The talk, from there, turned to gardens, then to birds, and then, in that associative way all conversations had, to airplanes.

Jim could feel the change. He felt the tension in the room, and though he knew that it was coming from Amelia, he could not imagine why. Usually, she poured herself a second cup of tea. Today, she didn't finish drinking the first; she just glanced at the clock and said, 'Is that the time already? I should go. I have to find a dress to wear tonight.'

She gave them both a smile, and rose, and left the kitchen.

Jim looked at Andrew Deacon. 'Did I say anything to upset her?'

'No. No, she doesn't like airplanes, that's all.' She'd left a handkerchief behind her, lying on the table. Andrew Deacon picked it up and neatly folded it, and tucked it in his pocket. 'Shall we start?'

It seemed to Jim, that afternoon, that Andrew Deacon's mind was somewhere else. The man was unusually restless. If he wasn't pacing the living room, he was standing in front of the window, hands clasped at his back, looking over the snow-covered rooftops towards Central Park.

There wasn't much left to go over. Jim went through the few final points, and then finished with a summary. 'The daughter, like I said, might be some help to you, so get to know her. She's a nice kid. I felt sorry for her, actually. She's not allowed to have much fun. But she's no fool – you'll learn a lot from talking to her.'

Andrew Deacon promised to remember.

'So that's it, really,' Jim said, with a shrug. 'I guess you're ready.'

'I guess I am.'

Jim didn't know exactly how to talk to that impassive face. 'It could be any day, now, so you'll have to be prepared. It all depends on when the Clipper leaves. There may not be much warning – they'll just send me to come get you.'

'And what happens to Amelia?' Andrew Deacon asked.

Jim knew his answer mattered. 'I'll take care of her, don't worry.'

From the hall, they heard the front door close, and then Amelia's cheerful voice called out, 'Hello!'

Jim's eyes were fixed on Andrew Deacon's face as he was turning from the window, and he saw a flash of deep emotion, almost like a private pain, that twisted Jim's own gut because he felt so damned responsible. It was because *he'd* failed with Ivan Reynolds that another man was being sent to Lisbon, and a married man, at that – a man with more at stake than Jim had ever had, and so much more to lose.

'Just see she gets home safely,' Andrew Deacon asked him quietly. And then he turned again to greet his wife as she passed by the open doorway of the living room. He told her, 'You're back early.'

'Yes, well…' She held up the dress bag. 'I found what I wanted.' She looked at Jim. 'Sorry to interrupt.'

'Oh, no. I was just going,' said Jim, with a smile. He didn't say anything further. Truth was, he didn't trust his voice.

He spent the rest of the day in a black mood, feeling angry with himself, and with the war, and with the world in general. He knew that, in his business, he couldn't afford to care what would become of the people he met. He had to keep his focus on the bigger picture if he was to be of any use to those he worked for. But in this case, he *did* care. He couldn't help it.

He was reading when the phone rang.

For a moment, he just let it ring, and looked at it. He knew that it was probably the call that he'd been waiting for – the call to say the Pan Am Clipper was preparing to take off from New York harbour, and it was time for him to pick up Andrew Deacon and escort him to the plane.

He considered what might happen if he simply didn't answer it, but he knew it wouldn't make a difference. Someone else would get the call, instead of him, and Andrew Deacon would still have to leave tonight and fly to Lisbon.

With a sigh, he reached to pick up the receiver, said, 'Hello?' and then relaxed when he heard Andrew Deacon's voice.

'Hello, Jim. Look, there's been a change of plans. We've left the party. If you need to find us, we'll be at the Roosevelt Hotel. In the ballroom.'

'Right. Thanks.' He wrote the information down, and hung up feeling happier. At least, he thought, they'd have a last night on the town together, to enjoy. And he might just have time to have that drink that he'd been putting off.

He rose to get it. Took the bottle from the cupboard in the kitchen. But before he could unscrew the cap, the telephone began to ring again.

They were dancing.

He could see them at the far edge of the dance floor, Amelia Deacon's red hair gleaming bright above the dress she'd bought that afternoon – a black dress, beautiful, with some kind of fringe on the shoulders reflecting the low ballroom lights like a shower of sparkling diamonds each time that she moved.

Her cheek was resting on her husband's cheek, and both their eyes were closed.

Jim couldn't bring himself to interrupt the dance. He motioned to the man who had come in with him to stand his ground, and listened for a moment to the orchestra, the song. It was from something he had seen a few years back, he thought, on Broadway.

The mellow-voiced singer was crooning the chorus again

for the last time, the swell of the music behind him a sign he was nearing the end:

'Might as well make believe I love you,
For to tell the truth,
I do.'

The music swelled again and stopped, and Jim saw the Deacons had stopped too. They stayed on the dance floor, still looking at each other, neither letting go the other's hand, as though even that small separation would be too much to endure. Jim felt his black mood returning as he walked towards them, with the other man in tow.

Amelia was the first to be aware of him. She turned her head a fraction, and Jim said apologetically, 'I hate to spoil your evening, but it's time.'

Andrew Deacon dropped his hand reluctantly and let go his wife's fingers.

Jim went on, 'We have to get you to the wharf in less than half an hour. There's a car outside, and your suitcase is already in it. Frank, here, will go with you.' He saw Amelia's eyes begin to mist, and quickly reached across her to shake Andrew Deacon's hand. 'Good luck,' Jim said.

'Yes, I…thank you.' Andrew Deacon took a moment to collect himself; then, looking at his wife, repeated, for some reason, 'Thank you'.

The reference was clearly a private one. Trying to smile, she replied, 'It was nothing'.

'No,' said Andrew Deacon, and he raised a hand to touch her cheek, a gesture of farewell. And then his fingers slid beneath her hair to gently cup her neck, and he leant close to her and murmured something not for Jim to hear, and kissed her forehead.

Amelia's face was hidden; Jim couldn't see her expression. But he saw Andrew Deacon's. He saw the passion in that kiss, and saw how the Englishman closed his eyes tightly as if to contain his emotions. He didn't quite manage it.

Straightening, Andrew Deacon searched his wife's face with a curious intensity, the way a man with failing eyes might try to make a memory of a thing he will not see again. And then he simply said, 'Goodbye'.

'Goodbye,' Amelia answered him, still trying hard to smile, but as her husband walked away Jim saw her give up the attempt. She looked away, biting her lip as she fought back the tears that were starting to well up along her dark eyelashes. Stepping in closer, Jim pressed his own handkerchief into her hand, trying to shield her from the curious eyes of the dancers around them.

Andrew Deacon had stopped at the door, to look back. Above Amelia's head, Jim met his eyes and gave a quiet nod of promise, and then slowly, with an effort, Andrew Deacon turned around again, and left.

'Come on,' said Jim to Amelia, and he took hold of her shoulder in an understanding grasp. 'I'll take you home.'

'Not home.' Her voice was shaking, just a little, but she dried her eyes deliberately, and raised her lovely, stubborn face to say, 'I want to see the Clipper leave.'

'Amelia...'

'Please,' was all she said.

He should have told her no. He should have said it was impossible; that he'd been given orders...but he couldn't, somehow, looking in those eyes.

He fetched her coat.

The drive was short. She didn't speak at all, just sat there with her hands clenched in her lap, her fingers working at the wedding band she wore, turning it round and round against her whitened knuckle. Her face looked almost normal…if you didn't look too closely.

Jim glanced at her. 'I can't let you get out of the car, you understand that. My boss would have my head if he found out I'd even brought you here.'

'I understand.'

He didn't go right to the wharf where the seaplane was waiting – they would have been seen – but he did park as close as he could, so she'd have a good view.

There wasn't much to see. The plane looked small against the dark sky and the harbour, rolling with the swells of water, at the mercy of the elements. A light, soft snow had started falling. Some of the flakes struck the windshield and melted to droplets that clung to the glass before losing their hold as the wind chased them off again.

Jim watched Amelia, as she watched the plane. She didn't cry. He found that worse, somehow, than if she had. It hurt him more to see her being strong; to watch her red-rimmed eyes shine bright with all the tears that she refused to shed; to see her lips compressing as she tried to stop them quivering; to see her look on steadily, unmoving save for that small, ceaseless turning of her wedding band. She sat like that, not speaking, while the Clipper made its final preparations, and she stayed there till the aircraft finally loosed its moorings, turned, and nosed its way into the blackness of the night, rising from the water like a great, unnatural bird on wings of steel, until at last it vanished altogether, and was gone.

Even then, she didn't cry. Her muscles tensed, as though she were attempting to hold on to something precious, something vital, that was being wrenched away from her. And then she pulled her gaze from where the plane had been, and turned to Jim, and in a very quiet voice said, 'Thank you. You can take me back to the apartment now.'

Not 'home', he thought. She hadn't told him, 'take me home'. Perhaps it wouldn't feel like home to her, without her husband there. Starting up the car, he wheeled it back the way they'd come and started driving, searching for the words to reassure her, to give comfort. But he couldn't think of any.

He glanced over at her, once, then wished he hadn't. Never, in his whole life, had he seen a woman look so lonely.

Talk to me, he thought, *I'll listen. Please, Amelia, talk to me*. But she stayed silent in her seat, face turned towards the window and the blur of whirling snowflakes, holding in the tears, as though to let them fall would somehow be a failing, on her part.

'He'll be fine,' Jim said. 'Don't worry. He'll come back to you all right.'

He saw her mouth curve, very briefly, in an effort at a smile. Then, to his dismay, he saw one small tear spill over and run down her cheek in silence. And she closed her eyes.

He kept his mouth shut after that. He saw her up to the apartment, switched the lights on, checked the locks, and turned to ask her, 'Are you going to be OK?'

There was no sign of that stray, solitary tear. Her face was perfect. 'Yes, Jim. Thank you. Thanks,' she said, 'for everything.' She held her hand out, formal, and he shook it. Gave it back to her.

'You're welcome. I'll be by to take you out for lunch tomorrow. Have you tried that little restaurant on the corner?'

'But…' She frowned, not understanding. 'But I thought, with Andrew gone…'

Jim smiled. 'You thought my job was over? Well, ordinarily, it would be, but your husband made me promise I'd take care of you,' he told her, 'and I always keep my promises.'

He tried his best, the next few weeks, to do just that: take care of her; to see that she was happy, or at least as happy as she could be, in the circumstances. They went walking, when the weather wasn't bad, or went to lunch, or even, one time, to the theatre. They talked, as they had always done, about small things – their families, mostly, and the way their lives had been before the war.

He didn't see her every day. He didn't want to harm her reputation; didn't want her neighbours thinking there was anything improper going on. So when the letter came for him from Lisbon, with its single, small request, he wasn't sure, at first, that he should do it.

But he did.

Amelia looked surprised to see him standing at the door with flowers.

'I can't take the credit for these,' he said, with a smile. 'They're from your husband. Happy birthday.'

She took the bouquet, wondering. 'I didn't think that he'd remember.'

'I hope I got it right. I had to go to a couple of florists before I could find what he wanted.' Roses, plain roses, he thought, would have been fairly easy to buy, in New York, but not—

'Tea roses,' she said, and brushed a pink bloom with a delicate touch. 'They're tea roses.'

'That's right.'

She looked quickly down and away from him, hiding her face, but he'd already seen her expression; the flush of emotion, the betraying brightness of her eyes. 'They're beautiful, Jim,' she said. 'Just let me put them in water.'

He wondered what tea roses meant in the language of flowers, but he didn't like to ask her when she seemed so overcome.

Instead he waited, and that evening he went past the public library, and went inside and asked if they had any books that listed all the flowers and their meanings, and they did. Tea roses, it turned out, meant: *I'll remember, always.*

A peculiar thing, Jim thought, to tell your wife.

Amelia Deacon seemed to understand, though. Later on that week, when Jim dropped by, he found the flowers on the front hall table, pink and blooming, beautiful. But in the room beyond, he saw a suitcase.

Frowning, he asked, 'Are you taking a trip somewhere?' Surely, he thought, they weren't sending *her* to Portugal. The journey was too dangerous.

She kept her head down. 'I thought I'd go home for a visit. My mother could do with the help just now, and I could do with the company.' Quickly she carried on, 'Not that you haven't been very good company, Jim, but—'

'I understand.' He saw her relax when he smiled. He asked, 'When are you going?'

'My train leaves tonight.'

'That soon? And when will you be back?'

'I don't know. I likely won't stay long. But then, you never know.'

He wasn't altogether sure how he would like New York without Amelia Deacon in it, but on the other hand he felt relieved that she was going home, to family, where she wouldn't be so lonely. 'Look,' he told her, as he searched his pocket for his card, 'if you need anything at all, just write, and I'll take care of it.'

She took the card and, looking at it, said, 'I will, Jim. Thank you.'

'And when you come back, call me, and I'll come and meet your train.'

'All right.'

She never called.

He waited all that winter. Every now and then he'd walk up West 73rd Street and look for signs of life in the apartment windows, but he always found them dark. A few times he even went into the building and knocked at the door. No one answered. And then came the spring, and the FBI sent him to Washington.

The work was busy. He forgot about Amelia Deacon – or, at least, that's what he told himself; what he preferred to believe, though the truth was he still turned to look when a redhead walked by, even though he knew full well it wouldn't be her.

And then, one day, it was.

He stopped dead on the sidewalk in surprise. It *was* her – there was no mistake. She passed him, walking with another girl, head bent in earnest conversation.

Jim called out, 'Amelia!' and he saw her slow her step and

turn, eyes searching, almost hopeful; then she saw him, too, and he could see the moment when she recognised him. At her side, the other girl said something, and Amelia hesitated; then she shook her head and turned away again and smiled at the other girl, and carried on as if he were invisible.

He followed her for half a block, and called again, 'Amelia!' but she didn't look around, and by the time he could push through the other people on the sidewalk she was gone.

That was in May. Late May.

Then D-Day had come, and the great Allied surge across Europe, and finally, the end of the war.

Jim had stayed on in Washington, settling into professional life there as much as his nature allowed him to settle. He worked, and he travelled. He liked the warmer destinations: Cairo, one year. Athens. Rome. In 1958 he went to Istanbul – he had a yen to see the Blue Mosque, and the Castle of the Seven Towers, and the tombs of Suleiman and Roxelana. He was standing in the Hippodrome, that great and ancient stadium, imagining the chariots with racing colours, red and white and green and blue, hurtling round in a dust-raising thunder of hooves to the cheers of the Byzantine crowds and their Emperor – when, quite by chance, he saw someone he knew.

Andrew Deacon had aged. He looked tired, and greyer, but Jim knew him instantly. The Englishman was wandering some little distance off, beside a broken column twined with serpents.

Jim didn't call out to him. They were, after all, in Istanbul, the gateway to the Bosporus, a stone's throw from the Soviet Union, and if Andrew Deacon was still in the business of spying for Britain, the last thing he needed was some damn fool blowing his cover. But Jim did take a moment to look round, to see if Deacon's wife was in the Hippodrome, as well. He didn't see her.

'Jim.' The quiet, friendly voice beside him caught him off his guard. He hadn't noticed Andrew Deacon moving; hadn't heard the man's approach. 'I must say, what a pleasant surprise. Are you here on a holiday? Come, let me buy you a drink.'

They found a tea room, off a side street near the Church of St Sophia. The tea was served in glasses, strong and fragrant. The proprietor – a huge Turk with a very black moustache – turned on the radio to entertain them while they drank. The songs were American, mostly.

Jim smiled. 'Sounds like home.'

'Are you still in New York?' Andrew Deacon asked.

'No, I'm in Washington.'

'Washington? I was there last month. A shame I didn't know...'

'Well, here, let me give you my address, and then the next time you're in town you can call me. We'll do something.' Jim wrote the address down; handed it over. Noticing the wedding ring on Andrew Deacon's hand, he casually asked, 'Is Amelia not with you?'

Andrew Deacon paused in the act of accepting the paper. He looked up. 'I'm sorry, I thought you were told.' Dropping his eyes, he folded the paper into crisp, neat squares. 'My wife passed away.'

Jim felt that like a blow to his own chest. 'No.' It was unthinkable – that bright and lovely woman, with the

450

laugh that could electrify a room. 'I am so sorry.'

'Thank you. It happened quite a while ago. I'm told one does adjust.' He felt his pockets for his cigarettes, and offered one to Jim. 'No? You don't mind if I...?'

'Go ahead.'

A match flared. Through the swirl of smoke that followed, Andrew Deacon said, 'She had an accident, you see, the April I was out in Lisbon.'

Jim fell silent. With new eyes he looked at Andrew Deacon's face. And then he said, 'But that's impossible.'

The Englishman had not expected that. 'What do you mean?'

'I mean I saw your wife in Washington, that May. And she was very much alive. She—' Jim broke off and frowned, remembering the circumstances – how she had been walking with another girl, and how her face had changed when she had recognised him; how she'd turned away. And then, all of a sudden, it made sense. He felt a growing sense of certainty; of wonder. 'Christ, she wasn't your wife, was she? She was... what? One of us?'

Andrew Deacon didn't answer right away. He exhaled smoke, and looked towards a corner of the room, as though deciding something. Slowly, then, he said, 'Not one of us. Not in that way. She was only a girl who was asked to do something quite selfless, to help with the war. And she did it, I thought, rather brilliantly.'

'Well, I'll be damned.' Jim sat back. 'I think I will have that smoke, after all.' He lit the cigarette and shook the match out, squinting hard. 'You two sure had me fooled. I would have sworn that you were newlyweds – you seemed so much in love.'

He was becoming used again to Andrew Deacon's habit of remaining silent, putting off a question with a small lift of one shoulder, like a shrug.

The tinny tea-room radio was playing Doris Day. It was an older song: 'I See Your Face Before Me', and her honeyed voice was singing words that Jim found quite appropriate:

In a world of tinsel and show

The unreal from the real thing is hard to know…

He looked at Andrew Deacon. 'You did love her,' he said. 'Didn't you?'

The Englishman stayed quiet for so long that Jim felt sure he wouldn't answer, but at length he raised the cigarette and brought his gaze around again, and calmly said, 'I should have been a great fool if I hadn't.'

'Then why, in God's name, did you let her go?' He wouldn't have, himself, thought Jim. If he had had Amelia for his own, he would have moved the earth to keep her. He felt curiously angry at this self-collected Englishman, for wasting such a golden opportunity. 'She loved you, too, you know that? I was there,' Jim said. 'I saw. It nearly killed her when you went away.'

Again the stretching silence, and the sideways sliding of the gaze. 'She had a fiancé,' said Andrew Deacon quietly. 'A pilot. Shot down over France, he was, not long before she got paired up with me. That's why she had a thing with planes… you might remember.'

Jim remembered.

Andrew Deacon carried on, 'I'm not a violent man. It's not my way to wish another person ill, but I'd be lying if I said I didn't hope, in private, that Amelia's fiancé was dead; that

452

he'd been killed in France. I held that hope, in fact, for quite a while.'

He raised his cigarette again, and in the pause that followed Doris Day sang mournfully:

It doesn't matter where you are
I can see how fair you are
I close my eyes and there you are,
Always.

Jim saw a faint twist of the Englishman's impassive mouth.

'And then, one day,' said Andrew Deacon, 'not long after I'd arrived in Lisbon, Jack Cayton-Wood took me to Caldas da Rainha. You knew it yourself, surely?'

'Where all the refugees were.'

'Yes, precisely. Our purpose, I was told, was to debrief a young man who had just arrived; made his way down, with his wits, out of Occupied France. Not the nicest of journeys, I shouldn't imagine. He was rather the worse for it. Had a bad arm. It had broken, I think, and there hadn't been anyone with him to set it. He'd done a fair job on his own, but one could see it gave him pain. Still, he didn't complain. He was that kind of chap. Quite impressive. The kind of chap I might have bought a pint for, if I'd met him in a pub. The kind one knows will make his mark in life.' He paused, to take a sharp pull of the cigarette. Breathed out. 'At any rate, we finished the debriefing, and then he and Cayton-Wood fell to talking, about where he came from, his family, his girl. His chief concern, as I recall, was how to let them know he was all right. And after that, how quickly he could make it back to join up with his squadron, and get back into the air. He was a pilot, did I mention that? Canadian.'

Jim felt for him. 'Amelia's fiancé.'

The nod was brief. The cigarette had burnt down nearly to its end. He stubbed it out. 'The damned thing was, I liked him. I admired him. And I knew he loved her too.'

The sad, clear voice of Doris Day sang on into the silence as the song came to an end:

Would that my love could haunt you so;
Knowing I want you so,
I can't erase your beautiful face before me.

Jim thought, in that one moment, that he'd always hate that song. He'd never hear it, after this, without remembering the buried pain in Andrew Deacon's eyes; those eyes that wouldn't meet his own, but kept their focus on the corner of the room, as though that small, fierce effort was the only way that he could manage the emotion, as a man might brace himself against the wind.

'And so I told myself, well, it's the chequerboard, you see. Like in *The Rubaiyat*. You've read *The Rubaiyat*?' he asked. 'Because that's all we are – we're only playing pieces, and we move where Fate would have us move.' His gaze slipped finally from the corner; angled down, to his left hand, and to the wedding band he wore. And then he raised his eyes to look at Jim. 'You asked me why I let her go,' he said, and smiled – a small, sad smile that stayed with Jim a long time afterwards. 'The answer is a simple one: She wasn't mine to keep.'

Somebody clinked a teacup near us. They were starting to clear tables in the little banquet hall.

'What did he mean,' I asked: '"The chequerboard"?'

Jim Iveson glanced up, and smiled – an echo, I was thinking, of the smile he'd seen in Istanbul, those many years ago.

'I looked it up,' he said. 'I was never a very good student, at school. Reading poetry wasn't my thing. But I got curious, myself, and so I looked it up. *The Rubaiyat of Omar Khayyam*, by Edward Fitzgerald – that's what he was quoting from. The part he spoke of goes like this:' And in his slow, deep voice, he said:

> *'Tis all a chequer board of Nights and Days*
> *Where Destiny with men for pieces plays:*
> *Hither and thither moves, and mates, and slays,*
> *And one by one back in the Closet lays.'*

The lines were lovely, resonant; made all the more so by his strongly felt delivery. In the silent moment that came afterwards, I thought about their meaning; thought of all the lives that had been played with – thrust together; torn apart.

Jim said, 'I saw a lot of sad things, in the war; heard a lot of sad stories. But I always thought Andrew's was one of the saddest. He never complained, mind you. Went on with life, in his own quiet way. But it might have been so different.'

I remembered how I'd thought that, myself, in my grandmother's kitchen, the night she had told me her story. I remembered thinking how life might have been for her, with Deacon, and I'd wondered whether she would have been happier if she had chosen him – but now I knew that Deacon hadn't let her make the choice. He'd stepped aside. He'd met my Grandpa Murray, and he'd liked him, so he'd sacrificed his own wants in one fleeting, noble move – a tiny playing piece discarded from the game board.

I thought of the few lines that Jim had quoted, and how perfectly they fit the private tragedy of Deacon and my grandmother. I thought, too, of the vicar of St Stephens; how he'd told me that there were no random meetings…and I had an inclination to believe he might be right. Perhaps a greater hand *was* moving us, according to its will.

I almost could believe that, after what Jim told me next.

The spring had come to Washington. The cherry-blossom time, when crowds of tourists filled the Capitol to marvel at the monuments and buildings, and enjoy the pleasure, long deferred, of walking out of doors, with winter fading to a small and distant memory.

Jim, having just passed his sixty-fourth birthday, had purposely slowed in his pace at the office, to give himself time to enjoy days like this one, and so, being in no great rush to get to work, he gave himself permission to take one turn round the Tidal Basin. The Basin, on that day, was perfect; smooth, without a ripple, catching clearly the reflection of the Jefferson Memorial, the arched rotunda shining white beyond the fragrant, pink-bloomed cherry trees that ringed the pool of water and made a such a brilliant show against the clear blue morning sky.

Breathing deep, in satisfaction, Jim felt good. So good, he was considering a second circuit round the pool when he heard someone laugh.

A woman. Low, and throaty, and infectious.

Stopping on the path, Jim held himself in check a moment,

not quite ready to believe. And then, he turned.

It *was* her. Older, like himself, but definitely her. Her red hair had lightened to something like strawberry blonde, but her figure had held. She was standing not ten feet away from him, holding the bar of an empty child's stroller and laughing at a little toddling girl with bright red pigtails.

Jim's voice didn't come, the first time, but he coughed and tried again. 'Amelia.'

As she had so long ago, again she turned round, slowly, and Jim thought, this time he understood the reason for the hopefulness he saw within her eyes. But he was not the man she'd been expecting. Not the man she'd wanted.

Still, she recognised him too. And this time, there was no denial. 'Jim,' she said, and smiled her wide, familiar smile, as though she were as pleased as he was by their chance encounter.

'How *are* you?' she asked. 'What a wonderful surprise. I'm afraid we'll have to walk,' she warned him, as he came across to meet her. 'This little one won't sit still in the stroller. She doesn't like being strapped in.'

'I don't blame her.' Jim crouched to the child's level, smiling. 'And what's your name?'

The little girl just looked at him with interest, and Amelia answered, 'Katie. She's my granddaughter.'

'She's beautiful.'

'Well, thank you. I think so, naturally, but then I'm biased.'

'Gamma,' said the little girl, and tugged Amelia's hand, and they began to walk. Jim took charge of the empty stroller, pushing it. He thought of all the ways he could begin their conversation, but he settled on, 'Just so you know, Andrew told me, a while back, that the two of you weren't married, so you don't have to keep up the fiction with me. Makes things easier.'

'Yes,' she admitted. 'It does.'

'I should have been able to figure it out from the last time I saw you, when you pretended not to know me. You were working here, then, weren't you?'

'Yes. I am sorry about that. I felt awful afterwards.'

'No need to. You were just doing your job.' He didn't ask her who she'd worked for. He already had a pretty good idea. As a Canadian, she'd likely worked for BSC – one of Sir William Stephenson's girls. He'd known about them, though he'd never known exactly what they'd gotten up to, in their offices at Rockefeller Plaza. Even now, with everyone grown older and the war reduced to pages in a history book, there still were secrets.

She said brightly, 'And you? Have you lived here all this time?'

And so they talked, as they had always done, of little things.

'You never got married?' she echoed, as though that surprised her.

'I never had time.' He smiled down at her. Glanced at the child. 'You did, though, I see.'

'Yes. I have one son,' she said. 'Katie's father. His wife died last year, so they're all on their own now. They live with us.'

'You must enjoy that,' said Jim.

'Yes, I do. Very much.' She looked down at the little girl, squeezing her hand with affection. 'I can't think what I'd do without her.'

458

'She looks like you.'

'Do you think so? There's the hair, of course…'

'She has your eyes.' Jim looked from one face to the other, certain.

'Well, let's hope she didn't get my temper, poor thing.' She glanced down, to check her wristwatch. 'We're supposed to meet my husband.' Then, on inspiration, she said, 'Will you come with us?'

Jim hesitated. Shook his head. 'I really should be getting to the office.'

'Please, Jim, come with us.' She held his gaze. 'I'd like for you to meet him.'

He was powerless, as he had always been against those eyes. He went.

He wasn't sure what reception he'd get, or how she'd choose to explain him – a man from her past – but he went, all the same.

Their hotel was the Willard, only two blocks from the White House, and not far for them to walk. 'My son,' she said, 'wanted to stay at the Watergate. He thought it would be more exciting. I told him that I'd had enough excitement in my life.'

Jim smiled. 'So he knows what you did during the war?'

'Oh, heavens, no, I've never told him that. I don't imagine he'd believe it, if I did. No,' she said in amusement, 'he thinks I'm a boring old woman.'

Jim didn't think much of the son, when he met him. A colourless young man, absorbed in himself; only vaguely aware of his child.

But the husband, Ken Murray, was different. Jim liked

him. Liked the firmness of his handshake, and the honest, level squareness of his gaze.

'So you knew Georgie in New York,' Ken Murray said. 'That must have been a time.'

It took Jim a few seconds to realise Amelia and 'Georgie' were one and the same. 'Yes,' he said. 'Yes, it was.'

Ken Murray didn't ask him what he'd done in wartime. Having been a military man himself, perhaps he understood the barriers of secrecy. He only asked, 'And what do you do, now?'

He was an easy man to talk to. In the coffee shop of the hotel, they sat and talked while Katie coloured happily beside them with her crayons. The son lost interest after twenty minutes, and went back up to their room. Jim didn't miss him. But he *did* feel at a loss when Katie tugged Amelia's hand, insistent, and Amelia rose.

'We'll be right back,' she said. 'Excuse us.'

Left alone, the two men settled back, as though each were deciding how to carry on the conversation. Jim spoke first. 'You were in the Air Force, in the war, as I recall.'

'I was. I wasn't very good at it. I got myself shot down.'

'Well, I would guess you had a few adventures.'

'Nothing much to tell,' Ken Murray told him lightly. Most men who had gone through hell and back again, Jim knew, weren't keen to talk about it. 'The people who helped me out, they were the brave ones. And there were so many of them. I remember this one man, in Lisbon – I never did learn what his name was; I wish that I had. He came with the SIS man, to debrief me. A real quiet guy, but he was so concerned about me having to go back into the air that he sent me a note afterwards, with the name of a British official he knew at the Embassy. Said

460

if I went to this man, he would find me a desk job. Intelligence. I didn't go for it, of course. My squadron needed me – we pilots were in pretty short supply. But it was nice of him to go to all that trouble, for a guy he didn't know.' He looked at Jim, and smiled briefly. 'That's what I took with me, from the war – what I remember. All the trouble people took, to help a stranger. Made me think the human race still had some hope.'

Amelia's voice asked, 'What did?'

Turning with a warm-eyed look, her husband said, 'Oh, we were just talking.'

Jim found his voice, and said, 'War stories'.

'Really?' Looking at the two of them with interest, she said, 'Ken never tells me those'.

'There's nothing much to tell,' he said again. He watched his granddaughter at play, and added, 'Anyway, it's ancient history, now. God willing, this little one will never have to live through days like that.'

They changed the subject, then, and talked of other things. It was going on for noon when Jim stood, finally, with reluctance. Said goodbye.

Amelia walked him out. Said the usual things, about keeping in touch. At the doorway she paused for a moment, her gaze on the floor. 'You said that Deacon told you we weren't married.'

'That's right.'

'When did he do that?' Her voice was casual, as if it didn't matter, but he wasn't fooled.

It took him half a minute to decide what he should answer. 'I met him in the Fifties once. In Istanbul. We had a cup of tea, and talked. He told me then.'

'I see.' She nodded, and he knew that she was also choosing her words carefully. 'How was he? Was he well?'

'He seemed to be.'

Another nod. 'I'm glad,' she said. And then she raised her head to look at him, and smiled as if to prove it. 'It was really good to see you, Jim. I mean that. Take good care.'

He never could find a convincing reason, later, why he hadn't told her everything – that he and Andrew Deacon saw each other once a year, at least, and wrote each other monthly; that they'd done that ever since they'd met in Istanbul; that Deacon wasn't married, though he'd never, to Jim's knowledge, taken off the New York wedding ring.

Jim felt a bit ashamed, in fact, whenever he looked back on his encounter with Amelia. Like he'd stepped between two lovers, who were meant to be together. But the truth was that, like Andrew Deacon, he had liked Ken Murray too. And he himself was only one more player on the chequerboard, who did what Fate decided.

The crowd was growing thinner in the banquet hall. Little groups of people were collecting by the doorway, as they started saying their goodbyes. I wasn't ready yet.

With clearer eyes, I kept my focus on Jim Iveson – this man who'd met me as a child. Perhaps that was why I'd felt so sure I should know him…though I hadn't been aware my memories stretched so far into the past.

I said, 'My grandmother…she's—'

'Yes, I heard,' he cut me off, so that I wouldn't have to say it. 'I am sorry.'

It occurred to me that this man, having been a friend of

Deacon's, was a target, too. I thought I ought to warn him, but I didn't get too far, because the minute that I mentioned the report, he said, 'You mean his accusations about Cayton-Wood. I knew about that, yes. I knew he didn't have much luck with it.'

'I might have more.'

'You'll have a hard time doing it. Especially,' he said, 'after last week.'

I didn't need to ask him what he meant. There was no way anybody could have missed the story – it had been in all the papers, and on all the nightly broadcasts. A woman like Venetia Radburn couldn't smash her car into a tree without it making headlines.

And the journalists and broadcasters had played upon the tragedy. A shame, they'd said, her family had been with her – her great-nephew, such a promising young lawyer, and his mother. All three of them killed, in that one accident. Then, tragedy on tragedy, her son-in-law (which was how they'd described the Colonel, notwithstanding he was her own age) had, in what the reporters liked to call 'a fit of grief', done the dramatic thing and gassed himself to death in his garage.

It had made for good news, but I wasn't completely convinced. The first three deaths – Venetia Radburn, Patrick, and his mother – those were real enough. I'd seen the pictures. But the Colonel had already died once in his lifetime, and I didn't put it past him to attempt the trick again.

Jim's thoughts were clearly running in the same direction. 'The British,' he said, 'do things very neatly.'

I half smiled. 'So you don't believe that he's dead either.'

'Men like Cayton-Wood don't kill themselves. He's likely

on an island, somewhere, soaking up the sun.'

And I would not be safe, I knew, so long as he remained there. I would always have to watch my step, to look behind me on the street, to never drop my guard. I didn't want to live like that, but it was how things had to be, as long as Cayton-Wood was living. And he *was* alive – I knew that in my heart. I knew his shadowy protectors had removed him from the path of justice once again, as they had done before.

'Don't worry,' Jim said. He was watching me as if he knew my thoughts; as if he knew what I had been through, and what I still had to face. He smiled kindly. 'No one lives for ever. But the truth survives us all.'

His face looked tired. We'd been talking for a long time, and the organisers of the small reception had begun to stack the chairs. Our interview was coming to a close.

I turned my tape recorder off, and started packing up my notebook.

'Did you get what you were after?' he asked.

More than I had hoped for. But I only told him, 'Yes,' and thanked him, even though the words seemed so inadequate, for what I had been given.

'If you have the time, I'm staying in Toronto for the weekend, at the Royal York Hotel,' he said. 'I'd like to buy you dinner while I'm here.'

I'd said no to Deacon, when he had invited me to dinner, and I'd learnt from my mistake. 'I'd like that. Thanks.' And then, because it had only just occurred to me, 'Do you need a ride back to Toronto? Because I've got my car here.'

'No, no, thank you, but my driver's in the parking lot.' He

checked his watch. 'Unless he's given up on me. I've been a little longer than I said I'd be.'

He stood, and helped me with my coat, and walked me out. A gentleman. The parking lot was busy, thick with slowly rolling cars and milling people.

'There he is,' said Jim. 'I guess I won't be stranded after all.'

I couldn't see his car at first. My view was blocked by a reversing van. But as it pulled away, I saw the long, black Lincoln Continental, and the man who stood beside it, leaning on the driver's door, arms folded.

'I believe,' said Jim, 'that you and Matt already know each other, don't you?'

Matt Jankowski's gaze met mine across the space between us, and he smiled.

I was so surprised to see him that I couldn't think of anything to say.

I slowly turned to Jim, beside me, and all of a sudden I knew where I'd seen him before. He had been at the next table over, at Dean and Deluca's, in Washington, sitting behind Jenny Augustine. My mind began to flip through memories, like a rapid slideshow: Matt's voice, telling me that Jenny would be fine. *She's with a friend of mine. A friend of hers, too, as it happens.* Further back, Matt saying how he had been sent to Lisbon by a former senior partner in his firm, a man who had been FBI...

I said to Jim, with certainty, 'You have a corner office.'

'Yes, I do.' His brows came down a fraction. 'How did you know that?'

I only smiled. So now I knew just how Matt's old man in the corner office had been able to identify me. Jim had been a friend of Deacon's; he had known of Deacon's death. He'd also heard about my grandmother's. And that meant he most likely would have known that I was missing. It would have been simple enough to compare the recent photographs of me that had been run in the Toronto papers to the ones that Matt had sent from Portugal.

I understood that now. And more. I gave myself a mental shake for missing all the clues. They'd all been there – he'd been in nearly every story I had heard, from the beginning, though he'd been different things to different people, filling many roles. A very active piece, I thought, upon the chequerboard.

'Be careful, now,' he said. I let him take my elbow; let him usher me between the cars, the people. 'Matt's a tough young man to read, sometimes,' he told me. 'That's a good trait for a lawyer, but…he's cautious when it comes to certain things, I've noticed. If that ever changes, well, you take my advice, Katie. Give him a chance. It wasn't for my sake alone that he did what he did.' As we neared the Lincoln, he said, in a louder voice, 'I'll let you two figure out the details of that dinner.' And with a briefly affectionate squeeze of my shoulder, he let himself into the car.

Matt stayed standing outside with me, shoulders hunched in his heavy black overcoat, hands swallowed deep in the pockets, and as the silence stretched he coughed and said, 'How are you?'

'Fine, thank you.' I waited, then asked, 'Did you get the tape?'

'Yes, thanks.' He looked at me. 'That was an idiotic thing

to do, you know that? You could have been killed. If I'd known you were going to do that, I'd...' He bit the end off the sentence, unfinished, and glanced away sharply, as I thrust my own hands defensively into my pockets.

'He'd have tried to kill me anyway. He still might.'

Matt frowned, as though the thought disturbed him. 'You're not back at your grandmother's house, are you?'

'No.' The lawyer, my grandmother's lawyer, had offered me the keys, but I had left them in his care. 'No, I'm staying with friends.'

He didn't ask with whom, or where. For all I knew, he might already have had Tony's address in his pocket; might have known exactly where I'd been. He only said, 'And the police are giving you protection?'

I shrugged, without taking my hands from my pockets. 'They've done what they can.'

The wind swirled cold between us for a moment, then he told me, 'I could do a better job.' His voice was casual, but his eyes, when they found mine, were anything but.

I was suddenly very aware of Jim Iveson, sitting in the front seat of the Lincoln Continental, with a clear view through the windshield. Not quite certain of my answer, I looked down.

Matt didn't seem put out. 'So,' he said. 'We're having dinner.'

'Yes.'

'And after that? What are your plans?'

'I don't know.' It wasn't so simple, I'd found, to just walk back into a life. Too many things had changed – it was like putting on old clothes that didn't quite fit. For the moment, I still had my job at the paper, but, 'I thought I might try my

467

hand at writing a book,' I said. 'I've got a good idea for one.'

'What kind of book?'

'True crime.'

'How does it end?' he asked.

I knew it mattered how I answered, but I really didn't know. I knew the figures on the chequerboard were shifting once again, but it was just too soon, I thought. Too soon.

He understood, I think. He drew himself up, in the wind, and found my gaze, and held it. 'Maybe when you get that figured out,' he told me evenly, 'you'll let me know.'

Afterwards

I've been told, by people more experienced at writing, that the hardest part of telling any story is the search for its beginning, and its end.

I learnt the truth of that.

All through that winter, and the springtime, and the summer that came after, I was writing. People helped me: Jenny Augustine, who, as she'd promised, used her publishing connections to arrange a solid book deal for me; Regina Marinho, whom I found, with Anabela's aid, in a remoter part of Portugal – in hiding, but, to my relief, quite safe; Manuel Garcia's widow, who was living in the north of England, and who kindly shared with me her memories of her husband, and her memory of the visit she'd had one week after that, from Deacon. He'd bought all her husband's paintings. Every one. When she had protested, he'd said that he was sure he would recover what he'd paid her, when he sold them in his shop. Meantime, he'd made arrangements with the British Embassy to honour their agreement with Garcia, so that, when the war was over, she could emigrate to England. What he gave her for the paintings was enough to pay her passage, and to buy a little house. 'He was a good man,' she had told me rather huskily. 'You must write kindly of him.'

She had sent me, too, a small sketch of her husband's, that she'd saved for all these years. Not the windmill – that would have been too much to hope – but a view over Lisbon, with its crowded streets and houses tumbling down to meet the harbour. Jim, when he saw it framed over my desk, was admiring.

'He had a great talent,' he said. 'Such a waste.'

Jim helped, too, with my writing. He called me daily on the phone, and visited in person when he could. And he bought me the dog. It was company for me, he said, though I knew he was really just trying to give me protection. He worried, a great deal, about my protection. So I was surprised when, in June, he announced he was going on holiday. Our wet and gloomy spring, he said, had left him starved of sunshine, and he had a sudden urge to see again the places he had travelled to, when he was younger – Istanbul, and Rome, and the idyllic isles of Greece.

I missed him, when he left, but I enjoyed the stream of postcards, and of course by then I was absorbed completely by the book. I was revising my first draft, then, and still searching for the ending.

And, at last, it came; not in the form of inspiration, but by messenger, with flowers, for my birthday.

The dog heard the knock at the door before I did – he usually does – and I opened the door with a hand on his collar. Without the dog there at my side, I would never have opened my door to a stranger. Not even a smiling young man holding flowers.

But the flowers were roses. Tea roses. And when I saw them I knew straight away who'd sent them. It was, after all, my birthday, and although Jim was out of the country I knew that he wouldn't have let the day pass without some sign to show he'd remembered.

With the roses came a box – not large, just the size of a bottle of wine, and about the same weight. It was wrapped twice: the first time in tidy brown paper, and under that, prettier tissue, with ribbons.

I sat down to open it, carefully working the knots. The box itself was very plain, and lined with wads of newspaper – Italian, from the look of it. I thought, at first, he'd sent a statuette, some kind of sculpture. It felt heavy in my hand. But then I turned it, and the paper fell away, and I could see exactly what it was.

The phone rang, and I reached for it with absent fingers. Tony, sounding cheerful. 'Happy birthday, gorgeous.'

'Thanks.'

I was still looking down, at the handle-sized, ivory white dragon's head carving, with lifeless red eyes. I could see, at the bottom, where someone had sawn off the walking stick. Clearly in my mind I could hear Jim's voice saying, like a promise, *No one lives for ever*. And I knew what he had done.

Tony's voice, forgotten, asked, 'Are you all right?'

'I'm fine. I'm just...'

'You were working, weren't you? Isn't that thing finished yet?'

I glanced toward the great untidy pile of pages sitting to the side of my computer; then my gaze went further – past the table to the window, and beyond, where I could see the two small rosebushes my grandmother had planted in the yard, against the fence. They were in bloom, now; pale pink, beautiful. I gripped the phone more tightly. 'Yes,' I said. 'It's finished now.'

And slowly, but decidedly, I set my birthday present down, and folded shut the box.

Author's Note

We writers choose our stories, sometimes. Sometimes, they choose us.

I still remember this one choosing me some fifteen years ago when, at a dinner party, I was told the sad tale of a man who'd witnessed something in the war, and who had written a report, and who had suffered for it. What struck me at the time, and what stayed with me, wasn't what he'd seen, but that this man, grown old and disillusioned in his search for justice, had at last arranged to meet a journalist, to pass on his report and make it public. 'But he died,' so I was told, 'before the meeting could take place.'

So Andrew Deacon grew from that, a grey and faceless shadow at my shoulder who would not allow me rest until I put him on the page.

It took four years to write this book, and in that time I had the help of many people, some who have themselves inspired characters — most notably the incredible Canadian women who actually went to New York in the Forties to work for Sir William Stephenson's British Security Coordination, and who so generously shared their memories with me. I'm indebted to the writer Bill McDonald, author of *The True Intrepid*, one of the best and most fascinating biographies of Sir William Stephenson, for introducing me to these 'BSC Ladies' – June Welsh, Mayo Lyall, Wynne Woodcock, Betty Noakes, Jean Martin, Bev Bible, and Chris Ruttan, without whose help Kate's grandmother would not have been the woman that she was.

I am indebted, also, to the FBI's Rex Tomb, who in the chaos that immediately followed 9/11, when the FBI undoubtedly had more important things to do, still found time to connect me with retired agent Kenneth Crosby, in whose gracious company I learnt of the realities of working in intelligence in the Second World War.

For details of Camp X, I was assisted by Norm Killian of the Camp X Historical Society, and by several of the veterans who had trained there, most particularly Leslie Davis, who not only suggested Deacon could be an instructor, but proposed the way that Georgie might be sent up from New York to meet him – plot points I'd been struggling with till then.

In Portugal, I owe thanks to Regina Gato, Fátima Da Silva of the British Embassy Consular Service, Anabela Matos of the York House Hotel, and above all to Robert Wilson, award-winning author of *A Small Death in Lisbon*, who went beyond the call of kindness to read through the book in manuscript to see I got my facts straight.

Closer to home, in Toronto, Sue Gariepy of the *Globe and Mail* patiently answered all my journalism questions, as did the incomparable Suanne Kelman.

And finally, my mother, as always my first and best reader, helped more than she knows.

PRAISE FOR SUSANNA KEARSLEY

'A deeply engaging romance and a compelling
historical novel. A marvellous book'
Bernard Cornwell

'Fabulous summer reading fun'
Gail Anderson-Dargatz, author of *A Recipe for Bees*

'Part ghost story and part romance, it is beautifully
imaginative, with a dream-like quality'
Bookseller

'A captivating book'
Woman's Realm

'Like vintage Mary Stewart by way of Rosemary
Sutcliffe . . . updated with a sprinkling of the supernatural'
Scotland on Sunday

'Like something out of the pages of Daphne du Maurier'
Daily Express

'A lovely, clever book'
Evelyn Anthony

'A strong first-person narrative tells the story of the past
and illuminates the present. If you liked *The French
Lieutenant's Woman*, you'll love this suspenseful novel'
Romantic Times

If you enjoyed *Every Secret Thing*,
read on to find out about more books
by Susanna Kearsley . . .

~∞~

To discover more great fiction
visit our website at
www.allisonandbusby.com
or call us on
020 7580 1080

THE SPLENDOUR FALLS

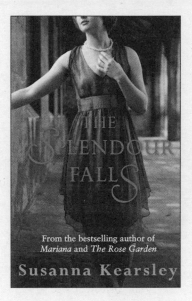

Emily Braden is intrigued by the medieval story of Queen Isabelle, and cannot resist when her cousin Harry, a historian, suggests a trip to the white-walled town of Chinon, nestling in France's Loire Valley. But when Harry vanishes and Emily begins to search for him, she stumbles across another intriguing mystery – a second Isabelle, a chambermaid during the Second World War, who had her own tragedy, and her own treasure to hide.

As Emily explores the ancient town of labyrinthine tunnels, old enmities, and new loves, she finds herself drawn ever closer to the mysterious Isabelles and their long-kept secrets.

SOPHIA'S SECRET

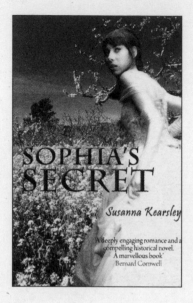

Carolyn McClelland, a writer of historical novels, finds herself with a familiar enemy: writer's block. A change of scenery leads her, and her book, in a whole new direction. Carolyn takes up residence in a cottage in Edinburgh, and feels inexplicably drawn to Slains Castle, and not so inexplicably drawn to the charming but somehow familiar Stuart Keith. Carolyn is soon writing with an unusual speed and imagery which leads her to wonder whether her 'fictional' character of Sophia is really so fictional after all.

Carolyn soon realises that she is somehow channelling the memories of her distant relative and that her story has a life of its own.

THE ROSE GARDEN

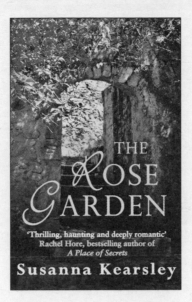

When Eva's film star sister Catrina dies, she leaves California and returns to Trelowarth, Cornwall, where they spent their childhood summers, to scatter Catrina's ashes and thus return her to the place where she belongs. But in doing so Eva must confront ghosts from her own past, as well as those from a time long before her own.

For the house where she so often stayed as a child is home not only to her old friends the Hallets, but also to the people who had lived there in the eighteenth century. Eva finds herself able to see and talk to these people, and she falls for Daniel Butler, a man who lived and died long before she herself was born. Eva begins to question her place in the present, and in laying her sister to rest, comes to realise that she too must decide where she really belongs.